*Celeste,
I hope you e[njoy the]
second time a[round.]*

★★★
NNP FLEET
MARINE

COLONY WARS

This is a limited print Author's copy. There may be errors that remain to be corrected in the final print release. Therefore, this copy should be treated as a collectors item.

G. VAN WALLACE

G Van Wallace

ISBN 978-1-64670-355-5 (Paperback)
ISBN 978-1-64670-356-2 (Digital)

Copyright © 2020 G. Van Wallace
All rights reserved
First Edition

All rights reserved. No part of this publication may be reproduced, distributed, or transmitted in any form or by any means, including photocopying, recording, or other electronic or mechanical methods without the prior written permission of the publisher. For permission requests, solicit the publisher via the address below.

Covenant Books, Inc.
11661 Hwy 707
Murrells Inlet, SC 29576
www.covenantbooks.com

Colony: a group of people who leave their native country to form in a new land, a settlement subject to, or connected with, the parent nation.

Green Gold: a super dense, highly compacted, multiuse clean energy source derived from eons of intense pressure and heat, combining a multitude of a planet's resources to create.

"Green Gold is the energy manna of the universe. We just have to go out and collect it, as the Hebrew's did in the Wilderness"—Bert Goor, CEO, Energy United Corporation.

"While the Coliseum stands, Rome shall stand; when the Coliseum falls, Rome shall fall; when Rome falls, the world shall fall"—Venerable Bede c. 673–735.

"You just don't get it until you've been there. It isn't that you can't get enough, it isn't the adrenaline rush. It is the man on either side of you. That is why we do it—for our brothers."—Lieutenant Colonel Rufus W. Eminster, Space Fleet Command

FOREWORD BY CLAYTON MARSHALL

An Uncommon, Un-sung, American (Devil Doc) Navy Corpsman

I came to know G. Van Wallace personally while reading his first book, *NNP Fleet Marine Six Weeks*. The second book, *NNP Fleet Marine Colony Wars*, is next in the series.

I thoroughly enjoyed this book. It was an awesome follow-up to *NNP Fleet Marine Six Weeks*. The story took me in an unexpected direction, that I think leads to a very real possibility for the future of society. G. Van Wallace has spun a multilevel story that keeps your interest and makes it hard to put down. I eagerly await the next book in this series.

I have experience as a combat Navy Corpsman in both Grenada and Beirut in 1983, with Weapons Platoon, Fox Company, 2nd Battalion, 8th Marines. Wallace has found a way to touch upon many of my true-life experiences. As a Corpsman with combat experience, there were times I actually had to put the book down as memories, both good and bad, came flooding back.

Wallace has a way of making you become, as I and my wife both did, a character in the story. His descriptions and details pull you into the tale of John Smith. As you transcend time and space through the characters, it is easy to relate to one or all of them. You find yourself eagerly turning the pages to follow the next adventure. *Colony Wars* is a story that will not only grab your attention but maintain it from start to finish.

G. VAN WALLACE

I can't imagine where Smith will end up, but I'm certain G. Van Wallace will tell his epic tale very well. I encourage readers of all interests and ages to read this series. You will thoroughly enjoy your time spent following John Smith as he grows in maturity.

Hospital Corpsman
3rd Class Petty Officer
Clayton Marshall

NNP FLEET MARINE TERMS AND ACRONYMS

AAR—**After-Action Report**; a summary of the actions by an individual or unit, mostly at the conclusion of a major event.

Abooe—Galleen military, low-level NCO, one confirmed kill.

A-Dose—A synthetic body chemical injection that feeds or replaces vital adrenaline and other nutrients to prolong optimal effectiveness.

AO—**Area of Operations**; could be used formally to describe a unit's immediate area that they are operating in or loosely to tell another that they are too close. "Hey! You're in my AO!"

Betty—**Basic Troop Transport Insert**; BTTI vehicle.

Candias—Galleen military, senior NCO/fighter, high morale.

Capt.—**Captain O3**, both Fleet Marine and Space Fleet, commissioned officer; may be referred to as the "Old Man," mostly at company level.

CI—**Cardinal Identifier**; see CP.

CO—**Commanding Officer** of a unit anywhere in size from platoon all the way up to division; sometimes referred to as the "Old Man," a more personal and honored term of respect.

CSM—**Command Sergeant Major E9**; the highest-ranking Fleet Marine NCO division level. This is the "Bulldog." CSM of the Fleet Marines is also an E9 but is the overall highest-ranking NCO over all division CSMs.

CPL—**Corporal E4**; low-grade NCO.

CP—1. **Command Post**; an area designated as the headquarters of any size unit in the field from platoon to division. 2. **Combat Pack**; the rucksack worn in combat that holds all the necessities and equipment needed while deployed for up to two months by all NNP military personnel.

3. **Cardinal Point**; a land navigational term identifying the OPD on which all directions are based.

CPO—**Chief Petty Officer E5**, Space Fleet, commonly referred to as Chief, but only if he allows it.

CQ—**Charge of Quarters**; mostly used in connection to in the rear or while in home rotation. The CQ duty ranges from lance corporal E3 to staff sergeant E6 and is charged with barracks security and administrative duties on a twenty-four-hour watch. A CQ runner will perform menial tasks during the duty time, such as buffing the Ops Room and main deck hallways, serving as errand boy. The runner duty will fall to the newest or lowest rank or the least squared away lower rank in the unit.

CR—**Combat Rotation**; a six- to eight-week combat tour.

CRL—**Company Recruit Leader**; the senior recruit during Six Weeks.

CSC—**Combat Support Company**; includes SS, medics, support systems, and armorers.

DCV—**Distinguished Cross of Valor**; awarded for exceptional acts of bravery and heroism, the EM equivalent to the DLC.

DLC—**Distinguished Leadership Cross**; awarded for exceptional acts of bravery and leadership while commanding troops; predominately an officer or senior NCO award.

EnE—**Escape and Evasion**; the tactical maneuver in which a unit or individual utilizes to withdraw from an enemy presence, hopefully unseen or in a cover and support manner to minimize or eliminate any pursuers.

EP—**Extraction Point**; the location that is designated as an exit point, escape route, or pickup point.

FP—**Fire Point**; a position that holds one of several characteristics, cover and concealment, offers good field of fire, good EnE, not easily accessible in counterassault.

Fire Team—a small unit of two to four marines, subdivided from a squad or handpicked from multiple sources.

Gunny—**Gunnery Sergeant E7**; company sergeant, highest-ranking NCO in the company; most often seen as the man that runs the unit while in the rear. The CO or captain commands the unit while in the field or combat. The CO is legally the caretaker but hands over the mundane, day-to-day rear matters to his gunny.

GBL—**Galleen Blue Laser**, the weapon system utilized by the Galleen military, as well as colonial rebels and others; a far less accurate, yet powerful laser that causes a high frequency of collateral damage in ricochet.

GLAR—**Green Laser Assault Rifle**, the sole personal weapon utilized by the NNP. All other weapons utilizing combustion or explosive force is outlawed in Space Fleet operations due to the danger imposed by either cataclysmic atmospheric destruction or the failure to perform properly under harsh environments.

HECS—**Hostile Environment Combat Survival** suit, a technology combining body armor and zero-gravity atmosphere protection to NNP military personnel; designed to withstand all known laser and space conditions from a wide range of temperature extremes. Classified.

HILS—**Heavy Insert Laser System**, a crew-served heavy weapon most frequently found on Bettys in a twin configuration and other vehicles; very powerful and causes massive damage.

HQ—**Headquarters;** base of operations from platoon to division while in the field; also referred to as CP.

IL—**Independence Leader**, rebel activist and agitator.

IP—**Insertion Point**, the designated area of offloading personnel or material.

IR—**Infra-Red**, the heat vison capability of night vision or poor-visibility situations.

LCpl—**Lance Corporal**, Fleet Marine E3, up-and-coming low-grade NCO, sometimes commands a squad, mostly a fire team.

LoL—**Loss of limb**.

LT—**Lieutenant**, O1–O2, a casual moniker for the platoon's leader by his men. Second lieutenant is the lowest, newest commissioned officer in the military; he will remain a "butter bar" or greeny for as long as eighteen to twenty-four months. First lieutenants enjoy a little better respect, surviving a bitter struggle of learning and command decisions that cost men their lives. Technically, as a commissioned officer, an O1 outranks even a CSM E9, but it would be a very naive and foolish young officer to overstep his rank above a staff sergeant E6.

LZ—**Landing Zone**, the designated area for Betty landing ops, either EP or IP; can be dangerous.

Marquis—Galleen military, young officer, aristocratic family.

MCPO—**Master Chief Petty Officer** E7, Space Fleet Squadron NCO, master chief.

MHG—**Medical Hospital Group**, three major medical facilities in the NNP military organization. The 301st MHG is located in Fraser, with each division having smaller satellite clinics to treat lesser medical conditions and daily "sick call."

Mowatt—Galleen military, conscript.

NCO—**Non-Commissioned Officer** starting at E4.

NNP—**New Nations Pact**.

OL—**Order of Leonidas**, an award ribbon, earned for either loss of life or LoL, sustained performing acts of valor and bravery while providing safety to fellow military personnel without regard to one's own personal safety.

Op/OP—1. **Operation**, a mission. 2. **Observation Post**, a position manned by one or two personnel out in front of their unit's main position to serve as an early warning of enemy contact.

OPC—**Officer Preparatory Candidate (Course)**, a three-month training course that trains potential officer candidates.

OPD—**Original Point of Direction**, navigational term for the base CI in which all directions start.

PFC—**Private First Class**, Fleet Marine E2.

PHA—**Power Head Auger**, a tool used in water operations to anchor personnel on the shallow bottom; also has a beacon to mark its location.

PO—**Petty Officer**, Space Fleet E4, equivalent to a Fleet Marine corporal.

PRL—**Platoon Recruit Leader**, a platoon recruit leader during Six Weeks.

Pvt.—**Private**, Fleet Marine E1, lowest EM rank.

RnR—**Refit and Retraining**, technically the time period just prior to deployment, but is seen wholly as the entire time when not on a CR.

RP—**Rally Point**, a tactical area prior to or after a mission objective; used for several purposes, regroup, mission rebrief, drop excess equipment, or jump-off point.

S1–S4—**HQ Staff Offices** from battalion to division that are responsible for essential duties, S1 Personnel, S2 Intelligence, S3 Operations, and S4 Logistics.

SS—**Scout Sniper**, Fleet Marine E6 and E7; generally performs one to two tours.

SCUV—**Small Command Utility Vehicle**, seats four, capacity six; lightly armored, 70 mph, 4WD; pronounced either scuv or scuvy.

SFP—**Space Fleet Patrol**, military law enforcement. The Space Fleet is responsible for both Space Fleet and Fleet Marine enforcement.

Six—Multiple meanings. "Six" is the direct CO or leader of a unit. Six also signifies protection or coverage, "I got your six." "Watch my six."

Six Weeks—Fleet Marine Recruit Basic Training, six weeks in duration.

SM—**Sergeant Major**, Fleet Marine E9, highest-ranking NCO in a brigade.

TDY—**Temporary Duty**.

Top—**First Sergeant** E8, highest-ranking Fleet Marine NCO in command of a battalion. Noncombat command NCO master sergeants are not frequently referred to as Top. The Space Fleet E8 senior master chief petty officer is called senior master chief.

XO—**Executive Officer**, second commissioned officer in command line of a unit.

"Y"—The "Y" or "Y Camp" is the location of Six Weeks, Fraser, Colorado, the site of a former YMCA facility.

Character list, NNP Fleet Marine/Space Fleet Rank and Unit Chart can be found in the back of the book.

PROLOGUE

The week had been rough, more so than last week, now with the Mars colonies mounting a full-blown rebellion and the colonists on Ceres One becoming more agitated and bolder in their behavior. This was the third public demonstration that had become violent in so many days. The platoon had been called out by the shift manager this latest time soon after the second work shift had arrived at the check-in building at 0700. The refusal to clock in and begin the day quickly escalated to destruction of company property and showing of independence paraphernalia.

Lieutenant Diaz ordered the crowd to disperse peacefully, but there was a brief period when most of the workers were unsure of what to do, though only briefly. The Independence Leaders or ILs took the unsettled moment to rally their cause and to set off several old flashbangs, which created the desired effect. The colonists, who had very little knowledge or experience with the devices, were in total chaos. The platoon had trained in preparation for this CR, Combat Rotation, in this and other associated IEDs, Improvised Explosive Devices, and had only just been advised this morning en route to the call out to be prepared and ready for any such deployment. The Fleet Marines standing with me were fully protected in our HECS, Hostile Environment Combat Survival suit, goggles, masks, and visors. The ensuing violence was almost one-sided in that the colonists were attacking us with whatever was at their disposal and we only used a defensive action, forming a phalanx, our GLARs, Green Laser Assault Rifles, slung downward by their slings, the eighteen lance corporals making a box with Corporals Alvera, Thomas, and Kidd and Staff Sergeant Williams in the center along with the lieutenant.

The punches and small hurled objects were taken in stride. We moved quickly and decisively toward the ILs, and the well-rehearsed maneuver was to divide into our squads on the lieutenant's order and quickly surround, isolate, and subdue them. Diaz gave the order and the trap was set. I moved with second squad with Corporal Alvera and my squadmates and we closed in. Suddenly, Lance Corporal Hughes was struck in the head with a folded metal chair from the back in a full arching swing, sending him sideways and to the deck in a crumple. The colonists pressed against us, and our phalanx formation collapsed. Again, we were fully protected from most of the physical violence, but the shock of one of our own going down and the escalating violence panicked Lance Corporals Yong and Stephanie, who should have had similar close-quarter action experience. The colonists were now using short clubs that appeared no doubt supplied and handed out by the ILs. My training and experience made me stick to the phalanx, but my combat medic training wanted me to protect and treat Lance Corporal Hughes. Sergeant Carpenter had advised and told me a couple stories about the chaos, violence, and quick decision-making while serving on a Riot CR, and I had soaked in his shared experience and knowledge.

This was our third week on the Riot CR, and Grigsby and I—along with the rest of the platoon—had learned from and experienced multiple callouts, but this was quickly becoming severe. Thankfully, we not only had Lieutenant Diaz from our long-ago Y camp experience, but newly promoted Staff Sergeant Williams as well. The corporals were all top-notch veterans along with the rest of the lance corporals, so it surprised me that our unit discipline was breaking down with two of them. Suddenly, a GLAR was discharged and I turned just in time to observe a colonist liberate Hughes' GLAR. Without thinking and in a sudden and violent action, I simultaneously broke the man's arm, hit him with a throat punch, and stripped him of the weapon in a downward disarming sweep. He fell to the deck, gasping and withering. I looked down on him with no compassion, no feeling, no sense of guilt. He could have been the one who attacked Hughes in the first place. The mob was slowly becoming aware of the injury of one of their own, and with the agitation of the ILs, the violence toward us increased.

First squad made it to the throng surrounding the ILs and quickly put them under arrest, while second squad reformed around me and Hughes. I utilized an armorer's trick and made the secured GLAR inoperable and knelt down beside Hughes to assess his injury. He was bleeding from the ears and a slightly tinged fluid was mixed in with it. I did not have advanced medical knowledge or training. *I wished Donna was here, well, not really.* I thought the fluid was, or might be, the fluid surrounding the brain. If that were the case, Hughes was in bad shape and needed advanced medical care ASAP. He was unresponsive, his breathing shallow and labored, and his skin color bluish. He wasn't getting adequate oxygen. He was going to die if we didn't get him out of here right now.

"Six, member is in bad shape, head injury."

We never said names of casualties over the air. I was one of a dozen trained combat medics in the highly trained and experienced platoon, but only Lance Corporal Sardinia, in first squad, and I, were designated medics. Our call and intuition were taken as the word.

"What's his status? Straight," Diaz responded.

"Six, I think he has ruptured cranial fluid from severe trauma. Would greatly defer to Two's knowledge."

This meant I wanted a second opinion from Staff Sergeant Williams who was a skilled, experienced, and knowledgeable caregiver in his own right.

"Man up or get out! I don't have time or patience for this crap!"

"He needs medevac ASAP. Critical."

He busted me right there in the open—either I had the maturity, knowledge, experience, and skill to act as the platoon's medic or I didn't. No room for hesitation. I looked at the man beside Hughes, now twitching in an obvious instinctive body reaction to asphyxia, and I moved to him and checked his status—blue face, nails, eyes wide open.

"Permission to treat local. Asphyxiation from blocked trachea."

There was a brief pause. First squad was subduing two ILs, while Corporal Alvera had broken off Grigsby and Lance Corporal Budner to cover me and Hughes and moved the five feet to assist with the arrest and containment of the objective. Grigsby and Budner now had their GLARs in hand and were not taking any aggressive behavior. The mob backed off.

"Apply necessary treatment. Camera rolling, affirmative?"

"Yes. Going to perform tracheotomy."

I had damaged his trachea and had to open his airway with a slit and insert a temporary breathing tube. I made an incision in the well of his throat, below his Adam's apple, and inserted a short rubber hose from my Med-Vest, specifically for this purpose. I wiped away the small gush of blood and taped the hose securely to his skin. The rush of air was loud. He had been suffocating, and now with his airway open, his color was returning to normal and his spasms calmed.

"Let him choke. He probably hit Hughes."

"Stow it!" Lieutenant Diaz was no doubt angry that one of his marines was injured, but he was going to maintain order and unit discipline regardless.

"Next marine that acts or displays behavior in an unauthorized manner will be brought up on charges!" Diaz was respected and looked up to; no one else said a word, all business.

Staff Sergeant Williams added, "Mind your fields of fire. Keep off the trigger. Keep your buddy in close. Move back to recover member."

All soothing, just like back at Six Weeks. Staff Sergeant Williams had that ability to calm others and bestow confidence while all around you everything was unraveling.

The platoon moved in a covering formation upon me and Hughes. Corporals Thomas and Kidd each maintained control over the arrested ILs, and Staff Sergeant Williams ordered Lance Corporals Tzenski, Cummings, and Hernandez to carefully pick up Hughes and carry him to the exit. I looked down at the injured colonist.

"What about him, Six?"

"Budner, Grigsby, secure the prisoner."

I guess he was going to be charged with the assault on Lance Corporal Hughes and the unlawful possession and discharge of a Fleet Marine weapon. No difference to me.

The platoon moved toward the exit, the protesters subdued now that the agitators were in custody. There was still yelling mixed with profanity and independence slogans and the call for my punishment for the attack on a peaceful protester and complaints about our apprehension of the three colonists. Lieutenant Diaz had issued the weapons ready position and the mob was unsure and neutered. Our Betty was circling overhead, ever ready for any show of aggression. Lieutenant Diaz called them down as we laid out the well-rehearsed and necessary Betty defensive extraction position.

The mob followed us to the safety limit of the Betty, but the flight crew was having none of this, and the door gunner fired off a single CC, Concussion Cannon, burst into the air, directly above the colonists. This action quickly and unequivocally dispersed the mob and allowed us to board unhindered with our wounded and prisoners. Now we could see that a larger crowd had started to gather in the street running from the check-in building to the small town square where the general merchandise, grocery, café, movie theater, and Grange buildings all were located. Word had evidently spread fast or this was a planned resistance movement.

The crew chief took control of Hughes immediately and directed him to be laid out carefully on the deck of the Betty. He carefully removed his helmet and performed a quick but knowledgeable assessment of his injuries and strapped him securely to the deck with two cargo straps. He instructed Staff Sergeant Williams to secure the prisoners. Williams personally performed this task, all but calf roping the three detainees.

I noticed three Bettys on the horizon, no doubt a company heading out on a mission from their frontier post, further west? Direction was all but relative to each location, planet, moon, or space rock we encountered. I watched them mindlessly through the open ramp door as I took my seat and automatically performed the required tasks, connect support tube, check GLAR, strap in, take a drink, raise my visor, pull down mask and goggles, perform an automatic check of each platoon member, and relax.

The crowd moved into the safety zone again and the gunner released another CC shot. The crew chief was distracted with

Hughes, more so than the usual injury, and that concerned me. Was he going to make it? The chiefs rarely left their position at the ramp during an extraction.

The Betty flight was tracking in a line diagonally toward us, but not to us. They were on a path that would close in on the town. The sun was past its midday point and there was no moon. The sky was cloudless, warm for Ceres One, but that was no impact for us.

The crew chief, I didn't know his name, was obviously agitated or bothered. I looked around and saw that the entire platoon was fixed on the scene that was unfolding a few feet away from us. Hughes suddenly went into convulsions and the chief, who was a trained corpsman—that's what Donna was aspiring with her corpsman certification, a crew chief position—started to vent the airway. He opened a box that he pulled out of a lower cabinet and hooked up a couple EKG pads. He looked up and caught sight of Staff Sergeant Williams and motioned for him to assist him, and the two worked feverishly for several minutes, all while the Betty was still on the ground. Unheard of. I had never sat on the ground in a Betty, anywhere, for more than thirty seconds.

In the meantime, Lieutenant Diaz personally unstrapped one of the ILs and walked him down the ramp and kicked him to his knees and stood there, facing the crowd with his GLAR pointed at the man's head. I had never witnessed such an intense show of brute power and authority. Hughes was obviously too critical to move through the wormhole, with the bumps and jumps.

Time stood still.

The Betty flight was almost past our field of vision, flying from a 0200 to a 0900 in front of us. I watched abstractly as a weird stream of smoke or fire shot up from the trees toward the flight. It wasn't a laser. I had never seen anything like it before. Lieutenant Diaz watched the fire trail too, caught in surprise and horror as one of the Bettys, the middle one, erupted in a ball of fire and plummeted to the ground, a black plume of smoke and red flames streaking in a tail behind it!

My mind shut down. This was Twelfth Division territory; Donna was assigned TDY, Temporary Duty, to this division. Was that her flight?

The crew chief abruptly came over the COMM. "Strap in! Betty down! Betty down!"

Lieutenant Diaz immediately grabbed the IL and shoved him into the Betty and pushed him to the deck, lashing a cargo net over him and cinching it down, with the help of nearly twenty Fleet Marines. The ramp raised slightly from a lowered ground-level position to an almost horizontal position. The COMM chatter was instantaneous and continuous between Diaz, Williams, the chief, and gunner and an unheard voice, either the pilot or division.

"Affirmative, one Betty down, enroute for security and rescue!" That was Lieutenant Diaz.

"…flight leader reports no movement. ETA thirty seconds! Hot LZ!" The chief.

"Weapons hot! Disconnect. Unstrap. Ready to insert!" Staff Sergeant Williams.

"…no sign of survivors, copy!" Diaz.

My mind was racing. The last time I spoke with Donna, she was with one of the newly formed companies of Twelfth Division, Third Battalion of Second Brigade. Grigsby was sitting right next to me and had to know what I was thinking.

"She's okay, man, probably not even her squadron." He was looking at me and put his hand on my leg.

"Yeah. Not even flying today, probably." I looked at him and then over at Hughes. He was completely still.

"Copy, heavy ground fire, too hot to insert." The chief.

"…negative, negative! Will insert and provide security for any survivors!" Lieutenant Diaz.

"Lieutenant Diaz, crash site under intense enemy activity. Pilot will not insert. We will perform air support."

"Damn you! Put my men on the ground! Those are your people down there too!"

"…prepare to jump! Weapons hot! LZ hot!" Staff Sergeant Williams.

We all stood up and shuffled to the ramp, tightly clumped ready to jump at the command.

"…negative, negative! Too hot, Lieutenant!" The chief.

"Make a slow pass at four meters, right on top of the site! My call! Do it!" Diaz.

"Confirm instructions. Lieutenant Diaz, slow pass, four-meter jump." The chief.

He was on the ramp, firing his GLAR at targets, the gunner blazing away on the CC and HILS, Heavy Insert Laser System.

Boom! Boom! Boom! Tck! Tck! Tck! Tck! Tck! Boom! Boom! Tck! Tck! Tck! Boom! Boom! Boom!

Lance Corporal Hughes was dead, we all knew it, and now we had the opportunity to save the lives of the Fleet Marines of a sister division, our brothers, and the crew of a downed Betty. We would sacrifice our lives freely and without hesitation; the same would be done for us.

A voice came over the COMM, a private channel. I looked around but no one else seemed to hear it but me, caught up in the imminent jump.

"Smith." It was the crew chief. I recognized his voice. "Intel is not clear, but Donna is flying with the 135th Air Wing today. That flight was Gulf 3/2/12, same wing, second squadron. I don't know if that was her flight. She was my classmate at academy. She talks about you all the time. I will crash this bird to pull her out, you got me?"

I looked at the chief standing on the ramp. He was looking right at me and momentarily paused in his firing of his personal weapon.

"I read you ten by ten, Chief. We will pull every brother and sister onto your ramp for extraction. You got our six?"

"To the end of the universe."

He turned and ripped off a long set. *Zik! Zik! Zik! Zik! Zik! Zik! Zik! Zik! Zik! Zik!*

"Coming to the jump site. Four meters. Prepare to insert!" Lieutenant Diaz. That was over thirteen feet. We had jumped that in the water but never that height on land.

"It's all now, marines! Give way, BLF, fall to your side. Just like we train—feet and legs together, fall, roll, defend. Form up on the Betty," Staff Sergeant Williams.

We packed in tightly on the edge of the ramp, each of us ready to die to save our brother or sister, eager for the jump. I could see the ground passing away from us, small trees, broken ground from the supporting Bettys overhead, and the flash of GLARs and GBL, Galleen Blue Laser. The rebels had both armaments. The wreckage of the Betty slid by, I could see activity around it, too close. The gunner, or someone, was firing nonstop at the advancing attackers. We had to get down there right now before it was too late.

"Next pass, prepare to jump, four meters! I know you can do it! Suck it up!" Lieutenant Diaz was nearly screaming. The highest jump on land from a Betty, a BLF, Betty Landing Fall, that I had completed was three meters. I was not even concerned.

"Ready! Ready! Speed is 5 mph on the jump zone. You do that in your sleep! LZ right on the ramp! Form up on the ramp in a Betty defensive position."

"I want status reports ASAP!" Williams.

"Ready! 3…2…1! Go!"

Diaz was the first off the ramp. I knew Staff Sergeant Williams was dying not to follow him, but he had to jump last, which was only a split-second later because we all followed Lieutenant Diaz, our platoon leader, in the same movement. I fell to the ground instantly and hard. This was not a normal training BLF in the sand or water. No, this hurt. We all landed within ten yards of each other and a little over six feet from the crashed Betty. I rolled to my knee and immediately picked out a target who was running straight toward me, a GBL in his hand, wearing a mismatch of body armor. I opened up. *Zik! Zik! Zik! Zik!* The last shot hit as he crumpled to the ground, his body torn apart by the GLAR.

I could see several bodies of fellow marines from the downed flight, burned but in an obvious defensive position, where they survived the crash but died fighting. My anger welled up. Discipline. I had to maintain discipline. Diaz and Williams would assess the situation and order the necessary actions, and my job was to perform my assignment.

"Second squad, maintain perimeter! First squad, recover casualties." Diaz.

"Pull all KIAs to ramp for extraction. Corporal Kidd, breach the flight deck!" Williams.

"Smith, Sardinia, pull back to crew cabin and set up aid station for survivors." Diaz.

I turned and quickly ran at a crouched position to the ramp and entered the Betty. The sight, it was a nightmare. Bodies of Fleet Marines were still strapped to their seats, burned, broken. There was a hole the size of a balled-up fist, the metal of the Betty savagely ripped, melted, and turned inward just midway on the right side. The armament, whatever it was, then exploded inside the cabin, maiming or instantly killing most of the occupants, blowing the ramp nearly off, and completely destroying the interior of the Betty. The crew chief's body was still strapped to his seat, never knowing what hit him; the gunner was pulled from his station and a surviving marine manned the big guns, defending the position until moments before we jumped, but was overwhelmed seconds before we could assist. I checked his vitals, gone.

A half-dozen bodies of rebels were inside the cabin. My helmet camera was rolling, I wanted to document everything I saw; this marine would not go unrecognized for his heroic actions or the three others that lay on the ground just outside the Betty, enemy dead around them.

I was in anguish, was Donna one of these… bodies? My thoughts and emotions were clouding my ability to function. *What if…?*

Sardinia was checking the men in the seats. He was methodic and experienced. This was his second Riot CR, and he had seen some bad stuff. Suddenly he called out as he looked at me; the whole platoon knew about Donna. We all knew about one another, our pasts, our family, brothers in other units, and the high ambitions we each had.

"Female. I can't ID."

My heart sunk. I was unable to move. I stared at Sardinia and then at the lifeless corpsman slumped in the seat, unmistakable with the Med-Vest and Space Fleet uniform.

"Grigsby, pull Smith out of there! Budner, replace Smith as medic." Williams.

I couldn't talk, I moved toward Sardinia and the body.

Donna. No! No. Someone grabbed me and shoved me back outside. I couldn't help but cry.

CHAPTER 1

The two-week Refit and Retraining, RnR, session passed without any notable occurrence, other than the guys all wanting to hear about the trip to the beach over and over again. I swear, Moon was able to tell the story of the week better than I was by the time we deployed on the CR. I was able to call and talk to Donna the night before we shoved off. I borrowed Lance Corporal Griffin's tablet again and decided I needed to get my own next chance I got. I asked him how I was able to do that and he told me laughing and asked me where I was from. I guess I was really not up to speed on this stuff.

I liked Griffin and he told me that he was about to go to PNCOC, Primary Noncommissioned Officer Course, and about the scuttlebutt going around about a major initiative coming soon. That added to what Corporal Davidson had told me, and the crazy situation with Jim Thompson during the week at the beach led me to believe him. I hadn't told anyone, not even Carpenter, about the experience with Thompson. I still didn't know who he was, and until he made contact with me again, if he ever did, I would take it as it came.

I still measured everything to Six Weeks experience and context, and I guess I would until I gained enough experience to do otherwise, so the RnR was way under the level of intensity and stress from that period of Y training. Sure, we ran and performed PT; practiced building search and entry, road crossings and ambushes, and tactical movement, had range time, and on and on. But it was with a unit of your buddies and we knew it, had experience with it; it was practical, everyday stuff. We mostly had hot chow at least once a day, no starving, and no sleeping in the wet sand. My first CR had clued me in to the real hardships of combat and there was no amount of simulated training that could mimic that. So the reality of what to expect and how and what we trained for and practiced was really on point. No need to be cruel and punitive.

Now, for the new boots to the company, that was a totally different matter. Second platoon got four new privates—Clark, Woolsey, Somersby, and Hackney—and I was so glad that the group of us, Moon, Grigs, Luke, Carlson, Jackson, and I, went straight into a CR, avoiding the prolonged anticipation, uncertainty, and stress. The whole thing turned out to be a blessing for us because we were not treated as or thought of as new guys since their arrival. Poor guys. Second platoon now numbered at fourteen, with the departure of Sergeant Custer, which was hard on all of us. He talked to Carpenter the day before we began the CR, and he had managed to "acquire" PFC Campbell into his platoon. The two of them were happy to reestablish. I was glad to know that they each had a buddy and that Campbell had someone looking out after him. It also turned out that there were a couple other long-lost marines that Custer and Carpenter both knew over at Charlie 1/1/7. That's how it was—after a little time in, completing some B and A courses and volunteering for a special CR, like Riot or Division Duty as an extra, you made friends that you would eventually meet back up with. Just growing up.

The day before we shipped out on the CR, we returned to the battalion barracks to get one last good night in a bed, a sit down at the chow hall, and to pack and repack our CPs, Combat Packs, and what we were leaving behind in the battalion supply room. It was odd—on one hand, it was stressful, knowing that tomorrow we were back on a fresh CR, and on the other hand, it was relaxed; we knew what we had to get done and we went about completing the small tasks. I called Donna that evening and missed her so badly. The time we had spent together a couple weeks prior was like a movie that I could rewind and watch over and over, but without the ability to actually touch her or be right beside her. It was painful. She was so deep into my emotions and thoughts that I spent my limited downtime in the field daydreaming about her. She was happy to hear from me but was also agitated; something was bothering her.

"Hey, how's it going? What week is this, two?"

Her video was blacked out.

"Oh, John! I miss you! I can't wait to see you again! This is worse than White Mountain Academy. But actually that is where we are, back on the Cali Coast. Can you come visit me?"

I could almost hear a slight pleading and hint of sorrow in her voice. I had heard the six-week Corpsman Training Course was above equal in difficulty, not only in stress but also physically challenging and way above the average White Mountain Academy basic training standards that the Space Fleet candidates were accustomed to. It made little sense to me to expect their best and brightest candidates to attend such a high-caliber course with expectations of success with the experience of the lower standard basic training.

"Sorry, babe." I had picked up the pet name in the last two days at the beach, and she seemed to like it. "You are probably going to be graduated while I'm out on this CR."

I could, I thought, hear a sniffle, a whimper.

"No, not really." Now I know I heard sniffling.

"What's wrong, Donna? What's the matter?" I was concerned about her.

"I…I, oh, John, you were right but I don't want to hear you say it. I failed the Entrance Physical Fitness Test."

More sniffling. I didn't know what to say. A long pause and then, "You are still such a bone. This is where you are supposed to tell me it's all right. I thought I had covered this with you already?" She gave a little laugh.

I wished I could hold her close and comfort her. I knew she was feeling horrible, but I wasn't sure about the process she had to move onward. "It'll be okay, Donna. You'll get another shot. You are on the up with the academia part."

"Oh, I'm still in, but I've been put in with ten others in a Preconditioning Course for two weeks! Oh, I hate it!"

I couldn't help but grin; she was recycled like the first weekers, living a nightmare of drill, physical training, discipline, and harassment. I bit my lip to keep from laughing.

"We have to wake up every morning at 0430 and do PT and then the remainder of the day is divided in the gym, the pool, and road marching. Road marching! What's that for? We have all our med gear and CPs, HECS, GLAR, and an additional thirty pounds! Thirty pounds in the CP. It's so hot, John. I wish you would come visit me on the weekends. I want to see you so badly."

"Listen, Donna, listen to me." I had to say something that would compute to her, something that she could latch onto that would encourage her to suck it up and drive on, but what?

"This is just a step, the first step. Don't give up in your mind, your attitude. You said to me way back that you had to make it yourself, earn your rank and position. You are going to do this and then complete the Corpsman Training Course. Then you are going to qualify for crew chief. It's not easy. If it were, the Fleet Marines would be doing it themselves, now, wouldn't we?"

She laughed and I could hear her breathing and trying to contain her sobbing. "Is that how you do it?"

"Do what?" I was at a loss.

"Walk off that ramp every op into certain danger and protect everyone around you?"

I couldn't tell her what made me force myself down that ramp, to control the fear, the queasiness, the feeling of absolute dread. I was repaying a debt. I owed my life to the brothers around me, and that's what drove me. No, she needed something else; her life had been much easier, and her abilities were much more advanced than mine.

"Look, the guys are all excited about this. They are planning and devising ways to be the first casualty that you have to perform mouth to mouth with."

She laughed and laughed; she finally turned her video on, and I could see her smile for the first time, that mouth open, her face so pretty, her eyes red from crying.

"You always make me happy. Thank you. Tell them all to stay safe and I will kiss them without them getting hurt."

She was sitting on a bunk in a shared room, and I could see the bunk above her and another off to the side. I wondered if they were separated by sex or if it was coed. That troubled me.

"You start in the morning?" she asked, wiping her eyes with a tissue. I looked at her and wished so badly to be lying beside her again, my little blanket thief.

"Yes. How much more of this 'Preconditioning' do you have left?"

"Another week! Then hopefully I pass the PT test and start with a new class."

I grinned. "So once you graduate, is that a promotion?"

"Yes! And yes, I will have earned it!" She thought she knew where I was going with this, but I outflanked her.

"So that means you get that goofy two stripe triangle thing, right? Chief petty officer?" I could barely retain my laughter. This was an old argument from our first date.

She laughed and shook her head back and forth. "No, petty officer and it's a bar!"

"Seriously, Donna, you have more to focus on right now than going out."

"I only want to go out with my PFC."

I put my middle three fingers on the screen and she put her small hand on the same spot. It was as close as we would get. "Be careful. Stay safe."

"Stop fooling around over there and get back and watch my six."

"John, I—" She began sniffling again.

"Me too." I had to hang up or I would be a mess more than I already was. I had to meet the guys for dinner chow in five minutes. "Bye, babe." I disconnected the call.

I walked out of the vending room and then stopped and turned back into the doorway and thought about that night. "I love you too, Donna," I said in a quiet voice.

The company was making its way down the stairs. I knocked on Griffin's door down the hallway on the main deck, one of the Permanent Duty rooms and returned the tablet. "Hey, you headed to chow?"

He looked at me surprised and said, "Yeah, sure."

The gang all sat around one table, as usual, and no one seemed to care that Griffin was with us. He had been around the entire down cycle, pulling CQ, Charge of Quarters, pretty regularly, and everyone liked him. He had been with Fox Company and lost his right leg below the knee several months ago and just couldn't make the transition back to a line company for a CR. He was a good marine, and Top and the battalion CO, Commanding Officer, Lieutenant Colonel Warner, were not forcing it. He would return when he was ready, or not, so they moved him to HQ. He was headed to PNCOC next week and was eligible for promotion to corporal after completion.

Our conversation was light, thoughts all on the coming CR. The usual cutups and jokes were interspaced.

"How's Donna doing?" asked Luke.

I gave a short laugh. "She's hanging tough. She's been placed in the Preconditioning Course for two weeks."

"What's that?" asked Moon. None of us understood fully the Space Fleet concept.

"She's been recycled." The table erupted in laughter, hands slapped the table, several guys shaking their heads.

"She lacked in her Physical Fitness Test. I tried to help her at the beach. I didn't know what to say. I did tell her about your guys' plan, though."

"No you didn't!" both Carlson and Luke said together.

"Maybe I should talk to her, try to pep her up," said Grigs.

I thought about that, not a bad idea; he knew how that felt.

Griffin looked at Grigsby. "You recycled? I thought all you guys went through together?"

"We did," said Moon. "He just started later." We all laughed.

"We'll bring you in too," said Carlson.

"Yeah." Several of us nodded and agreed.

Griffin knew he was accepted by us and was not an outsider. That made him smile, giving him much needed confidence. Not a single marine in the battalion looked down on him for his reluctance to rejoin a line company. Too many shared his pain and loss. He had to find his way.

"Hey! She did say for you all to stay safe and she would give you a kiss for that."

The laughter started again, and the conversation went all over. Soon it was time to go. Recruits were starting to come in and we needed to make way. I saw Corporal Breemer, who was now a sergeant, and I walked closer to him, not sure if he would recognize me or not and even if he did, would give me the time of day. He saw me and a smile came to his face and he waved me over.

"Well, I'll be! PFC Smith, congratulations Fleet Marine." He slapped me on the back. "Echo shoving off tomorrow?"

"Yes, Sergeant. How's the company?" That meant everything from the recruits, what week they were in, and the drill instructors.

"Running smooth. Hey, next cycle the numbers are increasing to 120. Two training corporals each platoon, another full training battalion. Gonna need you back here."

"So the scuttlebutt is true."

"Yeah, more than you know. Hey, we just got smoked in the range ambush this week. You're still the talk. I gotta go. Catch you later."

"See you, Sergeant Breemer."

I turned and headed toward the bilge and joined back up with the others. That was now several references and comments about the increase in tempo and numbers in the training battalion and coming changes. Was what Jim Thompson was planning a part of this?

The remainder of the evening slipped by—showers, final gear inspection and repacking for the sixth time, final visits with friends in other platoons, reading, and games of chess, cards, and Yahtzee—but hardly anyone slept. NCOs checked in and out, stopping and talking to this group or that, this individual or that one. We were told to go down to the TOE, Training, Organization and Equipment Room, to sign and draw three Full Meal rations, we could mix and match, and a rush for the stairs ensued to get the better choices. The barracks had to be cleaned and left in a condition that was acceptable in standards for the next company, of which there was already an Advanced Party from Fox arriving.

I finally pushed myself to turn in before 2130. First call was 0330, and company formation at 0400 with the march to the airstrip and load for deployment. I couldn't sleep. Private Clark had taken Larson's bunk and I could hear him above me, restless and unable to sleep himself. I didn't really know the guy and surely didn't know what to say. The four of them, like all new boots, hung out together and would until they became comfortable and familiar. Everyone in the platoon was friendly and helpful to them, but no "reach outs" had been initiated on either end and wouldn't until they experienced the CR. It was how it was done. The NCOs were different; it was their responsibility to settle them in and guide them. Sergeant Carpenter was good at that and Corporal Larson was excellent, taking them in and showing them how to do things. Sleep finally took me.

The bay lights came on and the CQ was not quite yelling, "First call. Echo Company formation 0400, thirty minutes. Take it to 'em, Echo!" He was gone.

Moans and curses and groans were exchanged between marines, some waking up this early the first time in weeks. Bunks were quickly stripped, sheets expertly folded and stuffed in waiting open duffle bags and then the blankets and pillows. We were deploying fully HECS up, so an odd and varied mix of underlayer was utilized by each marine, based upon their personal preference and experience. Nearly everyone had to some degree or other modified utilities and UAs, Under Armor, dressing in a combination of cutoff utility pants and UA, sleeveless blouses, cut-down UA shirts, and so on. The pajamas were put on next and then the outer armor shell.

Marines automatically double-checked their area, hoisted their duffle bag and GLAR, shouldered their CP, and made their way down to the battalion Training Room where coffee and a light breakfast were waiting. Talk was nonexistent. This was a personal reflective time. The banter would begin on the flight. I saw Corporals Larson, Olgby, Dettmer, Muniz, and Eddy on the bay deck, silently walking down the aisle, double-checking spaces, and pumping some marine on the chest or arm here and there. Larson talked quietly to his new privates, Clark and Hackney, giving encouragement and a pat on the back. No yelling, no screaming, no in your face intimidation—this was the real deal.

I ate a small portion of scrambled eggs and grits, grinning to myself, remembering Corporal Custer's remarks to CPO Ritter concerning my apparent, youthful, frightened appearance on my first Betty ride. I walked over to Grigsby and we stood together, having a cup of coffee. Moon was quietly talking to Lance Corporal Rich, Carlson laughing at something Jackson said, the company waking up, settling down, and having breakfast. No one knew what would be happening three hours from now. Lieutenant Green and the other platoon officer came in and mingled with their men. Gunny Scott and Captain Shupin walked in, but no official call to attention was announced. They each poured a cup of coffee. We were all in here again; the last time that happened was the day of the party two months ago.

Gunny Scott cleared his throat and the senior NCOs, that is, the staff sergeants, started *shushing* us. Gunny only said, "Stand at ease, Echo. Quiet down."

Captain Shupin looked around, nodding here and there, recognizing his men, saying the names of the marines he knew personally, respected.

"Before we fall out and start this CR, I want to take a minute and tell you, let you know, just how proud I am of this company for your hard work, dedication, commitment, and loyalty to one another. What lays ahead of us until the day we all meet back here in six or seven or eight weeks is unknown. We take it one day at a time. Protect the marine by your side and he will protect you. Work together to accomplish the mission so that we can all return home safe and healthy.

"Very briefly, there are some changes on the horizon and further information and details will be announced in the coming weeks. I will do my utmost to keep you up-to-date as they break while on the CR. The Fleet Marine divisions are about to undergo some growth and a new division is forming, the Twelfth."

He paused and looked around the room. It had been over fifteen years since the addition of a new division, and no one remembered how the process worked.

"There will be six phases, announced in planned two-week increments, starting today. Phase One, a volunteer call for senior NCO positions at the division, brigade, and battalion levels. This means that the Twelfth is filling sergeant major, first sergeant, gunnery sergeant, and staff sergeant billets straight from existing divisions, obviously. All officer billets will be selected randomly. I understand that we will lose some of you either voluntarily or in the coming phases. Opportunity for advancement in rank is no doubt going to be a factor. All requests for transfer will be accepted without repercussions by myself or Gunny Scott."

He looked around again, nodding. I don't think the NCOs had been aware of the announcement. He continued, "The other unofficial announcement is that First Training Battalion companies will be increased to 120 recruits and the scuttlebutt is that an additional training battalion is being formed. This means that we are really making a push on the Galleens and the rebel activity is heating up. That's all the intel on this that I have, and I will keep you updated. Echo! *Molon Labe*!"

We promptly came to attention and yelled, "Come and take them, sir!"

"Fall out for company formation," said Gunny and we worked our way to the quad.

It was now mid-March and windy, cold, and snowing—the perfect time to get out of Fraser. Early spring was probably the worst time of the year in the Rockies, since constant weather changes and freakish blizzards could occur without notice on a day that seemed to be breaking sunny and warm. "The Hawk," a term used to identify the cold, penetrating, and powerful wind, was unmerciful. The Hawk was flying today, whistling through straps and slings, forcefully blowing men weighing upward of 250 pounds with all their gear out of step and into one another.

We formed up, our visors up for the most part, the goggles in place to keep our eyes from watering. Thoughts of uncertainty ran through all our minds. *Wow, what a time to make that announcement, right at the start of the CR.* I wondered if any of the sergeants were going to actually volunteer. Who would want to leave the Seventh Division? What if they didn't get enough NCOs? What then? I quickly did the math. A whole new division would require a command sergeant major at division, at least three sergeant majors at brigade, and twelve to fifteen or even twenty or more first sergeants at battalion level. Good night! Thirty-six companies? Is that right? Thirty-six plus company gunnery sergeants! *Holy cow! And if they were selecting staff sergeants as platoon sergeants, or even taking sergeants, then that was... Let's see, I got to add, no, okay, just roughly... What! One hundred forty-four platoon sergeants!* Where were they going to get those NCOs from? That didn't even take into account the number of staff sergeants and gunnys in SS, Scout Sniper, platoons or headquarters, HQ, companies with cooks, engineers, maintenance, and who knows what else. And an even more interesting question, how were they going to replace them? A division had well over 1,400 odd Fleet Marines. This platoon, second platoon, can't even attain its full complement of twenty-four marines, nor could the other platoons of the company. On my very narrow and short experience with other units, I found that billet capacity was also lacking. So where were the numbers for another whole new division going to come from? It hit me like a ton of bricks. *Kids.*

Now I was putting the picture together. Jim Thompson was somehow a part of this, and his planned utilization of the orphanages around the NAC, North American Continent, to supply youth to fill the Fleet Marine divisions was, had to be, the solution. Were we in such a desperate situation? Were we losing, or was the scare of the rebels gaining independence that close to happening?

The company was formed up and the platoon sergeants did their report to Gunnery Sergeant Scott. Gunny then reported and turned the company over to Captain Shupin who then dismissed the gunny and platoon sergeants and called for the platoon leaders to take command over their platoons. All pomp and ceremony passed down from the beginning of man's formation of a military. The orders were to march to the airfield and load up and deploy on the scheduled rotation of Echo Company, Second Battalion, Second Brigade, Seventh Division's combat rotation. Proceed without delay. Gunnery Sergeant Scott was called back to the CO's presence, the platoon sergeants all returned to stand beside their platoon leaders, and a quick exchange of commands and authority was passed from the commissioned officers to the noncommissioned officers and we proceeded to march to the Bettys. Boy, this was fascinating just to observe.

Was this Sunday? It had to be. Just as we turned and started to route step on our way, a group of poorly clothed, frightened, and totally confused, fresh from Reception Barracks, recruits were chased down the sidewalk into our path.

The drill instructors yelling at the hapless victims, "Make way for a company of real Fleet Marines!"

"They are on their way to keep you safe while you try to figure out how to function as human beings!"

"Take your eyes off them. You aren't worthy enough to gaze upon them."

"Make way, holy maker of little green apples! That means move off the sidewalk!"

"For the love of God whose favorite planet is Earth, how did He make you so stupid? Move!"

It never got old. I laughed to myself. *Poor buggers, I was on my way to a six-week combat rotation, and I wouldn't trade place with them for anything.*

Gunny Scott started a cadence, "They say all the girls were crying the day you left!"

We replied, "Your right!"

"Your little sister cried. She said you left!"

"Your right!"

"Your momma cried the day you left!"

"Your right!"

"Your girlfriend cried when you left!"

"Your right!"

"She can't believe you said goodbye. You left!"

"Your right!"

"Jody was laughing on the day you left!"
"Your right!"
"You can never go back home again. You left!"
"Your right!"
"The Fleet Marines are all you have left!"
"Your right!"

He continued all the way to the airfield, never wavering, never repeating a line. Some were funny, and we laughed, hardly able to repeat our simple response and some were terribly sad and made us ponder. Gunnery Sergeant Scott was a bulldog, and I wondered why his promotion to first sergeant had been missed. Was this an opportunity for him to advance, move up to a battalion? Man, we were going to lose some good ones. I doubt they were going to take any bad NCOs.

The Bettys came into sight. The now very familiar activity surrounding the airfield was hardly an impression upon me—the flight crews busy readying their crafts and crew chiefs and gunners performing inspections and stowing supplies. I noticed a group, a company, standing off a hundred meters away. A training company about to set off on their Tactics Week were observing the activity and listening to their senior training sergeant. I looked around for a group of corpsmen to join us, but they didn't appear. I wondered if we were getting an SS, but none arrived to load with us. Echo didn't rate either of these two beneficial and highly trained assets.

If my previous experience with the working of the deployment of the CR proved to be correct, we would just orbit a moon or meander through a wormhole until there was an SS report on a suspected activity and we would respond. There didn't seem to be an existing conflict at present; otherwise, we would have been put on alert status. Too calm. At worse, the Betty crew would have to ditch us on some safe location where we would set up a camp and bivouac while they returned to Fraser for rest. That was always scary—we were alone and without air support for an extended period.

I performed the perfunctory tasks upon boarding, securing my CP, taking my seat, checking my GLAR, strapping in, connecting my support tube, taking a long pull on the drink tube, pulling down my goggles and then my mask, and looking around to see that we were all aboard. I was with second squad, with Corporal Larson, Lance Corporal Almond, PFCs Grigs and Carlson, and Privates Clark and Hackney. Luke, Moon, and Jackson were in first squad. Now the cutting up started. Sergeant Carpenter was sitting with us, and the lieutenant was facing him.

"So let me get this straight," Corporal Murray of first squad, the clown, even more that Custer was gone, started off. "If Staff Sergeant Ginny pulls out and heads to the Twelfth with Gunny and Top, Sergeant Carpenter will advance to staff sergeant and will take over first platoon. Staff Sergeant LaBoye in fourth moves up to gunny, and now that I have a clear and unobstructed pathway, am finally recognized for my hard work and dedication and am promoted to first sergeant and become the first corporal to ascend to a battalion level post with the creation of the new waiver system." The howls and whooping were instantaneous.

Sergeant Carpenter replied, laughing slightly, "I'll pass that on to Staff Sergeant Ginny. He'll be glad to know you have his future marked out for him. Gunny Scott will be interested too." The guys were laughing and adding their remarks.

"Come on, Corporal Murray. You hardly know where to stand in company formation, so how you going to know where to run to when Colonel Warner orders you to Post!" The laughter was stress-breaking.

"Well, at least he knows where the battalion Ops Room is. He buffed the deck in there enough as a struggling PFC!" Lance Corporal Rich added.

Lieutenant Green was holding a hand to his face, trying to cover his laughter.

"Okay, okay, so with your plan, where does that leave Lieutenant Green? Is the way open for him to move up to battalion with you? I thought the battalion CO usually brings his first career platoon sergeant with him?"

"Leave me out of this crazy talk. I don't want Colonel Warner to think I'm pushing him out." Lieutenant Green was openly laughing now.

"Yeah, if the colonel caught wind of the lieutenant's insurrection plan, he might head off the power play and transfer him to the new division chow hall as the mess officer, along with Sergeant Carpenter as the mess sergeant. What then? You'll have to take Ginny's place at first."

The joking continued for another hour or more, moving in and out of various scenarios where even the new boots were somehow promoted up to command sergeant major of the Twelfth. It finally died down and we all faded into our own thoughts, occasionally a buddy asking another buddy a question about this or that, the common time killer when it was slow.

It was looking more and more like we were going to be dropped off at the "neighbor's house" or have a boring night on the Betty. Lieutenant Green finally spoke and said, "Who's up for Alpha Centauri?" signaling our apparent destination.

That was just as good a place as any, and it was the closest solar system to ours and always had something going on. The system had three suns or stars A, B, and C. C was really a dud or nonbloomer, and the brighter one, Centurie Alpha, had multiple planets and moons in orbit. It was the dud sun, C's, little cluster of planets that I had had my fight with the Galleen Candias in the swamp. I still had bad dreams about that but didn't tell anyone.

Time passed, and we worked in and out of multiple wormholes, transitioning through the far reaches of space. Time not passing as had been previously thought and projected, rather space was bent, folded, so that we could travel through tremendous, unfathomable distances in hours and minutes. The system was four light years away, thousands of years in the previously earthen space travel transportation mode, but only required a skilled pilot with wormhole proficiency several hours or so. Now that we had a destination, I could peacefully take a nap. Nothing but an alternative callout could change our location now. I let the gas ease me into a restful sleep.

Chapter 1

PRESENT

Someone was standing next to me and calling my name. "Smith, it's time. Get up! You have to get ready."

A flashlight was in my eyes and I was really not quite sure about this whole thing. Corporal Larson moved over to the next bunk beside me and called out for Grigsby to wake up. The bay was still dark. Of course it was—it was only 0430 on Sunday. We only returned from the CR for our downtime cycle less than a week ago and I was enjoying the rest. I could see several other flashlights moving among the rows of bunks, the other platoon corporals waking their small collection of men. I sat up as I rolled my feet onto the deck. The morning was nice, a little brisk for the end of April. *But hey, it is the Rockies*, I thought. I stretched and stood up. Grigs was still lying in his bunk with his pillow covering his head, I'm sure trying to make this all disappear.

"Get up, Grigs. There's no getting out of it."

Without removing the pillow, he said, his voice muffled, "This can't be happening. It's too soon. I'm not ready."

"Too late. I'm headed for the shower. Get up."

I grabbed my shaving kit and towel and joined the other couple marines slowly making their way to the head. It was quiet, no one in the mood to talk. I quickly took care of business and Grigs walked in as I was drying off, the last straggler. I dressed in utilities, stripped my bunk, expertly folded the sheets and blankets, and carefully packed them in my waiting duffle bag. I locked the wall locker with it inside. My CP was hanging on the end of my bunk, my GLAR securely locked beside it. I waited for Grigs. The small group of us, seven total, all lance corporals, walked together to chow, still without saying much. The chow hall opened at 0500 and we were nearly the first ones in. Soon a throng of Sunday morning recruits were run in and out, followed by a First Week company and then a graduating Six Weeks company. Busy morning. Sergeant Carpenter walked in, along with Staff Sergeant Ginny and they sat down with us.

"You all ready?" asked Ginny.

"Aye-aye, Staff Sergeant," we all responded in a normal conversational voice.

"Look, forget about all the horror stories you've heard, all the bull. It's what you make of it, attitude. You all are young, green. I doubt that the cadre is going to make any concession for that, but you have limited leadership experience, so you don't have any bad habits. Every NCO has gone through it and made it. You all made it through Six Weeks. Suck it up and drive on."

"Aye-aye, Staff Sergeant."

"You know the deal. You all are volunteers for this, and at the end of this, you have a week off and then on to Drill Course, promotion to corporal before training duty assignments. It's a pretty good deal, fast track." Carpenter was looking at each of us.

Gunny Scott was gone, as were several of the senior NCOs advancing up a rank and moving to the new home of the Twelfth as Advanced Party. It had been a hectic and troubling past few weeks, not even counting the CR that we were on while all this was happening. There were a lot of holes throughout the other divisions as well, and midgrade NCOs were moving up to those spots, which left a tremendous opportunity for those willing to jump.

"Okay, change into your Alphas and report to the TOE room for dress inspection with all your gear at 0545. You have to report to Second Training Battalion by 0700." Ginny looked at me. "Wearing all authorized awards and ribbons."

"Aye-aye, Staff Sergeant," we replied.

I knew that was coming. We stood up together and deposited the trays in the window and walked back to Second Battalion.

We quickly changed into Alphas, checking one another over in the head where we could see better. Carrying all this gear and equipment clear across base without messing up our dress uniform was going to be a trick. Thankfully it wasn't raining or snowing. Two others had combat medic certification, and all had armorer, except for Grigs. He was the least diversified of the group, but that would change.

Staff Sergeant Ginny locked us up at attention and performed a thorough inspection, finding several gigs that would have to be corrected if there was time when we got there.

He stood in front of us and said, "Lance Corporal Alvera, take charge of this detail and report to PNCOC training straight away. Make it happen. Dismissed."

Lance Corporal Alvera was the senior among us; seniority counted in almost everything.

"Detail, fall out to the front of the battalion."

And so we moved off, picking up and carefully shouldering our CPs, assisting one another placing the duffle bags across the back of the shoulder resting between the CP and our head, and then looping the GLAR downward over the head and left shoulder. This was a lot of weight to carry in Alphas without ripping medals, ribbons, and badges off but it was part of the ritual, the passage right.

We had to stop a couple times; the burden was great. The average weight of our CPs was easily over eighty-five pounds, and the duffle with everything we owned was another sixty or more. HECS, GLAR, full water load, three brand new Full Meal boxes, Med-Vests, and armorer kits—I was dying. We marched in a single-file line with Alvera to our right, in route step, each in our own thoughts, knowing we were about to begin one of the cruelest, most stressful, and punitive courses in the Fleet Marines, rivalling Six Weeks training on a correlating factor of experience and fitness levels. It was how NCOs were made. Light contact was to be expected from the cadre, but if we struck back or even made a show of it, it would be the biggest mistake we could make. Self-discipline and control were very important when dealing with EMs, Enlisted Members, below us. Well, that was a challenge for me already, with my experience. They were going to push that.

All the cadre were senior NCOs and veteran drill instructors. They loved this school and many of them had been assigned so long that staff sergeants in the divisions had had them as cadre when they were lance corporals. *Oh man.* All divisions sent their young, aspiring, best, and brightest NCO candidates to this school and it operated out of three platoons of Fox Company, Second Training Battalion. Three weeks. We were all experienced Fleet Marines, anywhere from two to three CRs. All of us were below the one year of service requirement for promotion to lance corporal, except Alvera, and we had accepted the Phase Three deal, which waived the requirement and fast-tracked any marine that met the standards into a new training program and into A Course drill instructor slot.

The latest phase, Four, was announced last Monday, and the Twelfth was activated. A new base was nearly completed somewhere on the southeast coast and the advanced party of officers and senior NCOs had departed midweek. Nowhere near all the slots had been filled yet, so there were holes and the Third Training Battalion was gearing up at the same time. Recruits and boots were going to be rolling in heavily in the next coming weeks.

We neared Second Training Battalion and Alvera called us to a halt. We were all sweating profusely, our Alpha inner dress shirts nearly soaked. Breathing heavily, I was thankful for the stop, a chance to catch our breath; we had been marching for almost twenty minutes.

"Everyone pull out the marine's water in front of you and get a drink. We need it." We did and Alvera turned and I pulled his out for him.

"Listen, we have to help each other out. They pit us against one another and break us down just like at the beginning of Y camp. They want to break us, weed out anyone who doesn't belong. That lasts anywhere from a couple of days to the end of the first week until they are confident we are committed. If you don't have the heart for it, walk now, or you'll kill all of us."

Not one word.

"Brothers," he said.

"Brothers," we all replied. We took a last sip, helped each other replace the bottles, and gave each other a pump or hand on the shoulder.

"Let's do it. Detail, atten-huh. Lelf 'ace! Oward 'arch!" He had the voice pattern down.

"Stand tall! Lelf, lelf, lelf riot, lelf. I march all day, I march all night!"

We repeated the well-known verses as he called them out; we got in step and completed the last fifty meters to the front of the training battalion steps.

"I'll march your butt clean outta sight!"

"You say you called the marines to fight!"

"Well, pretty girl, you did just right!"

"Lay your head now and rest 'til light"

"This marine will hold you tight!"

"Detail, halt. Riot 'ace. Stand at ease. I'll report in and find out where we go."

He turned and met a staff sergeant coming out the door. There was another detail marching down the sidewalk to our right and yet a third just appeared from the direction we had come from.

"Fall back in! You're late!"

Alvera spun around as best he could with the weight of the gear on his back and started for our position. "Get back here! Come to the position of attention."

The staff sergeant was dressed in utilities and they looked pressed? Ironed?

"Where did you fall off from, Lance Corporal? Is that how you perform an about-face?"

The staff sergeant was right in his face, inches from touching Alvera's. There was no way we could be late; we had to report before 0700 and we left battalion at 0600 and the march here was twenty minutes with one brief rest stop.

"About-face!" he ordered.

Alvera performed it as best he could, but the weight made him become unbalanced and he took a step sideways before he recovered.

"Holy mother of little green apples! Are you yanking my chain? Do it again, correctly!" Alvera was facing away from him toward us and I could see his face; he was in pain. He performed it again, better but still sloppy.

The door to the battalion opened and three additional cadre strode out onto the steps, taking in the spectacle.

"This isn't Six Weeks, 'Cruits! That battalion is back that way. You missed your turn," one of the newly arrived cadre yelled.

The three walked down the steps and toward us, yelling at us to get in the "front leaning rest position."

We dropped to the ground, duffle bags rolling off our heads, GLARs striking the deck, the weight of CPs pushing us tightly down. We couldn't rise up, which was the point, but the yelling and abuse were horrific.

"For the love of the planet Earth! You can't even raise yourselves off the deck?"

"Get in the position! Get in the position!"

"Oh, for the love of my Fleet Marine divisions! Did you just let your weapon hit the deck?"

One of the NCOs now turned his attention and began yelling at the nearing details of marines who surely were witnessing our punishment. "You better double time it here right now! Move!" He then ran toward one of the groups and met them, stopping them and issuing the same orders we were under to them.

The staff sergeant now ordered Alvera to hit the deck and left him, running toward another group. One of the cadre remained with us and the other chased down a third group. I could hear the door open again and more NCOs walked out, splitting off.

"Get up! On your feet. Come to attention! Drop those CPs. Reposition your GLARs to remain off the deck in the position. Feet on your CPs. Move!"

Oh, man. This hurts. This was not a new position by any means, but it was backbreaking.

"What's your name, 'Cruit?" The cadre sergeant was standing right in front of me, yelling.

"Lance Corporal Smith, Staff Sergeant!" I yelled in reply, my face almost level with the top of his boots.

"I wasn't talking to you, you idiot! How stupid and uneducated are you? Don't you know your ranks by now? These are gunnery sergeant stripes. Get up!"

He reached down and grabbed ahold of my collar and yanked me to my feet; the rest of the guys were standing up too.

"Not all of you. Get back down. Only Recruit Smith here!"

My face was red from the position of the exercise already and the blood rush to my head. I came to attention, but felt weak, dizzy. My dress uniform had to be a wreck, nothing in place, tussled, dirty from the deck.

"Come to attention in front of me! This isn't back at the Battalion Bay After-Hours Club!" I stared straight ahead, my GLAR along my leg, my right hand holding the front sight. "How many stripes do you see on my collar?"

I looked, just to make sure it wasn't a trick.

"Can you count, Lance Corporal Smith?"

He was yelling in my face while at the same time poking me in the chest, not giving me an opportunity to answer, but he didn't want an answer. "I bet you can't. You just memorized the chart. Which one of you scumbags down there taught Lance Corporal Smith to memorize the rank chart?"

He began to yank up each of the members of Echo. It was a reprieve from the harsh position we were in, a brief relief from the pain.

"It was you, wasn't it?" He punched Simon in the chest so hard he nearly fell backwards. "No, it couldn't be you. You have three CRs." He walked the line and stopped in front of Grigsby.

"What's your name?" he demanded.

"Lance Corporal Grigsby, Gunnery Sergeant!"

"You taught Smith the rank chart, didn't you?"

"No, Gunnery Sergeant. He taught me."

"How did I know you were in the same training company? Now!" he said, grasping and jerking him so roughly by the jacket that a rip was heard.

"The lack of a CR stripe on either mine or Lance Corporal Smith's Alphas, Gunnery Sergeant!"

"Correct. Back down in the position. All of you," he ordered, pushing several down before they could react.

The other groups slowly but painfully joined us in front of the training battalion steps. The cadre yelled at us to straighten our backs or lift our heads, stop moving, or any number of insults. A roll call was completed, and it was found that we were missing three candidates from 3/3/2 and two from 1/1/7. My heart skipped; was Campbell coming?

We were all ordered on our feet and instructed to "stack arms" off to the side. The next task was to neatly stack our duffle bags near the bottom of the steps in a pyramid and finally to align our CPs in a single straight line in alphabetical order. That took a minute, as the cadre mocked and belittled us for not knowing the ABCs correctly. With the completion of that, the three missing marines from 3/3/2 arrived, taking some of the attention off us. They didn't suffer near the extent of pain we had because we had to move on. The two from 1/1/7 were identified as DNS, Did Not Show, and we were reorganized and separated into four squads, thirty of us total.

"You are Week One P, Fox Company, Second Training Battalion. There is no recycle. If you fail something, you will return to your battalion and come back another time. This is a three-week course to train you on how to become a skilled, knowledgeable, and competent noncommissioned officer of the Fleet Marine divisions. The course schedule is intense, physically active, and mentally challenging and has no room or tolerance for the nondedicated. Your uniforms are substandard, a disgrace. Your lack of preparedness shows that you are not proud of it, so you will therefore double-time up to the second deck, find your assigned bunk that is already posted with your name, change into utilities, make your bunks, and set up your footlockers and wall lockers. You have ten minutes to be at the foot of your bunks at attention and ready for First Sergeant's Inspection. Dismissed," ordered the unknown gunnery sergeant.

It had begun.

CHAPTER 2

Our arrival in the Alpha Centauri system the week before had been relatively quiet, unusual. For days, we slipped and skipped, flying into and out of two desert planets' atmospheres of the Centauri C system, CC-002048-01 and CC-002048-02, nicknamed Butch and Sundance. There were no scouting reports and division decided for Echo to insert on Butch and conduct patrols. *Great.* The average surface temp, even with the dud star, was 220 degrees and the daylight cycle was sixteen hours long; night temps only dropped to 175 on average, and there was no water, not for a long time. Mineral exploration samples had come up favorable for several known and unknown mineral deposits as well as a possibility of Green Gold, or GG, the superdense megafuel found throughout the universe. The topography of Butch was expansive desert plains as large as the island continent of Australia, along with enormous mountain chains and a system of canyons and deep, what was thought to be, long-ago dried-up oceans or lake beds.

The order was to insert at Mineral Sample Site 02103 in the Narmean Ocean Basin and determine if there had been any activity. First and second platoons inserted, while third and fourth remained in a cover pattern at two hundred feet. We performed the standard and well-rehearsed defensive perimeter and watched as the Bettys lifted off and left us in the blinding whiteout of coarse sand and heat shimmers. I would pity the colonist that would have to live on this rock if a substantial deposit of GG was determined to be worth the investment of a mining operation.

Lieutenant Green quickly located the core hole, a three-inch diameter boring from one of thousands of probes that randomly surveyed interstellar planets. A small beacon marker was located over the hole and would transmit for fifty years under all but explosive destruction conditions. There shouldn't be any presence of activity, but there was. The lieutenant ordered the platoon to make a grid pattern box search three meters apart going out fifty meters each direction from the hole. First platoon with Lieutenant Howard and Staff Sergeant Ginny moved straight out at 260 degrees toward an anomaly, a square-looking object formation one hundred meters away.

"Why does this sand have a different texture?" asked Private Hackney, one of the boots.

This was his third or fourth planetary patrol and of course he was still both excited and apprehensive.

"What do you mean, Hackney?" asked Sergeant Carpenter.

"Well, over there where we inserted it was coarse, big grains, but it is a smaller grain over here." He was on an outer edge, nearly thirty meters out.

Lieutenant Green bent down and scooped up a handful of sand and looked around. He walked briskly to Hackney and did the same thing, still holding remnants of the first handful. I knew he was talking to someone, but on the other channel. I was still only on the intra-platoon channel.

"We have mining activity here, Second Platoon. Look sharp. Form into squads," he said after reporting to Captain Shupin.

"Corporal Larson, on me. Murray, on Six," ordered Carpenter, moving toward the direction first platoon was moving.

I could see the subtle difference now, clever. The borings were mixed somehow with the surface sand, and overexposure to the heat and wind just blended in. There was no telling how old this activity was. First platoon was now at the object and halted, taking a knee.

We were in a giant bowl, thousands of miles across, at the bottom of a long-gone ocean, hundreds of feet deep, or below sea level, making Death Valley back on Earth look like a child's play sandbox. Several hundred miles away in some direction was a shoreline, but the horizon to us was just a washout of where the sky met the expansive ancient seabed. There were no clouds, no water vapor, only a very bright, hot sunlight of a dull blue. The wind was picking up, little dust devils swirling, picking up sand and dancing around before collapsing. The solar convection creates its own wind from heat shimmers and slight temperature variances along with other environmental and atmospheric conditions. Due to the depth of our location, we could be close to the epicenter of a weather creator, simply the heart of a regional wind-maker. The devils were getting larger and living longer. The temperature was fluttering now at 190 and 193 and this was closer to morning than midday; it was heating up and with it a wind was being created. This was not good.

There was hurried, excited activity to our front, among first platoon, and a huge plume of sand appeared out of nowhere and was engulfing them as they ran in a controlled cover and move deployment formation back toward us.

"Cover first as they fall back. Get into firing positions," ordered Lieutenant Green.

Sergeant Carpenter was now placing us where he wanted, Lieutenant Green feverously waving his hands and pointing, I guess to the overhead Betty, directing them to something.

"I've seen this before," said Corporal Larson. "Wow!"

"What is it?" asked the lieutenant.

"I think it's an evacuator, LT, blows the day's drilling castings out of the shaft. That was years ago on the first colony."

The wind was picking up the plume, and before we knew it, we were in the middle of a cyclone, the heat shimmers building to a crescendo and instant windstorm. Visibility was down to no more than our outstretched hand.

"Keep your positions. Move to prone. Switch to IR. Conserve your water. We might be here a while," ordered Carpenter.

I had never been in the birth of a windstorm before. This was absolutely intriguing. The infrared IR, sensors were on either side of the helmet just back of where the visor slides up into the recessed cover in the raised position. The visor acted as a screen and we could detect images through thermal display. The whole area was red with images of lighter pink and orange outlines to my left and right. The field of vision was anywhere from normal line of sight to near nothing depending on the conditions. The sand was causing a lot of interference, and visibility was only about fifteen to twenty feet. I thought about the exercise back in Death Valley, where we had to lie in the sand in the heat for four hours and how hot it was. This was much more comfortable with the HECS. It all made sense now.

"I know I've seen this before," I said, and the platoon erupted in laughter. Every Fleet Marine remembered that grueling part of Graduation Week.

"Don't fall asleep this time, Smith," Carlson said.

"What?" asked Corporal Murray.

"Yeah, he went right out, snoring so loudly Gunny Bryant thought he was choking," Grigsby added. There was more laughter from the platoon.

"That was right before the Land Nav exercise when he beat the crap out of his team to make them complete the course." Moon was laughing so hard he could barely say it.

"You're kidding," replied Lance Corporal Almond.

"Just stories, guys, tall tales these bored marines make up around the campfire," I said.

"How about when he stormed into the range pavilion and demanded a cup of the drills' coffee?" Jackson said laughing.

"Yeah! And he was punished with clearing the firing line of snow!" added Luke.

Everyone was laughing, even Carpenter.

"Just asking," quipped in Private Clark, I'm sure trying to fit in. "I heard he beat up four Second Division guys. Is that true?"

"No, Boot. It was only two." Grigsby was laughing. "And they were drunk!"

The laughter was a mental break, enjoyable in the harsh environment.

"Should I just put you on report now, PFC Smith, and wait to fill in the spaces?"

"Boom! Six! He nailed you, Smith!"

It went on for a few more minutes, the storm covering us with several inches of sand. An hour passed and then two. I had to sit up, because I was getting sleepy. The red light of the IR and the heavy blanket of sand covering me were making me drowsy.

I raised up to my elbows, gently stirring the sand off me; it was deep. I looked around but couldn't make out anyone. "Number Two?"

"Go ahead, Smith." The transmission was scratchy, static.

"Are you prone?"

"Affirmative."

"I had to sit up. I can't make anyone out. The sand is deep."

"Larson, Murray, report status."

"I'm buried. Rich, how about you?" Murray asked.

I could see someone walking now, just a fainter outline than the red surrounding it.

"I have movement to my front. Is that you, Six? Two? Where is First?" I asked.

"Negative. No one should be to our front, no one walking. Everyone freeze. What do you see, Smith?" asked Green.

"I have an outline a shade lighter than the screen moving from my 1100 to 0100. No, make that two outlines!"

I was whispering but my excitement and realization that we were being stalked was alarming.

"No one else move. Smith, remain still. Switch to normal mode. See anything?"

"No, Six, lost them. No visibility. Going back IR." They were gone. "I can't find them."

"Betty has us pinpointed but does not detect movement among us. They pinged you, roughly 270 degrees from OPD."

The only way to navigate on planets was to utilize an OPD, Original Point of Direction, and base all movement and direction from that point. "We are on a line 268 to 272. First platoon is to our rear. The square to our front. What did you see?"

"First it was a single definite outline, just lighter than the IR background, someone walking, and then a second figure. I know I saw it, Six."

"Affirmative. Close your eyes. Everyone ready. Betty is going to make a gun run to our front with HILS. On 3…2…1."

I had to close my eyes with the IR mode with a HILS run, or I would temporarily lose my vision, but I could still see the lasers through my eyelids. The stream and flashes and explosions on the ground were breathtaking. I opened them and was able to see several objects still burning with the intensity of the heat of the IR, that the HILS hit something. I saw the outlines, moving.

"I have movement and the HILS hit something."

"Affirmative. Betty observing afterglow but not what's causing it. Stand by."

My visibility was increasing, like the storm was dissipating, or at least the intensity. There was an outline on the ground where an afterglow was, now becoming clearer, another form beside it, and then it moved! It was coming toward me. I saw the superheated stream before I realized what it was.

Puc! Puc! Puc!

I returned fire in the split-second. *Zik! Zik! Zik! Zik! Zik!* It was on!

The outline went down. I'm not sure if I hit him, but I turned my head to see if there were any behind me or to my sides. No, not immediately.

"Report, Smith!"

"Six, there were two, one downed by the HILS and the other came at me and fired first. He's down, but I don't know if I got him."

"Rising, Smith, should be to your right rear," advised Carpenter.

I could see the movement where he said, he was only feet behind me, I never knew. Only his head and upper back came out of the sand, but he was still lying down.

"Where, kid?" He hadn't called me that in weeks.

"Just about to my 1130. The other one is 1100. You can see the heat on him."

"I got him. Good work. Put one on the 1130. Be ready to go prone. I got you."

I fired again and immediately went prone. No return fire.

"Move up. I'll cover," he said.

I inched my way forward in a low crawl, pulling my way through the sand until I was less than five feet away. The sweat was running down my face, soaking my neck and my back. I was breathing heavy, scared, the adrenaline pushing me forward. I was stressed out. He could have me in his sights or one of his buddies, just like Carpenter was covering me.

I stopped. *Push on. Keep going!* I was screaming to myself. I slid up beside the figure and found he was dead; his armor took a hit in a seam, rupturing, and the extreme heat took him out.

"He's dead. Checking the other one." I inched up and contacted the second figure; the HILS had really done a number on him. I looked around, and I could see other outlines. "I got multiple possible casualties. Betty can't see any of this?"

"Negative, only you and the afterglows. No figures. First squad, ease out of the sand in a prone. Second, remain concealed," ordered Lieutenant Green.

The storm was letting off now and I switched to normal mode and could make out the scene better.

"Six, wait till you see this. I make four KIAs. Looks like they were searching for us." I was on my knee now, and I could see Carpenter crawling to me.

"We have to get Division S2 out here, Six. This was cloaking for sure," said Carpenter.

I didn't know too much about that, but it was a scary thought to have them around us and not see them. So we discovered an underground-based mining operation. Terrific. They were using the planet's heat to create weather patterns to mask the operation. Slick. We found it purely by coincidence because we were right on top of it when they decided to expel the shaft castings. It had to be big under there, which meant that when the Galleens were aware that we had discovered it, there was going to be a pitched battle. We couldn't leave it, and they couldn't let us take it. It was all out in the open.

Third platoon was inserting now and first platoon moved up back to their original position before the storm. Second was performing a sweep of the enemy KIA and collecting them for intel when S2 would arrive. Fourth platoon remained in reserve. Captain Shupin inserted with Gunny Scott and inspected the site, laying out the defense plan and informing his two lieutenants—third didn't have one—that brigade was sending a company from first battalion ASAP and division was putting the first and third brigades on standby to pour in. This was a major find. There hadn't been an underground operation this large in years. There was no telling what they were mining. We now had to locate additional access shafts and be watchful for other storms. The CO then extracted and we set about our work.

The square object was evidently the exhaust cover and it was big, nearly ten feet square, but we didn't approach. It could be rigged to explode or even cave in. The bodies were examined, and we searched for possible nests and sniper holes, which was exhausting, stressful, and expansive. They could be anywhere, but these Mowatts, privates, and Abooe, corporal, came from somewhere. They could have just been an expendable squad whose only mission was to guard the site until relieved, whenever that might be. We searched for their bunker. The storm had added nearly six inches of sand and crushed rock to the area, waiting for it to be blown away and disseminated. What if there were another bunker, its occupants waiting on the next storm to attack us? Would a full-blown operation be initiated soon?

The day was sixteen hours long and the darkness was creeping in; this was the first anyone in Echo had patrolled this planet, and we weren't sure how drastic the temperature drop would occur, but if the increasing daytime heat caused the storms, so could the reverse. The one thing we now knew was that massive amounts of sand were capable of covering us and that we were blind during the storm, but apparently so were the Galleens. The three platoons on the ground set up a tight perimeter and set guard watches and established a Command Post, CP. We were set up in a circle, facing out, which meant anything coming in was a bad guy. Even before the sun set, the surface temp dropped ten degrees, and we watched the dust devils dance across the seafloor. They were much bigger than earlier, stronger, taller. This was going to be a wild night.

Chapter 2

PRESENT

The two-week Combat Medic Course I took—I don't know how long ago now, seems like forever—was hard physically and crammed full of academically challenging class periods and practicals. Of course, the combat field exercise was demanding, but the whole time we were treated with respect and given the due professional courtesy of being fellow Fleet Marines. But this PNCOC and the cadre were animals. They went out of their way to insult, humiliate, or downright attempt to provoke us. The morning had only gotten worse with First Sergeant's Inspection. There were at least two gunnys—the one, Goff, I had already had the displeasure of meeting and Castelle—and six staff sergeants. First Sergeant Alfonso was a real piece of work, a regular… He was mean. He stood a little over six feet, lean as a pole, dark-skinned, freckles, a face that looked like a ventriloquist's puppet, and wreaked of aftershave cologne. He personally tore sheets off the bunks, flipped over footlockers, tossed our wall lockers, and physically manipulated our limbs into the "proper" position of attention. This was totally different from what we had all experienced during Six Weeks. That harassment and punishment was deserved and taught us attention to detail, order, discipline, and command structure. This was blatant, undeserved, and wrongfully punitive. There wasn't a nonsquared away lance corporal in the group, we wouldn't be here otherwise.

There were two advanced class weeks on the same bay deck, and from the moment we ran up the stairs, none of them looked at us or spoke, busily performing their own assigned tasks on Sunday morning. The deck was being buffed to a high gloss, while dust bunnies were being chased down with towels. Every light fixture was dropped down and dusted, and bunks were being team picked up and moved by four marines. The windows to the bay were being cleaned inside and out, the screens removed and being hand cleaned. No one was wearing footwear but us and the cadre, and the guys buffing the deck were visibly upset that their work was being ruined. A small group of marines were getting anxious and were rushing the other group using the buffer, nearly pleading that they needed to hurry because it was needed to still do the commandant's office and CQ hallway.

After the inspection, we were ordered to fall out for PT, which, judging by what we had already experienced, led me to believe that this was going to be heartbreaking. I wasn't disappointed. The uniform was utility pants, boots, and the red water shirt. We just threw all of our uniforms and equipment into the wall and footlockers and fell out. There was no time to properly arrange it. PT took the remainder of the morning up to lunch chow. We went through every exercise in the manual, reciting each action and the corresponding directions or instruction.

"I realize that each of you has just blindly followed along with whomever was leading what minimal 'Organized and Daily Physical Training' period you may have participated in, but you will correctly lead and perform the required exercise routines in the correct manner as outlined in the authorized *Fleet Marine Physical Training Manual*," said Gunnery Sergeant Castelle.

He was a brute. He stood on a raised platform on the edge of the Second Training Battalion field, and we went through a set of each exercise. There were fifteen individual exercises broken into four different authorized routines, each containing a combination of six of the individual exercises. This was far worse than Six Weeks. After that, we went through each of the routines, one through four, with each of their six individual exercises. Then we performed each of the individual exercises again. Just so we wouldn't embarrass the cadre, who were already embarrassed enough being seen in public with such "a bunch of obviously low-IQ, deficient excuses for NCO applicants," we only did eighteen repetitions of each exercise instead of the prescribed twenty count. The cadre were humiliated enough with our poor performance and evident lack of knowledge of the exercises.

The *Fleet Marine Physical Training Manual* only recognizes or authorizes two run lengths, the three-kilometer and five-kilometer. Since we had had such an easy exercise period, and it was a beautiful day, we would embark on the five-kilometer run, which was 3.1 miles at an easy seven-minute-mile pace. We would run the first mile on the track here, which was six laps, and then exit the training field and run to the main gate and back and then complete the remaining distance on the track, approximately five laps. We would complete the full five laps just to round it up.

We began with Staff Sergeant MacGilly calling a well-known cadence, and the first mile passed by effortlessly. As we departed the training field, we took a strange route, not at all the way to the main gate. We headed toward the perimeter work gate, the gate that construction crews and vehicles entered. Most of us knew this from, well, experience and general knowledge. This route was going to easily add 2.5 miles depending on how we then proceeded to the main gate. My heart sunk as we turned and followed a work road toward the construction site of the new range. I knew this from my flyovers during Divisional Rapid Response Duty. Most of us knew we were about to put an additional four miles onto the run. The pace was also quicker than a seven-minute-mile now. The elevation and up- and downslopes were taking a toll. Finally, we turned toward the gate and turned around, but retraced our path back! This was a ten-miler. No water, heavy exercise period prior to beginning, this was going to drop some guys before we finished. That was a shame, because they were already recommended by their platoon leaders and sergeants as qualified and there was an emerging known shortage of corporals heading into the surge that was about to take place.

It started as soon as everyone realized the route was the same back. Mental games played in guys' minds. The thirst and physical pain were great. The feeling of dread was overbearing, killing intestinal fortitude. We tried to encourage one another to not give up; it didn't matter that we didn't know each other. The lance corporal beside me started wavering and weaving, his inner demons taking control.

"Come on, Marine. You can do this. Don't quit," I encouraged him.

"Keep your mouth shut. He's already quit, just looking for an excuse. What? Does your tummy hurt? We already have your gear thrown out on the steps. You can collect it when you limp in after chow," one of the cadre sneered mockingly.

"Don't listen to him. He can't hack a real CR. That's why he's hiding here as a bully." It's what I felt and it was the truth. These cadre hadn't pulled a CR in so long they were prima donnas and took satisfaction in pain and ridicule.

A hand grabbed me and violently threw me to the ground. I was stunned at first but recovered and knew I had beat them at their own game. This was bull and had nothing to do with making NCOs, it was worthless tradition that had little function in the operation of a cohesive unit fighting in combat. First Sergeant Alfonso was standing over me and glaring down in an absolute uncontrolled rage.

"You're out. Washed up. You can't control your mouth. How can you expect to lead marines in a squad when you can't follow simple orders and maintain self-control?"

I couldn't help but laugh out loud, which only infuriated him more. The platoon, Week One P, had stopped, and everyone was watching the scene unfolding. Only the six guys from Echo knew me, who I was, what I had already accomplished, and my obvious leadership traits and combat achievements. That was the funny thing—they knew that I was the humblest and most dedicated marine they had ever known. I always encouraged the best performance, the injured, and took the lead in whatever detail was assigned. My actions during the last CR on CC-002048-01, Butch, was a true testament of what a real NCO was, not how shiny the dagone deck was with a buffer.

I stood up and faced the first sergeant. I had faced real first sergeants before, and this was a fake, a Fleet Marine that was no more than a coward hiding behind a façade of institutional tradition. The drill instructors that trained new recruits during Six Weeks rotated in and out, serving in line units and training new marines based on a dedication to create a new Fleet Marine that would survive his first CR and become a part of the family. The senior drills were all SS and men who had lost two and three limbs but still volunteered for combat duty. Some like First Sergeant French who had over five known amputations or Loss of Limb, LoL, injuries and could not be assigned to an active line company anymore were role models of encouragement, but not Alfonso.

"When did it become wrong to encourage a fellow marine, First Sergeant?"

"Right there! Who do you think you are? Lock it up! Come to the position of attention when I address you, 'Cruit!"

"Professional courtesy dictates that you address me at my correct rank, First Sergeant. That is Lance Corporal Smith. I haven't been a recruit since before my awarding of the Order of Leonidas and Brotherhood Ribbon, both of which I am sure you are aware of."

Sometimes I just don't know where my mouth came up with what I said, but the company took notice. That was heavy weight I just threw out and something I had never used before and kept closely guarded. The recent visit with Donna I guess had begun to make me more acceptable of my achievements and actions. The ability to accept what I had accomplished and acknowledge that others had played just as heroic or significant contribution as I had made me finally realize my actions were commendable. I had to be proud of what I did and no longer feel ashamed in not doing more. My actions in combat required at the least respect and recognition of my dedication to my service in the Fleet Marines, and by the love of God's favorite planet, I was due at least that.

"You worthless ragtag orphan, you aren't fit to be an NCO in the Fleet Marines. You have no integrity, no honor."

"Tell me, First Sergeant, the first responsibility of a noncommissioned officer is trust and honesty. How many miles of this authorized *Fleet Marine Physical Training Manual* five-kilometer run have already been completed? I know from personal experience we have run well over six miles, and according to your route and the shortest route back at this point, we will complete no less than eight miles, well over the authorized five kilometers, First Sergeant."

I was completely caught off guard at the next series of events, milliseconds in their occurrence, but a slow motion happening of reactions. The first sergeant stepped toward me, his right hand and arm moving in a quick and direct line to strike me in either the head or throat in an unprovoked assault on my personal being. His arm and hand came up from his side in a well-known aggressive attack position, and my reflex action made me move to his right and bring my left arm up in a blocking position to deflect the strike. I could have performed several other countermaneuvers, such as breaking his wrist or his jaw or blowing out his knee, but I only defended myself from a flurry of strikes and kicks. The cadre stood in disbelief for a split-second and then descended upon me, two staff sergeants grabbing me from behind in a containment hold where I was now defenseless, and I was struck rapidly and full force three times, twice in the abdomen and then in the face.

Gunnery Sergeant Goff pulled the first sergeant away yelling, "Enough! Enough!"

The staff sergeants pushed me to the deck, where I was headed anyway. I couldn't breathe for one, and the blow to my head nearly knocked me out. I was dizzy and my left eye was killing me. Instantly Grigs was kneeling next to me and the rest of the platoon had moved in around me.

"Fall back into formation!" the cadre were yelling.

"That was assault! He struck him when he was being held," yelled Alvera.

"Fall in!" yelled Gunnery Sergeant Castelle.

The platoon slowly moved to fall in, except Grigs. I was gasping.

"Slow down. Easy. Let me stand you up and bend over."

"Leave him alone. Fall in!"

Grigsby didn't move, his hands under my arms lifting me up.

The staff sergeant forcefully pushed me to the ground by my head and Grigsby moved to a fighting ready position. "Touch him again and I might go to prison, but I'll break your neck."

The platoon, again, broke ranks now and several guys were helping me to my feet; there was a tense space of time with yelling back and forth and threats from the cadre.

The SFP, Space Fleet Patrol, arrived from a report by a Betty conducting security operations of a personal assault and a training run breaking down into a standoff between two groups. Two and then three SCUVs or scuvys, Small Command Utility Vehicles, appeared, emergency lights flashing, and the SFP quickly retained order by sending the platoon of lance corporals away across the road, two petty officers directing them to fall into a formation. Two CPOs, Chief Petty Officers, were now talking to the senior NCOs and initiating charges of insubordination against the EMs. One CPO walked over to me and helped me to my feet and then sat me down beside his scuvy and looked at me.

"I know you. You were in a fight a couple of months ago in town. You just can't stay out of trouble, can you, Lance Corporal Smith?"

I looked up and recognized the chief from that night at Linda's. "No, Chief Petty Officer."

"Looks like you lost this one. How'd that happen? You should have been able to take on one staff sergeant."

"Yes, Chief Petty Officer."

"You can call me Chief, Lance Corporal. What happened here? We're going to have to take you and have your eye taken care of."

"I can't leave now, Chief. I'll be washed out."

He looked at me and shook his head. "You're already washed out, Smith. You struck a senior NCO in front of all his friends during PNCOC. You'll be lucky if you don't serve five years at Salt Lake."

I held my head in my hands; it hurt to breath, but my eye was worse, and my head was splitting.

"Who struck you?"

"I fell."

"That's a shame. That girl of yours is going to miss you. She's the… You know who she is, right? Space Fleet Air Crew Operations Support Medal and an Air Medal for Valor device, she earned that the same mission you did your thing if I'm not mistaken. Let me go talk to your brothers over there. Don't get up." He walked across the road and was gone for several minutes.

In the meantime, one of the CPOs that had been taking the cadre's statements walked up to me and said, "On your feet. You're under arrest for striking a senior NCO."

I slowly stood up.

"Turn around. You try that mess with me and you'll be eating out of a straw the next month."

He shoved me against the SCUV and placed me in a wrist crossbar while he cuffed me, squeezing the cuffs too tightly, the metal ripping my skin. I flinched and he pushed me hard into the SCUV again.

"Whoa, whoa, whoa! Chief Reilly, that's uncalled for. He's my subject anyway. Remove those cuffs. That Fleet Marine's injured."

"What are you talking about, Chief Swan? He struck a senior, right there in a training run."

"Come here a second. Let me talk to you."

The two pulled back to the rear of the SCUV and I could hear them talking but not what they were saying. The third chief joined them. I was still in cuffs. The petty officer who had remained on this side of the roadway who stood between me and the cadre walked over to me.

"Something's not right. How come you're so messed up and the NCOs all have a different story? What'd you do? Hit one of them and they beat the snot out of you?"

"No, Petty Officer. I never touched the first sergeant."

He looked at me. "They really did a number on you, but I only see one visible mark. Who's this first sergeant you mentioned? Only six staff sergeants and a gunny over there."

I didn't say anything. He walked over to the chiefs and said something and then he jumped in a scuvy with the other chief whose name I didn't know and drove away. Gunnery Sergeant Castelle walked up close and looked at me.

"Hey." He was talking to the SFP chiefs. "How much longer? We have a schedule and they have to get chow."

Chief Swan walked up to him and asked, "How many of you were on this run, Gunnery Sergeant?"

"We started with thirty NCO candidates. We have twenty-nine now, with one in your custody, Chief."

"Sure, Sarge. So how many cadre?" The gunnery sergeant bristled, the use of such a disrespecting slang and of several ranks below his was not taken lightly.

"I have six staff sergeants."

"I was led to believe there was a first sergeant and another E7 on the run."

"Yeah, there were, but the first sergeant and gunnery sergeant had to get back and prepare for the next class of instruction."

"When was this?"

"I'm not sure. Look, we have to move on. The later we fall behind is only hurting these guys." The implication of retribution was just laid out.

Most of those marines across the road were not going to have a successful course completion. I had sealed all their fates. I ruined their careers.

"We're not finished with taking their statements, Gunnery Sergeant Castelle, and until the duty officer has a chance to get here and see what's going on for himself, we may be here for a while. Now, you need to return to your area over there, and if I see you approach Lance Corporal Smith again without my authorization, I'll charge you with tampering with a witness."

Man, this is it. I'm out. The gunny walked away and the NCOs all grouped together. Chief Swan turned me around and removed the cuffs. "You want to tell me the story? Or is this going to be an all-nighter?"

"There's nothing to say, and this is only hurting those guys." I nodded across the road. "Let them move out so they can continue with the course."

"What'd you do, mouth off, bump a gunny, make a threat?" He looked at me and shook his head.

"Lance Corporal Grigsby, come over here," said Chief Swan as he turned toward the class.

What was he doing? Man, now Grigs was in trouble. Grigsby quickstepped over and stopped in front of the chief.

"Yes, Officer Swan?" He was looking down.

"Look at your buddy. You Fleet Marines hold to this brother thing. How did your brother marine get so busted up? That's a pretty hard hit for such a skilled fighter, isn't it? One punch?" Grigsby was silent.

"Stand back. I want all of you to file over here. Petty Officer Toby, bring them over here."

Just then another SCUV pulled up and an officer stepped out. The two chiefs saluted and briefly reported the situation. The marines were standing in a line, waiting for instructions.

The lieutenant walked up and looked at me and then walked over to the group of NCOs and started asking them questions. Swan told the group to file by me and return to the other side of the road; they could sit if they wanted. Another SCUV arrived a minute or two later and several marines climbed out of that one, three walking straight over to the group of NCOs and the fourth to the marines on the road.

"On your feet, Platoon! Atten-huh!" It was a staff sergeant we didn't know but the group immediately fell in.

Swan ran over. "What are you doing, Staff Sergeant? These marines are involved in an investigation."

"Not anymore. Make way. You got questions, speak to the sergeant major over there. Right face!"

"Hold on! These men aren't going anywhere yet."

"Forward! March!" The platoon automatically and without hesitation began marching, disciplined to take orders.

The lieutenant was speaking with the sergeant major, who was dominating the conversation and was telling the duty lieutenant what was going to happen. The lieutenant had little recourse, while the NCOs ran to catch up to the platoon, and the sergeant major with the two he arrived with returned to their SCUV and drove off, following the platoon. The lieutenant walked over to me.

"You know, the next time anyone sees that platoon of marines is going to be late next week, out in the desert, and they are going to be so dehydrated and beaten down that they won't be able to function for weeks. But I guess you fell. We have First Sergeant Alfonso.

He blew a .09 BAC, that's pretty good for a Sunday morning drunk, but his problem is only beginning with being drunk on duty. Chief Petty Officer Swan, place this Fleet Marine under arrest for striking a senior NCO."

When Swan moved to place the cuffs back on me, I asked, "Which one? Which one did I strike, Lieutenant? Did he hit me back or did I fall?"

"It's too late for that, Lance Corporal. Right now all of those marines are being told who you hit and any of your buddies are being hit in the gut in front of the rest. Who hit you? Who knocked your eye nearly out of its socket?"

"The first sergeant hit me while I was being held from behind by two cadre. I don't know which ones. The first sergeant yanked me out of formation for something I said and pushed me to the ground. We argued, then he attacked me. Two hits in the gut and once in the face." I looked down at the ground, ashamed.

"Go get them!" the lieutenant yelled, but the SFPs were already moving. "Arrest the cadre and separate the EMs!" The scuvys flew down the road, spitting gravel and dirt, lights flashing.

He turned to his driver. "Get HQ. Tell the desk to send another team right now to Second Training Battalion. Notify the CO and the provost marshal."

He looked at me. "It doesn't matter what you said. That didn't warrant you getting sucker punched by a senior NCO. Get in. I don't know where to take you first, the MHG or the Duty House."

CHAPTER 3

The night was horrific. The plume of sand at the beginning was not as big as the one we had observed earlier, but the wind speed was up and down from 60 to 90 mph, the equivalent of a Category 1 hurricane. The Bettys dropped our CPs and extra A-Doses and water when third platoon had inserted. I wish they would have just taken us up. We knew the Galleens were here, and the Galleens knew we were here. Why did we have to sit in a sandstorm just to call their hand? If the wind increased much more, we would be in essentially a Category 2 hurricane, with winds of 96 to 110 mph. We were already taking a beating trying to remain in our positions. I didn't know it at the time, but later we were told that the storm followed a slight depression or ditch, and this was near the end of the course, the sand blowing in for hundreds of miles, continuing for another hundred. The good thing was that there wasn't as much collection as before, only two to three inches.

Sleep was impossible; with the wind increases at any time and variations, it was all we could do to keep our CPs from rolling away, strapping them on and sitting facing outward. The Bettys had to move off from their covering flight orbits, going to two thousand feet and moving out of the sheer path. That would have been disconcerting, if we had known, but we all knew that we were on our own anyway—they wouldn't be able extract us in this storm. Captain Shupin inserted at the last minute, the winds at a gust of 75 mph when he stepped off, Gunny Scott at his side. He was not going to have his Fleet Marines on the ground in this storm without him commanding them. A PHA, Power Head Auger, beacon was activated at the command post so that each marine had an orientation in the storm.

If the Galleens had the ability to see us in the sandstorm now, we were sitting ducks. The CO made an open COMM address to all of us. "Rest easy, Echo. They are just as blind as we are. The skirmish we had earlier proved that. I will turn the PHA on for one minute at the top of the hour for you to fix your position until the storm calms down to visibility. Hunker down! Echo Six, out."

I took a sip of water. I was hungry. We hadn't been able to eat since the insert; how long ago now? Ten or twelve hours ago. There was no chance of an energy bar, it was too hot to raise the visor and too much sand. The only thing we could do was mix a bug juice packet and siphon it in, but that was not possible in this wind either with no way to keep the sand out of the bottle to mix it. The temp had fallen to right around 160 degrees, still hot enough to get a heat burn on the face if we did raise our visors. You were in an awful position if your mask slipped now. There was just absolutely no way to replace or reposition it. This was really at the limit of our operating capability for more than a quick in and out op. Whoever made this decision didn't factor in this storm or how long it could last. We could all die down here from exposure if the Bettys were not able to extract us in a couple days or less.

I couldn't sleep, but I must have been dozing in and out; there was no way to tell time, there was zero visibility.

"Second platoon, give me a check. How you doing out there?" Sergeant Carpenter.

Each of us said a word or made a comment. We were tired, water was getting low from the long day. We had the gallon in our CP but could not go into that until given orders. I had just refilled my HECS with a bottle, but I had recycled first, so now I was down to just the one bottle and the liter in the suit. If I used the last bottle before I ran a bug juice mix, I would be without any energy or nutrient additives.

"Hang in there. We'll mix some juice in the morning," Lieutenant Green.

He knew our situation was getting dire. We had all endured long periods of activity with no water and food before, that's why we trained for it, but these conditions were dangerous if we couldn't replenish in the next twelve hours. The body had to have minerals and electrolytes that we were losing to sweating. The A-Dose would need to be taken soon while we were still hydrated, by sunrise. It just occurred to me, I hadn't thought of it—the day cycle was almost thirty hours here, sixteen daylight hours and about thirteen night hours.

"Beacons up! Second, steady now. First platoon has received a probe. GBL on one of their positions. Ensure the PHA is to your rear!"

First was to our right, and third to the left. We were in a tight circle, nearly double arm apart, because of the lack of sight. This was as tight as I had ever been in a company position. Captain Shupin made the change as soon as he touched down again and saw that we were too spaced in the coming dark night, and the holes were too big. I still couldn't see Grigs or Private Clark on either side of me.

"PFC Smith, what's happening?"

It was Clark. He was scared, so I shifted over two feet to my left and waved my arm around.

"Reach out your right hand," I said.

He did and I found it, grabbing it and scooting closer to him, butting my helmet to his and looking into his visor. We could see each other now, eye to eye. I could see through his yellow-tinted goggles, his face covered with the mask, but his eyes told me all I needed to know. I held up my thumb and shook it, patted him on the back, and then lightly patted his helmet and nodded my head.

"PFC Smith, is everything okay? How's Clark?"

The COMM was hollow, the private channel, I needed to find out more about this; it was Sergeant Carpenter.

"Secure?" I didn't want to broadcast the condition of Clark to the platoon.

"Affirmative. You are on Command channel. Keep it short. What's his status?"

"I'm with him. He's… This is closed?"

"Affirmative, PFC!" That was Gunny Scott.

"He's scared, Sergeant. Permission to stay with him?"

"Platoon leaders, pull your men back three feet, hand contact. Flight COMM, disconnect PFC Smith from Command channel…" That was Captain Shupin!

The hollow noise was gone. Lieutenant Green ordered, "Second platoon, move back toward CP three feet and establish hand contact."

We had practiced this, on various scenarios and conditions, most notably while in Water Training. I scooted back and away from Clark a little and then found Grigs' waving hand; we squeezed hard, reaffirming our condition. I loosened my grip and he gave me two quick hard squeezes, I responded with two back—we were good. I was still sitting with Clark.

"We have another probe on First. Can anyone see movement? Switch to normal and IR," Lieutenant Green said.

"Negative," we all responded, staggered.

"Report ASAP any movement or energy source. They are probing our perimeter. You should expect incoming. Hold return fire."

If we returned fire, they would know our position, they were only guessing, trying to find our line, maybe not even close. I saw an energy flow streak right in front of me, one burst.

"There! Right in front of me!"

"I saw it too!" Grigs yelled out.

"Right in front of us," Clark added.

It had just missed us! One of us would have been hit in the positions we had just moved from.

"IR?"

"Affirmative," the three of us answered.

"Smith, you are in the middle of that group. Switch to normal mode."

"Aye-aye, Six."

I was now acutely aware that Command had been and was currently monitoring all channels. I knew they could, but I didn't think much of it until now, and that was eye-opening.

"Smith, pull out your PHA and belt, activate it, and put it on," said Lieutenant Green. This was not leading anywhere good. "Drop your CP." I did.

Wherever I was going, I only had one liter of water now, in my HECS, and there was no recycle. I pushed my CP toward Grigs, who pulled it to him. Water was the only thing in there that was of importance, and the platoon would need it if I didn't come back.

"Second, we have a marine to your front, with a PHA active. Do not fire on his position. Smith, go prone and track that GBL back. Are you good?"

"Ten by ten."

I crawled out and made the turn where I thought the energy stream went by and continued. The sandstorm was masking my movement to the Galleens. I hoped. My heart was racing. This was an SS operation. This is what they were trained to do. Ginny was an SS, so why wasn't he doing this?

The hollow sound came back. "Platoon leaders, be advised. We have PHA outside the fence." Immediately I could hear the voices of platoon leaders and sergeants repeating orders to their platoons. It was eerie, a hollow sound.

"Staff Sergeant Ginny, take control of Smith," said Gunny.

"Listen, now, Smith, calm down. You can do this. Cake walk. You have it. This is what you are going to do. You are going to trace that GBL straight up to it origin, without giving away your position. You are going to *paint* the position. Betty is tracking you and will lay down a run to your front. You copy?" he calmly instructed me.

I was breathing heavily, sweating, somehow very cold. "How close to me is that HILS going to come?"

"They will lock on within two feet to your front. Don't stick your hand out." There was a couple of chuckles on the channel.

"Aye, One-Two." That was the call sign for first platoon sergeant.

"Ginny, for this little exercise," he responded.

"Yes, sir." More chuckles.

I crawled along the front of our perimeter, stopping every few feet, switching my IR back and forth. I must have crawled ten feet when a GBL energy burst streaked over my right shoulder off by two feet and off the deck about two feet.

"Incoming! Off my right line two feet to the company!"

"Roger, Jackson," Lieutenant Green responded on the platoon COMM, I was figuring out the noise differences in the channels now. "Keep off the triggers. They are only probing. They have no fix."

I corrected my course, but I could not tell where exactly the origin came from. My IR was nearly limited to three feet. It could have come from three feet away or twenty; there was just no way to know.

"How you doing, Smith?"

"I corrected my course, Ginny. I can't determine the range of origin. Sight limited to three feet."

"You're doing fine. They don't know you are there or you would know."

"Aye." My mouth was dry. I took a sip and rinsed my mouth.

I crawled another two feet and stopped. I switched the IR back and forth. The Abooe, Corporal, I had shot earlier was about six feet away when I was able to finally see him, and that was when the afternoon storm was letting off. This storm was still raging and was much stronger. I would be lucky if I didn't close less than three feet before I could make contact. Another thing occurred to me—what if they had some sort of affiliation with frequency, like our own whales and dolphins on Earth? Could they hear our PHA pulse? I switched mine off.

"Smith, are you good? We just lost your PHA?" said Ginny, concern in his voice.

"Yes, Ginny. Switch PHA on in CP. Off and then on again."

A GBL went by and then another. "Heads up!" I yelled in a hushed voice.

"Holy sour apple butter! Come on, son! A little more warning than that! That GBL travels at three hundred times faster than light!" Gunny Scott was breathless.

"They can hear our PHA, not very well. I think he knows I'm on to him, but the noise is probably distorted in this storm, he shot on reflex. I don't know much on sound wave stuff, but I think he had marker, not range."

"Scientists and politicians, PFC. Run your next idea by us first," the CO said.

"Aye, Six."

I crawled toward the intersect of the last two origins of GBL. There! I saw him! I could make out the slightly lighter shade of the red of the heat, which was in itself lighter due to the cooler temp. He was almost a deep rosy pink color. Very clear, I was close, four feet? I could hardly breathe. I was too scared to talk, sure that he could hear me. I saw another one, lying beside him to his right and a little farther back. They were oriented at a diagonal from my position, probably shifting on their last shot.

My voice barely a faint whisper, "Ginny, I have two, side by side, in a diagonal from my front. I corrected my line after the shots on the CP. They are four feet to my front. Does Betty have my position?"

"Affirmative, Smith. You are twenty meters to the front of the company. We are drawing a line from CP to four feet your front and going to light it up. Don't move."

The HILS rained down, just like before, and I closed my eyes but still could see the energy streaks, my face down in the sand. I looked up.

"I see two smoking, Ginny. Moving up."

"Betty has another afterglow behind them, five feet," replied Ginny.

"I got it, three now. These two are done," I paused as I crawled to the third. "That's three down. Moving ninety."

I crawled away quickly in case someone came to check on them. I had no idea from which direction that might be but decided a hard right turn was a good choice.

"Does Betty have any other afterglow?"

"Negative, you put out a sniper and his observer and probably a FO, (Forward Observer). Sit still. Good work. Do you still have visual on KIA?"

"Aye, Ginny. Have all three, lying feet to you, eyes on."

"Where did you read all this?" asked Captain Shupin, a reference to my Six Weeks reputation of reading the entire training manual ahead of schedule.

"Textbook, Six. He's a natural," replied Ginny.

"Nowhere, Six, just trying to make it back to you." The COMM was filled with laughter; it was still the Command channel.

"Very good. Lay low. Taking you off the channel for a few minutes. We can still hear you on the platoon net if something happens. Betty cut…" Captain Shupin was the last voice I would hear for hours.

They were discussing something above my pay grade. I did their hard work for them but didn't have the… *Knock it off! You are a Fleet Marine and performed your duty, your assignment. They owe you nothing.*

Okay, so here I am, isolated, lying mere feet from three KIAs. I was thirsty but didn't take a drink. There was no telling how long this was going to be. I needed to save my water. I was wide awake, but exhausted. I lay there for I don't know how long. Time was irrelevant. I was alone.

Chapter 3

PRESENT

It was as if a major black-market ring had been busted. The Duty House, the SFP main building, was chaotic and full of senior NCOs and midgrade officers. I was sitting in an interrogation room and still hadn't received medical treatment. Lieutenant Oliver, the duty officer, had just completed my full statement and walked out, and a corpsman came in and cleaned me up and put a bandage over my eye.

"Man, I know this hurts. They should have taken you straight to the MHG. You might lose some of your vision."

I looked at him and said, "I thought the eye replacement fixed that?"

"Yeah, the eye and vision from whatever trauma caused the initial injury. But, man, you might have optic nerve damage now, that's not repairable."

I just sat there; now I was mad. I wanted that piece of trash to pay for this. The corpsman looked at me. "Hey, do I know you? I've seen you somewhere."

"Hard to tell, Corpsman. We all fly around together."

"No, I'm not flight ops. Just graduated from White Mountain C Course. I've been ground support."

"Did you graduate this week?" I was joking.

"Yeah! That's it. You were there with a bunch of your buddies watching Ramsey graduate! You're her boyfriend. Man, Lance Corporal, you are one lucky guy. Every guy in class was hitting on her… I mean, you know?"

All of a sudden, he realized he was talking to a girl's boyfriend that was a number one Fleet Marine who just had his artificial eye, because his real eye was damaged in combat, knocked out of whack by a first sergeant in a fight. This guy was a wacko!

"Uh, um, I'll call the MHG and let them know your condition and try to get you an appointment other than a walk-in ER."

"Sounds good," I said. I grinned to myself.

Well, now I knew Donna was my girl for sure, not that that was going to matter, probably. The door opened, and First Sergeant French from Bravo Training Company and First Sergeant Clark from Echo 2/2/7 walked in. I'm sure they knew each other, and well, they were no doubt friends of Alfonso. *Man, not good.* French took a chair and sat down across from me and Clark sat on the corner of the table. Neither said anything, just looked at me for several seconds, silence.

"You know, you just keep pushing the boundary, don't you, Smith?" First Sergeant French spoke. I respected both of these men, these Fleet Marines. He turned to First Sergeant Clark and said, "You know who called Seventh Division and twisted arms up there when his age was revealed?"

"Yeah, the same guy who twisted Second Division arms when he busted up two of their guys."

They looked at me and then Clark spoke, "Smith, you have a friend up high that is the biggest rabbi next to God Himself. Don't get me wrong, your merits and combat service are exemplary, but you have a knack of being at the wrong place at the wrong time."

French now spoke, "I have had a problem with how PNCOC has been run for quite some time, too much menial garbage and focus on petty superfluous things, not on combat skills and small unit leadership tactics. We have a real shortage of qualified and knowledgeable corporals, especially now with this new Phase Initiative. I have been reassigned to oversee the PNCOC effective immediately. Are you willing to continue your course a week from now? I have to clean out the mess over there and the next class won't begin until next week."

I looked at both of them. "Who is Jim Thompson?"

They both laughed, then Clark said, "It's Colonel Thompson. He's Joint Staff, in charge of this initiative. He's big, should make his star soon, we both served with him in a company a long time ago. He found you and you have made an impression on him. That's all I can say."

"I can say this—that drunken excuse for a Fleet Marine will be sorry till the day he dies that he sucker punched you. That pig don't fly, and Goff and Sergeant Major Malone are going down with him. The rest of that cadre are marked for expulsion, loss of rank, and reassignment to either line companies or HQs in the Twelfth. They all acted with disgrace and actions unbecoming of an NCO." French was nearly livid.

They stood up. "We weren't here. Your orders will float in during the week, and as before, First Sergeant Clark will treat you no differently back at battalion than any other lance corporal, nonexistent. Your class, hopefully all of you, will resume next Sunday. I believe you have a clinic appointment to get to," said First Sergeant French.

I stood up. "Thank you, First Sergeants."

They walked out. I couldn't wrap my head around this—where, how, why—was I so special? What had I done to grab a colonel's attention, and what use was I to him in his plan, this "initiative"?

CPO Swan walked in a few minutes later, with Grigsby. Grigs was beat up, a black eye, busted lip, and sore ribs; we hugged each other, and he was nearly crying.

"I should have told them. I should have said it right there, reported the assault right then. I'm sorry man, I'm sorry..."

"No no no, Grigs. It's okay. You couldn't cross the line. I understand."

"The charges against you have been dropped," said Swan.

"I know," I said.

"Yeah, yours too, but I was talking to Lance Corporal Grigsby. He broke Staff Sergeant Simpson's arm and put Gunnery Sergeant Castelle in the ER with a crushed trachea."

I looked at Grigs. "Brothers."

"Brothers."

"Jeez!" was all Security Operations Specialist Chief Petty Officer Swan could say as he walked out the door and continued to clear up the massive mess that had developed.

The charges included—assault, dereliction of duty, drunk while on duty, actions unbecoming of an NCO, conspiracy to withhold evidence, falsifying reports of a crime, conspiracy to hide a witness or subject associated with a crime, aiding and abetting a known fugitive, conspiracy to tampering with a witness(s), threatening a witness(s), and committing assault against a witness(s). The orders had come down from the Air Wing itself, to leave no charge, however small, even an out of uniform violation, and to stack, as high as possible, each infraction onto each cadre of Week One P, Second Training Battalion, and to any other associated NCO of other training weeks that may be guilty of similar charges. Basically, the ball was dropped and someone was highly ticked off that senior NCOs had been caught mistreating lower EMs and the punishment was going to be severe and immediate. Career NCOs that were dirty were going down.

One sergeant major, one first sergeant, four gunnery sergeants, and two staff sergeants were busted down to privates and sent to Salt Lake Military Prison, for anywhere from three to five years for their actions and involvement. Six staff sergeants were reduced in rank to corporal and transferred to the Twelfth, two first sergeants were reduced to staff sergeants and retired, two gunnery sergeants were reduced to sergeants and retired, and eight staff sergeants were retired. It was a full clean house.

The court-martials were brief and vicious. The period of over-rated, bully, privileged, long-overdue-for-line-company-rotation senior NCOs who were doing no more than sandbagging in the rear was over. First Sergeant French brought a new and clean rebirth to the PNCOC. It was still difficult, but in a professional way, full of hands-on, practical courses and expectations, training new corporals to become effective and qualified entry-grade NCOs into the Fleet Marines and removing the dread and dark stain over the necessary and needed course.

CHAPTER 4

I remained alone and in position for the remainder of the night, never falling asleep, not even a nod off, and I was spent. Besides just my physical exhaustion, I was stressed to the max and becoming mentally unstable, hearing voices and having daydreams. I was talking to myself, out loud, I guess, talking to someone about a girl named Anne recounting *a date we had had. I told her that if she would marry me, we could go away and raise a family and never have to worry about governments again. She was beautiful, with auburn shoulder-length hair, green eyes that looked at me full of happiness and trust, a smile that gave me all the confidence in the world, warmth, and a strong will that oftentimes overpowered me. Later we had children, a beautiful girl named Celia, and then a boy and then another boy named Micah. Oh, I was so happy with my family, but I had to work all the time.*

"Smith, are you all right? Talk to me, son. Where are you?"

"I'm right here, Daddy, where you told me to stay, under the house."

"Smith, wake up! Snap out of it. It's Ginny. Wake up!"

I shook my head. "No, no, it's not true. He's just working late. He'll be home tonight. Go away!"

"Carpenter, go get him," I heard someone say.

"Is that you, Corporal?"

"Yeah, kid. Where are you?"

"I'm under the house waiting."

"Come out of there, kid. I need you to do something for me."

"Yes, Corporal. What do you need me to do? I'm coming."

I started crawling and bumped into something. "What the heck?" I crawled straight into one of the dead Galleens and came straight back to reality. "There's no movement on the site. I just confirmed visual."

"What's your status, Smith?" asked Carpenter.

"Good, no movement. What do you need me to do? Remain in position?"

"No, can you make it back to the perimeter, Smith?" asked Gunny Scott.

"Yes, Six-Two. Heading back to perimeter."

Wow, I felt weird. The storm was still raging, daybreak had to come soon, and hopefully this storm would stop and we could get out of here. I had a sudden memory of my mother, a picture my father had of their wedding day, her long, shoulder-length auburn hair and green eyes. I hadn't thought of that picture in years, it was left behind in the house when I was sent to the orphanage. I crawled right into Corporal Larson who grabbed me and I at first thought he thought I was the enemy, but he just held me and bumped his face into mine.

"Glad you're back!" he said.

"Me too!" I said, wondering what was wrong with him.

Chapter 4

PRESENT

We were all in one room, the four of us who couldn't be released and had to be held overnight for observation, myself, Grigs, Alvera, and Simon. Alvera was in first platoon and Simon was in third. Grigs was probably the most busted up, a possible concussion and a bruised rib, in addition to the black eye and busted lip. Alvera had a sore throat from a punch that nearly crushed his larynx, the Fleet Marine's favorite attack point in putting down someone, and Simon had a "green twig" rib, or a possible broken rib. Either way, it hurt for him to breathe and he had to wear an oxygen mask. We laughed and made up super stories of his heroism in "the brawl" as it would become known, which had ensued after the cadre had gotten the platoon away from the SFP protection. This only made him laugh and then scream out in pain, whispering for us to stop.

Being in the hospital was kind of fun for a night. Hopefully we would all get out of here in the morning, but in the meantime, we were in a room to ourselves, had chow in our bunk, and had a TV. The entire PNCOC platoon that we started with was scheduled to restart next Sunday and to expect drastic changes. I had come out of eye surgery a little over an hour ago, with a bandage covering my left eye wrapping around my head, just as these guys were being moved into the room from their exams and treatments.

The door opened and we all looked up from our joking and making Simon laugh in painful contortions. Command Sergeant Major J. Kennedy walked in our room, the Seventh Division Command Sergeant Major! We all made to get out of our bunks and stand at attention, we all recognized him from various experiences and chance meetings. I knew him especially from the awards formation a couple months ago.

"As you were. Don't get up. You are all busted up to some degree." He took a moment to look each of us over and I thought, *Holy moly! He's going to bury us.*

"This is hard to say. The Fleet Marine divisions are hard-pressed in the coming months for new NCOs to take the place of those that are moving up and to other assignments. The blight and cancer that was limiting the induction and training of our NCO corps was long overlooked and ignored. The actions of you and your fellow platoon-mates brought that situation to the immediate attention of command, not that your physical contact and assaults toward senior NCOs are in any way condoned. Your actions are not going to be a part of your permanent record. Let me be very clear, any future assaults on a senior NCO or any officer on your part will be dealt with swiftly and to the utmost length of military punishment under the *Guidelines and Laws of Military Discipline and Judgments.* Am I clear?"

"Aye-aye, Command Sergeant Major!" we all responded, even Simon, who started coughing uncontrollably.

"Lance Corporal Smith."

"Aye, Command Sergeant Major." I'm sure he was not positive who I was; why would he?

"I see you have found a group that is just like you. Off the record here, boys, just the five of us in this room, the only five, get my meaning?"

"Aye, Command Sergeant Major." We had no idea what was about to come next.

"You fought for one another, protected your own. You'll be blood brothers to the end of time, Valhalla! You're tighter now than you know. Corporals soon, then sergeants, and moving up the ranks—that's a special bond, fighting and defending what's right. Keep that in your hearts."

He turned to walk out the door but then turned to look at us again. "Try to keep from choking Simon tonight, Marines. You need anything?" We all laughed, even Simon, who started coughing again.

"No, Command Sergeant Major. We're good." He was gone.

We all started talking about what had just happened. We were marked. I knew Alvera and Simon, not well, but not in a bad way either. Alvera was one class ahead of Simon, who was two classes in front of Grigs and me. Simon had had Carpenter and Custer as drills, while Alvera had Corporal Valmer as a drill. First Sergeant French was there with all of us and Staff Sergeant Adams had just rotated into Bravo Training at the end of Alvera's training from an SS rotation. Man! It was crazy that we were so linked and didn't realize it. Alvera and Simon and the other lance corporals of our PNCOC platoon from Echo all had three CRs, though Alvera had started with the company during a CR like me and Grigs, but only had two weeks in and it didn't qualify.

The door opened again and the next visitor we had was Staff Sergeant Ginny, the acting company sergeant. He walked in and looked at us. He stood there at the door and shook his head.

"I don't know how many corporals, sergeants, staff sergeants, and I am sure a couple of gunnys have attended that course with most of the same cadre. But I send seven of my best lance corporals to a time-honored and revered institution of PNCOC and they bust it wide open—I mean wide open for the corruption, dereliction, abuse, and noneffective training that it has been for at least five years. Marines, good job. I apologize on behalf of the entire Seventh Division that you had to make that sacrifice. But don't take a swing at me."

Carpenter entered just then. "Or me, because I will flat lay you out. And you know it!"

We all hooped and hollered, sending poor Simon into convulsions again, and a corpsman came in and worked on him, scolding all of us for getting him roused up and into a fit of breathing difficulty.

She was cute, and I know I had seen her somewhere. She was one of Donna's roommates, the one Grigs had been trying to impress that night we all went out. What was her name? Kristy? Carla? Kate. She had been trying to ask me about my OL and Grigs steered her off. I looked at Grigs, all while Ginny and Carpenter were talking about something, and I motioned toward her with my head. He looked at me with a puzzled expression and then, finally, recognized her. A light bulb was turned on in his head. He looked at me with a deer-in-the-headlights look and I mouthed, "*K-A-T-E*." He nodded.

"Awh!" Grigs winced with pain.

Kate looked at him, and since she was just about finished settling Simon back down, who was in real pain and was having trouble breathing, she moved over to Grigs who had to think of something that was hurting. I guess, to be honest, we were all in some pain, busted lips and concussions and sore ribs, but that was just normal.

"What is it? Where does it hurt?" she asked, doing her job.

Ginny and Carpenter just sort of paused and the room was looking at Kate. She was a looker. This had to be like the hundredth time she was stared at by a room of marines. I had to get the conversation back so that Grigs didn't land flat.

"So do we get to skip PNCOC now and go over to Drill?" I asked.

"What? Are you out of your mind?" Ginny exclaimed. Then he continued, "Are you not listening to me? I just said that you will..."

He continued explaining the next series of events. Sergeant Carpenter took a step back and put his hand to his lowered head and was shaking it back and forth. He saw what had just occurred and was trying to control his laughter. At the next chance, he took Ginny by the arm and whispered in his ear and they both started laughing.

"Report to the TOE Room when you get released. Get some rest," Ginny said, and they walked out laughing.

"Who has the remote?" I asked, to keep everyone off Grigs and Kate.

"Simon had it last," replied Alvera, laughing. Kate looked around at Simon, and then Alvera said, "Nope. Here it is. I have it." He turned it on.

"Hey, Grigsby, is it okay if we watch *the Newlywed Game*? I love that show!"

Simon was coughing and trying to laugh and breathe.

Kate and Grigs were talking; she remembered him now and it looked good.

"Hey, Alvera, turn it to that Military Channel. I want to see how they used to ride horses into combat," I said.

"Okay, I remember that was on yesterday." He was laughing. He stopped on some channel that was advertising a local spring training baseball game. "You like baseball?" he asked.

"Yeah. Is there a game on?" We watched a spring training game between the Cali Dolphins and the Great Lakes Coasters. Kate left and the TV was switched off and we all looked at Grigs.

"I got her number! Thanks, guys. Sorry, Simon. Are you all right?"

Simon pulled his mask down and said, "If she has a friend, you owe me." He was barely able to talk a word or two without going into a coughing spasm.

"You have to take that up with Smith. They're roommates." It was understood that he meant the girls.

"Dang!" said Simon. I didn't mention Steph, the other friend, but I think Moon was already working that angle. Grigs winked at me.

"She said that she was going to be talking to Donna later tonight and that she would mention you were in here."

"No! Get her back in here. I don't want Donna to know about this."

"Is that the chick that was at the party back when we got in last time?" asked Alvera.

"Yeah, that's Smith's girl," said Grigsby, trying to head off any potential conflict.

"No, no, don't get me wrong, man. Nice girl. I'm not going to dish on your girl, man. I have a girl back home, and like, we want to keep going, you know. It's hard in the Fleet Marines to get anyone from back home caught up to you. We have been trying to get her a job and moved up here to Fraser. I know there are plenty of jobs here, especially now with all the new construction. So Donna must be in the Space Fleet, huh?"

"Yeah, she just completed corpsman. She may have been a gunner on one of your flights," I said.

"What? Are you serious? She's a door gunner? Man, I thought all that was bull. You are all right, Smith!"

We all laughed, well, all but Simon, who was nearly red from coughing.

CHAPTER 5

I sat in the middle of the CP, a couple feet from the PHA, which made me a little nervous, but as long as it wasn't turned on again, I guess it was all right. I took my first drink in several hours. Wow, maybe even six or seven? I was so thirsty. I was exhausted, but I knew all the other Fleet Marines on the line were just as overwhelmed as I was, sitting blind, not knowing if any second you were going to be hit with a GBL. Echo Company needed to get some rest and a meal or, at the least, an A-Dose and a water resupply. A figure waddled up to me. It was Gunny Scott.

"Here, Smith, siphon this in. You empty?" He was holding out a water bottle, his probably.

"Thanks, Gunny. No, I probably have a half liter." I took it anyway.

"Finish yours up. That's mixed, so don't dilute it." Wow. How did he have a mixed bottle still untouched?

He put his hand on my shoulder and stared into my visor. "I'm going to miss you, Smith. You are one gutsy marine." I looked into his eyes, through our goggles and visors. No! He was leaving? Transferring to the Twelfth?

I started to speak, but he shook his head and held up his hand. "Siphon that up and hold onto the bottle. I'll get it back later. Try to sleep. You're fried."

"Aye, Six-Two."

I sat there and thought about what his departure would mean to the company. Gunnery Sergeant Scott leaving—I couldn't wrap my head around it. He was a fair, honest, and straight-shooting senior NCO, he was the company sergeant. He had been the gunny with the former CO. He had been the gunny that had spoken to a group of us one weekend during Six Weeks when we were returning from a movie. Lieutenant Meese was the other marine present that night; he was the second platoon leader who was killed before I joined the company. Who was going to replace the gunny? Who was going to watch over the CO? How could the company operate without our gunny?

My mind was moving in a dozen places. I pulled on the straw in my mask, sucking down the last of the water in my HECS reservoir. I connected the bottle that Gunny Scott gave me and it siphoned in automatically. I took a drink. *Ooh!* It was hot! The HECS hadn't had time to cool it down. I could still taste the bug juice though; the flavor and nutrients were a startling change from the dank water. I leaned back on the stack of water canisters that had been off-loaded for our resupply. I let go—.

Chapter 5

PRESENT

We were settled down; dinner chow had been delivered a couple hours ago and the conversation had waned. Each of us were, I guess, in our own thoughts. The TV was on some really old comedy show replay from long ago, *Friends* or something. It was funny, but no one was watching. They had held all four of us another day and we were bored out of our minds. Simon was much better, Grigs had had his head x-rayed during the day, and my bandage was still on. Kate had checked in on us later in the afternoon when her new shift started, remaining in the room for almost half an hour, talking to Grigs. No one minded at all, just listening to her voice, not even staring, just looking up at the ceiling, enjoying the voice and company of a female.

The door opened, and to my utmost surprise and total bewilderment, Captain Ramsey entered our room! I was scared. After the last meeting I had with her, her total barely veiled hostile attitude toward me, I was taken aback at her presence. She strode into the room without a pause and stood in front of the four of us. She was all business and gazed at us. Her eyes quickly fell upon me and she walked straight toward my bunk. I was hardly able to keep from running away. What did she want? Why was she here? What could she possibly want to report me for this time?

She removed my chart, a medical tablet, from the foot of my bunk as she walked up, glancing at it and flipping through the screens, almost in a fit of anger. She looked at me, her stare penetrating my inner soul, making me squirm. The rest of the guys were completely silent; not a single officer had entered our room since we'd arrived. Alvera turned the TV off.

"Lance Corporal Smith, how is your eye? Are you experiencing any pain?" She paused for a few seconds. "Related to your injured eye?"

My mind was blowing! This woman despised me. Her loath was so heavy it could be scraped from the wall. I could think of no reason for her being here other than Donna or their father. *Holy moly! No way.*

"No, ma'am. No real pain. I was told that I might have lost some of my vision? Is that true?"

She looked at me and then back at the chart. She flipped a screen back and forth, I guess analyzing the results or information. "I will have to examine your eyes in a couple of days, when the bandages are removed. If you show up to your appointments." She stared at me.

Jeez! This woman, this officer, hated me.

"Yes, ma'am."

She looked around the room, staring down each of the occupants, forcing them to turn their gaze away. Captain Ramsey looked back at me. "Lance Corporal Smith." Her voice was a little less stern, but still icy, and much quieter. "My sister is concerned for your well-being, and the Air Wing has"—her eyes were piercing through me—"requested my involvement. You will not share our mutual connection and I will do my utmost to restore your vision to operational standards. I just hope that scout sniper wasn't in your plans, because that is now not possible."

That floored me. She had taken her best shot at decapitating me as an operational Fleet Marine. The inability to progress to the level of E6 SS and the onward climb up the divisional NCO ladder were now dead. I was numb.

"I will check in on you tomorrow afternoon."

She looked down at me, hesitating, almost like she was torn. "Donna is concerned about you. You will talk to her, inform her that you are all right."

"Yes, ma'am. I will talk to her as soon as I can."

Just then the door opened and Kate entered the room. She caught sight of Captain Ramsey and nearly tripped, balancing a tray of stacked-up hospital meals and a cloth bag draped on her arm.

"Oh! Excuse me, ma'am, Captain. I was just…" Kate's voice trailed off.

Captain Ramsey replaced my chart at the foot of my bunk, walked next to Space Fleet Corpsman First Class Daniels, and quietly said, "As you were, Kate. Have you got a tablet?"

"Yes, ma'am."

"Please allow Lance Corporal Smith to talk with First Class Ramsey. Carry on."

"Yes, ma'am."

Kate obviously knew Captain Ramsey through her association with Donna. Her possession of extra, unauthorized, hospital rations, meals, were overlooked. The captain exited the room.

Kate nearly exploded. "You marines are nothing but trouble!"

The room exploded with laughter.

She looked at me while she set the tray down on a rolling shelf. "You! You will call Donna right now. She is out of her mind crazy! She has called and left messages all day. Now you have—" She stopped. She knew that what she wanted to say was a secret, and she needed to be more discreet. "Here. Call her now." Kate handed me her tablet.

I was at a loss. I didn't have her number. I had only used Griffin's tablet. Kate's was different, I didn't know how to call her. Kate was staring at me, almost glaring. "You got to be kidding me. Really?"

Grigsby spoke up. "Come on, Kate. Don't be a jerk."

She immediately looked down in shame. "Sorry, John. Here." She took the tablet and dialed the number from the screen preset.

The number rang and I looked up at Kate. "I don't want her to see me. How do I turn off the video?" Kate hesitated and Grigs leaped out of his bunk and grabbed the tablet, just as Donna answered.

"Hey! Donna!" Grigs said.

"Uh. Hello, Grigs." Donna's voice was surprised and distant, almost hesitant, hearing Grigs on her roommate's tablet.

"How you doing? Have you got an assignment yet?" The other marines were staring at the spectacle, locked into the strange conversation.

"Uh, yeah, I'm assigned to the new 135th Air Wing. Grigs, are you with John?"

"Yeah, he's in the head. I was just wondering, Donna, I got to go to the Combat Medic Course in a couple of weeks. Is it as, you know, hard as the Corpsman Course?"

There was a few seconds pause. "Grigsby, I know he is right there next to you. I will get Moon to beat the life out of you if you don't let me talk to him, right now." I could see Grigs fooling around with the tablet, the different screens, and then he handed it over to me, with a blank screen.

"Here he is, Donna. Oh crap! What did I do?"

"Hey, babe! How you doing? So you landed with the 135th?"

I took the tablet from Grigs as he quickly scrambled back to his bunk, suddenly aware that he was only dressed in a very short hospital gown and Kate was staring at him.

"What happened? Are you okay? Why is the video off?" her voice was heavily ladened with concern.

"Heck, Donna, I don't know. Can you see me? I can't see you. Are you okay?" Alvera started laughing and Simon started coughing.

"John, please, are you all right? Tell me the truth! Kate? What's going on? I swear…" Her voice trailed off.

Kate grabbed the tablet and fiddled with it, not able to get the vid back up. She glared at Grigsby. "Hey, Donna. I'm here with the boys. They're all okay, just, being typical marines! You know. Grigsby messed with my settings, you know, trying to learn something." She handed him the tablet and stood with her fists on her waist.

"Kate, tell all of them that the moon is a lonely place and Salt Lake is worse!" She was mad.

"Hey, come on, man. Get the vid back up! This chick is for real." Alvera was stressing.

"Come on, Donna. I'm okay. You're acting crazy. The crazy captain was here a few minutes ago and I'm all right. I have to make the next appointment."

"John, are you all right?"

"Yeah, babe. I'm fine. Don't worry about me. Really. I'm good. Tell us. We want to know what's going on. The 135th Air Wing, that's new. You're with the Twelfth? Where? Can you say?"

There was a moment of silence, security, thought, indecision. "I can't say that. Who is there with you? Why won't you turn the vid on? You're scaring me, John."

I looked at Grigs; he tapped something and I could see the light from the tablet.

"Hey. There you are. You are looking good, Donna!" Grigs said. Of course, he was probably the worst-looking of all of us, his busted, swollen lip and black eye.

"Oh no! Grigs, are you all right?"

"Heck yeah, Donna, feeling great. Hey, I been meaning to ask you about that girl who was with us the other night. What was her name? Do you think she would let me call her? What was her name?"

Kate grabbed the tablet from Grigs and spoke to her roommate. "These guys are idiots. Really, Donna, what do you see in them?"

Donna laughed. "Kate, I swear, run away as quickly as you can! But it's too late. Grigsby is like the fifth best second choice of the group." The laughter was loud in the room, Kate was even rubbing her eyes and covering her mouth.

"Oh! Come on! That was mean," said Grigs, a little put off.

"Kate, let me talk to John, please."

"Okay, but he doesn't look anywhere as bad as Grigs." She laughed and passed me the tablet.

"Hey, babe." I held the tablet off me, slanted toward the ceiling.

"You are really, really, making me mad. Let me see you. Right now."

"You know—"

I really didn't want her to see me in the patch and head wrap, and I had looked in the mirror when I went to use the head earlier in the day and saw that my face was swollen and my right eye was blackened and my lip was even slightly swollen. "I'm good. What are you all upset about? I'm okay, Donna. I just don't want you to worry about nothing."

"John, please, let me see you. Are you okay?"

"Yeah, it looks worse than it is. Captain Ramsey is going to check it all out. See. All good." I moved the tablet down and smiled at her. I could see her, my Donna. She moved her hand to her face and made a gasp. I could see her facial expression change from a concerned, worried expression to a more traumatized, frightened look.

"Oh! What happened? Tell me. Grigs? Right now. Who else is there? Kate? Who is in that room? Tell me! What happened?"

"Calm down, Donna. It's all good. We're all okay. Grigs looks the worse, but that's just Grigs." The laughter erupted in the room.

"Come on, bro! That was harsh," said Grigsby, but Kate was standing next him, holding his hand and laughing as she bent down and kissed him on the check, and he was all smiles.

"What happened? John, tell me. I heard you hit a first sergeant! Tell me what happened."

"No, Donna. I didn't hit anyone."

"I did!" yelled Grigs. "I busted the coward right in the face who sucker punched my brother!"

"Me too, Donna! I broke that lousy poser's arm who held him down! I'll do it again!" yelled Simon, who then started coughing violently.

"I broke that lousy goldbricker's arm that pushed my brother down to the ground! I'll break his other arm! Let me go!" yelled Alvera, climbing out of his bunk, in a rage.

"Holy! Who is that? Tell me your names? How many of you are there? Are you all okay?" I could hear the breaking of her voice, her concern, her compassion.

Alvera spoke. "All of us stood together. We are all brothers!"

"Brothers!" we all yelled.

Silence. Donna didn't speak. Alvera climbed back in his bunk. Kate stood next to Grigs, still holding his hand. I held the tablet and looked at Donna. She was looking at me, just staring into the vid, her eyes darting around, taking my appearance in.

I smiled and said, "I see what you are doing. You are using your x-ray vision."

"You know," she started and gave me a half-happy, half-worried smile. "I know you have it under control, that you are just 'taking it a day at a time.' I love you, John Smith. I want you to know that."

The words hit me like a hammer. There were people in the room. They could hear me, us. I squirmed. I felt it too, but to voice something like that out loud and in front of these guys.

Kate quietly said, "You better not leave her hanging. You might wake up tomorrow feeling icky."

"Donna, here? Yeah, babe. I do. I…I… You know I do." I looked around and everyone was staring.

Alvera said, "Say it, man, if you mean it."

"I love you too, Donna. I do. Don't worry about me, us. We're all good. Please stop pushing, you know, for outside help here. Please." She knew what I meant; her sister had said so.

She looked at me. "I had nothing to do with that, that came from somewhere else. Maybe from your camping buddy. I only talked with Kate and Chris called me yesterday and told me about it."

"Who?"

"Chris, my classmate. He treated you at the Duty House. He said, well, he told me what happened. Otherwise I wouldn't have known. I have to go. We're running back and forth with the advance team. Call me tomorrow! Bye." She hung up.

Just like that. I handed Kate the tablet, Alvera turned the TV back on, and Kate said, "I brought you guys some extra dinners, and I have gum and a couple of magazines."

"Great! Thank you, Kate," everyone was saying and looking forward to another meal. They were too small.

Tonight, we had a chicken patty and a tiny scoop of mashed potatoes and even less gravy and a single twig of broccoli. And that's what she brought us, and it was gobbled up in an instant. Even the green Jell-O. I would have loved another carton of milk, but wasn't going to say anything, because this was already way over-the-top nice.

She left and we passed around the magazines, female stuff, *Hot Stars! How to Find the Right Guy! Dressing for Success for Less!* These couldn't have come out of their quarters? None of them seemed to be this girly.

"When are we getting out of here?" asked Simon.

"I don't know about all of us, dude, but I think you're here a little while longer. You still can't breathe," said Alvera.

I wondered what was going on back at battalion, what the news was going around the base. I thought about Donna, a part of Advanced Party with the new Air Wing and division. What was her assignment? What was she doing? Where were they?

CHAPTER 6

I woke with a start. I dozed off, not for long, I don't think. It was still dark; the wind was letting up. My backstop of water jugs was gone and I was flat on the ground, a thin layer of sand covering me. I sat up and looked around. I flipped the IR and normal screen back and forth and I could see more now with the IR.

"Good, you're awake." Corporal Larson was sitting beside me. "I didn't want to wake you but you are assisting me with the A-Doses in a couple of minutes. Gunny and Six put together a little shelter. We're going to file the company through and mix bug juice and resupply water."

I just stared at him. *What?*

"Listen, it's still hotter than a firecracker. You have to stick these guys quick through their open visor in the neck before they blister." He was all matter-of-fact, telling me what I was going to do.

"That's over forty-five marines, Larson. I gotta stick all of them? I've never stuck anyone but myself."

"Well, you're about to become a pro. You have the smallest hands."

"I drank some mix a little while ago Gunny gave me. It was hot. Won't the A-Dose burn?"

"Yeah, the ones we have on us are all probably ruined now. The resupply doses are in a temp-controlled box, so you have to be quick. Take one out, prep it, and stick it. Seconds, they'll heat up quick."

He looked at me. I was very unsure about this, and he saw it.

"It's not a matter if you can do this, Smith. You have to do it. In another hour, it will be too hot to lift our visors."

"Wouldn't it be easier to stick these guys in the wrist?" I asked.

"Can't do it. In this environment, if the glove wrist seal is broken, the suit will lock up the closest tourniquet band and may not release."

"This is really poor design."

"Are you through? Because we got to move." Larson was agitated.

"Sorry, Corporal. Where do we go?"

He led the way to a long, narrow, barely three-foot-high makeshift tent tunnel. Gunny and Captain Shupin had combined several Shake-n-Bake shelters, stacked CPs in parallel lines and covered them with the fabric, creating a tube. The ends were capped off and the structure was nearly free of the wind and blowing sand. Ingenious.

Gunny Scott was just outside of the "Hole" short for watering hole, a clever take on an old Western time saloon term, and would ensure that each marine's HECS reservoir was empty so that he could refill with a fresh mix. Each marine in the company was run through in the next forty-five minutes, starting on the one end, crawling in and sitting facing me and Larson. Larson would check them out as best as he could, ask them a few questions, and then tell them to quickly raise their visor so that I could stick them in the neck with the A-Dose. It was extremely painful, the heat as hot as an oven.

I had to open and close the box quickly, rip the protective package off, remove the safety cap on the one end and insert it on the plunger end and reach into the face area of the man in front of me who was withering in pain, find the muscle along his neck without disturbing his face mask, and push the spring-loaded plunger in to activate the auto injector.

We had all experienced the A-Dose countless times, and in the neck was nothing new, but these conditions just made men cry out in pain. The marine would lower his visor and then crawl another foot or two to the CO, who was busy mixing punch. The marine would siphon off a bottle to his suit and receive another mixed bottle and a refilled plain water, trading out his two empties. Lieutenant Green was beside the CO, hurriedly refilling water bottles. The marine would exit out the other end and the next would enter. The eerie red lights of our helmets lit the interior of the "Hole," giving the grisly process that was taking place inside an even more hellish atmosphere. We had to get out of here.

We had two boxes of A-Doses, fifty count each, and there were forty-nine total Fleet Marines on the ground. Two of the doses failed to inject, which was bad enough, but horrible for the men who had to endure the process even longer. When each marine had come through, it was now time for me to inject the CO, Gunny, Lieutenant Green, and Larson, who would stick me. The fail rate was 1:50 per box, so the two bad ones were close to margin. There was no sure guarantee that we wouldn't have the same failure rate on the next box, tonight, if we were here that long. I knew the numbers, I knew we were short one dose, but I didn't say anything, sticking the CO last, before my turn. Larson reached in the box but I didn't lift my visor, and his hand came out empty. He stared at me with cold eyes.

"I can't believe you did that! Dagone you, PFC!" He was mad, though I'm not totally sure at me or because he got one and I didn't.

The CO looked at us and then said, "Corporal Larson, give him the dose."

"There are no more, Six. Two failed out of the box."

Captain Shupin turned back to me and pointed his finger.

"What makes you think I won't break open the other box?"

"Six, we can't risk it. The box is sealed and we may have just as many or more bad ones in it. I'll be fine, sir."

He slid up next to me, his face right into mine; the COMM switched over to the Command net, he said, "This is private, just you and me, Smith. I just want to let you know if you ever upstart me again, I will bust you down to recruit and send you to Division Supply. You never, ever, place yourself in front of Command on the short."

"Sir, I'm the least important here. If you go down, we all go down."

He shook his head. "You're first tonight. I'll stick you myself."

"Aye-aye, Six."

He pushed himself back, hit me on the shoulder with his hand, and said, "Back to Command net, Betty. Keep Smith on until further notice. List him as company medic. Sergeant Carpenter, instruct PFC Smith on proper Command channel SOP ASAP. Let's get these platoons spread back out to tactical perimeter. As soon as the sun rises, I want second platoon to recover enemy KIA for intel and a sweep performed. These creatures are crawling out from somewhere and I want to find out where. Gunny."

Gunny Scott started barking out orders and instructions to his three platoon sergeants who were on the ground; fourth platoon was still overhead, unable to insert just yet. The storm was dying down, and the cycle was over for now. If this were the cycle, midmorning as it heated up, a six- to eight-hour hurricane came alive and then dissipated, followed by an early evening storm that was created with the cooling temperature for the whole of the night hours. It didn't look like we were extracting, at least not right away. What if the next storm was longer?

Surely the CO wasn't doing this; he was following orders from above. We had to stay until relieved. My thought went back to yesterday with the first probe, as I had thought about the Mowatts and Abooe, how they had to remain on this planet until relieved. Was Echo going to eventually end up like them? I made my way back to the perimeter where second platoon was, Larson right behind me. He grabbed me to a stop and came around to face me.

He looked in my visor, closed his eyes, and shook his head. He opened his eyes, then nodded his head, and gave me a thumbs-up. He took me by the shoulder and turned me around, saying, "Behind us is the CP. Second right in front. You are over there." He pointed with his left hand.

"First, third." He moved me around, showing me the layout. I knew it in my head, but it was nice to have the visual. "Just like back at the Y, the platoon sergeants and officers are just behind, placing each marine, and he knows where each of his men are, always. The 'square' is over there." He continued pointing in the direction where second and third platoons merged. This was the importance of the lesson during Tactics Week Four, "Fields of Fire," and the diagramming of the individual unit positions now came to life.

"Original Point of Direction (OPD) is, basically, the 'Hole.' Gunny and Six are CP there. Betty has limited COMM channels, but enough to separate the four individual platoons, the Command channel, the CO's private chat box like he tore into you with, and the private one we are currently on, which the CO, Gunny, and Betty Operations/Flight Support Officer, (O/FSO), also monitors. So what the heck were you thinking? You don't have that privilege of making that choice, the decision to not administer the A-Dose, pass yourself up. That's the CO's decision, his authority, his call!" He grabbed me by the shoulders and stared at me; he was angry. I had never made Larson angry.

"Don't you ever pull that kind of a stunt again! You really showed up the CO, put him in a position where he went before his men. Captain Shupin is a fine officer, a skilled leader, an experienced warrior. He may have designated you as the company medic, which, by the way, congratulations." He patted me on the head and then continued, "But you embarrassed him in front of his leadership team. Come on, Smith, you have performed above and beyond out here the past day, but you got to use your head." When he was through, he looked at me.

I was barely able to keep my eye contact. He was right. I really messed up.

"I wasn't trying to show the CO up, Larson. I knew we were short. He had to get one, stay focused. So does Six-Two and the other leaders. I watched you, listened to what you asked each marine. It was always different. You knew each man, talked to them, calmed them down. Larson, you knew their needs and capabilities. I don't have that. I had to skip out. I was the least important."

Larson shook his head. "Where did you come from? How do you have this much maturity and knowledge at fifteen?" He grabbed me. "Sergeant Carpenter needs to chew you up next. Then I guess we need to sit you down. You're running on empty."

He pushed me toward the hole between Private Clark and PFC Grigsby and returned to his own area. The sun was beginning to appear on the horizon, but without the presence of water and other gasses in the atmosphere, the sunrise was different—a bold blue sphere, the glare of the white sand reflecting it, the sky turning purple and blue and red. It was still beautiful, just not usual, normal. But what was anymore?

Chapter 6

PRESENT

I sat in the chow hall with Grigs, Moon, Carlson, Jackson, and Luke. And it was silent. As a matter of fact, there was hardly any talking, among Echo or any other permanent party of the battalion that shared this dining facility with First Training Battalion. Yep, the news was out and there were a whole lot of NCOs that were friends with the cadre that had been severely punished in the PNCOC scandal.

"It's been like this for days, don't worry about it," said Moon. "None of them had the guts to do what you guys did, and they're embarrassed."

Grigs looked at me and I looked around for Alvera; he was eating alone. Simon was being held over for a fourth day. The other three marines from Echo who were involved were not eating right now. They had been released late Sunday afternoon after giving their statements; their injuries were light, but all three had taken part in the fight. Grigs, Alvera, and I still had the evidence of the fight, blackened eyes, swollen lips, and my bandaged eye. I knew that not all the NCOs were angry with us, Ginny, Carpenter, and a few of the corporals. I had passed Captain Shupin earlier in the afternoon, and after I performed the proper salute and divisional greeting, he said, as he walked past, "Glad to have you back, Lance Corporal."

I got up and walked over to Alvera. "Hey, join us over here." He looked at me, the group that I was a part of; his platoon had disowned him.

"We're marked, Smith. They hate us."

"Nah, they don't know how to react yet, Alvera. They're watching us, even now, seeing how we handle it. You, me, Grigs, Simon, and the other guys, we're the same marines that ate in here together five days ago. You were our leader then, Alvera, and you still are. Don't fold."

He looked at me. "Smith, if I were half the leader you are, I'd be good."

"Don't cut yourself short, man. It ain't your style." He laughed and stood up, grabbed his tray, and walked back with me. All eyes were on us.

As soon as we sat down, Moon, in as loud a conversational tone that pushed the limits of obnoxious, said, "So tell me again, it took how many SFPs to pull you guys off those busted-down, washed-up, sandbagging, low-life CR-dodging wanna-be Fleet Marine has-beens?" The table roared to life, Grigs and Alvera laughing and started talking at the same time, telling what happened.

"Hey!" A staff sergeant from one of the training companies walked up and glared down at us. "Keep your pieholes shut! I know several of those NCOs and they are fine marines. You punks just destroyed several men's careers and lives, not to mention a long-standing A Course. You should be out on the street."

"As you were, Staff Sergeant!" Sergeant Major Golden, Second Brigade Sergeant Major, stood up from a table in the corner, where he and several other battalion-level senior NCOs had been sitting and observing.

"All of those men have been convicted of crimes and charges that no self-respecting NCO should be associated with. I should hope that you have more character than that. I see that we need to bring this issue to the front, expose it, and address the questions and unresolved issues of the incident. While I do not condone the striking of, or assaults upon, senior NCOs, I neither condone the same behavior from those NCOs to under EMs. The fight that these marines were retelling is no different than the banter and similar stories we all share of our exploits of combat. Here, the difference was that these marines were justified in retaliating against the unprovoked and violent assault of one of their brothers. All those involved, from sergeant major on down, acted in a manner unbecoming of an NCO, from assault, lying, aiding a known fugitive, tampering with witnesses, threatening witnesses, and possession of alcohol or being under the influence. Do you have alcohol in your quarters, Staff Sergeant, while actively training those recruits sitting over there?" His look was stern. He wanted an answer.

"No, Sergeant Major, of course not. That would be unethical and against regulations."

The staff sergeant was now small, and the stares of the entire chow hall were weighing down on him; a sergeant major was dressing him down in front of not only a company of Fleet Marines but also his own recruits.

"All of those marines, unfortunately, being replayed in this account, had alcohol in their system, Staff Sergeant, the rest of you marines here." He walked to the center of the room. "That is not acceptable! I fully understand our tradition of having an after CR throw down, and I am not addressing that situation. It stands. What I am calling out is under the influence while on duty, especially while presiding over recruits, A and B courses and in the field. It stops now! Right now. I am clear?"

The room stood up at once and replied, "Aye-aye, Sergeant Major!"

"Carry on." He returned to his table and their conversation started right back up. Ours did not. We quickly finished chow and left.

The remainder of the week crawled by. All of us went to visit Simon, who would not be released until Friday afternoon, and then it was still up in the air if he would be physically able to resume on Sunday with the rest of us. The six of us decided to approach Staff Sergeant Ginny Friday morning and formally request a special waiver from First Sergeant French for Simon's injury. My eye was still bandaged and I had a second appointment to have it examined this afternoon.

"Or what? Is this your idea of a mutiny? Are you making deals now? Let me tell you Lance Corporals something!" His voice was on the verge of making me crumble. We had not envisioned a threat or any such tit for tat. We only wanted to request a fitness waiver on Simon's behalf.

Ginny was standing now, only a foot or so from us. The TOE Room was small already. Now there were the six of us, Ginny, the CO, and Lieutenant Howard from first platoon. This was an NCO matter. The officers really had no oversight or interest in PNCOC, and the current discussion was out of their realm. NCO business. Staff Sergeant, promotable, Ginny could handle the situation without the CO's involvement. Captain Shupin sat watching, as if entertained by a play.

"No, Staff Sergeant!"

He glared at us, his experience as a drill instructor not lost on us or his reputation as an SS and self-defense instructor; he had trained Sergeants Carpenter and Custer and who knows how many others. He was highly respected by all of us. His disfavor with us cut to the core, even more with Alvera, who was a member of his former platoon.

"Either Lance Corporal Simon will be physically fit enough to attend PNCOC on Sunday or he won't be. There will be no special waiver. I suggest the rest of you worry about your own ability to pass the Fitness Test. You have not PT'ed all week. This is not going to be a walk in the park, Marines. First Sergeant French can still run a 3K in under eleven minutes, even with his... He'll smoke you. Then he will laugh at you while you lay face down in the muck while he pumps out a hundred push-ups in under two minutes. Sunday morning inspection 0530, utilities. Everything else is the same as last week. Dismissed."

We were already at attention, so we performed a smart about-face, and Alvera led us out of the office.

"Lance Corporal Smith, stand-fast," said Captain Shupin.

Ugh, I just want to blend in, I thought, as I halted and let the others pass by me. I did an about-face and remained at attention. The door closed and I stood there.

"Lieutenant Howard, excuse us for a moment, if you will," said the CO. Lieutenant Howard, who I barely knew, walked out.

Ginny was back in his chair and passed a piece of paper to Shupin.

Both of them were looking at me but said nothing. After a few seconds, Captain Shupin said, "At ease, Lance Corporal Smith. Your actions and behavior continue to astound me and others. I have not had the moment to address several of your actions that took place during Echo's recent CR. And with this latest, situation, Division is—" He was looking at me, almost in a saddened manner. "Well, it is not thought to be a good idea to recognize you openly for your contributions and actions at this time. With that said, I also have the latest examination results performed on your sight. It is, difficult for me to inform you, Lance Corporal Smith, that your vision falls below the standard for entry into the Scout Sniper Course and barely meets operational standards. You will remain on active duty until that falls below Op standard, or you are reclassified."

He stood up and Ginny followed.

"Lance Corporal Smith, it is with my highest honor and privilege to present to you the Fleet Marine Distinguished Leadership Cross for your actions and gallantry during the campaign on CC-002048-01, Butch, in which you were solely responsible for the elimination of no less than a dozen enemy combatants, the continued fire suppression and leadership of your fire team during the…"

I stood there, his words barely registering in my consciousness. My sight was failing, and I was only a whisper from being placed in a rear support position. I was out of the fight. I was somewhere else as the CO pinned the DLC onto my left breast pocket flap of my barely "Service and Inspection" condition utilities, the continuation of reading for the award of an Oak Leaf to my Achievement Ribbon, and the awarding of a Commendation Medal for the combination of actions during the CR. I stood frozen, lost in, well, a feeling of loss. I barely was able to return the CO's salute and shake Gunny's hand, well Staff Sergeant, promotable, Ginny. I walked out of the TOE Room and leaned against the wall, sliding down to sit on the deck. I was still there when Grigs and Alvera found me on their way to fetch Simon.

CHAPTER 7

Carpenter had instructed me as to the proper SOP on the COMM channel for low-grade NCOs, which was basically shut up, be brief, listen, and learn. I was not to talk unless I was specifically called upon. No net info/intel was to be shared with unauthorized personnel, and the old "what happens in Vegas, stays in Vegas" adage was shared. I didn't know what that meant, I'd never heard that before, but I figured I was given a special insight and I was expected to behave accordingly.

Morning broke and the earlier sunrise spectacle was only upscaled in the majesty and beauty. The deep purple, brilliant blue, and scarlet red was breathtaking. God really was a magnificent artist. Due to the lack of water vapor, the rainbow of other colors was absent, pink, violet, and orange. There was no wisp of clouds, only the blue of the star Centauri C and the purple and red caused by the refraction of dust particles in the light spectrum. The heat climbed steadily from the low overnight of 168 degrees, the sun quickly lighting up the vast empty dry ocean bed. The storm ceased. This was our chance. We had to extract before the next cycle began and trapped us for the next sixteen hours.

I heard the CO calling the Bettys down for the extraction, fourth platoon would insert and cover our exit. *Oh, the thought of a cool drink and something to eat was so...* I wanted to remove my helmet and scratch my face, rub my head and my eyes!

Puc! Puc! Puc! Puc! Puc!

The GBL came from behind the KIA positions. Their nests.

"Second platoon, advance in a cover formation! First, sweep to the right flank. Third, hold and cover!" The CO wanted this rabbit hole. "Fourth platoon Betty, insert to the rear of Galleen activity."

We were going to finally find their hole, root them out, and make aggressive contact.

"First squad, cover! Second, advance five! Move!" Lieutenant Green ordered.

I raised up and ran in a zigzag pattern, my drop position already in my mind. I hit it square, a little mound of sand formed by the wind. I looked ahead of me, toward the area where the GBL came from, and saw the pattern of sand rivulets and choose my next position. I fired three short bursts of my GLAR—Zik, Zik, Zik!—anticipating the "Go!" order from Carpenter. I watched as first platoon took a long swinging arch to the right, the enemy's attention supposedly focused on our frontal assault. Both platoon maneuvers were actually a distraction, as fourth was inserting just to their rear.

Carpenter yelled, "Go!" I fired another short burst, moving as before, but in an opposite pattern, so as not to give a sniper a set pattern of my movement. I hit the berm as a trail of GBL whizzed over my head! That was close. This was definitely a sustained aggressive defensive contact. It didn't make sense. First squad ran past me.

"Go!" yelled Carpenter. I rose and fired, running straight, then a zigzag, dropping on my preplanned sand berm. I looked at first platoon, now cutting back in, on a line to take them astern of the Galleen firing positions. There were three firing positions, spaced fairly evenly, over a twenty-five-meter distance, in a row. Fourth was advancing from the rear.

It didn't make sense. These were well-concealed Firing Positions, FPs, over seventy-five meters away from the KIAs; it would take us days to find them. Why give it up?

"Go!" I fired and kept firing. *Zik! Zik! Zik! Zik! Zik! Zik! Zik! Zik! Zik!*

We were close now and had to keep their heads down. First squad was laying it down too. I slammed into the sand, barely, before a stream of GBL streaked where I was a nanosecond before. I blindly fired my GLAR in the approximate direction of a FP.

Zik! Zik! Zik!

"Carpenter, something's not right!" I forgot I was still on the Command COMM.

"Keep the channel clear!" Gunny Scott yelled.

"Go!" Carpenter yelled again.

We were close now, only forty meters to their front. Fourth platoon was almost at their backdoor.

The ground gave way under my feet, a huge plume of sand, dust, and rock filled the air around me, covering me, enveloping me to the point where I was totally blinded. The dust was thick as the earlier storm but was dense, more of a finer particle than the sand. I felt myself sliding, falling, sinking, below the desert floor! It was an absolute feeling of panic! I heard the curses and yells of my platoon-mates as they disappeared into the void. A thick dark gray cloud rose into the air and hung over us.

"Grigs! Clark! Moon! Luke!" I yelled.

"Second platoon, stay calm. Get your bearings. Stay calm." It was Carpenter.

Had he ever experienced this before? Surely. This was just another day. Stay calm. He was going to get us out.

"Six, Larson, Murray!" It was Carpenter. "You okay?"

"Yeah." I was on the Command channel. "I'm deep, probably fifteen, twenty feet. I'm stuck. Sand up to my waist, bro. They caved a tunnel in on us, sucked us in good." Larson had experienced this then. Okay, good. He knew how to get us out.

"Second platoon, what's your status, Two-Six?" the CO asked, but no answer.

"Carpenter, take command of the platoon, gather your marines, and set up a defensive position facing the FP. Copy?" Captain Shupin said.

"Copy, Six. It's zero visibility, up in five."

"Quicker than that!"

"Aye." I could hear the doubt in his voice. We were in trouble.

"Larson, are you clustered?" He asked if we were together, not the other meaning.

"Aye, we were running a tight pack. I can't move."

"Murray, what's your status? Have you got Six in contact?"

"I got Moon, Luke, Jackson, Rich, and Woolsey accounted for. Missing a boot and Six. He was just behind me when the deck caved. I'm searching for him."

"Every marine that can climb out, get topside now and set up defensive position."

A few seconds passed. "Conserve your water, Marines. It's going to be a long day."

My heart sunk. I was already exhausted, I was starving, I was weak. But I was alive, which may not be the case with some of my platoonmates. I scampered toward the top. I knew Clark and Grigsby were to my left and right.

"Clark, you doing all right?"

"Yes, PFC. Are we getting out of here soon? I want to get out of here."

"Yeah, Clark. We'll get you out as soon as we can. Hang in there."

"Grigs, you good?"

"Ten. Keep going." He was good, he wanted me to move to the next guy.

"Carlson?"

"Yeah, man. I got free. I got Hackney with me. I can see daylight."

"Clark, move to your right, to me." I moved a little left. There he was. I grabbed him and I could feel him shaking. I looked into his visor, it was covered in dust. There was no way he could see. I wiped it off with my gloved hand and held onto him with the other. He was white as a ghost inside.

"Grigs, come to me."

All the while there was sporadic COMM chatter in my helmet. It was hard to concentrate on a singular conversation. I had to constantly flip the tiny switch that was in the front of my helmet, centered on my chest. I missed the switch and repeated, "Grigs, come to me, to your left."

The CO was instructing his platoons to engage the FPs. Third was to hold. That meant that we were on our own. We had to dig out.

"Larson, what was your position?" I asked.

"I was three steps behind you to your right. Nice run patterns, by the way. Going to get you to teach that class in the next RnR."

I held onto Clark and moved back to my right, swerving in the near darkness, trying to meet up with Grigs. *There, a figure.* I switched my IR and normal mode back and forth; the figure moved back up the slope.

"Grigs, look to your left. See a red light?"

"Yeah, I got you." He moved toward me, only a few feet away, but nearly invisible in this collapsed ditch and suspended dust.

"Take Clark up. I'm going down for Larson."

"No way, man. I'm going with you." I could see in his helmet; his eyes squinted, and he was shaking his head. "It's going to take all three of us to pull him out of this sand. Let's go." Grigs was not letting me go alone.

"PFCs, what is going on? I ordered you to get topside to form a defense position."

I held my finger up in front of my face, and Grigs caught on. Clark was the weak link. He needed to get out of here. He could jeopardize us. I didn't want to send him up alone, but I pushed Clark up toward the top and hit my helmet with my hand and made an expression of confusion. I could see light now, at the edge of the sunken ditch. I pointed to it and shoved him onward. Grigs and I turned toward the bottom of the ditch, and Clark followed us. I stopped and pushed him back up.

"I know you can hear me, PFC. I'm staying with you guys," Clark said.

I hung my head, that was the very last thing he needed to say.

"PFC Smith, I ordered you topside to prepare a defensive position."

"I can see him! He's just a few feet away." We slid down on our butts, Clark in the middle.

"Switch back and forth, Larson. We have our red lights on. See us?"

"Negative."

"Are you on slope or at the bottom?"

"Dude, I am waist-deep, blind, one arm under me. How the heck do I know if I'm on the bottom!"

"So you're saying that you can't undo your fly, or it would be difficult?" I heard several bursts of laughter on the COMM net.

"I can tell you this, you little upstart. I will undo you if you keep… Hey, I got a light on my four o'clock. Turn it off." I turned my spot light off and then back on again.

"I got you! Move to your ten o'clock. Sweet mother of green apples. Smith, is that you guys, really?"

I could hear the flood of relief in his voice. "We're on you, Corporal. You have to tell me more about this mining business. Was it a family thing or something you picked up before you became interested in the Fleet Marines?"

"I don't know whether to hit you or give you a hug!"

We circled around him and started digging him out. As soon as his right arm came out from behind his back, he grabbed me and pulled me tight. He was much more than waist-deep. He was nearly up to his helmet, both arms buried. It took the three of us almost an hour to get him loose. The sand on the slope kept sliding down, once nearly covering him totally back up. If Lieutenant Green were similarly stuck, he would die very soon, lost forever.

"Corporal Murray, what was last known position of Six?" Larson asked.

Everyone was up on the top now except for the four of us, Lieutenant Green, and Private Somersby.

"I think he was behind me, center of the platoon, overseeing our deployment. I'm not sure of his position."

It had been quite some time since the initiation of the attack on our position. I had lost track of time. Our visibility was very limited, and the sliding and collapsing properties of the sand into the deep ditch were physically draining as well as mentally fatiguing. We searched for hours, laying out a grid pattern and setting one of us as a reference point. Nothing. We attempted several COMM contacts with no success, the overhead Bettys weren't able to get a positive fix on either one of them, which meant they were deep, under tons of sand.

We sat together, the four of us—Larson, Grigs, Clark, and myself—and felt totally worthless; we couldn't retrieve, much less find, our lost brothers, our platoon leader. I was near hysterical, he was due more than this. Lieutenant Green was a great officer, a true leader, and he loved his men. I couldn't abandon him to the sand. Private Somersby was only seventeen, just a kid himself. I thought of the irony and shook my head. I was still younger than any recruit.

But I had aged. I was experienced, I was a tested and tried Fleet Marine. Why was I bothered over some boot private? I wanted him to be alive. I wanted to, at the least, find his body so that he could be returned home and to his family. His mother was… Did he have a mother? I didn't know him. I would talk to Privates Clark, Woolsey, and Hackney and learn about them. They were somebody, I cared about them. I had to find Lieutenant Green! I started digging again. Here, there, over there. Up that slope, farther down. Up.

I was crawling on my knees when Larson pulled me to him. He held me. "You can't bring him back. He's gone, Smith. He's gone. Let him go."

"No, Larson. He's waiting for us. He's right there, just like you, buried and waiting for us to find him!"

He held me, as I squirmed to get free; my fingers were on fire, the fingertips of the HECS raw and heavily worn.

Chapter 7

PRESENT

Oh man, I hurt—not only my eye, which was killing me, though I didn't say anything, but also my whole body. This was still not anywhere near the discomfort of a CR, with the constant stress and unknown around the corner. No, this was way different. This was voluntary, so I guess you couldn't complain, or if you did, so what?

Ginny had been right—First Sergeant French may be old—in his thirties, with multiple LoL and prostatic replacements, PRs, but he flat wore us out at PT. He brought changes to the course all right, but didn't make it physically or academically any easier, just more relevant to the skills, knowledge, and demands of what a new corporal in the divisions was expected to have. One of the changes was that all three Platoon Weeks had morning PT together. Streamline. The over-the-top punishing exercise segment was drastically changed, though still teaching the regulation routines, but in a more professional and knowledgeable manner. Arrival and reporting on the first day was changed to utilities, and the introduction was also professional, courteous, and in recognition of a Fleet Marine's service and commitment to a higher level of responsibility.

The days were filled with a combination of classroom and practicals, or fieldwork. There were still inspections and barracks cleaning, but nothing like it had been; there were way too many important issues and topics to be addressed. Duty day ended after evening chow and study groups went until 2000, and then we had personal time. That had to be the biggest change that the present two weeks that had been "frozen" were absolutely having a brain blast over. All the changes were greatly appreciated by them, but the 2000 to

2100 off time before lights out and the resumption of the next day at 0430 were unbelievable. They had suffered through near twenty-two-hour-long days, every day. Now, weekends were free from lunch Saturday to dinner chow formation Sunday. If anybody on the whole base loved us, it was Weeks Two and Three P.

PT this morning was a killer. We had started with the normal exercise opener, two full routines, Third Week leading them, and now were running Two-Mile Peak and Bad Girl, two wildly infamous hills on base. This was an eight-mile run, performed at a six-and-a-half-minute-mile pace. We carried water packs, a small-liter capacity bladder pack. Every marine from last week's course was back, even Simon. And Campbell was here too. He had been scheduled, he was one of the DNS, but his company, Charlie 1/1/7, was on a CR and they didn't make it back on time last week. Man, Grigs and I were glad to see him on Sunday when he walked up. We laughed, punched, and asked about each other and shared what other guys from Bravo were doing. It was great. He asked about Carpenter and Moon, and we asked about Custer and he laughed.

"Oh," he said, "Custer is a hoot!"

The first day he arrived, he had gone into the TOE Room to report to the gunny, who he knew, of course, and made a swap. He said he would give up having his first three casualties in a trade for an unknown private in fourth platoon. The gunny had laughed and asked how he was supposed to know when that happened. It was rumored Custer grinned, sat on the gunny's desk, and said, "When I report the fourth marine is hit, Gunny!"

We all laughed, and then he said, "So Gunny says, 'I got two privates in fourth. I'm assigning Jeters to your platoon.'"

"Can't take him, Gunny."

"Who the heck do you think you are?"

"The deal was an unknown private for three casualties. You told me Jeters' name. I'll take the other one." We fell out, laughing and slapping each other.

Simon was wheezing and having a hard time, and he started falling back. He had been able to do the other runs, but he was still in pain and this was probably not helping his rib. He had barely made the sit-up minimum, spitting blood when he got up. He was in my squad, so was Campbell. Alvera was closer to my size, while Simon was a little taller, but only about 140 pounds. We were almost done, only another two miles. If he fell out, he was out. This was Friday, and if he could just make it, he would have the weekend to get better. I turned and looked at Alvera, and he knew what I was thinking. We had practiced this in Combat Medic, a three-man run. It was simple—the middle man put his arms around the shoulder of the two outside men, who would grasp the waistline of the middle. Weight was taken off the injured man just enough and he was slightly lifted but was still mobile.

Alvera and I broke ranks and came up beside Simon. "Three-man," said Alvera and we grabbed him, while Simon put his arms around us. The training instructors—French had changed that too, replacing cadre to training instructors, whom he personally interviewed and selected—didn't say a word. An NCO is supposed to help, instruct, be a role model, and be a leader to his men. Helping one another overcome adversity and achieve the mission is the goal.

After a mile, Alvera and I were nearly spent ourselves, so Grigs and Campbell came up from behind. "Switch out," said Campbell. They took him on in.

First Sergeant French, like Gunny Bryant from back during the Y, was barely showing any sweat. It was rumored that he ran twelve miles a day and did his two hundred push-ups and one hundred sit-ups every day. Every other month, each sixty days, he submitted his request for a line battalion and was rejected. It was said, though not in his presence, that the division command sergeant major had finally told him one day that they couldn't risk him going back into combat and losing another limb, that the Galleens would have more of him than the Fleet Marines and we would surely lose fighting a Galleen French! First Sergeant French had allegedly stormed out of division and the next month sent in six requests, one for each of his LoLs!

He stood in front of the formation of the three platoons and issued the orders of the day—shower, chow, prepare for morning inspection, formation, inspection, and continue training. He ordered the senior training gunnery sergeant to Post, transferred the platoons over to him, and executed a smart about-face and retreated inside the Second Training Battalion. Gunnery Sergeant Chavez repeated the orders to his training platoon staff sergeants, who were at the head of each platoon. Staff Sergeant Harris from back in Bravo was a training instructor for the platoon just in front of us, Week Two P. I didn't know any of the others. Our platoon staff sergeants were Patte and Tzenski, who were tough as nails and former drills. Well, they all were, as well as SS.

They came from all the divisions and had anywhere from seven to nine years, countless CRs, and all passed up moving to the Twelfth and getting a gunny promotion to be training instructors at PNCOC. They all knew and respected First Sergeant French, and when he called each of them, they yanked their applications for the new division. French evidently had a lot of pull with Colonel Thompson, who had a lot of pull somewhere. French got every senior NCO he requested. We got all this information from our old friend, now Corporal Griffin, who was the duty NCO at Second Training Battalion. He was the first sergeant's aide, driver, runner, etc. He had been in the second to last class to graduate before it was overturned. He told us he wished it had happened sooner.

This morning, we were continuing our instruction on the duties and responsibilities of small unit command. Staff Sergeant Tzenski had been the lead instructor in this class the entire week. Prior to lunch, we would fall out to the Second Training Battalion drill field, the quad, and practice formal formations, the nuts and bolts of all the underlying formalities and where we were supposed to go in each position of rank and responsibility in each unit from squad to division. Then, we would organize into combat roles and review and role-play those positions. Who takes command in the absence of each unit organizational level? We had to be ready to step up and take command at squad-, platoon-, company-, and battalion-level NCO positions, especially as we moved up in rank. ANCOC, for staff sergeants, prepared them for senior NCO command level and went more in-depth into the battalion responsibilities and beyond.

"A long way yet," Staff Sergeant Tzenski laughed.

It was now the end of the second week in May, and even though the nights were quite chilly, the days were getting warmer, but there was still snow in the forests and on the peaks. The wind could be extremely cold, especially after working up a sweat running around and then standing still and walking through formation positions. First week was almost all in utilities. Next week, we would do more field maneuvers and small unit tactical command maneuvers.

"No no no! Lance Corporal Grigsby, if you are first platoon sergeant and the order from company CO is for 'First Sergeant, Post!' you…"

The morning rolled on, Staff Sergeants Tzenski and Patte laughing at us for being "uneducated combat warriors" one minute, wondering out loud how we had made it this far, and then nearly turning red the next because we couldn't step out the battalion-level change of command formation that we had gone over the hour before.

"Are you yanking my chain, Campbell? You got to be doing this on purpose. I know you were the CRL for your training company. Do it again! From 'Platoon sergeants, Report!'"

We all took our turns, but it wasn't any easier after watching. Each marine messed something up, so there was something wrong with each sequence. Every night in study groups, we would go step by step, breaking down the various formations. Last night, a group of staff sergeants from ANCOC came down and practiced with us, helping us out, giving us simple reminders, and telling us to relax, that it wasn't as hard as it looked. To our surprise, Sergeants Williams and Mean were with them. They had been recently promoted and were on their way back to line companies as platoon sergeants.

Man! The contacts and number of Fleet Marines that you knew or had associations with just accumulated. The marines from the other divisions also knew staff sergeants in ANCOC from their own experiences, so it was interesting to make all these connections and contacts with other NCOs of other divisions and know that one day you might meet again. The staff sergeants in ANCOC were not too chummy with us; they were now E6s and we were not yet E4s, a wide gap. Professional etiquette had to be maintained, but they wanted to see us succeed. Almost half were on their way to the new division.

It was Friday night; study group was over and I sat on my footlocker looking around. One more morning and Week One P was over. Tomorrow, Week Three P would graduate, and those guys were walking on the clouds, happy as could be, laughing, cutting up, and preparing their Alphas. I watched absently as two of them walked down the middle of the bay toward the head, having to pass my bunk. They stopped right in front of me and started talking to me.

"Hey, Smith, right?" one of them asked.

I hadn't really been paying attention to them in particular, just in overall observing the general activity of the bay. I was pulled back into the here and now.

"Yeah, what you need?" I wasn't alarmed or in any way defensive or in a mind to have to jump up at attention; we were all lance corporals, same rank, no seniority over another, equal.

"My name's Smith too. Allen, from Dog 2/2/1, hopefully still am next week." He stuck out his hand. I took it, and we shook.

"I'm Martin, Charlie 1/2/1. Nice to finally meet you. You the guy that punched Gunny Castelle, that lousy sadist? Biggest excuse for a gunny I've ever run across," he said as he held out his hand.

"No, I never hit any of the cadre. It's all scuttlebutt."

I remained on my footlocker. My wall locker was open, and my Alphas were hanging, like everyone else's. My awards and ribbons were in place, the newly awarded DLC as visible as the OL.

"Holy smokes! It is true." Smith walked by me and toward my wall locker. "May I? I've never seen the OL so close. How did you earn the DLC? I thought that was mainly an officer medal?"

Grigs was lying on his bunk above mine and started reciting, almost in a monotone voice, the subsection of the DLC exemption for awarding parameters for EM. "Under situations when the condition in which a smaller size unit is commanded by a lessor rank of E4 and the marines under his control are engaged in heavy and/or close-quarters fighting and the outcome of such combat would be detrimentally different had command and direction not been given, EM is authorized awarding of Distinguished Leadership Cross."

He looked down at Allen Smith and Martin. "Smith there was in charge of a fire team during a sandstorm when a…" He continued the story, not skipping a beat.

Campbell was on the top bunk on the other side of the locker listening. Alvera had lived his own part of horror that night as well and got up to go to the head.

I got up and walked down to see if Griffin would let me use his tablet. Grigs kept talking, telling the story, others now gathering to listen to the action of the ravine. He had played a major role too, and I hoped he included his part. He was up for the EM version of the DLC, the Distinguished Cross for Valor, and Oak Leaf for his Commendation Medal for other actions. I hadn't talked to Donna all week, and I wanted to hear her voice.

CHAPTER 8

Echo Company sat and waited the daytime storm out, quiet, knowing that two marine brothers were MIA, torn between guilt not being able to find and recover their bodies, not wishing them dead, but hoping they weren't POWs either. The four of us, Grigs, Larson, Clark, and myself, crawled to the edge of the vast ditch and flopped down, exhausted. I was hot, somehow the exertion not keeping up with the HECS or the lack of water not taking place of the missing food. I was confused, and my thinking was "numbering" my brain activity. I was out of water, had been for a while, even the recycle, which wasn't much. I looked around for the sky; it had to be up there, unless I had crawled up to the bottom of the ditch. And we were perched on the slope looking onto the bottom. Nothing. Maybe that's why I was so hot.

"Larson?" I asked.

"Yep," he answered. I could hear the tiredness in his voice.

"Did we climb up or down?"

There was a pause, and then he laughed and said, "Up, I just checked."

There was a soft round of laughter throughout the platoon, guys momentarily pulled from their somber inward selves to the close-knit band of friends.

"How did you do it?" asked Almond.

"I let sand fall from my fingers."

"What if the planet's gravity mixes it up," asked Carlson.

"Yeah, it's been flying sideways most of the time we've been here," added Jackson.

"No, I'm on my stomach and it fell," replied Larson.

"Well, what if Smith is right, and you are at the bottom and lying on your back, then it would have fallen upward," said Rich.

"No, no, it fell back from where I grabbed it from. Here, I'll put my hand up higher, where the sand is swirling around." Just then a flurry of GBL streaked by the four of us.

Puc! Puc! Puc! Puc! Puc!

"Holy smokes! They're right in front of us, Echo Six!" exclaimed Larson.

We returned fire.

Zik! Zik! Zik! Zik! Puc! Puc! Puc! Zik! Zik! Zik!

There was a continuous firefight on, not just a probing skirmish. There had been little activity since the cave-in. Fourth platoon had reached the FPs but found nothing, no holes, no trace. First platoon had visually marked the positions but came up short as well. The snipers had vanished. The next storm came in a couple hours later as the search for Lieutenant Green and Private Somersby proceeded. With Larson's arm up in the air, it had given the Galleens the first target in hours. The other two platoons had fallen back twenty meters and set up in an "L," but the problem was fourth platoon was facing directly at us. Now we were shooting blindly toward them while trying to return fire at the GBL, which seemed to be in the center of the three of us. This was bad. They had to be just feet from us to see his hand.

"Cease fire! Cease fire!" yelled Carpenter, Captain Shupin, and Gunny Scott all at once.

The GBL kept coming in.

"Cease fire! Cease fire!" yelled Carpenter again.

"I don't think they're on our channel, Two," said Murray, the platoon COMM erupting in a roar.

Even in our extreme predicament, a combat Fleet Marine still found humor in the direst of situations. The GBL was lowering, digging into the sand now, seeking us out in our fighting positions. They had us zeroed in.

"Dive! Dive!" Corporal Larson yelled. "They have us!"

I slid down several feet, and I could feel Grigs falling into me and Clark slipping farther down in an uncontrolled slide, the sand giving way. Larson was on the other side of him, I was sure, sliding down for cover as well.

"This is heavy contact, Six! This is aggressive behavior. They're about to assault!"

I could hear Larson's voice change to something I had only heard from him a time or two—the last was at the small derrick at the end of our last CR, when we were outnumbered and about to be overrun. I closed my eyes and relaxed for a brief moment. *Do the best you can and be the best you can. You'll rest with your fallen brothers tonight, Valhalla!* I thought to myself.

"Smith, take your team to your right ten yards and come up even to the top. Wait for the breach!" ordered Larson, his voice different.

"Almond, slide down with your team a few feet. You should be just below to the right or in with Smith."

"Corporal Murray, you are to the left, take first squad, and hold position. Ready to attack from the rear," said Carpenter. We were blind in this ditch.

"Larson, what's your status?" Carpenter asked.

"I'm headed for the bottom, Tim… I can't…"

Chapter 8

PRESENT

We were almost all here, the old gang.

"Hey! Come on! Come on!" yelled Campbell, his face telling the truth, he was not sure about this at all.

"It's all good, bro. Smith's girl vouches for this place. We had a bad night, man." Moon was patting his best friend on the back, so happy to be with him again.

The laughter and joking and stories were all at the same time, making it hard for me to listen to any one in full. It didn't matter. We were all so glad to be together again, laughing and in each other's company—not since, well, almost six months.

"Hey! Hey! To old times, Bravo 2055-07!" yelled Luke, raising his glass.

"Hoo-aah!" we all yelled.

The place was empty except for us and a couple other locals, trying to keep from staring, laughing, wishing they were a part of a group again. Ski season was over, the spring melt full on, the tourists gone, the locals relapsing into the off-season until summer brought in a different group, the Lake Crowd.

The original Linda's Group, Grigsby, Lewis, Luke, Campbell, Moon, Jackson, Carlson, Andrews, Blaine, Bennett, Hackney, Cartwright, Hawkeye, MacCauley, Baumgardner, Feekas, and myself—we were not all here. Lewis, Bennett, Hackney, and Cartwright were gone, so were Douglas and Hatch from Bravo Training Company. That was six Fleet Marines from our training company, gone. KIA. Not even a year. High casualty rate, over nine percent, and we hadn't reached our first year yet. Others from the group were deployed with other brigades and battalions and were out. Somehow, Moon had contacted all those that were available, even those that weren't on a CR were in B Course or Division Duty. Still, Luke, Grigs, Moon, Campbell, Jackson, Carlson, Andrews, Baumgardner, and I were having the best time. Others joined us too, Alvera, Simon, Yost, Griffin, and Maliki, from PNCOC.

Earlier this afternoon, as I was just hanging around the bay after we were dismissed for Saturday lunch chow, Corporal Griffin had sent a CQ runner up to find me, saying I had a phone call. When I ran down as fast as I could—we were at PNCOC—I heard Moon on the other end saying we were all meeting at Linda's for dinner chow. What?

Now, here we were, even guys that didn't know one another, but had a connection in some way. It was over-the-top fun. Hardly anyone was drinking a beer or alcohol, just sodas or iced tea, but having a blast. I still hadn't thought of something to do to remember our friends from Bravo, but now I had lost someone in my immediate family, a good leader, Lieutenant Green, and Somersby. We had to do something; they couldn't just be forgotten, no one to know their sacrifice, lost to our consciousness in a year's time. It was already getting hard for me to remember Lewis' smile, his voice, his love for life, and his total commitment to the Fleet Marines. I don't know why, but I had brought my Bravo platoon graduation group photo with me and my OL.

We had Linda's to ourselves, practically, and Linda was so glad to see us. We were all seasoned and experienced marines now, and Linda was astutely aware of that fact. She recognized me from the start and Moon and Grigs from our last time here. All of us were in civilian clothes, but you could tell, eyes, hands, arms, and scars. This was still not a bar. It was a nice little family restaurant, struggling in the in-between season; and Linda was very, very, glad to see a group of mature, nondrinking, veteran Fleet Marines eating at her establishment in mid-May. We weren't looking for a "deal." We had more credits than we could spend. We only wanted a place that was fair and welcomed us.

I pulled Linda to the side and said, "Look, we aren't here to tear the place apart or get rowdy. I think I can help you, if you can do something for us."

She looked at me with a quizzical expression, "What are you suggesting?" Her business senses bristling.

"Let me hang a picture over that table there," I said, pointing to a little two bar-chair high table at the corner of the room, next to the narrow hallway that led to the head. "And every time I come in, I'll buy an extra drink and taco."

"What!" She almost laughed, her eyes wide, her mouth open in a smirk. "I haven't seen you in weeks!"

"Watch," I said and turned back to my buddies. "Hey! Let's toast my friend, PFC Lewis, OL recipient, posthumously, Wound Badge, and Commendation Medal recipient. Hoo-aah!"

"Hoo-aah!" the room exploded.

"Linda, please, I'd like to buy my friend a drink and a taco at that table," I said, pointing to the empty table I was just discussing with her.

"Me too! My friend is thirsty!"

"Lewis, for all the wanna-be drill instructors that ever tore his kit apart, was better than they ever were! I'm buying my best bud a drink," yelled Andrews, wiping his eyes.

The table was quickly so full of plates of tacos, whiskeys and beers, and margaritas that it couldn't hold any more. The guys from the other training companies and all of us from our personal losses from active-duty units bought our brothers who had "gone on to Valhalla" a drink and a taco. That's how it was, and it has always been that way with warriors from the beginning of time. We needed a place to remember our brothers—it was that simple.

We ate and laughed, cried, and told and listened to stories of brothers that we knew and didn't know, until tonight. Their memories were not forgotten.

Linda came up to me later and pulled me away, tears in her eyes. "You hang your picture. It will always be welcomed, as all of you are for as long as I own this place."

She gave me a hug. She held on a little longer than I was expecting, and I felt her quietly sobbing, her body limp in my arms. She was overcome with grief, or guilt, or some other emotion, but she was a true believer now.

I pinned the graduation picture of Bravo 2055-07 on the wall above the little table, the heads of the Fleet Marines that had died in battle, circled in red. I pinned my OL above that, with a line in marker connecting it to Lewis. Each of the marines present looked at the picture, rubbing their eyes or completely breaking down, reaching toward the picture, not seeing it in months or ever, seeing the young and innocent faces of brothers they had spent their first six weeks in the Fleet Marines with.

From that time on, Linda's became *hallowed ground*. Fleet Marines would silently hang a picture of a fallen brother, buy a drink, maybe sit and retell a tale, and leave; all divisions, all Fleet Marines. Linda's became a legend. No recruits ever entered again. It was our place now, and Linda's was never empty.

CHAPTER 9

Puc! Puc! Puc! Puc! Puc!

An endless stream of bluish laser energy bursts streaked overhead. If not for the life-threatening consequences of the streaks, it would be a breathtakingly fabulous sight. I didn't know what Larson's condition was, he didn't say, but the objective of the moment now was to stay alive, with the guy to my left and right. I could feel my body tensing; all remaining energy reserves were being pulled from wherever and I was alert and responsive as I could be.

"Ready, Clark, right here. Right here. You're good, Marine. Follow my instructions. You're good." I pulled and pushed him to the position I wanted, at my left boot. "I'll tell you when, and you burn that GLAR up. I'll buy you a new one, you got me?"

"Yes, PFC. You've seen this before?"

"Oh, heck, yeah, Clark. This is every day, been getting bored. You'll be okay." I patted him on the back.

"Grigs, I want you on my right shoulder. Cut 'em to pieces, bro. We may be dancing soon. I'll lead. You keep the music in time, got me?" I wanted him to stay on the gun, while, if I needed to, I would go hand-to-hand out in front.

The thing was we couldn't see, and I don't know if the Galleens were able to see us better through an advance we didn't have yet, or they were just as blind as us. The fact that they were taking an aggressive assault on a full company of Fleet Marines was astonishing. They either had overwhelming numbers or were suicidal, both were cause for concern. Second platoon was already at a disadvantage by being in the collapsed ditch and practically isolated.

I felt, rather than saw something, someone pass in front of me. Without thinking, I reached out my hand and grabbed a hold of a leg, feeling the body trip and fall before me!

"Fire! Angle to my front!"

The green laser energy of the GLAR penetrated the darkness. GBL crisscrossed the void, intertwining the two laser energy forces in a spectacular show of green and blue just over our heads! Eerie shadows were created by the incandescent glow of the two laser energy flows, dancing on the sand, making a ghostly and rather scary backdrop. The surge was constant, a flow of bodies straight and seemingly endless, at least in my mind's perception, into the ditch we occupied. The assaulters quickly fixed on my fire team and conveyed alternative route paths. I was locked in mortal combat, protecting my team, still directing their individual shots.

"Clark, straight up. Grigs, he's down to my front. Finish him! Right! Right! One coming at you!"

"Almond, light 'em up. You see our positions?"

"Fire Team Two, watch the laser. Follow the GBL into the source! We got you, Smith!" replied Lance Corporal Almond, the marines of his team now revealing their positions, just to the bottom left of the first team.

"Steady, now, Murray! Hold! Let's suck them in a little—" Sergeant Carpenter's voice was soothing.

I was caught in a sudden physical assault, but what isn't sudden in combat? We grappled, our bodies falling or rolling over the several bodies already dispatched to my front.

"Clark, pop him! Pop him! Right here, to your front."

I kicked and punched and slugged it out with the Mowatt in my grasp, only slightly confident that he would be taken out before I was.

Zik! Zik! Zik!

The body in my hands became deadweight, his lifeless soul freed to travel to its judgment. I barely had time to reflect, as I wrestled with another, just before he managed to enter the safety zone of Grigs. I reached into the void just between where the helmet and chest protector shielded the neck. It was a terrible design flaw, and my only thought was that they had left it on purpose to give their soldiers a little more flexibility in a trade-off for up-close protection, thinking it would never come to that. I crushed his throat as I was trading knee kicks and punches; he fell to the ground gasping for air and life, out of the fight. We would recover him later for intel, if he didn't die first.

"Leave the squirming one. He's choking," I said, moving onto the next one in the small pocket, cracking his ribs, breaking a knee, finishing him off with my GLAR.

"Go ahead, Murray. Light 'em up. Clear the field. This push is over," I exclaimed out of excitement.

"Check that, PFC! Hold your shadow, Corporal Murray. You are unknown, stay low, Murray. PFC Smith—"

My Command COMM was hectic!

The CO was directing, "Fourth platoon, move in behind the assaulting Galleens. First, hold. Second platoon, keep the assault alive!"

"Smith, you do not issue orders above your command! You do not realize the overall... Good night, Smith! Scientists and politicians, wait for your orders," responded Carpenter, calmer now, almost coaxing me.

"Aye, Corp...Aye Two-Six."

I was lost; the sudden and hectic change of command status was numbing. I could faintly see the looming sunset. Oh, the day was almost over! *Please, please, let us extract*, I thought to myself.

I caught another poor Galleen conscript as he blindly stumbled over the edge of the ditch and into the unknown, a certain death, thinking, *What pushes them onward? Do they know that they have no strategic favorability attacking down into a blind, fire-superior position?*

Lance Corporal Almond's fire team was dead-on in their targeting, just below us, seeking out the GBL sources as the Galleens stormed the ditch, not being able to adjust their fire on the decline until it was too late. My team basically stood them up and slowed them down, and the bodies slid down or caused the Mowatts to trip.

Because our fire was travelling upward at an angle or away from fourth platoon, fourth was now able to advance and find the exit points and plug the holes. First platoon now moved in to assist fourth, and third platoon finally was put into action, skirting the ditch and swinging to the right, following first platoon's original course.

"Six, we've breached the anthill," Staff Sergeant LaBoye proclaimed.

He was the highest ranking in fourth platoon, the platoon leader, effectively. Echo was down to just one lieutenant now, First Lieutenant Howard of first platoon. If anything happened to Six, Captain Shupin…

The daytime storm was letting up now, starting to wind down as the surface temperature leveled off, cooling as the sun slowly sunk into the distant horizon. Relief from the blowing sand and hurricane force winds for a limited period, as we now knew, would follow for only several hours, before the real storm started sometime after nightfall. Now was the time to extract. The Galleens had purposefully sucked us in this morning, essentially trapping us for another cycle.

Please, please, please, Captain Shupin, pull us out. We can't go another sixteen hours. The Galleens would decimate an entire company tonight as we would be too weak to continue.

My Command COMM was busy, the platoon leaders and sergeants reporting their positions and status. "We're rested, Six. Let third root out the tunnel," pleaded Staff Sergeant Oliver.

I did not really know him well, but he seemed to be highly respected by his marines.

"Six, the men are running on fumes," added Lieutenant Howard.

"Give me the 'go,' Six. Fourth is right here. We can clear these tunnels!" Staff Sergeant LaBoye was forceful. "We are the only platoon that is truly fit, rested."

"They're sucking us in again, Six, just like this morning." Staff Sergeant Ginny was the voice of sanity. "They know we're exhausted, and that's why they hit us, wrapping it up as a present. We'll lose the company if we miss this extraction window."

"Second, what's the status of…" Gunny Scott asked, he wasn't sure what had happened to Larson. None of us were.

"I'm here, Gunny," answered Corporal Larson. "I'm below my Fire Team Two. I'm…" He stopped. I knew he was hurt, and this was all on the Command channel, so the platoon couldn't hear him.

"Lance Corporal Almond, make contact with Larson and advise," said Carpenter over the platoon COMM; none of the platoon, other than Larson and Murray, knew I was on the Command COMM. "Smith, slide down and assist."

"I need it straight," he added on the Command COMM.

"Aye, moving," I replied on the open channel.

Chapter 9

PRESENT

"What are your orders, Lance Corporal?"

Staff Sergeant Tzenski was quietly demanding, squatting down just in front of me, lightly tapping my shoulder with a short stick.

I liked him, but he was not easy on any of us.

"I was directed to lead my squad in a move and cover maneuver around that small knoll, Staff Sergeant." I knew I had made a mistake and he caught it immediately.

"You can't very well support the other squad, running on the far side of this little ravine, can you, Lance Corporal? You just split the platoon in half. You should have directed your teams either up the ravine or on the near side, there." He pointed with his stick. "Fix it!"

"Campbell, cover! Budner, cross the ravine to that aspen."

The afternoon was warm, and we were in our utilities, web belt, CPs, and the water pack. The CP was of course combat loaded, and with the HECS packed inside, the weight and cumbersomeness were staggering. The snowmelt was adding to the absolute discomfort and near ineffective maneuvering speed, the soggy, muddy, and icy slushiness only making the conditions exceedingly uncomfortable. We were well-fed, rested, not under direct threat, or otherwise overly stressed. We did everything in our HECS while on a CR or RnR, so the absence of the suit was painfully evident in our diminished physical ability and reaction.

Week Two of PNCOC was just a tactical continuation of Week One. This was Tuesday and I couldn't imagine the next three and a half days.

"*Puc!* You're dead, Lance Corporal Smith!" Staff Sergeant Tzenski said, after expertly hitting me in the chest with a slushy loose snowball composed of grass, mud, and snow.

"Who's next in command? Quick! Quick! Quick!" He was making another snowball. I was soaked and now cold, hoping he was not going to hit me in the head with the next one.

"I am, Staff Sergeant," answered Hernandez. The slush ball exploding on his CP, just at the top of his head, running down his neck and back, causing instant discomfort.

"No, you're not, Lance Corporal. We discussed this last week. Who is next senior? Time *and* grade."

Staff Sergeant Patte was busy admonishing the other squad, to our left, upending their shallow comfort zone as well.

"When the platoon is split up into squads or even individual fire teams, the next senior member in attendance will immediately take command of the unit. Smith"—he called me out by name—"who replaced your squad corporal on Butch during the *assault in the ravine?*"

The battle was quickly becoming a classic tactical study.

"Lance Corporal Almond was next senior, Staff Sergeant." My mind wanted to forget that period.

"You continued to direct the squad. Why?"

Why? I didn't want to think about it, the darkness, the chaos, the fear. Why? Why was he bringing this up? Let it alone. It was the heat of battle, and decisions had to be made. *I liked Almond, but he just… He was not… He didn't want to take charge. He wasn't ready, but I…* Was Tzenski hitting me? Was this his way to exact revenge for the PNCOC episode two weeks ago? Was he trying to make me look bad?

"Lance Corporal Almond is a good marine, Staff Sergeant."

"I know he is, Lance Corporal. Why did you overstep his command?"

I stood there, frozen, self-doubt trying to creep in and question my decisions.

"Never hesitate in a fight, Lance Corporal Smith. You've heard that before, yes?"

Of course I had, numerous times. I saw Corporal Larson now, lying in the sand, Almond at his side, not able to react or speak. I had to push him away so I could…

"Lance Corporal Almond was not able to direct the squad, Staff Sergeant, so I took the lead."

"Exactly. You have got to know your platoonmates, Marines. You have to know one another's weaknesses and strong points. Hernandez, you are longest in time, but not in grade. That would be who?"

"I am, Staff Sergeant," Lance Corporal Cummings said, unsure if he was about to receive a slush ball to the head.

"Carry on, Cummings. Smith, recover as a squad member, out of command rotation through the remainder of this exercise."

I took Cummings' place in Fire Team One. The afternoon wore on, and every man was rotated through, carrying out a part of the mission—the objective, Command Structure.

We were marching back to Second Training Battalion, down a sloppy, muddy, dirt road. All of us were tired and hungry; our day had been full since PT this morning. Lunch was on the run, from a full-day box meal, and I only had been able to eat an energy bar and drink on bug juice all day. Dinner chow was going to be so good.

Senior Training Gunnery Sergeant Chavez was leading the platoon. We halted in front of the battalion barracks and stood at attention, waiting on the final orders of the day, anticipating the chance to clean up and go to chow.

My eye felt much better, but I could tell the loss of vision, since I had to strain to see clearly, closing my left eye sometimes, not able to focus close-up. Reading was difficult, and I hated that.

We were soaked, muddy, sweaty, and cold. We were ordered to clean up, chow, study groups, prepare, and clean equipment for tomorrow. Same drill. Dismissed. I was relieved, I was beat. Grigs was standing a few feet from me, Alvera next to him. They had been in the other squad. The platoon kinda just stood there, with everyone tired—too tired to move up the steps and clean up.

Our CPs were filthy, everything in them wet. The staff sergeants had found a nice mudhole earlier this morning, and we had been ordered to prepare for Field Inspection. Everything was laid out, as we had been taught long ago, the entire contents of the CP displayed in precise order, on our blankie. The added weight of mud and water was tremendous. It all had to be cleaned and dried and repacked tonight. Over and over, it had been drilled into us that corporals had to lead the way in example and be ready always. I remembered the Corporal's Bay, their CPs hanging on their bunks, everything inspection-ready. The corporal was always prepared to move *right now*.

There was no chow for us tonight, since we would all be preparing and cleaning our gear, and that was our expected action. We all knew it. Sacrifice. Lead by example.

Staff Sergeants Tzenski and Patte were standing off to the side, laughing and talking together, almost as muddy as we were, although without CPs, only their water packs. The platoon slowly headed up the steps, talking quietly, making internal assignments for a more efficient equipment cleanup.

"Smith, come here a second," called out Staff Sergeant Tzenski.

I immediately changed my physical manner, pulling myself to an energized attitude and approached the two staff sergeants in a respectful and professional manner.

"Yes, Staff Sergeant Tzenski." I stood at attention, the best I could with the over ninety-pound pack forcing me into a forward slouch.

"Stand at ease, Lance Corporal. I don't want you to think I was beating you up over Butch. You did the right thing." He was standing in front of me, Patte just behind him, watching.

Tzenski was about five foot ten, short-cropped, reddish hair, and with a full drooping mustache. He was thick, about a hundred and eighty pounds, solid. He spoke with a heavy European accent, but had a hearty laugh. His eyes were green, original. His teeth were not perfect or gleaming white, and he was one of the few senior NCOs that I had encountered that indulged in the habit of tobacco. His right cheek was extended, swollen, with the chaw of a chew.

"I know Ginny and LaBoye and Oliver. They all said the same thing—the AAR has been studied and picked apart. The Galleens changed their tactics on us. You got a head for tactics, Lance Corporal.

I noticed you're missing your OL off your awards card. Tomorrow, when we come back in, you head straight over to the PX and order a replacement. You need that for Saturday inspection. Dismissed."

He surprised me, he rubbed his chin, spat on the ground, and turned away from me, back to Patte, without the formalities of the formation. I spun around, as best I could, and retreated to the second deck of the barracks, too tired to ponder what had been said. I could dwell on that later. I had work to do. We all did.

CHAPTER 10

I forced myself calmly and professionally to evaluate and then treat, as best I could, Corporal Larson's hand. It was obviously mangled, but he had self-treated as best he could, knowing that the platoon was about to be assaulted and not wanting anyone pulled off the line to assist him. I could see the darkened sand near him, still damp, but drying quickly, where he bled. Sometimes the laser wound would cauterize and there would be little to no bleeding, and sometimes it didn't, resulting in extreme loss of blood. We were all dehydrated, and the blood was not as thin as normal, but on the flip side, we were in extreme heat and stressed with quickened pulses. Larson had managed to apply the tourniquet band around his wrist but couldn't apply the "cup," a heavy-duty rubberized fabric that capped the end of a severed limb. He hadn't lost his hand, so the cup wouldn't secure. His HECS glove was still in place, the seal intact, so the suit didn't tighten as it normally would have. The heat of the atmosphere had to be horrible as well as the loss of blood. I knew my friend was in severe pain.

He looked at me through his goggles and visor, watching me as I worked on his hand. I had learned so much from him on treating wounds. He was always talking, joking, asking guys the dumbest things while he fixed them up. I was too tight, too inexperienced, worried that I would make a mistake.

"Hey, I thought I showed you how to talk it up. Your bedside manner is unnerving."

"I'm going to administer your Med-Dose. You're going to be all right."

"I know. I wouldn't want anyone else working on me but you. I know you read the book."

"No, see, I got you all fooled. I just read the bold type and the end of the chapter summary. Tells you everything to pass the exam."

He laughed. Larson had never yelled out in pain, just lying there waiting for us to find him. He didn't want to Med-Dose and be unable to fight if it came to that. I stuck him in the wrist, through his torn and burned glove. The pain relief gradually taking effect. The Med-Dose also contained a combination of antivirus, anti-inflammatory, anti-infection, a host of super vitamins, and a small A-Dose to feed the body.

"Ah, that's better," he said as I felt him untense.

"Six, I've got junior Two dosed, relaxing. He's lost some blood, I can't guess without a better exam. His right hand," I paused as I looked at my friend. He was lying back, he was spent. The exertion, the stress, the injury, and the Med-Dose, he was out. "It's gone."

"Luke, Jackson, Clark, slide down and prepare to drag him out of there to the CP side. The rest of the platoon, cover," said Sergeant Carpenter.

"Oliver, bring third in to assist with pulling casualty out and cover. Fourth platoon, fall back and join with first. Prepare for extraction," Captain Shupin ordered.

Finally, we were going to get out of here.

It was hard going, dragging Larson up the slope of the ravine, since the sand just kept collapsing and sliding away. This was near impossible, and it was hard enough climbing to the top yourself, but trying to pull someone else. We were getting nowhere, the side of the ravine just kept collapsing. There was no way a Betty would come down here, so close to the anthill as LaBoye called it. I think the vibration would just cause the shifting more. This reminded me of an insect trap. I couldn't remember if it was an ant killer or a spider that would dig a hole in the loose dirt and would wait at the bottom, covered and hidden. The insect prey would become trapped in the hole, with the sides collapsing, like this, and would eventually be killed and eaten by the hunter. Why did I have to think of that now?

I could finally see the sky above me and for the first time, in the fading light, grasp the enormity of the ravine. The floating dust was still very thick, wafting aimlessly, caught in the confines of the cavity.

It looked like the space between the two opposite edges was well over thirty or more meters wide, bringing the edge closer to the Galleen FP nearly up to them. That would explain how they saw Larson's hand so well—we were right in front of them. I still couldn't see the bottom, but I could now see how much farther we had before we reached the top and it was almost the same distance as it was wide! I shook my head. I have to keep going. I saw a Betty overhead.

"Echo Six, we finally have visual of the landscape."

"Yes, Betty One-Six. How's it look?"

"That ravine is massive, chock-full of dust. Can only make eight, nine of your second platoon. Alpha 1/2/7 is preparing to insert now. I will patch you through to them next. Where do you want extraction?"

The COMM I was listening in on was switched to another channel, but I didn't mind. I just wanted out of this ditch and to get on a Betty.

We pulled and pushed, even tried three-man, but the effort was tremendous for little gain. For every two hard-fought steps in the sifting sand, we lost one. Captain Shupin had coordinated with the CO of Alpha 1/2/7, and they were inserting in our CP area and laying out their defensive perimeter, preparing for the night.

First and fourth platoons were moving back around the far end of the ravine, somewhere to our flank. I don't know how far it stretched. Third platoon had moved up to the edge we were now fighting to climb up to, covering our withdrawal. So now the remainder of second could slide down to the bottom and start their climb up this side. They finally met up with us, and even though they were tired from their quick-paced maneuver, Moon, Rich, Carlson, and Woolsey grabbed Larson and plowed up the bank to within five meters before sliding back down half of what they had accomplished. It was so frustrating. Their second attempt took them to just feet of the edge, so several marines from third platoon made a human chain and grabbed Larson and pulled him over the top. Moon and his team barely crossed the top, falling to their knees or lying on their back. The recovery must have taken an hour or more, and it was nearly dark.

The little dust devils started their dance, the sand lightly blowing, and the Bettys circled overhead, prepared to give cover and fire support, if needed.

The extraction of Echo was completed. I almost fell into my seat, my hands shaking, not from fear, but from a total energy washout. I was barely able to connect the Support Tube and took several long drinks then unlatched my helmet, letting it fall to the deck, nearly ripping my goggles off, and then pulling down my mask so that I could finally scratch that itch on my nose. I forcefully rubbed my head, ears, and eyes and opened my mouth wide. Everyone else was doing the same thing, since it had been over forty-eight hours without touching our faces. Everyone's faces looked sunburned around the outside of the eyes and mouth from the heat.

"Look at that. Look at the bodies," said Corporal Murray, who was sitting on the end, across from Carpenter.

"We counted seventeen on the slope that we could see," said the crew chief; he was kneeling on the deck, taking care of Larson. "Here, this is new. All of you grab one."

He opened a box and started it off on the end nearest him.

"These are chilled. It's a gel energy supplement. Thought you guys would like it."

The box made its way up one side and was passed over to the other. I took one. Chilled was all I needed to hear. I quickly looked at the "Tear Here" directions and sucked and squeezed it into my mouth. Oh, that was good. The chief passed down energy bars next, all the while we were taking drawls on the bug juice from the Support Tubes. I could feel my HECS being cleaned and the reservoirs rinsed and filled.

We were circling, I didn't know why, but I could see the landscape and the ravine, the darkness closing in. Then I could see why we were circling. GBL was streaking across the ravine at Alpha 1/2/7. In the next instant, the door gunner opened up!

Boom! Boom! Boom! Tck! Tck! Tck! Tck! Boom! Boom! Boom!

No…

Chapter 10

PRESENT

The day had been mostly fun, for me anyway. The training day had started with a quick review of Map Reading and Navigation in the classroom, and then we loaded up on a Camel and set off. There was no talking and the flap was down. It was a strange mode of travel for us, in this truck, and I could feel us climbing a mountain and then going down.

Staff Sergeant Patte was sitting in the back with us and after a while started talking. "Anyone ever been to the moon Rizour?"

One of the guys from First Division said, "I have, Staff Sergeant," kind of in a haltingly way, not knowing where this was headed.

"Did you like it?"

The guy laughed. "Are you serious, Staff Sergeant?"

"Yeah. What? It's a straight duty, mostly flat. Go in, stand your watch, patrol the perimeter, off for a twelve, and repeat. You didn't like it?"

Patte was leaning on his knees, looking down the middle of the truck at us.

The guy was staring back at Patte. "You're yanking my chain, Staff Sergeant. You couldn't possibly have enjoyed that assignment."

"Enjoyed it? Oh, heck no, Lance Corporal Cassidy. I hated it. I was just asking if you liked it."

The Camel burst into laughter. Patte was all right.

"What's that planet, Staff Sergeant, where it freezes up and then nearly boils?" asked someone.

"That's in the Alpha Centauri system, Hephaistos, named for the Greek god of fire and volcanoes. That's a bad place. I set down there once, twice. You have six hours, twice a day. Too close to its sun. It's a mystery why there is so much water present. That's why we go there, to study the environment." This was interesting.

"I'll tell you another one that has the biologists and botanists all worked up, the Xavier moon in the Centauri C system. Enormous amounts of water and heavy vegetation with the slightest of light. They can't figure it out."

He looked at me. "You ever been there, Lance Corporal Smith?"

He knew I had been. They knew everything about us.

"Yes, Staff Sergeant. Echo 2/2/7 patrolled it a couple months ago. It's creepy."

He smiled, nodded his head, and then laughed. "Yeah, I guess so."

He sat back up and listened to the platoon talk. He did that on purpose, to lighten us up and take our minds off the next assignment. I knew what was coming, I'm sure we all did. The Camel started to slow and then stopped. Staff Sergeant Tzenski appeared at the flap and whipped it back. We were on a dirt road somewhere in the mountains, the sun lighting up the early, chilly morning.

"When Staff Sergeant Patte calls your name, jump off. You will be in groups of three. We'll drop you off at intervals. You've done this before, only there is no EP, Extraction Point. You make it back for dinner chow, or you don't. If you miss one point, you'll probably miss them all, because it builds in a sequence. No need to talk with other groups if you happen to cross paths. Be aware of firing ranges and Six Weeks training companies, you know. Try to act like you are combat veterans and remain undetected. Drill instructors love to find PNCOC students. This means you are operating in tactical mode. Once you hit the ground, HECS up, open the envelope, and find your way home."

Staff Sergeant Tzenski walked back up to the cab and started the Camel.

"Campbell, Yost, Budner!" Patte called their names, then the truck started moving, and Patte threw the envelope out the back. "Quickly! Move! Off my Betty!"

We all laughed. He would not make a good crew chief.

My name was called on the tenth team out of twelve. I was with Cummings and Maliki, they were squared away. We tossed our CPs out the back and hopped off the slowly moving Camel. I retrieved the envelope and shoved it in an outer pocket of my CP. We quickly got off the road and HECS up, completely aware that we could have been dropped straight in the middle of a Week Four tactics training area. I just remembered we had to hurry. I had to go to the PX and order a replacement OL this afternoon.

"Anyone see anything striking?" I asked, hoping for a prominent Cardinal Identifier, CI. It was how we were going to orient ourselves to figure out where we were.

"Man, I thought the desert was hard. We can't see anything over the trees," said Maliki. He was from 1/1/7, with Campbell.

I was looking at our map, the other two joined me kneeling around the map on the ground.

"I know where we generally are, I think," I said.

"Yeah, me too," added Cummings, who was First Division. "Somewhere on the map, hopefully." We all laughed quietly.

"Look, there is only one road on this side of the mountain, halfway up, here." I pointed. "I know we went up and over." I traced my finger along a single road that started on one lowered side and then went up and around and back down.

Cummings and Maliki were staring at me. "If you say so," said Cummings.

"There is no other road, until here, at this trail intersection."

I pulled out a smaller sheet of paper from the envelope that was folded and read it out loud, "'*Your fire team was separated from your platoon during an ambush cover and move tactical withdraw. Your team must head to RP 6, a group of three large black boulders. This will be your OPD, Original Point of Direction. Mark it as such with your protractor when you reach it. Head due south from IP to creek, follow the creek back up to its spring, and move at a two-hundred-degree direction to OPD. Call in for EP.*"

"That's it? We got to find the RP and call in for an EP?" asked Maliki.

"I doubt our day is going to be that short," Cummings said, half laughing.

"Okay, we're somewhere along here. Here's the stream. We hit the stream and trace it back to here. Then we can find these boulders, here." I was tracing my finger.

I could now see several other possible RP locations, but none of them were marked. I tapped on them to point them out to my teammates, and they nodded.

"Yeah, I bet we are going to get to climb that peak and play in that swamp too," Maliki said, with a hint of sarcasm.

"Guaranteed." Cummings was shaking his head. "Keep the map, Smith. We'll switch at the call in."

"Sounds goods. Let's go. Maliki, take point. Let's keep five. Cummings, sweep."

We all knew what we were doing. It only takes a good platoon sergeant and a CR to reinforce the tactics learned in Six Weeks, and we had been dry-running this exercise the last two days.

"Prepare to road cross tactically."

We spread out on the road, five meters apart, and looked up and down and across, watching for movement or the smallest sign of an ambush.

"Go!" I said and Maliki sprinted straight across, his CP swinging wildly from side to side on his back, the heavy load cutting his speed in half. He fell flat several feet into the forest, looking for movement.

"All clear! Go," he said.

I ran at a diagonal toward him and fell flat next to him and then quickly turned and faced back to the road. It felt good to be back in the HECS.

"Go!"

Cummings ran straight at us and repeated but facing slightly off down one way of the road. We waited several seconds, watching, listening.

"Move out," I said.

Maliki raised up to his knee and then stood, checked his position, and started walking south. I got up on my knee, and when he was several feet to my front, I followed. I checked his direction, stopped, fixed on a landmark to his front, and reconfirmed his direction. Good.

"I make that scarred pine tree up there, see it?"

"Yeah," he replied and shifted just a little to his right.

I turned back and faced the road again, looking for something to mark. Cummings was moving now, so I turned back and followed Maliki. Cummings' responsibility was to watch our rear and flanks, he did not have to worry about which way we were going, not his job. I pointed and kept Maliki on task and was constantly checking and rechecking our route, looking for the next marker, and peering over my shoulder every few steps to ensure we weren't zigzagging. Maliki followed my direction while also on alert for ambushes, traps, and any movement. We were all nervous, just knowing that any moment the instructors were going to light us up in an "idiot ambush," something so simple an idiot could have spotted. Without the fear of actually being killed, this was still stressful, but enjoyable at the same time.

Maliki stopped, his left hand slowly easing up to a halt signal, and then he took a knee. I repeated the signal and went to a knee. We had been walking, maybe twenty minutes. We should be coming to the stream shortly.

"I got it," he said, "but it's the boulders."

"Moving up," I said and joined him, moving crouched over.

I scanned the area ahead of us. There. We both saw at the same time; another group broke out of the trees to the southwest. And the boulders were white. This wasn't our RP. I moved back and set down on my knees and pulled the map out of my arm pocket. Here's where we were. Cummings moved up.

"Man, I didn't see this before. We're good. I was putting us farther back on the road, but we definitely know our location now. We can bear to the west southwest and hit the creek or this trail then the creek and follow it up to here."

"Yeah, I see it. I was thinking we were on the other side of the intersection too. Along here, but this is where we dropped. Yeah. You think they know we are going to deviate from the instructions to head south to the creek once we made our real location?" Cummings asked.

It was a valid point. What would be the point of continuing south to find the creek if we now knew our true location? They couldn't just straight out and say, "You are here. Go here."

Maliki was still watching the other group, making sure they didn't come our way. "I hear what you guys are saying, so this team is probably seven, eight, or nine, arriving the same time we did. I say we slice over like you said. We can always turn back south if we encounter another group. You got our fix, right?"

Our fix, our location.

"Oh, sour apple butter! They're headed this way. Down!" Maliki said with a start.

I went flat and then quickly turned toward the approaching team.

"Quick! Remove your CP. Prepare FP!"

We still had several meters between us, and the giant hump on our backs would surely give us away. I just hoped it wasn't Campbell, Grigs, or Alvera. Those guys would spot us any second. They were good.

"Fire Team Ten junior, what's your status?"

My COMM crackled, making me jump. I was not expecting any communication. I wasn't sure if the others in my team were receiving the COMM traffic.

"Six"—I guessed, made sense—"my team is close proximity to unknown team, advancing toward our concealed position." Sounded good. There was no telling what was about to be played out.

"Copy. Remain concealed. Take them out if detected. Monitor their movement and then continue to RP. Out." I wasn't sure if that were Gunnery Sergeant Chaves or not.

"Maliki, Cummings, did you copy?" I asked.

"Affirmative, Smith. You are good. Stay low and whack 'em if they spot us," said Maliki.

"Ten by ten," replied Cummings.

I dared not turn to check his position, just hoping he had been able to turn toward the threat.

"Check safeties, man. I pray we are on training mode."

I was sure they were, since they had been checked and rechecked multiple times, and we had not had a live fire exercise at all in PNCOC. My armorer training was pinging me, making me nervous. The HECS could take a GLAR hit in all the life-threatening areas, but a live incident would cause some damage, if not a loss of limb if the location were right. Several of us were armorers, and I had gone through with Hernandez and Johansson. Some of these guys, including Alvera, Cummings, and Budner, were also combat medics.

"If they spot us, light 'em up. We have the advantage and superior position. Cummings, you take their point. I got the nav. Maliki, take out the sweeper," I confirmed our targets.

We each had our kill assignments; they were passing into our red zone, off our right flank by no more than seven yards. My heart rate was above normal, but not frantic, this was not life and death. The point man missed us, and I could see that he was just walking, not even in weapons ready. The next man was not actively plotting their course or paying attention. How they found their first RP was beyond me. The sweeper was a little better, trying to monitor his rear and glancing more to his left than to the right, toward us, for some reason.

"Team Ten junior, what's the situation?"

"Six, they are passing within fifteen feet. Have not made us. Continuing to observe," I whispered.

"Take them out, Smith. They're careless."

I sighed. I hated to do this to a classmate, but they were going to lead Fleet Marines in the future and could get men killed by this lackadaisical patrol behavior. Perhaps this could help teach them, but then these were seasoned vets, so they should know better.

"You have your targets? On my mark, 3, 2, 1, hit 'em."

The green laser energy glows streaked through the midmorning, amidst the rocky landscape of the forest and found their marks easily. *Zik! Zik! Zik!* The three marines never had a chance. They didn't see it coming. The middle lance corporal, the navigator, had his GLAR slung on his shoulder!

"Team Ten junior, perform an intel and resource search. Strip the enemy of valuable supplies and proceed with mission."

"Six, I am unsure of my orders." I did not understand what I was searching for, other than their pride and embarrassment.

"Team Ten junior, I want you to confiscate all food and energy products and pour out all water reserves except what is in HECS, copy?"

I looked at my team. This was harsh. It wouldn't hurt them, our victims, but this was going to make the remainder of their day very uncomfortable.

"Copy, Six. You heard it. Take your man and dump his CP, all food and energy packs, dump the water. Move out."

Cummings and Maliki stood up and approached the KIAs. It was hard for us to do, because these were our friends, our classmates, but they had been lazy. I upended my guy's CP. I didn't want to know who it was, but I saw his name stenciled on the flap anyway. I shook my head. He wasn't a close friend, but I knew him. He was looking down, too embarrassed to look up, which didn't help much. The team evidently received orders to sit and surrender their CPs without argument. I took all the food in his pack and then poured his water, hoping he had some in his reservoir. We had received additional orders to leave the larger water cube untouched, I'm sure for the weight, and they would not be able to use it. It had also been stressed for us to search and confiscate any bars or mix in their HECS pockets—a thorough clean-out. We moved on.

I set the course direction for us to hit the creek shy of the trail crossing and we picked up the pace. We were on the side of the mountain, maintaining a nice gentle downward slope. An hour passed, and Maliki motioned for us to halt.

"This is it. This time we have the creek," he said.

I moved up to him, Cummings closing the gap but not joining us.

"All right, let's stay on this side until we cross the trail, and we'll switch over upstream."

"Copy," responded Cummings.

I patted Maliki on the shoulder, and he moved out, tracing the stream, keeping us a safe distance. He was good, he liked being out front, and he knew what he was supposed to do, what to look for. Another ten minutes and we reached the little trail where it forded the stream. This had to be an RP, had to be; it was too good a location to be wasted.

"Look sharp. I bet we are not the only team at this junction. Fall back to Cummings, Maliki."

I covered his retreat, and then I followed him. We formed a huddle, the map on the ground between us.

"We're here. I say we move north a hundred meters and then cross the trail. If they spaced us out evenly back up on the road"—I took my pencil out of my pocket and made a mark and then counted backward nine additional marks—"either some of those teams went north or we are really thick down here. I see maybe eight good possible RPs south of the road. The Y is here. I'm sure of it now." I pointed to a point on the map. It was unmarked, but I knew the roads and the small peak east of there was Bad Girl. We ran her last week.

"Sounds good."

"Team Ten junior, can you give me your location?" They both looked at me.

"Affirmative, Six. We are twenty-five meters northeast of trail junction on creek."

"Give me your map coordinate, Smith." Oh.

I quickly looked at the edge of the map and intersected the X longitude and Y latitude axis and pulled the protractor out of my sleeve pocket and laid it on the grid square, rechecking my grid letters, and I responded with a six-digit alpha and numeric coordinate.

"Good work. Pass the map to Cummings and take point."

I did what I was ordered and waited for instructions from the new team leader. Our orders were changed, and Cummings was to mark our current position and label it RP 1, OPD. All future directions would be based from here, the CI. The trail we were just off of took a second major turn, northbound at thirty-five degrees from the OPD, and we had to move to that elbow and call in.

"Man, I hope I can do this half as well as you did." Cummings rubbed his face through his raised visor and marked the RP and then drew a light line with the protractor to the elbow. It was thirty-five degrees. He studied the map, looked up and around, and got his bearings, which was hard without a magnetic compass, and back down to the map again.

He looked at me. "All right, Smith, we're going to cross back over the road up there again. Be sharp. If anything, I will veer us to the left to hit the little trail before the elbow so we don't miss it, but not before the main road. Maliki, you ready?"

We had all taken the brief moment to slurp down one of the new energy gels that were now being supplemented with the Full Meal boxes and to refill our reservoir with our bottles.

"All good, on you," responded Maliki, already visually sweeping the thin forest.

We were close to the tree line elevation where the tree growth really becomes sparse. The undergrowth, mixed with holly, small cedar, willows, aspens, and all various brush, is quite thick; this was the main reason we had been nearly undetectable to the team we ambushed earlier. Another team could be just feet away, waiting for the orders to exact revenge on us.

"Smith, start toward that tree there with the charred trunk. I'll correct," he said, pointing to a stunted pine that had obviously taken a lightning hit several years prior.

I moved out. It was past midmorning now, the sun sending streaks of light and long shadows onto the forest floor. The night had been chilly, dipping back down into the forties, normal for this elevation and time of year. The mist from the warming sun added now to the shadows, not to mention the abrupt and sudden blinding sunlight as it peaked through the newly leafing hardwoods and the new green needles of the pines. A moss covered the forest floor mostly, some bare earth and patches of grass where the tree growth opened above enough for it to grow. Spring was full on and small flowers dotted the plants and bushes. Birds and squirrels and chipmunks were all out, playing and talking and enjoying the fresh day. Mule deer and even an elk were spotted earlier. I wondered what we were supposed to do if we came across a bear. I remembered that time with the shark. I looked up. Did we have a Betty overhead watching over us? I had my visor up but reached up and pulled it down, just in case.

"Take a lean to the right. See that log with the thick bush?" Cummings pulled me back. I was scanning and looking for signs of movement, just subconsciously, habit.

"Copy."

I was taking a good pace, not too hurriedly, scanning above the growth, then the floor, and in the trees and repeat. My head moving constantly, my GLAR followed my sight. It was a technique Sergeant Custer had taught us. We should make the road, unless there was a problem, in an hour, down from the spot we started.

CHAPTER 11

The chief had to leave Larson for the time being—he would be okay—and oversee the ongoing assault and hectic activity.

"Throw your A-Doses in this box. They're no good," he said, grabbing the almost empty gel box and thrusting it at Corporal Murray.

The Command COMM came to life. "Get your marines ready to redeploy. I want A-Doses taken, suck down a couple of those gel packs, ensure reservoirs are topped. Two minutes. First and Third Brigades won't be able to deploy until morning. We will assist Alpha through the night."

Immediately after the CO ended his direction, Sergeant Carpenter ordered, "Second platoon, prepare to insert! Everyone take A-Dose, suck down another gel, mix a bottle, top reservoir, suit back up. Two minutes!"

The Betty was chaotic. We were all scrambling to mix at least one of our bottles; some guys had lost theirs, others passing one of theirs down so that each man had something. A fresh, sealed box of A-Doses was passed, each of us grabbing one and sticking ourselves, mostly in the wrist, before redonning our gloves. The chief pulled a new box of gel packs and we squeezed them in our mouths, then taking sweet, cold drinks of bug juice, rubbing our faces and heads one last time, and then pulling our masks securely in place and then our goggles. We looked around at each other, gave a thumbs-up, and lifted our helmets over our heads and fastened them.

"Thirty seconds! We are inserting right behind the FPs and will light them up. You know the drill. We will take the pressure off Alpha and then fall back to a tight perimeter. The storm will quiet them down until sunrise. CO says morning we are out of here. Keep it together, Marines." Carpenter was standing and looking at each of us as he spoke.

"First squad, Corporal Murray, Lance Corporal Rich. Second squad, Lance Corporal Almond, PFC Smith. Same teams, Chief." Carpenter handed over the insert to the crew chief.

"Disconnect tube!" the chief yelled.

"Disconnect tube!" we repeated.

Boom! Boom! Boom! Tck! Tck! Tck! Tck! Boom! Boom!

It was dark, and the windstorm was getting stronger, the sand blowing into us. The Bettys were almost at their operational limit, though we inserted as a company strong. Fourth platoon being the best rested was in the center, flanked by first and third. Second just to the rear, in reserve. It made sense, kind of, since Sergeant Carpenter was the least in rank and commanded the platoon now. Captain Shupin and Gunny Scott were with us, second platoon. Second quickly established a perimeter, the four fire teams holding, or marking, an area for the other three platoons to withdraw to later.

Now there were two full companies on the ground, nearly blinded, for the Galleens to possibly obliterate. Was this their plan? Echo was spent, we had been continuously deployed without rest or food for almost seventy-two hours, and Alpha was brand new and didn't know the territory or the hardships it faced.

For some reason, either the Alpha 1/2/7 CO didn't understand the dire situation of the sandstorm or he wanted to get his company into the action, but he ordered three of his platoons into the ravine in a frontal assault, essentially trapping them.

"No no no! Pull back, Alpha! Pull—" Captain Shupin was yelling in our Command COMM and then transferred to the Alpha net.

He had been observing and ordering Echo's deployment when he saw what was happening, too late. I couldn't see any of it from my position on the bare bones perimeter we had set up. The Galleens were intensifying their fire on Alpha as they poured into the ravine.

"I want first and third to sweep the flanks of the FPs. Fourth, take the heat off Alpha. Do not, I repeat, do not, follow them in their holes! Copy?"

"Copy, Six," replied LaBoye.

Fourth platoon swatted the hornet's nest and the bees or, rather, the anthill, as LaBoye referred to it, and the ants swarmed out. They headed straight for the ravine. I could see the flashes of green and blue in the growing storm. Commands and cursing from all platoons on the Command net started at once—Staff Sergeant Ginny repeating orders from Lieutenant Howard, LaBoye directing his platoon to shoot directly into the now disclosed FPs, and Staff Sergeant Oliver ordering his platoon to the edge of the ravine and to aim at the sources of GBL.

"Second platoon, move up!" ordered Gunnery Sergeant Scott, taking direct control of the platoon as senior NCO, not a slight to Carpenter in the least.

One of a gunnery sergeant's responsibilities was to take command of a platoon in absence of a ranking senior NCO. This was a dire situation we all were in now, as if the past two days hadn't already been a butt-buster. Alpha was in serious jeopardy of being wiped out, if the Galleens could collapse the ditch again, sacrificing their own men for the humiliating morale killer that the massacre of an entire Fleet Marine company would bring.

"Do not enter that ravine! Do not enter that ravine, Echo! Fall back to the FPs." Captain Shupin was nearly screaming at his platoon leaders.

The ground shook, as a huge cloud, visible in my normal-mode visor, billowed up, rolling over and over on itself and then whisked away by the storm, straight at second and the rest of Echo. I was immediately blinded with black and gray dust and pelted with heavy particles of soil. Clots and rocks, not sand, and a heavier, denser soil stratum. This was the planet's crust surface, below the sand layer.

"Fourth, keep hitting those FPs. Melt the sand! Second, join fourth. Howard, take first and monitor the new edge. Mind your step. This whole surface may give at any time. Third, I want you to sweep to your right and give me a sitrep on the size of this thing, all the way around. Can you do that, Oliver? Straight up, I know your men are beat."

"Copy, Six. We just had dinner and a bath. We're good to breakfast."

I could hear Staff Sergeant Oliver's complete support for his assignment and the importance of getting an eye on the scale and scope of the situation.

The likelihood of encountering any other enemy combatants was minimal, they had just sacrificed a whole platoon or more in the second cave-in, taking nearly a whole NNP Fleet Marine company down at one time. This was devastating. This was crushing. I knew that Lieutenant Green and Private Somersby had been buried in the sand. The collapse of a layer strata was certain death to every soul in that ravine.

The night wore on, the unending green laser bursts of our GLARs at the mouths of the Galleen FPs. Intermittently, a COMM would come from Third, reporting their progress. They had turned an hour after their start, working their way back toward the original CP and the remaining platoon of Alpha.

Alpha's CO had charged into the hole after his company when it caved in and was assumed MIA/KIA, along with first, second, and fourth platoons. Their gunnery sergeant was also MIA and the highest-ranking remaining member of the company was an NCO, Sergeant Grimes, of third platoon. The platoon was stationed on the edge and trying to keep it together. Captain Shupin had taken temporary command of the company. When Staff Sergeant Oliver made contact, I could almost hear him losing it; his concern and mutual sorrow for the survivors was evident in his request to remain with the platoon. Captain Shupin approved the request, almost making me wonder if he hadn't sent Oliver over for that reason to begin with. They were all alone, losing friends and brothers in a horrendous, sudden action. Some forty-eight to fifty plus Fleet Marines gone at one time. It was heartbreaking. It was unheard of.

"I see GLAR, Six! There is GLAR activity below us, two, three separate sources. We have possible survivors down there!" Lieutenant Howard exclaimed, hours after the cave-in and midway through the night's storm.

"Copy, One-Six. Maybe a ruse to lure us in. There has been no COMM contact and Betty has no fix in the ravine. Continue to monitor."

I know Captain Shupin was dying inside, but he couldn't send his men down, not until we could see. He knew that if there were survivors, we probably couldn't help them anyway. I knew that after my own experience down there. The hole was deeper now, the bottom probably unescapable, the sides collapsing, trapping anyone that attempted to scale them.

The night slowly wore on, the storm hardly noticed, our thoughts on Alpha. Second platoon was ordered to pull back and rest, as was a squad from fourth and first platoons. I couldn't sleep. There was too much to think about. We rotated in, relieving the squads on the edge and FPs.

Morning finally broke, the sky in its beautiful light blue and red purple colors. The wind died down and finally stopped. The sun rose over the horizon and scorched the planet's surface as it had for a millennia. I gazed at the ravine, it was massive. It stretched in either direction almost a kilometer, the gap wider but not much, and to my surprise now that the wind was gone, a cloud of dark, grayish dust continued to waft up. I was kneeling, posted near the edge, and could see several meters down the slope; it was steeper, the sand cascading down every few minutes. Lieutenant Howard had set up a five-meter marker sometime during the night. I was standing right in front of it now, peering over the edge, and it was growing at a slow but steady pace.

A swarm of Bettys off-loaded two, maybe three companies and a free-standing hexagon dome structure was quickly set up in the original CP area. Supplies of water, boxes of rations and A-Doses, and other items were hurriedly passed hand to hand from the Bettys into the dome. Another dome was set up and then a third.

Fleet Marines, I think—they were wearing a different camouflaged pattern HECS—filled bags with sand with a machine, and stacked them along the outside of each dome, now over four feet high. A fourth oblong dome tent was then put up, and the sandbagging procedure repeated. More Bettys inserted two additional companies wearing the same pattern HECS, just behind our position, essentially relieving us from the continued assault we had deployed against the FPs for close to twelve hours. Echo fell back to the Bettys and onloaded, heartbroken, devastated that we couldn't help our brothers.

Captain Shupin was the last man to board, double-checking with Gunny Scott that all were present or accounted for. He was standing right in front of second platoon. I watched him, not even guessing what was going on in his mind. He scanned the ravine, hung his head, and slowly turned and boarded the Betty with us. He stepped onto the ramp and sat in a seat in the middle of the cabin, hooking up and strapping in. He removed his helmet and pulled his goggles down and then his mask after taking a drink.

"You did good out there men. You did good," he said and held his hands to his face as he leaned over and wept.

Chapter 11

PRESENT

Cummings brought us back to the road, though it didn't look familiar, so we had jumped off the Camel farther up. I looked down the road. The three of us were scanning the road, listening, watching for any movement. I did not want to get hit with an ambush. I figured if Cummings could take us close enough to the elbow of the trail, maybe, just maybe that's all they wanted to see, if we knew what we were doing.

"That rock with the limb hanging down, that's your mark after we clear the road," Cummings said. I nodded. "Go!"

I ran straight across and hit the deck in three steps of the other side. I checked my front and flanks. "Clear!" I said.

Cummings followed and then Maliki. We waited, and then we waited to a slow count of ten. We all, of course, trained the same way, so we had to throw a curve ball. Nothing, I got up on a knee and scanned again. I quickly started off toward the marker, my pace fast. I wanted to get this road behind us.

This past Sunday, the latest phase, Phase Five, had been announced and it was a kick to the gut. One full battalion of each brigade in each of the four standing divisions was redesignated, pulled out, separated from their division, and either assigned in whole as a new battalion in the Twelfth or broken up and used to strengthen the first four divisions. That was twelve battalions, nine going straight to the Twelfth Division. The new Third Training Battalion was filled out, and the now missing battalions were set up as "ghost" battalions—a first lieutenant, gunny, corporal, and three EMs maintained a presence until they could be reactivated. Obviously, if your battalion wasn't selected, things didn't change much. A couple guys sat in shock when hearing they had lost their division and were heading to the Twelfth.

One of the benefits of the deal we had taken was that after we completed our drill rotation assignment, we could choose our unit. I guess the whole Phase Initiative was built around a surge of new NCOs to train replacements and refill the older divisions. That was the thing—the Twelfth was starting out full strength. It was the other divisions that were going to get the bulk of the new boots. None of us, Cummings, Maliki, or myself, lost our division. Cummings was in First Division and Maliki in Seventh. Most of us in our class were going straight to Drill A Course after this, another three weeks, and then to either First or Third Training Battalion as a drill corporal. Wow, I never thought I would want to do that.

Cummings was doing a good job of directing me and keeping the next landmark out front. We were heading back up the mountain at an angle to the slope, which was hard to keep on direction. He was constantly checking and bringing me back on course. I never heard a word out of Maliki in the back. We were in very sparse and open ground now and he was, I'm sure, doing his best to keep our six secure.

We had been nonstop, other than back at the road crossing, uphill now, for close to an hour. The terrain was rough, rocky, with underbrush, and warming. I mean, you know, I had experienced a few tough times, the heat on Butch would never be forgotten, but this seventy-six-degree rating of the HECS was bogus! This hump up the side of this mountain with full CP was a buster. I could feel that my under armor was soaking wet, and I was hot; the fan didn't seem to be blowing cool enough. I know that once we stopped for a few minutes, the temp would regulate and the sweat would start to be sucked out. But, man, put me back on the beach any day.

Huh. I thought about that beach we went to off from Butch. Now that was a nice place, except for the reason we went. I thought about Donna and our beach week. *Put me back there. Now that was good times all around.* I hadn't thought much about Donna these last two weeks, too much to do. Talking to her last Friday was great, she was still shuttling back and forth, moving supplies and assisting with the Twelfth's advance party. She hadn't been on a CR with an active unit yet, and she was getting upset and thinking her father had sabotaged her combat assignment. I assured her that it was just a rotational thing, with the new division. Once the division was in place and running CRs, she would probably be getting all the corpsman ops she wanted. She wasn't new with the ops; during her course, she had spent a total of nine days with three different-length deployments with different heavy platoons.

She had asked about my eye, and I lied. I told her it was fine. She challenged me and said she knew differently. I asked if that wasn't a breach of doctor-patient privilege.

"What? Are you reading law books now?" she retorted, laughing.

I would call her again this weekend. Corporal Griffin said he was going to take me to the PX Saturday afternoon and help me buy my own tablet, not that he minded at all letting me use his, but that I needed to get my own so I could call Donna every day, he said. I wondered if she hadn't put that in his ear.

"Smith, we should be coming up soon. I'm sure I have kept us on course, but I want us to head straight north now, just to make sure we don't overshoot it." Cummings was feeling the pressure to get this right.

"Copy. What do you see for me to head to?"

I bet the trail was not far at all, and I would throw in Guard Duty rotation that he was within ten meters of the elbow.

"Make for that willow to your left. She's all by herself." Yep, they usually grew several together.

I took several steps and held my hand up. *Bingo!* The trail was just ahead.

"You hit it. Let's see if you got the elbow. Stay to my right flank and we'll parallel this trail."

I scanned the area to the trail and in front of me. Maliki moved automatically at an angle to me and to my rear, forming a triangle. We skirted the trail about fifteen meters and there it was.

"You had it perfect, Cummings. If we had stayed on your course back there, we would have hit it dead on. Man, that was good dead reckoning."

"Six, this is Team Ten junior. We are at elbow, coordinate…"

He was instructed to mark the spot as RP2. Good work. Rotate. Maliki was now team leader and was seriously stressed on continuing our record. His assignment was to investigate an SS report of sporadic GBL activity, five degrees from OPD, and report. Great. We were headed to a training company weapons range. At first, Maliki made the fateful error of drawing a five-degree heading from our present point, and it was all I could do to keep from helping him, but I knew better. He had to do it on his own, even if it meant that we walked all night. He shook his head.

"What the heck was I thinking? For the love of God's favorite planet, Smith, Cummings! I know you would have followed me off the map, but jeez! I got it. OPD. Five off OPD, stupid. Okay, I'm good. It's right here. I see the range. Let me adjust the heading to our position. Got it. Looks to be two hundred eighty. Slight downgrade. We will approach to the FP's left, facing us, and then monitor activity. Cummings, you're point. Smith, sweep. I got—" He looked around, got his bearings, looked at the map on the ground, oriented himself to a zero heading, and then used his nonmagnetic compass and shot an azimuth, looking for a good landmark. "Okay, Cummings, as soon as we clear this crossing, see that bush with the little purple flowers?"

"Yeah, I got it."

"That's our way."

"Copy, bro."

We had a good couple minutes rest. I ate an energy bar, not feeling too guilty about those poor guys we hit earlier. Man, I bet they were dying about now. I refilled my HECS with a mixed bottle.

"Go!" said Maliki and Cummings sprinted across the road, diving nearly on top of the poor little purple flower bush!

He did his scan and gave the all clear. We crossed without incident. Within the hour, we were settled in on the left flank of the firing range in the woods—the very woods Week Four Monday ambush was oriented around. We all knew the layout, the range, the Pavilion, the Sauna, and the road. We all knew where we were. Down that road thirty minutes at a double-time run was the First Training Quad. It was the end of lunch chow, Wednesday afternoon. It was so weird looking at it from here, since this was where we would all be in another month or so. I didn't recognize any of the DIs, and neither did Cummings or Maliki. Maliki did his call-in.

"Six, Team Ten junior. We have range training ongoing at coordinate…"

He continued with an excellent byline of Mowatts, Abooes, and Candias and even a Marquis was present. The numbers were overwhelmingly against us, and if our presence were discovered, we would be hard-pressed to EnE.

Permission to fall back to a secure area to observe.

"Good work, Maliki. Team Ten has it together. I have an enemy sniper reported in your area, hunting you. EnE to EP forty-three degrees OPD on far side of hardball." Hardball is a major paved road. "If you make him first and score a kill"—he laughed at us—"I don't think so. Won't happen. Get moving."

We looked at one another. *Scout Sniper A Course!* The map was laid out on the ground. I quickly found our position. I hadn't looked at the map since I passed it off this morning. I drew the azimuth from the OPD back at the trail creek junction. The line went to a group of rocks on the far side of Highway 70, between the overpass foot bridge and the tunnel a kilometer past it. I knew the rocks. That was the turnaround for Bad Girl.

"Here." I pointed. "Bad Girl turnaround."

"Yeah. If he doesn't nail us any minute now, he'll just off us as we cross 70," said Maliki.

"Smith, why don't you get us there." Cummings was looking at Maliki who nodded his head in agreement.

I was thinking. They had not set any parameters. This was a "get it done" mission, and they wanted to see what we could think of against the odds. In a real situation, you use whatever means necessary to achieve the objective.

"Maliki, you take point. This is going to be a quick pace. We've got, hmmm, a 4 or 5K run. Take it a seven-minute-mile, okay?" He was looking at me, nodding his head.

"This is going to be dicey in daylight but should take that sniper off our scent for a little bit until he figures it out. Here it is…"

I laid out the plan, over the COMM, so I know First Sergeant French was listening and would stop me if it was out of line. We were going to space out and hit the training company, hopefully scoring multiple kills on their HECS, rendering them unable to fire their GLARs, while performing a move and cover. This of course was going to send the DIs into a full-blown meltdown, and the woods were going to be overrun to find the unlucky perps and beat the snot out of them for firing on their recruits. We would then proceed along Troublesome Road, in the cover of the woods to the construction road, and cross the highway at that little bridge, well up from the foot bridge. Just another training exercise, so no one would bat an eye. We would drop our CPs at an RP along Bad Girl and set up on the EP to either take out the sniper or extract. Questions?

They both looked at me. "You got a gel left? Suck it down, refill your HECS. My sight is bad now. I can't hit a house, I'll take your CPs up with me there." I pointed. "Grab them as you withdraw. Who is the better shot?"

Maliki said, "I scored a SS qual last range time."

"Take it. We all lay down fire at the same time and then move and cover, right?" replied Cummings.

"Yep, two shifts. I won't move. I'll have the CPs further back. That will make it look like a bigger force than we are. Ready?"

They both removed their CPs and I picked them up and ran back twenty meters, huffing with the weight in my hands. Maliki moved nearly to the edge of the wood line. Jeez! That was close, but he was going to drop several recruits and kick the nest for sure. Cummings was five meters behind him.

"Two moves and then we beat the bushes. Those DIs are going to be hot and run us down if they get the chance. Hopefully they'll flush that sniper out or pin him down for a minute," I said.

I was just going to shoot, I really couldn't focus on a target now. I probably couldn't even qualify my next range time. I took a knee. I wondered if shooting at a training company was a judicial offense.

"Set?" I asked.

"Affirmative, Team Ten junior," replied Maliki.

"I knew you were trouble, as soon as I saw you. Ready, Six," said Cummings.

He had actually been very active in the brawl, but his injuries weren't serious enough to land in the hospital with the four of us.

"Open up!"

Zik! Zik! Zik! Zik! Zik! Zik!

I fired at what I thought was the command post, hoping to hit a DI or a recruit in between. I was too far back to make any real target. My objective was to just lay down a continuous covering fire. Maliki had several targets picked out, all recruits finishing their lunch, sitting on their CPs. Cummings took out a couple recruits in line for the Potty Palace, a wholly sadistic attack, and as the guy inside came barreling out undone, as the story goes, Cummings nailed him!

"Cover!" yelled Maliki as he raced back and hit Cummings on the shoulder as he ran past and took a new position five meters to his rear and then resumed firing at other targets.

Zik! Zik! Zik! Zik!

The range was thrown into total chaos, as recruits hit the deck and went into the prone position. A few returned fire, which was live, and the drills were yelling conflicting orders, trying to figure out what was going on.

Cummings took his last shot and yelled, "Cover!" coming to a crouched position and running, now acutely aware that live GLAR was being sent his way. We hadn't thought about this.

He was laughing, yelling, "Won't that just be a kick in the—'Decorated First Division Fleet Marine with Distinguished Cross for Valor killed in freak training accident by Week Three training recruit!'"

He tapped Maliki as he ran past, setting up his next position, firing nonstop.

Zik! Zik! Zik! Zik!

The activity and disruption we were causing was staggering. The DIs from the Sauna came running out, assessing the situation and the highest-ranking NCO—I'm not sure if it was a gunnery sergeant or a staff sergeant—screaming for a cease fire, which was not being obeyed.

Maliki yelled, "Cover!" running to his last position, tapping Cummings.

I yelled, "That's enough. They're going to hunt us down clear to the quad! Cummings, move. Maliki, cover!"

It was textbook. Cummings retrieved his CP as I ran back another five. "Go!"

Maliki turned and raced for his CP, Cummings and I relentless on the cover fire.

"Take point! As we planned. Go!"

Maliki grabbed his CP, hoisting it on his back as he ran for the edge of the road, ten meters inside the tree line, a direction not in line with our firing lane. We had deflected our EnE route. I followed behind him, Cummings acting as our rear guard, giving us a couple seconds. Then he too turned and ran at an angle toward the road, completely away from our line of assault. The pace was killer, the CPs swinging wildly, not being fastened properly. The hunt and pursuit against us was going to be relentless. The DIs wanted blood. We had assaulted their training session, which to be fair was sort of off-limits, and made their DIs look inept. Yeah, they would pound us into the ground if they caught us. But my real concern was this sniper. He was standing in our way of the rest of the afternoon off.

"Scuvy!" yelled Maliki as he hit the deck, and we followed instantly.

The vehicle came tearing down the road at a dangerous speed, heading for the range. Oh, yeah, that was a first sergeant or some officers; we started a fire for sure.

"Come back inside another five. Let's move. They're going to have a Betty on us any minute. We got to put some distance on it."

Maliki was a natural; he angled back in and quickened the pace, so we were now at a 6.5-minute-mile. We couldn't sustain this for long, but time was critical. We had to get out of the search and kill radius. Of course, the drills should know this, as well as the first sergeant who was probably losing a head gasket about right now.

"Down!" yelled Maliki again, as two SFP scuvys with blue lights screamed by.

Oh no. I didn't think about that. I guess this was seen as an unauthorized training exercise.

"Got it. Pick it up," said Maliki as we ran headlong into the forest, which at this point was denser, a little below the tree line.

After another ten minutes, I said, "Okay," breathing heavily, almost not able to catch my breath.

We had put one and a half or two kilometers behind us. "Take a knee. Grab a drink." A pause almost between each word. I was sweating profusely, my legs ached, my back sore.

"Get those CPs on correctly before we blow a spine."

Cummings laughed. "I've heard of a blown knee, but never a blown spine!"

We all laughed. This was crazy. I had the right guys with me, not knocking Grigs or Campbell or anyone else, only meaning these two were with me, not like Sirus or Cortez or Stark. I laughed thinking about him. I wondered how he was doing.

"You know where we are?" I asked.

"Yeah, the PT field is coming up next, so we need to skirt around that and then slice back toward the construction road. How we going to get out the gate?" asked Cummings.

I knew from my Division Duty flyovers that there was a stretch of barbed wire fence down past there, never made sense, but it is what it is. I relayed my plan.

"Yeah, it's up this side of the walkover bridge, not on the map. There's a divided median there, so we can make a run for it and be covered both ways. We can dump our CPs on the other side and set up and wait for the sniper, hopefully. He is traveling lighter than us, from what I've heard, bare bone CP, if that."

We had been there almost a minute. *Too long.*

"Let's move."

CHAPTER 12

Third platoon, as well as the remainder of Alpha, was picked up at the same time as us. The ramp came up and we all just sat in silence, trying to wrap our heads around the enormity of the loss. I didn't know anyone in Alpha, I didn't think, but that didn't matter. I unlatched my helmet and let it drop to my feet, holding it there. I pulled my goggles down and my mask. I wasn't thirsty. I peeled my gloves off and looked at my fingers from where they were blistered from the day before. *Wow, I needed new gloves. How did I go about doing that?*

I rubbed my head. I was filthy, sweaty, and raw. My body was tired of nonfood and my gut was in knots, and I wanted to use the head. I looked over at Carpenter and he was talking to someone, but not on the Command net. *So a private line? Hmm. Who could that be?* He looked up and caught my gaze and smiled and gave me a thumbs-up.

The Betty was circling again. I don't know why, but we couldn't see anything and there were plenty of other units on the ground now we shouldn't have to go back. We straightened up after a few minutes and were going somewhere; anywhere was better than here.

Captain Shupin regained his bearing and put his helmet back on, to hear the COMM better. Gunny Scott was on board also; he followed the CO everywhere while deployed. He was engaged in COMM chatter also. I half listened, though none of it was within my control anyway. I felt like switching my COMM back to the platoon net but knew that Carpenter wanted me to listen and learn about Command structure. There seemed to be an argument going on between the CO, the gunny, and the senior noncoms—obviously not between themselves, but with a third party that I couldn't hear.

Captain Shupin looked at me as I was watching him, but he continued talking, making little sense to me, and then abruptly informed the Betty O/FSO to cut out all but senior NCOs and officers. Well, that took me out, as well as Carpenter, since the rank of sergeant was not senior, and Corporal Murray, and I guess all the other platoon corporals and sergeants.

I pulled my mask up to take a drink. I sat back and relaxed, or tried to, but I was wound too tight. The past two days, is that right? This was the third morning, but the days were so long. I just realized that none of us had our CPs, they had been left back on Butch, making the "Hole." Marines had grabbed their bottles and clipped them straight onto their HECS wherever they could. I just remembered I had Gunny Scott's bottle. I still had my web belt on from crawling around with the PHA and I hooked it onto that. I unclipped it. Yep, his name was written in marker on the bottom, "Scott, F." He was sitting across from me, a couple seats down, next to Carpenter. I tapped it on my leg, just absentmindedly.

Whatever the company leadership was discussing came to a close and my COMM clicked back on and Captain Shupin was saying, "...yeah, when we get there, no need now. Okay, advise your men that we will have company formation and go over the guidelines and get our bunk assignment. Strict adherence to Authorized Area. They won't mess around down there, guys will disappear. Two days, maybe three. Division S2 is standing by for AAR. Gunny, advise second and then turn the platoon back over to Carpenter. Okay, Betty, bring the Command COMM net back up."

"What!" Shupin exclaimed.

Captain Shupin and Gunny Scott both looked at me at the same time, staring, their goggles down, but masks up, so that they could talk without being heard. I was still lightly tapping the bottle and looked at one and then the other. Was I not supposed to hear their conversation? It didn't make sense. We were setting down in a high secure area. *Yeah, so?*

I heard a subtle click again and Gunny Scott was talking to me. "PFC, what did you hear? When did you come back on the net?

Straight now, Smith. This is important. You need to level with me now, son. Put your helmet back on now and pull up your mask."

I did what he said. Scott was even tempered and calm. Carpenter was still, obviously, out of the loop. Whatever I heard, Carpenter didn't. The Betty O/FSO had mistakenly connected me too early.

"Gunny, I swear I only heard the click a second or two before Captain Shupin realized I was on." I had a strange thought that at any moment I was going to be gassed and never wake up. "He was saying something about when we get there we would go to company formation and get the rules. It was strict. We would get bunk assignments and S2 was going to do AARs and we would be there for two or three days. That's it. You're turning the platoon back over to Car— Sergeant Carpenter." I was sweating. I don't know what I heard, but it put a stinger in the CO.

"PFC Smith, where are we going?" cut in Captain Shupin. His tone was reminiscent of when he was the XO teaching a class to a bunch of Week One recruits, hostile, caustic, and demanding. He didn't even use this tone with me over the A-Dose incident the other…whatever it was ago.

"I don't know, sir. You didn't say. Honest, sir, my COMM only clicked back on when you said we would have company formation and get bunk assignments and rules. Gunny Scott was turning the platoon back over to Sergeant Carpenter." I was really tapping the bottle on my leg now.

"Have you played back the tape? Lines up? Okay, Betty archive that section. Smith, I will talk with you at some point on the ground. Until then, you will not, I repeat, not share this conversation to anyone. I am clear?"

"Aye-aye, sir."

Another click and Gunny was talking to Carpenter about when we set down we would have a company formation and get an orientation, expect a debrief, and further information would come. He apologized for pulling the platoon out from under him, he was a good NCO and his abilities were not being questioned. Carpenter replied that he understood and he had a lot to learn yet.

Gunny Scott said, "Sergeant Carpenter, you are one of the brightest and most talented marines I have ever known. It has been a privilege to have you under my command. You are the future."

"Thank you, Gunnery Sergeant. When are you pulling out?"

"You are observant. Soon. I need you to hold these boys together now. Then you need to go back to Bravo and train some more."

"Aye, Gunny. We'll cross again, yes?"

"Yeah, count on it. Pop that twin of yours in the head for me."

"I'll do it."

"Keep that pup of yours on a tight leash now too." They both looked my way.

They were sitting next to each other, talking on a private line. They were tight somehow, in some way I hadn't gotten privy to. Rabbi? Was the gunny Carpenter's mentor from way back?

COMM traffic started in earnest soon after that, platoon leaders relaying the information to their marines, and the flight settled down into restless talk among friends. I removed my helmet and pulled my mask down, rubbing my head and face. I looked around. Everyone was dirty, somehow, I guess from rubbing their faces with their gloves still on. Beard stubble was several days old and faces were gaunt, burned, and tired. That was a rough three days.

I searched for Private Clark, who was sitting with Hackney and Woolsey. "Hey, Clark," I said, loud enough to be heard by most of the platoon. "Now that was some fine shooting you did down there. What? You took out seven, eight Mowatts?"

"Heck no, man! When you were goofing around with that one you were trying to choke out, he popped three or four that had you dead to rights. Saved your bacon! Clark took out at least a dozen or more," added Grigs, propping up the timid private's reputation.

Clark's group of buddies popped him on the shoulders and started asking for the details. He looked over at me and smiled, and I grinned back. Yeah, he did all right. He turned back and retold his action in the ravine; the other two had been in Corporal Murray's squad and hadn't participated in the assault. I would have to remember to make a point of his actions in my AAR. He deserved recognition for his contribution to our survival and Grigs too.

The platoon came to life and the banter and stories started, as they always do, of this marine doing this or seeing that and the laughter and joking continued for the next hour. The added presence of the CO and Gunny only intensified the tales. Evidently Captain Shupin had come up in another brigade and was not too well-known before taking command of Echo. Our loss of Lieutenant Green was heavy, but we adopted Captain Shupin as our temporary platoon leader. He joined in on the fun and stories, becoming a lieutenant again of a platoon, if only for a short period, letting his hair down, so to speak. I could sense in his manner that wherever he had come from, he was admired by his former marines and he missed that relationship. Word came that Corporal Larson was all right, and he would rejoin us in a couple days. Man, that was fantastic news, and we all cheered.

We had been in a continuous wormhole the whole time, traveling unknown distance of space. Usually, there were in and out, connections, or transfers from one dimension or bent space to another, but not this trip. The flight was smooth, relatively quiet and fast. I could almost sense an increased speed of our journey, but I had no idea what our Betty's cruising speed/distance capability was. This felt different.

The Betty shuttered out of the portal or wormhole, the familiar bone-rattling vibrations and ear-shattering noise interrupting our conversation. I automatically looked around to ensure that everyone was strapped in, and that's when I noticed for the first time that the door gunner and crew chief were wearing the same pattern camouflaged HECS that I had observed with the companies that set up the fortified CP. Now that I thought about it, the chief had not issued any commands, we had just followed normal procedure.

The chief was strapped into his seat at the front of the cabin. The pattern was totally different aside from the color, which was almost white, a light pink, and a very light brown. I bet if the crew chief laid out in the sand of either Bruce or Death Valley, I would be hard-pressed to see him until I was very close.

The Betty nosed in, making us lean heavily toward the front of the cabin. This was a strange maneuver, unless we were plunging into water. I felt the impact, and it was not a gradual slip in. We hit at a speed—well, I'm not sure what speed, but it was jarring. We all flew up out of our seats against the straps and crashed back down again. Man, a little heads up from the chief would have been appreciated, but he just sat in his seat, not moving. The Betty continued her journey, wherever that was for another half hour or so before I could distinguish the slowdown and hovering maneuver that indicated an underwater insert. Wow, we were deploying somewhere, underwater.

"Gunny, ensure GLARs are deactivated," Captain Shupin ordered. "We'll form up and then make the beach. After orientation and bunk assignments, let's get them to chow and showers."

"Aye-aye, sir."

Now, wherever we were, we were safe enough to be unarmed.

"Platoon sergeants, deactivate GLARs, sling upside down over left shoulders. Company formation on the Pad, then on the beach for orientation. Give me all clear when you have double-checked all weapons."

He turned to Sergeant Carpenter. "Have Smith deactivate. You double behind him. Give orders for neutral arms."

"Aye-aye, Gunny," replied Carpenter over the COMM net. Then he ordered over the platoon channel, "Unstrap and disconnect tubes. Prepare for Inspection Arms. PFC Smith will deactivate GLARs and I will follow him. Sling neutral arms after I check you."

It was strange that the chief wasn't assisting with the insert prep. He was still in his seat.

I had to quickly pull up the necklace from around my neck and grab the armorer's key. I had not been authorized to disarm or arm until now. Larson had that responsibility for the platoon. I was nervous. I didn't know which way to go, which end to start from. Was I supposed to do Gunny and the CO too? Carpenter was an armorer, and I think Corporal Murray was too, so why was I doing this? I was four seats in from the ramp and the CO was two down from me, while Gunny and Carpenter were on the other side. I walked to the ramp on my side and started there, with Lance Corporal Almond, just as good as any place to start, I guess. I took his weapon and made the change, hoping above all hope that I was doing it correctly. Safe weapon was center position, armed was clicked toward the muzzle, and training mode was to the butt. I double-checked, moving the selector to the middle, then to training, and back to the middle. Okay, that was completely disarmed. Can't fire a shot at the deck to double-check. That's why Carpenter was going behind me. I was feeling more comfortable now. I knew how and what I had to do, just had the jitters. I stepped in front of Captain Shupin and I digressed. He stood there, not quite at Inspection Arms, not at attention, more of a relaxed and interested state of presence.

"Sir, may I have your GLAR?" I asked, not at all believing that I was requesting the CO's weapon.

He moved to a casual position of Inspection Arms and presented me his GLAR. I took possession of it and made the mode change and held it out for him to recover. He took it and I moved down and then crossed over to the other side. Gunny Scott was last, and he presented his GLAR and gave me a wink. Carpenter was right behind me and checked my weapon and I checked his, hoping beyond all hope and favor that I didn't accidentally reactivate his by mistake!

"Neutral arms!" ordered Carpenter, and the platoon slung their GLARs upside down on the left shoulder, signifying that we were nonaggressive. I had never performed this action other than in Six Weeks drill. This was basically a surrender or passive stance. The ramp lowered. The chief finally became active and took his place for the insert. HITS, High Impulse Tension Screen, was obviously active and I could see a beautiful clear blue body of water just inches away. The bottom was an intense clean white sand and I thought I could see the glare of sunlight just above. We were not too deep, but the environment was calm. That was weird, at this depth there should be tidal action or we were in a lake, lagoon, or other protected enclosure.

The platoon leaders had all reported confirmed deactivation and Gunny Scott relayed that to the CO.

"Insert and form up the company, Gunny," said Shupin.

The order was given, and second platoon walked off the ramp and formed up. It was the clearest open water I had ever been in, second to the giant pool, and we quickly formed into a company. I was able to look around; third platoon Alpha was not with us. The formalities of command were quickly dispensed, a formal company roll call was performed. Second platoon reported two MIA, one casualty at MHG. Echo Company then proceeded to march toward the breakwater and the beach, where we would receive an orientation briefing, bunk assignments, hot chow, and showers.

Man, I was looking forward to this.

Chapter 12

PRESENT

I had never been to this section of the base before, only the flyover. We were lying at the edge of the forest, looking at the open field and road in front of us. The barbed wire fence was fifty or so meters out, about fifteen meters on the other side of the little gravel road.

"I don't know. That's a long way," I said.

Maliki was on my right. "Yeah, it does look different from down here." He obviously had done a flyover too.

"This is wide open, almost like they set it up as an invite," added Cummings.

I was trying to think of what we could do, how to get across. I was sure that the assault on the training firing range was now a hot issue. The gates were going to be closed, the roads were going to be under surveillance, they didn't know who hit it or where we were headed. Time was critical.

"We got to move. The longer we wait, the tighter the noose is going to be closed. I'm sure the other teams have been redirected to avoid conflict where possible. We made our bed."

"Yeah," replied Cummings.

"The only avenue is here. The footbridge and tunnel are sure death traps. We can't cross up at the construction gate. If we move tactically, we'll be picked off or stopped for sure. I say we bebop in a Land Nav formation and act like we are lost. We work our way close to the fence and cross to 70. We really have no other choice."

I looked at Maliki and Cummings. They nodded. I took the map out. "Here, this is our story. We came from…"

I shot a direction and drew a pencil line from the elbow of the trail to the walkover bridge, we were close to being on course, yet far enough away from the range. I erased our points and direction to the range.

"If we get stopped, we are just lost and trying to get to EP at the rocks. Good? We'll break out of the wood line in classic Land Nav formation, nontactical, and say that we are avoiding the bridge because of a sniper report." They were nodding. "Okay, Maliki, nice and easy, straight ahead."

We stood up and walked straight into the open, several feet apart and as casual as could be, not a care in the world. There had to be Betty activity now and we were sure to be picked up to be checked out.

"You know, tactically speaking, this is suicide, but crazy enough to work." We were coming to the road.

I saw the scuvy tearing down the road from the direction of the construction gate heading toward us at near full speed.

"Easy, guys, whole different game from combat. Act unbothered. We have no idea about anything other than this mission." How many times did I have to lie back at the orphanage to keep from being punished?

We came to the road and stopped, clustered together, and looked at the map and turned around and pointed and stared at where we came from. If this weren't so serious, I would laugh, but I hoped we weren't overdoing it. The scuvy braked and skidded to a stop a few feet from us and the SFP jumped out and ordered us to shoulder our GLARs.

"What's going on? This isn't a secure area, is it? The map doesn't show it secure," I said to the chief petty officer stepping toward me.

"What is your training objective? What unit are you assigned with?" He asked, now right in front of me. "Where'd you come from? What's your assignment?"

The tactic was to barrage me with questions, to get me confused, to get me to make a mistake or contradict myself. I spent almost six years learning how to overcome incriminating myself over missing food from the kitchen or breaking a lamp while playing catch in the hallway. Stick to the story.

"We're trying to find our next point. We're with Second Training Battalion, PNCOC."

"Where'd you come from? Are you in charge? Why did you fire on the range? Who's in charge of this detail?"

He persisted, adding the charge of the range assault to get my reaction. Maliki dropped his CP and reached in for a meal, ripping the top off and eating a packet of chili mac cold. Cummings mixed a bottle of juice and ate an energy bar.

"We're trying to find our next point. What? No, we haven't had range time today. I don't know, we're all lance corporals. Maliki, are you senior, or, wait, when did you enlist?" Another scuvy was headed our way.

"Why are you here? Who's in charge of this detail? Why did you fire upon the training company on the range? What's your name?"

He was pounding me, already receiving several of his answers. He was looking for deviation. The second SCUV pulled up and its riders hopped out. I knew better than to fiddle with anything, like a water bottle or my face, as it shows an attitude of guiltiness. I just had to answer the questions over and over, the same way.

"None of us are in charge, Chief Petty Officer. We're trying to get to our next RP. I told you we haven't had range time today." I failed to disclose my name on purpose so he would have to ask again.

I almost laughed when I recognized Chief Swan as he walked up and joined us. I was not sure how he was going to proceed, but he recognized me I'm sure but didn't waiver.

"I asked you your name. Why are you coming from the training range? What's your assignment?"

"Lance Corporal Smith, Chief Petty Officer. We are trying to find our next RP. We haven't had range time today. We came from—" I turned around and pointed toward the general direction of the elbow of the trail, over five kilometers up the mountain behind us, a good ways away from the training range. "Over that way. I think," I added, trying to look unsure in a positive deflection.

"Lance Corporal, let me see your map," injected Chief Swan.

Finally, I hoped that my eraser marks weren't visible. Maliki had not traced them too darkly anyway. I had retraced all our azimuths and circled our RPs and written SS with a question mark between the footbridge and tunnel and circled that as well.

"We are trying to get to here, Chief Petty Officer. There is a possibility that a SS is along here. That's why we are searching for another crossover. Any suggestions?"

He knew me. He knew that I knew him, and it was all in his hands. No one was hurt, and it was a training exercise involving the Fleet Marines only. The SFP didn't really have a horse in the show.

"We detained a Second Training Battalion SS candidate that was found in the area of the incident that was hunting a three-man team that's, well—" He looked at his watch. "That was ten minutes ago. You three would have had to have busted out a pretty good pace with combat load CPs to be here from there. I can't give you a route, Lance Corporal. On your way."

He handed me back the map but held on to it briefly. The other CPO turned and walked back to his SCUV.

"That was the gutsiest maneuver I've ever seen. Good luck."

I took the map but didn't say a word, still not sure if he was playing me.

"Okay, Maliki, let's head to the fence."

I smiled at Chief Swan and turned to my team. We had a couple minutes on the sniper, and our plan worked. We might make our EP after all.

CHAPTER 13

The beach was incredible, white sand, the smallest wave action, really just a gentle lapping. There were no discernable tidal marks, a constant shoreline. I sat in the sand with my feet in the water. The temperature was a pleasant warm, maybe low eighties, and a cool breeze came in from the sea, perhaps the ocean, or bay? I looked out and as far as I could see was water. Our camp was behind me, several hundred meters back from the shoreline, nestled really, in a grove of palm and, I think, mango trees. The sun was bright, warm, and yellow. It was nice to have a semblance of home. We had marched in, literally, no tactical formation at all, straight onto the beach from the water. We received an orientation briefing, which laid out the rules and guidelines that we were expected to follow, for our own safety as well as the safety of the local inhabitants. Infractions would be dealt with immediately and harshly. None of the rules seemed to be difficult—we were to stay within our assigned area, do not cross any water, and do not interact with any local unless invited. Our GLARs were secured in an arms room adjacent to the bunkhouse.

We had showers, a chow hall, the bunkhouse, an activity building, and two or three days off. Yeah, this was great. Division S2 was here, and a schedule was set up so that each marine performed an AAR. Second platoon was scheduled for after breakfast in the morning. After dinner chow, we lined up to be issued a "comfort kit." Our CPs were somewhere, and we would reunite with them sometime, but until then we received a new complete shave kit, utility shorts, and water shirt. Wow, that was all we needed.

I sat on the beach, fed, showered, wearing shorts, my HECS and other uniform neatly folded on my bunk. This was great. I had no idea where we were, other than what the man who gave our orientation called it, New Garden. Grigs walked up and sat beside me.

"Man, this is gorgeous. How's the water?"

"Feels good, not too warm. Beautiful sky, huh? Look at that sunset," I said.

"Hey, I just wanted to tell you thanks for back there. You held it together. I think you were pivotal in us getting out of there. I wish we could've found Lieutenant Green and Somersby."

I pondered his comment. I thought about what had happened, our near destruction.

"Grigs, you ever wonder about," I paused, I didn't know how to say it, he would think I was crazy. "Are you a believer?"

Grigs was brought up in a wealthy family, he and his stepbrother enjoyed a rather privileged life, nice house, good schools, and college. He was from what used to be known as Texas.

"Yeah, man. God, you mean? Sure. It's hard to equate what we see out here to what was taught to me as a kid. But, yeah, Smith, God made all of this. It's all under His control. I can't figure out the lapse of the timeline, but I think we have entered a new or different age. There are obviously multiple worlds, and for some reason, we are interacting with one another. Don't get blinded by what you can't figure out. You just have to accept what information He has given us."

I thought about that. I had no idea where we were. There was just no way that all of this, what I had seen already, was accidental or chaotic. Look at this water, the sand, the beach, the sky, and sunset. This was too close to Earth, but this was not Earth, and the sun was different. The water was not being affected by currents or tidal pull, and I bet there was no moon tonight.

"Let's go for a swim," I said.

"Yeah, man," Grigs replied as he dashed into the water. "Oh! This is great."

I stood and ran in, diving as I reached above my knees. Soon nearly the whole company joined us and we swam and goofed off. A volleyball appeared, and we started a game. We played until it became too dark to see. No moon rose and there were few stars, very few stars, very odd.

Chapter 13

PRESENT

We had dropped our CPs just off the road, in the trees after crossing over Highway 70. Now we were lying among the rocks that overlooked the walkover bridge. The tunnel was several hundred meters farther down. We made our EP but, well, the attraction of scoring a sniper kill was too tempting to quit now. The problem was, was he going to set up on this side or the far side of the hardball? He had to be racing at a pace that was at or faster than ours had been. His discovery and containment no doubt was embarrassing not only for him but also for the instructors of the course. A team of lance corporals had sprung a trap that he was caught up in. The question was, was he thinking like us? Did he know we were going to cross somewhere else? He couldn't cross at the bridge or the tunnel, so he had to use the same route we did and was gambling that he was quicker, lighter, even with his delay.

"He's going to be mad that he got caught. Could that toss him from the course?" I queried.

"No. I know a staff sergeant in First that was caught twice during the course but went on to have an excellent kill record on his tour. He told me that it's a learning experience. You have to keep your head, not let it distract you, and continue the mission. This guy hunting us. He's awake now and knows we are too." Cummings was to my right, scanning the direction we came from.

"I don't think he is stupid enough to use the bridge or tunnel. I think he is going to cross like we did and either try to pick us off on this side or the divided median. Can he shoot across the road?" Maliki asked.

"I think that is a safety issue." I laughed. The assault on the firing range was a safety issue.

"That's got to be an ROE violation," I added. Rules of engagement, ROE, spelled out what actions could and could not be taken in combat or, in this case, training. Our own ROE said we could not fire across the road.

"What if he sets up on the other side?" asked Maliki.

"Nah, he's been given our EP. He doesn't know where we might cross, so he could miss us. He's got to take these rocks and wait for us," Cummings said.

The sun was starting to slide to late afternoon, a nice sky, blue, no clouds, with little breeze. The temperature had climbed to the midseventies but, again, at this elevation in the Rockies, with a bright sun, the radiant temperature was quite warm. We had cooled down from our earlier exertion. Lying in the rocks was almost relaxing. We had recovered, and the rest gave us a better position of superiority.

"There he is!" said Cummings, almost sounding like a kid seeing Santa.

"Incredible, we been here for almost ten minutes. How could he possibly think he beat us here? After he was detained?" wondered Maliki.

"I don't know. Is he coming straight here? He's got to be." I was shaking my head. Was this a trick? "Maliki, check our six, easy movement. Is this a setup? No way he is running that quick and without caution, unless he is pushing his luck."

"I been watching our rear, Two. No movement. Unless they were set up already, then they would have popped us before now. Right?"

"This is too easy," I said.

"I don't know, we're just stupid E3s. These guys are cocky staffs, and he may not know the reason for his detention. He may think that he has to beat us here. It's all open." Cummings was playing the devil's advocate, laying out different ideas.

"How close are we going to let him get? We can pop him anytime now, score a kill, before he smells us." Maliki was right. We had not reported in that we had reached the EP, although they knew it, were monitoring our COMM.

"I'm going to report in. Six, this is Team Ten junior. Reached our EP and have possible SS approaching our position. What are our orders?"

"Team Ten junior, it's about time you called in your status. If approaching contact is alone, treat as hostile and eliminate. Confirm when objective complete."

"Maliki, you take the shot. I don't want us to reveal our strength, in case this is still a setup."

"Roger, Two. I'm lining him up. Is it a go?"

"Take out hostile."

I was essentially giving an order to take a life, in practice, but the significance was not lost on me. It was just as if I pulled the trigger.

Maliki was good. He hit the SS dead-on, three kill shots in a tight group. Zik! Zik! Zik! The SS dropped to the deck, but he knew he was dead, or at the least mortally wounded, in the open, less than thirty-five meters from the rocks. His prey had become the hunter. He didn't return fire, he had no support, he was in a poor defendable position, and he had been careless. He was not sure if his demise had come from his quarry or another unrelated team. It didn't matter, he was dead. His COMM was directing him on his next actions, as he lay in the open field, just off the little road that served a combination of purposes, but mostly as the route for a run that was known as Bad Girl. He would forever remember this lesson. My only thought for him was that I hoped it saved his life in the future.

"Six, hostile down. Is this a confirmed kill? Over."

"Wait one, Team Ten—"

None of us said a word. This was unbelievable. Had we actually, successfully, outmaneuvered an SS candidate and scored a kill?

"Team Ten, you have confirmed kill. Report for AAR. Mission complete."

"Copy, Six. That's confirmed objective. We'll take those steaks medium. Copy."

There was no response, but Maliki and Cummings yelled and hooted and nearly fell on top of me as I was lying there, still not believing that we had succeeded in taking out our sniper. The three of us rolled on the ground, bumping heads and slugging one another in the chest and shoulders. A passerby would have thought we were locked in a fearsome fight.

"You did it! You did it! I can't believe you pulled it off!" Cummings was shaking me with his right hand as he was latched onto Maliki, shaking him as well.

"Man! Smith, you are top-notch. That was awesome tactics, dude! Unbelievable! I'll team with you any day! Wow, Cummings! Can you believe this?" Maliki was patting me on the helmet. I was reaching out for both of them, trying to settle them down.

"We all did it, you two. We did it together. Okay, okay. We got to get our CPs and get out of here."

I raised up on my knee and looked over toward the sniper who was now sitting in the spot he went down. We had to pass by that way to retrieve our CPs, and I didn't want to do anything to further his possible embarrassment.

"Let's go. Try to avoid, you know."

"Yeah, I know," said Maliki.

"No problem."

We walked past, avoiding eye contact, passing within ten feet of the SS candidate.

"I didn't know what you had done. I was suddenly and totally surrounded by angry drills and SFP. Real world conditions, I thought the DIs were going to literally pound me. It got rough. SFPs had to pull them off." He looked up at us, his helmet off. I didn't know him. "This here was my fault. Anger at you and pushing to get you cost me. That was incredible maneuvering. I don't think you're going to be welcomed in First Training anytime soon." He stood up. "How did you come?"

I thought about it. They were going to analyze our COMM traffic and our route anyway. "We deflected the direction of the assault and made toward the construction gate crossing at the median over there." I pointed.

"How did you get across the open field?"

"How did you?"

He laughed, I didn't have to tell him everything.

"I sure hope I get the pleasure of serving with you one day, Lance Corporals."

"Same here, Staff Sergeant," I said.

He laughed again and walked toward the road and back to the training battalion for his debrief. We collected our CPs and followed behind him at a distance. This was another 3K, but we were walking on a road and our mission complete. What a day.

CHAPTER 14

My AAR with Division S2 was completed after breakfast and was as nerve-wracking as my first one had been. I had participated in several now and knew the routine. Basically, the interviewing officer had the general knowledge of the action and built from each interview forward. Some marines had little to no relevant information, while others were a wellspring of intel. I recognized the major from other AARs, but he looked familiar in another way. He let us tell what we knew or had experienced, and then he would direct his questions to points that he needed more info on or, if we opened a topic that was new, would expand on that. He questioned me on the action in the ravine, the search for Lieutenant Green and Private Somersby, the assault, the treatment of Corporal Larson, the last night, and lastly whether I recalled Captain Shupin ordering Alpha into the ravine. I stared at him in disbelief.

"No, sir. Captain Shupin to my knowledge gave no such orders. He was beside himself trying to stop it, sir. He gave Echo direct orders to not enter the ravine, before the collapse."

"He did not suggest Alpha to engage the Galleens?"

"No, sir. Echo inserted to the rear of the FPs to take the heat off the assault of Alpha. We were to fall back into a defense perimeter the remainder of the night. I don't know why Alpha went into that ditch. It took us all day to get out of it."

"That's all, PFC. You're dismissed."

I stood up and came to attention. "Aye-aye, sir." I hesitated but then started out the door.

"I know you've been trying to figure it out, PFC Smith. Just so you can enjoy your stay here, I met you at the cookout and your fun run. That's all."

I looked at him, but he was already writing something in his notes. I walked out.

The guys were on the beach or in the water, some swimming way out. We were told that there were no sharks or other dangerous wildlife either in the water or on land. I wanted to take a walk, so I turned and followed the tree line and came to a trail. I took it. The pathway was worn, a mixture of sand and a loamy soil, soft, comfortable in my bare feet. I was dressed in my shorts and water shirt. Our orders were very casual and to rest and relax. The morning was warm and humid, not hot and not too muggy. The coolness of the trees out of the sun made the walk very enjoyable, and I soon found myself at an easy stroll, listening to the birds and insects. I did not recognize some of the trees and plants, which some bore fruit. The jungle or woods, or whatever this might be categorized as, was teeming with various fruit-bearing species. There were mango, pineapple, orange, papaya, banana, and coconut. This was a small paradise. The trees and plants mixed in with one another, random wild growth, not cultivated or seemingly planted. The pathway meandered through the grove.

Sunlight peered and streamed through the canopy and cast shadows that really mixed in well with the not overbright daylight. The ambiance was calm, cool, and comfortable. I stepped around a tight bend and walked into a small glade with a little running brook cutting the opening across the top corner. A man was peering down into a little pool, his legs straddled over the two banks, his hands suspended just above the surface. In a flash, his hands darted into the pool and a wild splash of water erupted, and he brought out a small fish, wiggling and flipping. In the same moment, he turned his head and caught sight of me, and briefly, his concentration was lost on the fish and it flipped out of his hands back into the water as he frantically and wildly fought to regain his grasp while losing his balance and stepping into the brook. The whole incident was in a twinkle and the sudden frantic movement, with the stepping in the water, caused the man to slip, sending him stumbling in an uncontrollable sequence, unceremoniously, backward, sitting in the water! He let out a roaring, deep laugh, almost as though he enjoyed the whole incident, including the accidental soaking.

"Hello, friend! Don't be afraid," he said, hardly stopping laughing at himself. He stood up and looked down, laughing some more. "Go ahead. It's okay. That had to be funny to watch."

He stepped out of the water and gave the pool a glance. "You won again, little fish, but I will see you again soon."

I smiled; the man did not mind losing his catch or getting soaked. I was unsure of what to do, since we were not supposed to interact with the locals, and he was surely not one of us.

His hair was longer, a wavy deep brown chestnut color, hanging freely. He wore a type of wrap around his waist, like a towel or small sheet, that was secured with a belt, the length just to his knees, and a loose pullover shirt open at the neck, the sleeves falling at his elbows, where it was rolled up. He was tanned and muscled, a laborer, I was sure. He bent down and retrieved a small satchel or bag from the bank and looped it over his head and arm and flipped it around to his back.

"It's okay. You are not bothering me, and I have talked to you first, so you are not breaking the rule. I know you, who you are. You are one of the soldiers visiting. Your world has many issues, experienced some troubling things. Oh, pardon me. I am… Where are my manners? Are you thirsty? Would you like a drink of water? Come, drink. The stream is clean." He waved his hand toward the flow, stepping aside.

I was really not sure what to make of this now. He took a large broad leaf, breaking it from a nearby plant, and rinsed it in the running water and then quickly folded it, making a cup, and dipped it back down filling it. He stepped toward me, extending the dripping leaf cup. "Take it. It's refreshing, and the morning is warming."

I was thirsty.

I reached out and took it. The leaf was surprisingly sturdy, a full cup, more than enough to drink at once. The man smiled, as I took a drink.

"That's cool and tastes good. Thank you." I smiled.

I guess if he somehow tricked me and poisoned or drugged it, I would soon know. He laughed.

"There is no trick. It is only water."

Bizarre.

"Join me on a walk? I will show you some things and we can talk."

"I don't know. I'm not sure it's a good idea." I liked the man. He was intriguing and kind and I would enjoy talking to someone from this world and learn about them.

"It will be fine. You cannot cross the water boundary and I have invited you to join me, so you see you are not breaking the rules."

I consented, and we walked together down the path, talking casually as if we were friends for a lifetime. I asked him if the place we were was really named New Garden and he said yes, and that was one of many names it was called.

Chapter 14

PRESENT

Chow tonight was downright hilarious as word quickly spread through not only our class but also the entire Second Training Battalion of the assault on the First Battalion firing range and the successful EnE and SS kill. First Sergeant French decided to let the news run its course, either as a lesson or for a little esprit de corps. Staff sergeants in both the ANCOC and SS courses were watching the three of us closely. The PNCOC scandal was already over two and a half weeks past and life had somewhat returned to normal. The upper A Courses had little to do with us, but this newest situation was an attention-grabber. Staff Sergeant Williams, one of my Y drill instructors, walked over as he was leaving. He stopped at our table and smiled at me and motioned if he could join us.

"Yes, Staff Sergeant, please," I said almost too excitedly.

We were in a nontraining, nonformal setting, so there was no need to jump up. It still felt very weird not to break out and stand straight at attention, though.

"Lance Corporal Smith, I heard scuttlebutt that it was your team that hit the firing range today and successfully scored a kill on the SS. You want to take a wild guess at which company it was that you kicked and jabbed a finger in the eye to?"

He looked at me with a grin spreading across his face.

"No, Staff Sergeant Williams. You're yanking my chain."

There was just no way I could have hit the same training company twice.

"Yep, you took out Alpha again. You know they feed First Division. I suggest you give that division a wide berth. This your team?" he asked, now giving the table his genuine attention.

"Yes, Staff Sergeant. Maliki from Charlie 1/1/7 and Cummings from First," I said almost laughing.

"Fantastic op today, Marines. The rest of these guys know your history, Lance Corporal?" he nodded back to me.

Also seated at the table were Grigs, Alvera, Campbell, and Simon. "Of course, I know these two and you too," he said looking at Grigs and Campbell and lastly at Simon. "Great bunch of future corporals here. How'd you get mixed up in this bunch?" he asked, talking directly to Cummings.

"Fate," he replied. The whole table burst out laughing, even Williams.

"Yes, you better not reveal your part." He paused and laughed. "I hear there was a turkey shoot at the Potty Palace!"

Several of us laughed. That was a story that would continue to grow for years. Williams stood up, and we all made to stand as well. "As you were, Lance Corporals. It was good to talk with you all, you especially, Smith. I'll keep you tucked away in my memory. Best of luck, all of you." He walked away.

"I don't remember him," said Alvera, motioning to Williams.

"He was third platoon sergeant for us. Corporal Valmer and then Corporal Carpenter took over," I said.

"Yeah, he was third platoon for me as well. I was first with Mosher and Breemer. Carpenter I think was fourth," added Simon.

"Naw, Sergeant Mean was second platoon and Staff Sergeant Ginny just came out of SS rotation. Corporal Carpenter, I think, just came out of drill school and was assisting, maybe."

The conversation weaved in and out, but I tried to steer it back to common ground, because poor Cummings was the only non-Seventh guy with us. He sat with us tonight away from his usual group due to the excitement of the op, and I hoped this wouldn't make him leave us. I liked him, and he fit very nicely in with us. As a matter of fact, he joined right in, telling his own stories of Y Camp, making us laugh at guys we didn't know.

He asked, "What did the staff sergeant mean when he said you hit Alpha again?" Half the table laughed, even though only Grigs and Campbell knew the story firsthand.

Cummings just stared at me as Campbell, Grigs, Simon, and Alvera took turns telling the story, all of us laughing. Cummings said, "Man, Smith, you really do understand tactics. I said it this afternoon, and I'll say it again—I'll stand with you any day."

We all laughed and got up to go to study group. What a day.

All the teams made it in for dinner chow, and they had all been diverted away from the ensuing chaos of the search, even to the point of a direct approach being set up to the Training Battalion. All of my classmates had showed that they had a good grasp of Nav, and only more experience would strengthen their skills. The AAR was performed as a team and highlighted the assault on the range and the EnE with the kill. Nothing was said to us either way as to our decision or use of training fire mode on an unrelated noncombative force, that is, the training recruits, to divert attention to a suspected SS in the area. First Sergeant French, along with the first sergeant of the SS A Course—I didn't catch his name—took part, asking a couple questions.

I was able to ditch my gear in my wall locker and double-time to the PX to order my replacement OL ribbon and return just in time for chow. I was running down the steps of the battalion on my way to the PX when First Sergeant French called after me.

"Lance Corporal Smith, a word," he said as he followed me out the door.

I stopped so suddenly I almost fell over, recovering and nearly tripping down two steps. "Aye, First Sergeant!"

I turned and came to attention facing him at the entry to the Training Battalion barracks.

"That was quite a performance today. You can't help yourself. You are grabbing the attention of… Tell me, was it the thrill to hit a bunch of recruits, the completion of a mission, or the desire to take out an SS? What was in your mind this afternoon, Lance Corporal?"

I was caught off guard. He was not trying to trick me or in any way hurt me, I knew that. He wanted to seriously try to understand what drove me, my thought process.

"First Sergeant, it was the mission. I wanted my team to successfully complete the Nav course. The SS was thrown in really in our way, I'm sure, just as a 'what can they do' or even as part of his training process. I don't know but I looked at the problem only as a mission, First Sergeant. I looked at where we were, where we had to go, what was in our way, and how I could complete the mission. That's it. If you had come over the COMM and stopped us, I would have come up with an alternate plan."

"So now you are dumping this on me?" he said, not angrily, almost in bewilderment. "You knew I was monitoring your COMM and thought I would step in if it were outrageous?"

"Yes, First Sergeant. If what I was planning were against the rules, I thought you would interject or stop it. I was given a mission, no limitations, no boundaries."

"Let me get this straight, you would assault a group of civilians if not stopped?" He was almost incredulous.

"Absolutely not! That is not a fair comparison, First Sergeant!" I was almost yelling, my anger taking control over my respect for French.

"They were a group of Third Week training recruits, Lance Corporal." He was provoking me, although I didn't see it.

"Over seventy strong, with weapons! Am I to evaluate the training level of every company level unit in my path, First Sergeant? My intel had an SS hunting my team and I had to reach an EP to get them out. That was my mission and I did the best I could!"

"You better check that attitude with me, son! You are still so wet behind the ears and full of baby teeth that a wet nurse should be your doctor! I can knock you on your butt and you won't know it's Christmas until the snow starts to melt next August! You better figure out who in God's favorite planet is talking to you right now and beg for mercy. I don't care if Crazy Thompson is your rabbi. He won't miss you like a pass of gas!"

I was truly humiliated. What came over me? What the heck was I thinking? I was yelling at a first sergeant, an E8. Not only that, but this man stood up for me, two times that I know of, not to mention he was a first sergeant. I had lost my mind.

"Forgive me, First Sergeant. I'm, I'm—" What do you say? How do you apologize to a first sergeant? Holy moly, lance corporals don't even talk to first sergeants! I was way over my head, this shouldn't even be happening.

"First Sergeant, I don't know what I was thinking. Forgive my insolence. You, why are you talking to me?"

He stood there, bigger than life. This man was a legend, staff sergeants and gunnys queued on him. What the heck was he even addressing me for? What brain malfunction did I have that allowed me to become too familiar with him?

"That psych exam might not be a bad idea. I think you are suffering from altered inflated ego, Lance Corporal."

"Yes, First Sergeant." I was truly embarrassed. I was still locked up at attention.

"That's better. Your action today was unconventional and challenged some on the command chain. I like it. You think on your own. You are mission-driven and desire the best for your men at the same time. Where are you going?"

The last part caused me as much confusion as any other part of the conversation. Where was I going? He had a multitude of levels of NCOs to keep up with my whereabouts and movements. Why was this a concern for him?

"I'm running to the PX, First Sergeant."

I was now almost shaking from the earlier exchange, now that my brain had caught up to my actions. How stupid could I be? You don't yell at a first sergeant, much less argue with one.

He looked at me with a questionable gaze, almost in doubt. "This isn't back at home, Lance Corporal. You don't run to the 'store' when it suits you. You have duties to attend to. Did your platoon sergeants authorize this?"

Oh, man, digging the hole, can't climb out. "Yes, First Sergeant. I was instructed to order a replacement ribbon for Saturday inspection."

He looked at me. "I find it hard to believe that you arrived at PNCOC without all your authorized ribbons, Lance Corporal? Which one are you missing?"

Okay, maybe that was a really bad decision I made. The significance of the whole situation that was now unfolding was not lost on me. This was not an everyday occurrence. First sergeants didn't make conversation with E3s, this was beyond normal.

"I have to get a replacement for my OL, First Sergeant."

His gaze was burning through me, and I could see a glimpse of astonishment and question. "What exactly—? How—? Where, Lance Corporal, is your OL ribbon? Do you realize that that ribbon is precious? Where is your OL?"

He stepped toward me, coming to within inches of me. "I swear I will knock you out if you... What did you do with it?"

"First Sergeant, it is, I...I pinned it to the wall over PFC Lewis' picture at Linda's in town. He was awarded the OL posthumously and I wanted to honor him, First Sergeant. He was my friend. He shouldn't have died. He was just... He did the same stupid thing I did, only I made it and he didn't." I was broken.

I couldn't maintain my position or composure, so I looked down, my head bowed. What happened next totally caught me off guard. First Sergeant French put his arm around my neck and leaned in close, his head next to mine.

"You can't change it, Smith. You can't bring them back, not Lewis, not Green, Somersby, not Alpha. You can't undo what you did. You have to move on. I know you have demons, son. We all do. You need to come to the meetings. Ginny was supposed to bring you in. You need to let us help you."

I didn't know what he was talking about. He pulled away and stared at me. "I want you to come to the Senior NCO Chow Hall Sunday morning at 0800. There is a room that will say OL Private. Just come in. Now, for the love of God's favorite planet, you need a copy of your OL Award Letter. Do you have that?"

"Up in my locker, First Sergeant."

His look was borderline comical and distain. "You can't just walk in and order an OL ribbon, Smith! And for your sake, you better hope that your original ribbon is still at Linda's! I have to go fetch that tonight. You can't leave that lying around. Linda's? Are you out of your mind? Carry on."

CHAPTER 15

Our two days off relaxing at New Garden ended sooner than we had wanted but accomplished what it was intended to do—take our minds off the massacre of Alpha Company. When we formed up on the beach as a company prior to the underwater extraction, we were given a briefing to treat our visit as confidential and not to discuss it either with others outside the company or even among ourselves, to just let it pass. It was a beautiful place, and the less anyone knew of its existence, the better it would be. We would no doubt visit again during our service. That was good enough for me, and I couldn't wait to return.

Our departure was linked to the expanding rebellion taking place on Mars with the colonies and we were needed there. The Bettys contained our CPs, each hung above the seats we normally sat in. The contents had been removed, inspected, and cleaned and missing items replaced such as the shelters, water bottles, and meals. It was fantastic. Evidently a headquarters quartermaster supply platoon had landed on Butch after we had extracted, and the abandoned CPs had been discovered and arrangements made to reunite them with their owners. *Outstanding.* There was nothing in mine of a personal value anyway, so it was much to my surprise and happiness to find that several items were new.

I didn't say anything to anyone about my meeting with the local, having thoroughly enjoyed his company and the things he had shown me. We parted on a trail that came out of the jungle forest above where I had entered, which was odd because we never crossed any water and kept, I thought, the ocean to our right. It seemed to be a long walk, but when I came out and joined my friends, it was well before lunch. It was almost as if time stood still.

The Bettys now were making their approach to a landing or insert, the crew chief stationed at the ramp, ready to lower it. Almost as soon as we had boarded, the CO and Gunny Scott ordered weapons activated and to resupply A-Doses that were passed around. The CPs had a full resupply of meals and supplements, but we grabbed a couple energy bars and stuffed them in our pockets as well. *Hey, near starving makes you hoard.* We had been fed plenty of good food, fish, and local vegetables that looked like broccoli and squash and so much fresh fruit that I had never had before. I squeezed and sucked down a gel pack. It was good, but I'd rather have a banana or a fresh ripe mango or orange! I was going to miss that.

"Disconnect!" yelled Sergeant Carpenter.

"Disconnect!" we all yelled in return.

We were back in the routine. I looked around. All of us were here but Corporal Larson, well, and Lieutenant Green and Private Somersby. Larson was recovering from his replaced hand and would rejoin us in a couple days. He was ready, Carpenter said, to come back right away but had to have therapy and retrain with the prosthetic. Captain Shupin and Gunny were with us, second platoon, but Carpenter was once again our platoon leader in the absence of an officer. That meant that the two squad leaders had to step up and lead. Corporal Murray was doing great, but Lance Corporal Almond was unsure. Lance Corporal Rich in first squad was also young, who was I to say that, and was not ready to step up either. I was only a PFC but had shown I was ready for a more advanced leadership role, but rank is rank, and the Fleet Marines observed that, in theory. It was an unspoken truth that I was in command of second squad when the action started, but Almond was the de facto leader. I didn't flaunt it or, I think, want it but it was what it was.

The briefing over the Command COMM informed us that we were going to insert a kilometer away from a surface colony and tactically approach. Betty support would transfer back to our assigned squadron, the Second of the One Hundred Twentieth, 2/120, Air Wing. It was still very confusing, but each division was assigned three air wings, a massive, complex entity in itself, basically a brigade, but much more complicated because it included not only the Bettys and all their equipment and personnel but also all the ground support. I really had no idea of the actual numbers and depths to which it spanned, but it was massive. Donna had tried to break it down for me at the beach but grew tired of the relapse of overlaying assignments and berths of personnel, I'm sure much like the Fleet Marine structure was to her. At any rate, our assigned flight, usually four Bettys, was going to provide air support for us.

The colony was enclosed with a huge domed biosphere or energy field, basically a protective covering. Massive amounts of energy, from green gold, were spent in maintaining the gigantic force field that enclosed the entire colony. A satellite was kept in orbit above the surface at, I don't know, some altitude, and the "dome stations" were interspaced at regular intervals in a circular pattern around the entire colony. Several miles in radius, encompassing thousands of acres, were under the umbrella protection of the dome. It was very secure. That's what the Fleet Marines did, provided security and regular patrols. There were several of these settlements, or colonies, all laid out and constructed similarly.

First Division was primarily responsible for Mars and maintained frontier posts or bases, scattered nearby the settlements, but totally disconnected from them. It was a harsh, brutal, almost depressing, assignment. Other divisions would rotate in and relieve a company, or even a battalion, to give First Division some Earth time. Echo was going to relieve a unit that had oversight of three stations for the next two weeks. Constant patrols, security watches, and boredom were our plight for the next two weeks. This made Division Duty look like a visit to the fair.

Each station had an underground bunker that served as bunkroom, galley or small kitchen, lounge, and head. Aboveground was a small guardhouse adjacent to the Systems Control Room for the station. No one was authorized to enter the control room except those on the daily roster. The four platoons rotated from their station to patrol duty. I don't know which I liked better or worse. It was all four on, eight off. The monotony was fatiguing. I don't know how First did this every day. This was truly what used to be known as border duty, going back to the Cold War in Europe with old armored cav units.

We were essentially at the edge of the dome inside the settlement or colony. Every day there were riots and demonstrations and attacks on patrols. To attack a dome station was out of the question. That would endanger the whole settlement. Our security was focused on outside aggression, assault from the Galleens or the Mars natives themselves. I mean who would want to destroy their own home and possibly kill their family and neighbors?

Captain Shupin and Gunny Scott took up their CP in the Patrol Bunker, obviously. It was the command post overseeing the three stations. That's how it was all set up. One equivalent full-strength battalion at a time was engaged on the dome stations, and we were just one company.

I was amazed at the atmosphere inside the colony. It was very pleasant, the sun—our sun, Earth's sun—Sol, was not as bright or radiant with heat. It was odd to stand on a planet in our own solar system and look around. I remembered that cold morning on the range when I asked Sergeant Mean about our constellations and Staff Sergeant Adams gave us a short astronomy lesson. I looked up, because of the position and distances, nothing was the same, completely different constellation groups. I wondered if the Martians—that was funny to say—had their own stories and legends. Surely they did; they had to use something to try to explain their existence and place in the universe.

I looked down at the ground, the earth—really that's what it was called to us, the ground, earth, meaning exactly that, soil, dry land. Terra Firma was Earth's ground. It was boggling our knowledge was so confined to our tiny speck of all of this! Earth was the name of our planet, or Terra, which meant ground, so really I was looking at Terra Firma, dry earth. We were so self-absorbed as a planetary race for nearly all of our history, believing that God had created the entire vast universe for our own little existence. How vain could we possibly be? There were numerous races scattered throughout the universe, all in their own confines of space and knowledge. Some had intertwined and gained more overall understanding of Creation, and that's where we were right now. I don't know all the answers, though I had just as many questions, but the NNP Fleet Marines were at the forefront of gaining some valuable knowledge to the makeup of the answers.

I squatted and scooped up some dirt. The regeneration of a sustainable environment was years in the making here. Mars at one time had a bountiful amount of surface water, but it disappeared suddenly and caused catastrophic damage. The inhabitants, either then or afterward, were forced underground when the planet's atmosphere collapsed with the lack of water, oxygen, hydrogen, and other necessary life-sustaining elements.

There was a theory that stated the huge amounts of water involved with Earth's massive catastrophic Great Flood were drawn from both Mars and Earth's own moon, Luna. At one time, the planetary orbits of Mars and Earth were very close that some biblical scholars believed God used the water from these two celestial bodies in the preplanned event, giving the historical Noah the warning and means to survive the deluge from a gravity-fed universal event. What's to say a hundred other systems haven't experienced a similar occurrence?

Terra forming, the procedure of regenerating a soil to a sustainable condition, was fully underway. The atmosphere inside the dome was life sustainable; green plants, water vapor, photosynthesis, oxygen, and carbon dioxide conversion, life. It all was happening.

The colony, a small community, really, lived in constant realization that if the dome failed, all would be lost. The colonists lived under the rigors of catastrophe. Anytime they were not inside a structure, they wore a Zero Atmosphere Suit, ZAS, basically a civilian version of the HECS. There was an alarm warning system, and drills were performed monthly, for the event of a failed dome. After years of constant living under a threat of a dome biosphere collapse, the colonists became more and more complacent in their personal protection, almost to a point of laissez-faire, allowing children to play without the ZAS, working and going about personal activities as if they were on Earth. It was a tremendous stress factor.

Somehow, through natural human will and determination, the colonies had organized and become united, even though their separation on the planet was as great as from Earth itself. I couldn't help but think of myself as a red-coated British soldier and these colonists were no different than the long-ago American colonists that fought for independence. What irony. I sympathized with their grievance. They had endured separation, hardship, life-threatening conditions, and attacks from the indigenous people and from an outside civilization. This was so similar to past history that it was eerie. I wanted no part in forcing them to comply under the control of the billionaire industry. I think most of us were of the same mind-set. But that's not why we were here. Our mission was to protect the colonists from outside aggression, maintain an open trade route of free-flowing assets, and maintain order. We were the police while on patrol and the security guard while at the stations. Captain Shupin taught a refresher course on Civil Unrest and Urban Policing to each platoon as we rotated in to our first patrol duty. Gunny Scott performed frequent and surprise inspections on each guardhouse and bunker complex.

Echo was just settling into our two-week routine when Corporal Larson rejoined second platoon on the second day of our rotation assignment. You could equally say just in time or fatefully. He was just as glad to see us as we were to see him. The day went bad from there.

Chapter 15

PRESENT

This was beginning to be a regular Saturday night event at Linda's. Most of us from last week were here, plus add-ons from everywhere, Y, PNCOC, Echo, and even some First Division guys that were in town that Cummings invited. The place was packed, and when Linda saw me, she came right up to me and gave me a hug.

"You will eat for free every time you come in! And I had to almost call the SFP on a first sergeant that tried to steal your ribbon and picture over there," she said, motioning toward the table.

I quickly looked over, frightened that he took it down. He never spoke to me the rest of the week, and this morning during First Sergeant's Inspection, he barely gave me notice. It was still there, but the area around it was growing with additional pictures and medals and ribbons.

"You have a wonderful soul, Lance Corporal Smith. You were right. There is never any trouble. Marines come in all day long, some stay for several hours and stare at the wall, and some just buy a drink for that table and look at the pictures and leave."

"Thank you, Linda. That's very kind. I'll take your offer, but I'll pay for my table tab, okay?"

She looked at me and smiled. "Deal."

I stood there, my curiosity getting the better of me. "Linda, what did the first sergeant do or say? Anything?"

"It was kind of weird, you know. He walked in, still dressed in his utilities, but I recognized his rank right away. The big ones never come to town still in uniform. He glanced around, and that's when I really got kind of nervous, and he walked over to your table. He stood there and looked at the graduation picture. There were several others over there by then and a couple of other medals and such. He just stood there staring at it and then he reached up to that pretty ribbon you tacked up and started to remove it! I yelled at him, 'Hey, you can't take that! That belongs to the marine that is circled. That's his ribbon!' I was mad. No one all week has tried to steal anything, and I was not going to let him start. I told him if he didn't put it back, I would call the SFP. There were a couple of marines sitting at a table close by and they stood up and told him he needed to leave if he couldn't show proper respect. He walked out."

I almost couldn't believe it. I wanted to laugh, but I didn't know what to think about it. I was going to see him in the morning and he was going to jump all into me. That's why he hadn't said anything to me the rest of the week.

"Thank you, Linda. Good job. How's business?"

She gave me a squeeze and said, "It's dinner rush! Look at them coming in. I have to go work. Remember on the house!"

She grabbed some menus off the bar and a rag and walked to the table of guys that just entered, talking them up and patting or rubbing their shoulders, her smile as wide as her face. She was a natural-born smooch.

My guys were gathered around two tables they bumped together, and the conversation was pretty loud and obnoxious, joking, laughing, backslapping, and head rubbing. Some of these guys hadn't seen one another in some time, you could always tell. Larson was in the middle of it, talking to a couple marines I had never seen before. Who were they? Cummings was with them. *Oh, okay, First Division. Wow, how did Larson—? Never mind, dumb question.* Sergeant Carpenter walked in just then. I'd never seen him off base. He joined the table, looked at me, shot an index finger at me and a wink and smile, and joined in with Larson.

"Hey, Carpenter, is that the runt?"

I was standing across the table talking with Alvera and Maliki, who knew each other from their Y time.

"Yeah, that's him. Not as big as you thought, huh?" replied Carpenter.

"No, Custer said he was a little puke. Is he the same one that hit us this week?"

Now I knew they were talking about me and the Alpha Training Company incidents. Carpenter knew this marine. He was older, tough, and hard. A drill instructor? No, please don't let it be an Alpha Y DI.

"Hey, what's your name, little guy? Why you keep hitting Alpha First Training Battalion?"

The table broke out in laughter. Some of the marines at the other tables took notice and watched. "This the guy that hit Alpha this week? Took out an SS? Great job, man!"

Other comments could be heard between the tables and groups.

My inquisitor continued, ignoring the comments and cheers. "You know they contained and questioned an SS trainee over that, almost tore him up."

"Good thing they didn't catch us then," I said, still my mouth engaged before my brain. "That was the plan. He was on us."

"Yeah, it didn't bother you that you disrupted training? Not to mention your ambush trick several months back."

I looked at him. I couldn't read him, he was good. This was all off the reservation, no rank, but I was experienced enough to understand that of course outright disrespect would follow you back on post. This was off time, no uniforms, just guys blowing steam. He was doing the same. We were measuring each other up. I was adding it altogether. Carpenter knew him, so Drill Course or other A courses. Riot? No, that was all in-division. Had to be A and B courses. Larson knew him, so PNCOC instructor? No, they were all gone. Larson was older, been around, and was highly respected, former military. Cummings knew him. His DI, platoon sergeant, or squad leader? He mentioned Custer, so they were all old friends. Had to be Drill Course.

"Sorry, Sergeant, I didn't catch your name. Were you an Alpha DI? No disrespect."

I figured I would eat crow, be humble. The First Division guys laughed, along with Larson and Carpenter.

"That's Gunnery Sergeant, Lance Corporal. And yeah, you could say I was an Alpha DI." He broke into a smile, "Now which one of you little jokers shot up the Palace?"

Maliki and I started to laugh, and Cummings froze. The gunny looked up at him and said, "You gotta be kidding me, Cummings? That's gonna cost you. That was a down and dirty hit and just as sneaky as you are. Good execution!"

We all laughed. Then the gunny reached his hand over to me. "You are one gutsy marine, Smith. Glad to meet you. Gunny Jacoby, HQ 3/2/1, TDY."

I shook his hand. He admired me. I wonder what his TDY was.

The evening passed by, and a round and then two were ordered as well as a feast of tacos and other entrees for a number of fallen marines we knew or just learned of. Dinner was enjoyed, a couple new pictures hung. Goodbyes and good nights. The gunny and a couple others had cars and rides were arranged, so no one had to ride the bus. Carpenter had an old beat-up junker he shared with Custer that they parked off in the storage lot, hardly ever used.

The whole group walked together for a little bit until we had to split off, most of us heading back to the PNCOC barracks. Carpenter was walking and talking to Larson a few steps behind the larger pack.

"Hey, kid, let me tell you something really quick," said Carpenter.

He was the only one that called me that. It was a good night, fun times with a bunch of friends. I did miss not seeing Donna, but I could talk to her tonight when I got back to the barracks. Griffin kept his word, and right after we were dismissed this afternoon, he took me straight to the main PX and helped me pick out my own tablet. We must have shopped for an hour, looking at and comparing the various choices and finally deciding on a model that, among several features, had a Kevlar shell, an antitheft tracking mode, five-year full warranty, and lifetime GG battery. It put me back a hundred and fifty credits but was CR-approved and secure, meaning it had a nontrackable mode that I could enable and disable. If I was separated or it was stolen, I could enable its tracking from a separate system. Pretty cool. I couldn't wait to call Donna tonight and play with it.

I stepped off the pack, and Grigs pulled up, waiting for me but not intruding on Carpenter's space. "Hey, Grigsby, come over here, you'll want to hear this, too."

Grigs was well-thought-of by the entire platoon back in Echo, and Carpenter and Larson knew we were the best of friends, he held both of their respect.

I had no idea what Carpenter wanted to tell me that he couldn't have said all night, unless it was more bad news concerning my sight. Larson was just standing there, rubbing his hand. It was an absent-minded reaction. There was no reason for him to rub his hand, it wasn't there. Ghost sensation I believe they called it. There wasn't supposed to be any pain or feeling, but guys complained all the time of numbness, pain, or tingling from severed limbs. I knew Larson had experienced another LoL years earlier, his lower right leg; he was a two-time Wound Badge recipient. That was years ago, so his hand was really bothering him. He put his arm around me, pulling me in.

"Hey, kid, I just wanted to tell you. Larson too. Grigs, I don't think you know this." Carpenter waving him closer. "I, we, want to wish you." I was at a loss.

"Happy birthday, kid! Sixteen, right? Finally, old enough to join the NNP Fleet Marines. I'm off the hook. Larson will you sign his waiver so I can move on?"

He grabbed me in a headlock and playfully punched me in the arm and chest. I was dumbstruck. I had not even thought of it. What day was it?

Grigs grabbed me too, rubbing my head. "What? You didn't say anything all week! Sixteen, you got to be kidding me! He's just now legal to join up? Dude, I am not going through all that crap again with you. Sorry, Carpenter, but once was it."

Larson was still holding me. "Happy birthday, buddy. Thanks for everything." He smiled at me.

"What's the date? Is this really the twentieth?" I had no idea. It was Saturday was all I knew.

"No, it was yesterday, but hey, we're busy," Carpenter said, laughing. "Custer wanted to come, but they have Division Duty. Hey, let's go harass him at the gate!"

We had passed through unscathed. I had no idea he was working it, Sergeant of the Guard. Good for him.

"No, we better not. You know my reputation might trigger something," I said, laughing.

"Yeah, sorry there was no cake or anything." Carpenter sounded almost, guilty.

"Are you kidding? This was great. I can't believe you remembered. Thank you for this, Sergeant."

"I told you, Carpenter, unless we're in formal, Smith, and you're welcome. I hope you have a good rest of the day, night, weekend."

We all stood there a few seconds and then it was time to move on. "You talking to Donna tonight?" he asked.

"I hope so."

"Tell her, you know, hello."

That was weird, like he wanted to say something else, but didn't.

"I will." I looked at him.

Yeah, it was him. He put that together a couple weeks ago and maybe Larson too.

"We got to get this company up to strength, you two. You'll be moving on to a Third Training Battalion company or back to Bravo. Got to get us some new boots in here." Carpenter said, quickly moving on.

"Well, Gunny Scott told you to get back to Bravo yourself and run them through here," I said, referencing the conversation I overheard between Carpenter and Scott.

"What?" Larson exclaimed. "You're not leaving again, are you, Tim? Come on, man. That means they're either going to pull another E5 in here, or don't say it." He was giving Carpenter a stare down. "Man, I'm not doing it! I'm not taking a sergeant billet. You guys forced this corporal thing on me, but I'll leave. I'm serious. I'm not taking the platoon. I'm not taking three stripes, Carpenter." He was rubbing his hand.

Carpenter reached his right hand out and laid it on his old friend's missing hand. "You'll be all right, bro. You'll be fine. I'll be back in a couple of months and you won't want to give it up. Shupin put the promotion in yesterday. It's done." They both stared at each other.

"We need to shove off. Last week coming up. We gotta make sure we have our AO up." Grigs was trying to pull us out of the tension, and I made the move.

"Yeah, Donna told me to call before 2300 and we got to run. See you guys next week."

Grigs and I started a light jog up the road toward Second Training Battalion, another ten minutes away. I had no idea that Larson was about to be promoted and take the platoon, while Carpenter returned as a drill for who knows how long this time. Larson was going to be all right. He was going to be a great platoon sergeant. Grigs and I were soon headed to A Course Drill and would no doubt meet up again with Carpenter, but on the same side of the chaos. The thought of that combination gave me a sense of excitement! Maybe I really did yearn to become a drill instructor after all.

CHAPTER 16

The day we had arrived and been assigned our dome station and bunker, second platoon walked into the "Two O'clock Bunkhouse" and made ourselves at home. The interior was painted red and yellow and decorated surprisingly well. A hand-painted lettered sign above the main hatchway leading down the steps to the entryway read, "Mars Colony #3. Welcome to Bunkhouse Two O'clock, Home of First Division, Spearhead! Don't Forget to Water the Plants, Feed the Roaches, and Take the Trash with You. Courtesy 111. Enjoy Your Stay!" We all laughed and thought a little humor had to make this place more livable.

Not too long after the day Corporal Larson returned, most of second platoon were topside in the actual guardhouse, talking with him, when a scream came from below, in the bunker.

"Get it off me! Get it off me!"

We started for the steps to descend into the bunker.

Zik! Zik! Zik!

There was total pandemonium, cursing, furniture and equipment being tossed around recklessly, another short burst of GLAR. *Zik! Zik! Zik!* Several marines were down there. I wasn't sure if the outer door had been breached or what sort of assault was being levied against us, but it was aggressive to say the least! Jackson and Hackney were taking the brunt of it.

COMM traffic was immediate from the CP. "What's your status, Second?"

Gunny was demanding as calmly as he could with an unprecedented attack on a dome station seemingly underway.

"He's over here, over here! Get him, Jackson! Kill him! Kill him!"

Zik! Zik! Zik!

"Situation unknown. We have assault on bunker with unknown force inside, Gunny!" responded Carpenter as he hastily rushed the steps, quickly calling his marines into a reaction force.

We all had our weapons but were mostly only dressed in UA or utilities except for those actually on duty.

Carpenter, Larson, and Murray were in the front. "First squad, cover! Building assault! Go!"

We charged down, weapons in up and ready position into the unknown.

"Aargh! Get him off me! Don't shoot! Don't shoot! He's getting in my helmet! Aargh!"

The screams were bloodcurdling, Jackson screaming. The agony of battle and the fear of pain and mental as well as physical torment were all too real. I was pressing down the steps, ready to get in the fight and assist my brothers.

"What the heck is that? Back! Back! Back! It's running this way!" Murray yelled, tripping on the steps and falling into Larson who then became unbalanced.

"Get off me! Stop pushing!" yelled Larson.

Zik! Zik! Zik!

"There's another one! Right there! Right there! It's on you, Jackson. Pull it off, Hackney!" Carpenter was yelling.

I scrambled down the steps and into the bunker. The place was destroyed, laser burns and streaks on the deck and walls. Hackney was in his shorts and was alternately waving his arms over and around his head and kicking his feet. Jackson was running away from us toward the head and then turned back to us, total fear and horror in his eyes and face, wearing only his skivvies, HECS helmet, and his GLAR in his hands. A huge, ugly, I don't know what it was. It was…it… It was terrifying! An alien creature was crawling over his bare shoulder and onto the back of Jackson's helmet, blackish rusty brown, almost a foot long and four inches wide with huge antennae and black eyes. It flew off and toward us, its wings flittering and making a swish, clicking noise.

We scattered, bumping into each other and yelling, complete hysteria in our voices.

"It's huge!"

"What is it?"

"Move! Move! Move! Get out of my way!"

"Kill it! Kill it! Kill it!"

"Where's the other one? There! There! There! It's under the table!"

Zik! Zik! Zik!

It was total chaos! There were now at least three of these huge beasts flying, fluttering around the room, darting in and out of the marines, occasional GLAR fire streaking in the small confines of the bunker, shouts and orders and screams intermingled with curses and, finally, laughter.

"Status, Carpenter! What's happening? I have fourth platoon en route to assist. Do you know the size of assaulting force?" demanded Gunny Scott, his voice full of barely controlled emotion, realizing that his men were under a full-blown attack and he had received no sitrep since the initial COMM.

"All clear! All clear! Situation under control Echo Two. Pull reaction force back into patrol. Repeat, all clear," responded Carpenter, breathing heavily.

I was standing with my back to a wall, scanning my front for any movement. The smoldering whitish gray goo with pieces of exoskeletal wing and abdomen shell splattered a few feet away from me making me want to bolt outside. The guys were slowly reorganizing and stepping cautiously amidst the jumble of bedding, mattresses, furniture, equipment, and clothing scattered throughout the entire room. Jackson had been thrown to the deck viciously by Larson, while Carpenter grasped and flung the beast off his head onto the deck, where several of us fired at it at the same time, exploding it across the room. I had seen at least two, so there was another one, maybe even two more, somewhere.

"Everyone, calm down. Where's the other one?" asked Carpenter, trying to regain composure and a sense of leadership.

"I saw three. There were three! Where'd they go?" said Murray, standing on the first step, looking like he wanted to run up into the guardhouse.

I looked around, Private Hackney was still feverishly waving his hands and arms, excitedly turning in circles, gripped in utter panic. Jackson was balled up on the deck, his helmet still on, visor down, and his arms wrapped around the bottom edge, evidently in an attempt to secure his head.

"There it is! Over by Hackney. Look out, Steve! It's by your foot!" yelled Woolsey. They were best friends since the beginning of Y.

It was, had to be, one of, if not, the strangest things I'd ever seen. But Hackney looked like he flew as he turned and ran past all of us and up the stairs. I swear, his feet never touched the deck!

He was screaming as loud as he could, "It was on my face! It was on my face!"

The alien was now in a free fire zone and the GLAR intensity was massive, with nearly the full platoon firing into that section of the bunker.

"Cease-fire! Cease-fire! Check your weapons. Perform complete room search for possible…" Carpenter was saying.

"There! There! It's on the wall by the head!" called out Luke, and a flurry of green laser energy streaks exploded on the wall along with the hideous creature.

"Cease-fire! Cease-fire!" Carpenter continued, as he himself finally lowered his own weapon.

"Sergeant Carpenter, what is happening? What is status of assault? I have reinforcements with me and we are ETA your position in thirty seconds. Advise our deployment!" Gunny Scott was both excited and furious with the lack of intel on the situation.

"Echo Two, situation contained. Please redeploy patrol on assigned duty. Two o'clock station is under control. Repeat dome station is secure."

Carpenter was now starting to regain composure and logical thinking. I remained with my back firmly pressed against the wall, constantly moving my head in all directions, including above and to my sides along the wall. What the heck were these things?

Moon, Carlson, and Clark were up in the guardhouse on duty with all this going on, maintaining security on the position. Moon called down, "Sergeant Carpenter, looks like Gunny's QRF, (Quick Reaction Force), is tactically advancing our main hatch."

"Copy, Moon. Corporal Murray, return to your post." Murray was the SOG on watch. Murray didn't hesitate, leaping up the steps and into the guardhouse.

The room was a shamble. There were laser burn marks on every wall as well as the deck and ceiling. Nasty intestinal creature goo was splattered everywhere, on everything, uniforms, equipment, furniture, and even on us.

"Spread out. Search everything. Jackson, where'd they come from?" Carpenter finally regaining control and a sense of order and direction.

Jackson was still in a ball, but managed to talk. "I don't know, Sergeant. Hackney started screaming and I looked over and that thing was on his face. He flung it off and it ran toward me! They were everywhere!"

"How many did you see? Two, three?"

We were all walking in a line now, kicking sheets, throwing CPs against the wall, our GLARs in the ready position.

"There were, I don't know, Sergeant, three, four, five. One flew straight at me, and I don't know. I shot at it." Jackson was standing up now, his visor up, trying to fall in line with the rest of us.

"I need it straight now, Jackson. How many did you really see?" Carpenter was in a mixed state of caution and humor.

"Sergeant Carpenter, I am breaching the hatchway, all clear?"

Gunny Scott inquired testily. I could almost sense his anger and frustration at his lack of updated intel involving the incident.

"Negative, Gunny. Do not, repeat, do not open hatchway. We have unknown life-form contained in bunker and do not want it to escape. Copy?"

Carpenter was now on very thin ice with the gunnery sergeant. Firstly, he informed Gunny that the situation was clear and then he admitted that there was still a possible threat. I was correct, in the next instant Gunny responded furiously.

"Carpenter, I will… What is your situation? Is the dome in danger?"

"The dome is in no harm, Two. I swear. We have an, as yet, unidentified life form contained in the bunker. Three have been destroyed and an active search for any remaining beings is underway. I do not want them to escape, if possible. We have no casualties, and dome security surveillance is unaffected. Will advise when all clear. QRF can be redirected to assigned duty, Two. We have situation under control."

"Negative, Sergeant. If you had the situation under control, I could enter and make that assessment myself. Standing by, out."

The pressure was extreme for Carpenter. "Larson, you ever see anything like this?" he asked, cautiously continuing his search pattern.

"Negative. This thing isn't a natural species. Must have been brought in by First Division. We can't let it out. No telling how it might affect the ecosystem."

Larson was beside me, Grigs to his right, and Almond between me and Carpenter. We walked in a line, systematically now, picking up everything and shaking it, upturning CPs, boxes, containers, everything, and anything that these things could hide in. Bunks were overturned, mattresses flipped and tossed, cabinets swept out, and drawers turned upside down. I laughed to myself. *So there is an actual purpose for tossing a bay!*

The overhead lights were stared at and Carpenter said, "Cover me," as he pulled a chair to step up on and reached up to unfasten the cover.

My heart was racing. Nothing. He stepped down, I'm sure relieved as all of us. There was a giant planter box along the back wall with several flowering plants and a running vine on a trellis. It added some natural beauty to the bunker, was out of the way, and was thought of as a little fresh oxygen source. We had paid it little attention other than to ensure that it was watered every day. We now noticed that the soil was disturbed and broken, revealing three large cavities. Those dagone First Division guys had played a massive practical joke on us that could have gotten somebody seriously injured or killed.

"Gunny, advise all other platoons to search for planters in the bunkers and to perform detailed inspection of the soil. Be on alert for possible large insect, most probably a giant cockroach of some sort." Carpenter took no chance and aimed his GLAR and opened up, destroying the planter.

Our quarters were a wreck for a practical joke. I couldn't help but laugh, then others joined me, and the cursing and joking began.

"Those guys are toast! We got to get them back!"

"Holy moly! Are you serious! They set us up?"

"Man, I swear I hope I never run into a Spearhead. I'll knock him out!"

"This was wrong! Did you see Hackney? That guy's a mess!"

"Look at Jackson!"

We all laughed. He was standing there, in his skivvies, helmet, GLAR in his hands, skinny white legs, barefoot. He was furious.

"Are you yanking my chain? That was a giant cockroach! Those pukes are going to pay!" Everyone was laughing.

"Gunny, come in. Watch your step. All secure," said Carpenter, barely controlling his composure, looking around at the bunker.

When Gunny stepped in, I saw his face change from concern to anger to confusion to amusement back to a normal gunny authority disposition. "Report, Sergeant Carpenter. What exactly happened here?"

He gazed around the bunker, taking in the burns, the destruction, the complete chaos, the marines in front of him in various stages of dress, all armed, all ready to defend their position. That was the most observable item of note. His marines had fought off an attack of unknown origin and were at the instant ready to fight.

"Gunnery Sergeant, it seems that several large, giant, insect casings were planted to activate at some time and cause confusion and disorientation. My platoon reacted in a controlled and effective manner in eliminating an unknown possible threat in short order. Several marines are to be commended on their quick and stalwart action in protecting each other and alerting the remaining members of the platoon. Gunny."

I could barely contain my laughter. I swear, if Hackney and Jackson walked out of this with an Achievement Medal, I was going to die!

Gunny just looked around, shaking his head. "How big were they?"

"Huge!" answered Jackson, almost unconsciously. He had managed to remove his helmet before Gunny entered and appeared to be like the rest of us, normal.

"Get this bunker squared away, Sergeant. Submit those names on your AAR. Carry on."

He turned back toward the door and then suddenly jumped back and shouted, pointing, "There's one!"

All of us instinctively came to ready arms at the same time jumping back, a single *Zik!* slicing through the room at the wall. Gunny Scott continued out the door, laughing hysterically.

All bunkers, including the CP, were found to contain giant roach casings that were planned to activate within days. For some reason, ours had hatched out early, preventing a full-blown company crisis. I have no doubt that the other platoons would have reacted in a similar response as we had. The things were terrifyingly ugly and large and could bite. Orders came down from Captain Shupin to remove, after complete inspection, all planters and to restore to condition the stations, except for painting and other burn markings, to their original condition.

It took second platoon several hours to thoroughly clean and dispose of the insect remains, wash and repack our equipment, and return to a ready status. Shupin also made it clear that any plans of individual retribution or schemes would be dealt with harshly and immediately. All ideas were to be submitted through the proper chain of command and a companywide plan would be enacted. Yeah! Payback! Every marine in Echo thought of a way to get back. I thought extremely hard.

Chapter 16

PRESENT

I woke up, took a shower, and got dressed to eat breakfast. I was unsure of the proper uniform I was expected to wear, and First Sergeant French hadn't said. It was a dilemma. I was going to the Senior NCO Chow Hall for some meeting, so did that mean I needed to wear my Alphas? If I was supposed to wear my Alphas, surely he would have said so, right? Unless it was just so simply obvious, it was not even needed to be stated. What was this all about? Should I just wear my duty uniform, utilities? No way I was showing up there in civvies. Who was going to be there? He said that there were people there that wanted to help. Help with what? Staff Sergeant Ginny might be there, but he was too far to run and go ask, plus he might not be awake. I looked around, guys were starting to wake up, and the barracks would be alive in a few minutes with the new week moving in shortly. Grigs looked at me with a puzzled, sleepy expression.

"What are you doing up and dressed already for? You didn't go run, did you?"

He stretched and made an attempt to get up and then just laid his head back on the pillow. "I guess I need to get up for chow. I'll shower later." He started a second attempt to get up.

"It's okay. I have to run, well, go somewhere right after anyway, I'll catch up with you before lunch."

"What? Where you going? Is Donna here?" he asked getting up for real now.

"No, she's not here. Hey, that reminds me, when was the last time you talked to Kate?"

He looked down at the deck. I couldn't remember him saying anything about her, now that I thought about it, since we left the hospital. "I don't know. She doesn't want to talk to me. What was I thinking? That was just a fun one-time thing."

I looked at my friend, maybe my best friend, and gave him a strong, sudden, jolting push on the shoulder, sending him backward in a violent manner.

"Are you out of your mind? Grigs, Kate likes you man. Are you crazy? Here." I turned and opened my wall locker and grabbed my tablet and tossed it on his bunk. He had sat back up, staring at me in bewilderment. "You still have her number, right? Call her. Call her now. Wake her up or leave a message if she's on duty. For crying out loud, it's been over two weeks."

"Did Donna say something to you?" He picked up the tablet and fiddled with it. Of course, he could figure it out. He was a techno nut. "What's your password?" He was already on the main screen.

"No, she didn't say anything about Kate, but that doesn't mean anything. I don't have a password."

He looked at me in amazement. "Serious? Anybody could steal this, and it would be gone."

"No, I have a tracking device thing."

"It's off, dude, and you haven't set it up yet. I thought Griffin helped you out?"

"He did. We didn't set anything up but my account and Donna's number, there." I was pointing. "See it?"

"Oh, for crying out loud! That just means that whoever steals it gets Donna as an extra. I'll set everything up for you, but I just might lock you out of it." He was laughing.

"Whatever. Call Kate, invite her to breakfast, or go for a walk, something. Do it! I'll let you use the tablet whenever to talk to her."

"Yeah, well I was going to say that to you after I lock you out of this thing. Where you going?"

"I got something I was asked to do, and I have to go alone." Grigs looked at me quizzingly.

"You going to church? Nothing to be scared about. I'll go with you." He stood up.

"No-ooh! I'm not scared to go to church. What's wrong with you? I got to go. Messing around with you has made me late. Call Kate. When I get back, I'm checking the call log thing to see."

He laughed. "You don't know where to look for that. You have no clue."

I headed for the stairs, shaking my head. I had decided on utilities. I had to hurry and grab a quick bite and a cup of coffee and run to Seventh Division Boulevard. I think senior chow was behind Division HQ.

I woofed down a quick plate of SOS and a glass of milk. I let my cup of coffee cool for a minute and then enjoyed it a few sips at a time, leaning back in the chair. Second Battalion Chow Hall was pretty lax on Sunday mornings. It was actually the most relaxing time I'd ever experienced in chow. There were no First Week PNCOC students, graduations were all yesterday, classes didn't start up again until after lunch. The only marines that officially ate here were the ANCOC, SS, Drill, Recruiters, and PNCOC course attendees and instructors. Of course, there were the permanent party and other sneak-ins. It was a good chow hall, relatively quiet, small, private. Sunday morning was so sparse, you could practically order anything you wanted, as long as you didn't mind waiting a few minutes. The SOS gravy was on the line, but you could order pancakes or waffles, crepes, an omelet, or hash browns. I even watched a guy last Sunday have steak and eggs!

A couple NCOs walked in and looked at me and made their order to the cook that had sat down at a table and was reading the paper. While their eggs were on the griddle, they walked over to the beverage area and poured coffee and headed toward me.

One of them asked, "Mind if we join you, Lance Corporal?"

"Sure, but I gotta run in a minute, just so you don't think I'm ditching you."

The one marine laughed. I noticed he was a staff sergeant, the other was too. "That's good." They sat down.

The cook yelled over, "Hey, I don't have grits. I can make some up if you want to wait a couple of minutes?"

"That's okay, Wright. Just put my eggs to the side and cover some potatoes with gravy," said the one that had talked to me.

"Yeah, it's good. You got biscuits?" asked the other one.

"Sure, how many you want?" replied the cook. We were just a row from the steam line.

"Just split one, SOS on top, some bacon."

"You guys are ready."

The cook returned to his paper, his routine barely interrupted, two plates steaming on the counter. The nontalker went to fetch them. He returned while the first staff sergeant was sipping on his coffee, sitting back in his chair, watching me as if we were old friends.

"Are you two instructors or in a course?" I asked, trying to get a feel of what was going on.

They knew who I was. That wasn't being conceited or self-gratifying. There was no reason for two staff sergeants to sit and talk with a lance corporal they didn't know on a Sunday morning.

"We're in the recruiting course. Pretty laid-back class, I got to say, the easiest two weeks I've ever had." He laughed, a wide smile crossing his face.

"Yeah? Hadn't thought about that course much. How many of you are there?"

"This course only rotates once a month, no revolving, like all the other ones. We got, what, Jones? Eighteen, twenty?" he asked his partner.

"No, only seventeen of us. It's nice, nothing like Drill or ANCOC or even SS. Gonna be a sweet four-week tour."

"I hear you, man. But I can't wait to get back to Dog Company." He cut his eggs and took a bite. "Perfect eggs, Master Sergeant. When you transferring to First Training?"

"Ha! Not on your wildest dream, skinny six." Skinny six is a nondisrespectful reference to an E6, the single rocker even though denoting the first level of a senior NCO, some may say midgrade, appeared to be "skinny" compared to two or three rocker stripes. "Give up this? I put myself on the duty roster on purpose Sunday mornings to have some peace and quiet."

The three of us laughed. Yeah, he had a point. He was a master sergeant? An E8? You got to be kidding me! Pulling Sunday chow duty in his own chow hall? I'm sure he had a couple privates in the dish room. He was only working the line, enjoying the leisure walk-ins.

"The scuttlebutt is you were recruited at fifteen, that so?" I was done with my coffee, but I didn't mind the question, or the company, though I had to go soon.

"Master Sergeant," I asked, hoping Sunday morning leisure time included me, "is the senior chow hall behind Seventh HQ?"

If it was, I could stay a few minutes more, have another cup, and network some.

Master Sergeant Wright didn't even look up, skip a beat, or lose his place. "Yep, Lance Corporal. Take you about, hmmm, five-minute jog. Just go around the left side, along the Colonel's Walk. Senior chow will be the first building behind it, big sign. You could've had breakfast there. Thanks for shining a little light on my day." The two staff sergeants laughed.

"Let me grab another cup. Be right back, Staff Sergeant." I thought if I was going to push it, I might as well go all the way.

"Fill one of those pitchers and take it back to the table with you, Lance Corporal. Save everybody from getting up," the Master Sergeant replied.

Hmmm, I'd never used one of them before—a whole pitcher of coffee on the table. Wow! Grigs was going to love this.

I returned to the table and sat down, refilling my cup and then passing the pitcher off to Staff Sergeant Jones.

"That's right, Staff Sergeant. No secret now, I guess. Why? Is that the directive now for recruiting?"

He looked at me. He had finished his breakfast while I was up getting the pitcher.

"My name is Lloyd. But no, actually, we have been specifically ordered to not recruit under the age requirement. That's, well, you'll know soon enough. Where are we? Phase Five? Last phase will spell it out. That comes out today? I'll be, no, wait." He looked puzzled. "Next week. Can't tell you. Anyway, you were a one-shot wonder, a chance in a million. No offense, Lance Corporal. You are the top of your league, a fine marine. I'd be glad to serve with you any day, but no, sixteen is firm for recruiters."

We all sat there, drinking coffee, looking over our raised cups, sizing up the other. He meant no harm. I think he was genuine, searching for a key, a secret formula to pull in some qualified and highly motivated recruits. That was his mission now, fill the 120 spots each week.

"You looking for the golden egg, Staff Sergeant Lloyd? I don't know what to tell you. I don't know what they have taught you or what the statistics or method you will employ. I wanted, needed, a change, a chance, a way out, a way up. I don't think the military, the Fleet Marines, let alone the Space Fleet, is remotely seen in a positive light by the general populace, at least not where I came from. The people are misinformed, poorly educated on who we are, what we do. That may be part of the government and billionaire scheme, to undermine a strong military arm, but I don't know. Why did you join? How did you get here?"

He laughed. "I was drafted, to be honest, but I fell in love. Like you said, it was not what I was led to believe. I guess it took me the first three years to figure it out, that I liked it, I fit in." He gazed in thought.

"See, what? How many you got in now, Staff Sergeant Lloyd, six, seven years? Drill, an armful of CRs and hashes, SS tour, your next stripe coming soon. Go out and sell that. Corporal—Sergeant Carpenter, I can't even remember what ribbons he had on his Alphas, but that's not what pulled me in anyway. It was… Who was he? You got, I'm sure, more than he did. Educate your potential enlistees. Most of them are kids, right? What's your target? Seventeen? Eighteen? This is way better than out there." I jerked my head.

Staff Sergeant Jones was just looking at me. Master Sergeant Wright spoke up, "That, Lance Corporal, was the best recruitment spiel I've ever heard. But if you're going to get there on time, you need to move."

I was taken aback at the master sergeant's comment and the fact that he had been listening, but senior NCOs did seem to take in a lot of information.

"That was very insightful and helpful, Lance Corporal Smith. Thank you. Good luck. You're going to make a great NCO," Staff Sergeant Lloyd said.

I got up. "It was nice to talk with the both of you, but excuse me. I have to run."

I took my tray and slid it down the window and walked out and then started a light jog toward Division HQ. It was warming up, almost June, spring full on. This week was going to be warm, I was already sweating. I followed the master sergeant's directions and came to the chow hall, not overly impressive, just another building, nothing special. A large sign denoted the "Senior NCO Chow Hall" and I skipped up the five or six steps to the small porch that led to the main door. Here goes.

CHAPTER 17

We were all on edge from the practical joke the day before, so it was no surprise that the next night when an attack alarm sounded, most everyone was awake anyway. I was in the middle of my guard shift up top, it was a little after 0100. The initial reports came in that Dome Station Nine was taking fire, to its rear. This meant rebels were attacking the guardhouse from inside the colony. That hadn't been done before. We were immediately put on alert. The first reports were confusing. First, it was reported that it was the "Nine" taking fire, and then it was reported that it was Dome Station Eight. Soon Twelve, Ten, Five, and then Three all reported incoming fire. This was now a full-blown inside attack on the perimeter guardhouses. There were four patrol platoons from the four different companies on the stations. Each patrol now reported being under fire as they had reacted and rushed to assist the stations. This was a well-thought-out and delivered assault on the Fleet Marines.

"Prepare to deploy and set up defensive perimeter around bunkers, Echo," ordered Captain Shupin.

It was the SOP. Grigs, Woolsey, Larson, and I were in the guardhouse, everyone else prepared to exit and clear the area around the bunker. Then we got hit. Multiple laser shots exploded on the hatchway and along the outer walls.

"Incoming. Incoming. Taking fire on Station Two. Single shooter, to our ten o'clock," reported Corporal Larson, calmly.

The fact that the dome was protecting the atmosphere of the colony and the progress it had made to the terra forming made it impossible for the Bettys to provide flyover security inside the dome, so their mission was outside security. We were on our own to deal with the assaults inside. Larson had Grigs maintain observation on the outer perimeter and shifted me and Woolsey to provide a covering fire directed at the shooter. We opened up and laid down a heavy suppressing fire while the remainder of the platoon rushed out of the bunker and made a quick and direct assault toward the position. The shooter faded away. Now a different one began firing at seven o'clock. This was their game plan, harassment. They weren't large enough or heavily armored to take a platoon or bunker down, but if they could deploy a couple shooters to several stations, they could disrupt our routine and keep us unbalanced. This had opened up a whole new chapter.

The night wore on, dawn edging on a calm as the shooters disappeared and the new day began, the rebels melding in with the populace. This was an age-old tactic, fighters hidden among the civilians. It was a rough night; a couple minor casualties had been reported throughout the entire perimeter units. Our own third platoon had sustained a wounded marine that had been hit in a crease in his HECS and was taken to the Echo CP. I was ordered to report ASAP and be prepared to remain at the CP.

The patrol led by Gunny Scott arrived and I departed. It was a temporary assignment, I was sure, but I felt a tinge of sadness in leaving my own platoon. Each platoon had at least one combat medic, so it was odd that I should be pulled away in this case. It turned out that there were several reasons for the CO to shift his medics, and it only became clear to me after I arrived at the CP. Now each patrol would carry a medic in addition to each platoon having one. That made sense. I was just one of five that now were stationed at the CP. The patrol that picked me up had gone to each of the Echo stations and collected them. Second platoon had already rotated to the CP for patrol a day ago. It was really about the same, a little bigger, there was a separate room that served as the Ops Room and where the CO and Gunny slept, if they ever slept.

I was assisting the treatment of the PFC that was wounded. He had suffered a deep four-inch burn across the back of his knee. It was painful, of course, and required stitches, which was above our training level. A Space Fleet corpsman was attached to another company on the perimeter, and he arrived with a small security team and assessed whether the marine should be evacuated. The corpsman set up quickly, we had already prepped the wound and closely watched as the stitches were closed up with a little stapler tool. A local anesthesia was administered, and it was decided due to the location, the stitches would probably tear, so we readied the man for a trip home. The corpsman had some surplus supplies and passed them out to us.

"Hey, Smith, right? I remember you," he said as he finally had a minute to look around. He was my field training corpsman, Space Fleet Senior Corpsman Chief Petty Officer Weaver.

"Hey, Chief Petty Officer Weaver, good to see you again." I was glad to see him. What a surprise. This was the first time a corpsman had treated anyone in Echo since I'd been here.

"Looks like you're doing okay. You medics did a good job here," he said looking around at all of us.

That made us feel good, coming from a senior corpsman in combat. He wouldn't have taken the time to say it if it weren't true.

A thought occurred to me. "Are you taking him back?"

"Affirmative. I have to instruct a section in a couple of days back at White Mountain. Why? Is he a buddy of yours?"

"No, I just, could you pass something on for me when you get there?"

My thoughts were racing. This was crazy. He was going to think I flipped my mind.

He eyed me with a quizzical expression. "What you got?"

"A note. Can you give me a minute?"

He laughed, still not sure what I was asking him. "Sure. Make it quick."

I looked around and saw an empty piece of thin sheet cardboard from a Full Meal box and pulled it out of the trash and flattened it. I took my pen and quickly wrote a short letter:

> *Dear Donna,*
> *Just a short note to say hi and to tell you we are all good, mostly, all that you know. Don't worry. Can't say much, but you probably heard. Seeing the universe, looking around for you! How is the course?*

I hope you are doing well. I miss talking to you. Got to run.
    John

    I folded it up and taped it closed with some med tape around the edges and then ripped a piece and put that over the printed writing of the Meal Box and wrote her name, "Weapons Specialist First Class Ramsey, Donna. Space Fleet Corpsman Course, White Mountain, Cali."

    I handed it to Senior Corpsman Weaver. "You got to be kidding me? Do I look like a postman?" he laughed. "Yeah, I'm going that way. Nothing intel sensitive in here?"

    "No, Senior Corpsman. I was vague on where and what. Just letting her know I'm okay, you know, because of what happened a couple days ago."

    "You were there? Sorry about that." He looked at me with respect. "Okay, let's go. Gunny Scott, your guys going to assist your man?"

    "We'll patrol out with you and just continue from there," Gunny called out. "Second shift, saddle up. Someone grab PFC Trottier's gear, three-man, rotate out."

    They departed, and I was assigned to third shift patrol, which would go out in four hours. I was up all night and all day yesterday and found an empty bunk and laid down. Everyone was beat. I guess the games would start again at dark tonight. I fell out, waking up to get ready for my patrol three hours later.

Chapter 17

PRESENT

I walked in the door and immediately saw about, over two dozen men all in civilian clothes. *Great, wrong decision.* Several had shorts on, T-shirts, or flowered-print sun shirts and a couple looked like they were going to play golf this morning. I recognized several, but most I did not know. A group of three looked at me and quietly walked out of the room through another door. I didn't even get a good look at them. Staff Sergeant Ginny was standing beside a table just to the right of the door I came through. It had two coffee urns and several trays of biscuits and a large bowl of fresh fruit. Man, I could have had breakfast here. He walked over to me, a giant smile on his face and his hand outstretched to me.

"Smith, good morning. Glad you came. Top said he had invited you. Sorry I didn't get you here myself. Next time, civvies is okay. Welcome."

Uh, this was weird. "Good morning, Staff Sergeant Ginny. What's going on?"

"Let me take you over here. Grab some coffee and a biscuit. You didn't eat already, did you?"

"Yes, Staff—" He cut me off, waving his hand.

"Ginny. It's informal in here, no rank, but be polite and respectful. If someone introduces themselves to you by rank, go with that. Otherwise whatever they tell you their name is, got it? I know, just here."

He took me by my arm and led toward the corner beside the table, to give access to the table of those that didn't want to make contact with me, I suppose.

"Go ahead, grab a cup. I know you are a coffee drinker."

I poured a cup to help relax and give me something to do.

"Listen, here's the deal. All of us in here are OL recipients. It's a special bond we have. I think you have realized it's a separate group that has earned it. Many marines have experienced wounds and LoLs and even, well, like you earned the Brotherhood and DLC and DCV. But the OL is different. There are basically three levels to a group that has been organized by those that earned the OL. All of us earned it. The first level, Lifetime, can't deny it, never lose it. The next is Inactive Lifetime, someone that has been nominated to join this organization but has not yet made the decision or is not currently participating in meetings or functions. The third is Active Lifetime. We meet here the third Sunday every month, go over some business, check up on one another, and share personal problems. Your name was thrown into the mix almost immediately. Your actions were highly commendable, under any circumstances, but your additional actions on the Xavier moon with the Candias and your initiative and leadership during the ravine proved it wasn't just a fluke. You're the real deal. Now you have the PNCOC thing, and just to push it over the top, this past week you nailed an SS candidate. You're moving up quick. I'll be honest, Smith, it's not a hundred percent, never really is. There are a few that don't like you." He paused.

I said, "Like the three that walked out when I came in?"

"Yeah, them. Those are good marines, but they just aren't sold on you yet and some others. But don't worry about that. Your nomination was tabled, waiting. Today you will, if you want to stay and observe, see what's going on a little bit. Take your time. Decide what you want to do. You don't have to make a decision right away. Think about it. Other OLs will search you out and talk with you about it, answer questions, like I'm sure you have now. Go ahead."

I looked around, and a few men were watching us, talking in small groups, giving us, me, room to talk with Ginny. "What? What is it? What do you do, just sit around and tell stories?"

Ginny laughed. "No, this isn't a war stories club. We do, we can, help out marines that are having problems, whatever. Everything stays in here. Nothing you say goes back out there unless it might endanger other marines. Not saying you do, but guys have bad dreams, can't let things go, feel responsible for things, have problems adjusting. We can get the right assistance to help that can't be arranged without certain problems at the company level. You know what I mean?" His look was unchallenging.

I looked away and quickly diverted to another subject. "You said you do other business. You're not selling stuff, are you?"

Ginny laughed. "What you mean, like food storage bowls and napkins?"

I laughed. "Yeah, that and insurance door-to-door."

He put his hand on my shoulder. "No, we aren't selling anything. We start at 0800 with an informal gathering like now. Then any minute now, we'll be called to order by the president. That's Dixon over there." He nodded. "He'll proceed with the meeting, probably announce you, nothing to get worried about, and then continue. We'll have some closed things to take care of, but that'll be at the end. You can wait in the hallway there or just leave, but some of these guys will want to say hello to you. Remember though, this all stays in here, okay? We felt that you had the bearing to accept that. You won't be asked to join today, so don't worry. Any other questions right now? We'll sit toward the back here, and you can ask me questions if something comes up, or later back at the company, but always to the side. I know you are tight with some of the guys, but you can't share this with them or anyone else, agreed?" He looked at me.

"Agreed, I got you, Ginny. I understand."

I felt, in one way, kind of honored that I was being asked and given an opportunity to join this group. I could see they were all older, mature marines. The S2 major was one of them and a couple gunnys, French and Clark. On the other hand, what the heck was this group? And what was going on?

Ginny nodded to Dixon and the president started up. "Okay, gentlemen, let's get started. I think everyone is here that is going to show up today. It's getting busy out there."

We moved to our seats and Ginny motioned me to a chair. I'd never been to a formal meeting before. This was interesting. Dixon, I have no idea who he was, began with a head count and a secretary was given the command to mark those in attendance. The call for old business was made and several items that the group had discussed previously were brought up to be discussed and either finalized or carried over. None of it made sense to me, until all of a sudden my name was mentioned in the form of a nomination vote that was going to be conducted, but a motion had been made to delay the vote until a future time after more members that were absent could have a chance to review the nominee. Huh? The nomination was tabled, and Ginny was selected to "bring me in," the same way First Sergeant French had said it last week. Dixon then called my name and asked me to stand.

"Thank you for coming, John Smith, fellow Order of Leonidas. We are glad to see you here and you are welcomed. Ginny will serve as your mentor to assist you with any questions and help in any way he can. After the meeting, please stick around if you can, as some of the members would like to talk with you, but I realize you may have prior commitments." There were a couple of quiet laughs. I sat back down with Ginny nodding to me.

New business was called for, and a marine stood up and said, "Some of you may not know, but the widow of Staff Sergeant Adams of Alpha 1/2/7 had their baby girl last week. I wanted to make sure that we had the scholarship set up, and she needs some help. It's been really hard for all the families, but she's…" He couldn't help himself, another marine stood up and put his arm around him and they sat down.

Dixon let the moment pass and then said, "Yes, it's been done. The chaplain visited her at the maternity ward too. We are going to give her everything she needs, the other families with children also, as much as we can. Thank you, Cooper, for bringing that up."

I looked at Ginny, who leaned over to me and quietly said, "We will set up a savings account for the family of the OL and help with all children until they reach sixteen."

I was shocked. How many scholarships were there? That could be a lot of credits. I had to pay to join? As if Ginny knew what I was thinking, he added, "Not what you think. Relax."

A couple other issues were brought up, though it was getting kind of boring. Dixon finally said, "All right, time for private business. Smith, if you would excuse us for a few minutes. You can wait in the hallway. Stick around if you can. If not, that's fine. I hope you attend again next month. Thank you for coming."

I got up and walked to the door, I wasn't sure if I was going to stay or not. I didn't want to be rude, but I didn't want to stick around either and find that nobody really was waiting to talk with me. I walked out. Gunnery Sergeant French followed me out, which caught me off guard.

"Hey, Smith, you got time to stick around? Really, there are some guys who want to meet you. It would be good." His expression was unchallenging, inviting.

"Yes, First Sergeant. How long?"

"We'll be done in here another ten minutes, total half hour more of your time. You can wait in the dinning hall."

"Okay."

He walked back inside. I walked down the hallway toward the main dining hall. I should have grabbed one those biscuits. A couple of old marines were sitting at a table, and one of them saw me. He smiled and waved me over. I walked up.

"Hey, Lance Corporal, passing your day visiting odd places?" I saw the stripes on his collar. He was a sergeant major.

"No, Sergeant Major. I'm waiting for someone. Sorry, I didn't mean to barge in the senior chow hall." I was at attention.

"Stand easy, Lance Corporal. Who you with?"

"Echo 2/2/7. I'm attending PNCOC right now, Sergeant Major."

He was taking me in, and his partner was doing the same, though I couldn't see his rank.

"You wander off the street or something? Don't you have duty this morning?"

Was he testing me? Surely all the NCOs, everyone had heard of the PNCOC shake-up by now. He had to be from another division, just landed for, whatever sergeant majors do, a meeting or something.

"No, Sergeant Major, not until lunch chow." I didn't think I was supposed to mention the meeting.

"Around the corner, the OLs? I guess we're waiting for the same thing then." He waved at a chair. "Join us, Lance Corporal."

I was at a total loss. What was I supposed to do? He invited me to sit, but I didn't know what for.

"I'm waiting on my… I have someone in there I have to accompany, you know. Both of us." He nodded to the other Fleet Marine with him. They didn't, on purpose, introduce themselves. I was nervous.

"Relax, I won't tear you apart. How long you been in?"

"Seven months, about, Sergeant Major." I was sweating.

"Seven months? You have lance corporal and are in PNCOC with seven months? What the—? See what I mean? This is what I'm saying." He was addressing the other marine and then back to me. "You don't have the experience to lead other marines yet, Lance Corporal. That's why we have time structure and minimums. It's not your fault. You were promoted too fast, but you don't know what you're doing yet. You haven't led marines in combat. What, you rotated a couple CRs and been in a firefight or two? This is too fast. This phase plan is going to destroy the Fleet Marines. Probably his plan."

Now I was uncomfortable and a little angry. He didn't know me. He was old school, nothing wrong with that, but he didn't want change. He had his slice of the pie. I held my tongue. This was a sergeant major. I wanted to get up, but I didn't think I could.

"May I be excused, Sergeant Major? I need to wait in the hallway."

"Did I hurt your feelings? Are you mad because I challenged your little setup? Who did you say you were waiting for, Lance Corporal?" I had gotten him agitated. I didn't want that.

"I think I should leave, Sergeant Major. I didn't mean to anger you."

"Stand fast, Lance Corporal. I'll tell you what you should think and when you will be dismissed. You are too inexperienced to realize that you have wandered into an area that even staff sergeants are uneasy in entering. You wander into a building where it clearly says on the sign out front 'Senior NCO Chow Hall' and you stand around almost as if you want to have your hands in your pockets, sucking on a straw. You are too inexperienced to realize that there are two sergeant majors having breakfast and you casually approach as if you were walking up to your sister's house. I am not your friend, Lance Corporal. I am not your squad corporal, not your platoon sergeant, nor your nice, good 'ol gunny, or friendly battalion Top. I oversee a brigade. Do you know how big that is, Lance Corporal? Do they still teach that at Six Weeks?"

He was staring at me, looking for a sign of weakness in me. I wasn't going to give him the satisfaction. He continued, "My boss is a brigadier general, and I guarantee you he expects me to pull it off every day. Twelve years is the minimum for this rank, you think you're going to get it in five? Is that your thought?"

"No, Sergeant Major. I believe you earned every one of your promotions by the book and by personal merit. I am out of my place and do not wish to agitate you further."

I wanted out of here. If he ever let me go, I was out the door. The heck with the meeting.

"Who said I'm agitated, Lance Corporal? You again don't have the experience in dealing with midgrade NCOs, so how do you expect to operate around senior NCOs? Who are you waiting on?"

What was this? "I'm waiting for the meeting to adjourn, Sergeant Major."

"That was not the question, Lance Corporal. Now you are trying my patience, because you are not listening. Who are you waiting on?"

His eyes studied my face for subconscious indicators of fear, panic, uncertainty, or hesitation. But he had agitated me.

"I am not at liberty to say, Sergeant Major."

Really? Was I? I was told specifically, instructed by Staff Sergeant Ginny, to not disclose information of what happened inside the room, and I figured that meant who was in there as well.

"Listen, you little pup, I asked you a direct question. I'm done fooling around with you. On your feet! Stand at attention."

I immediately jumped up and came to the position. I should have stayed at the barracks. I should have gone to breakfast with Grigs. I should have told Ginny and French that I had to leave. But I was not going to tell this sergeant major a thing more.

"Who are you waiting for? Why are you in this chow hall? What makes you think you belong here? How on God's favorite planet did you attain the rank of lance corporal in only seven months and why are you in my presence and not buffing the deck on the second bay of PNCOC Second Training Battalion on Sunday morning, Lance Corporal? Tell me what I want to know."

He was not yelling, but his manner was demanding of a man that had achieved the rank he had and was speaking with a nobody Fleet Marine. Yet his authority and stature were overwhelming. He was at the top of a rank structure that was centuries old. This man was demanding answers from me when he usually received them when he only initiated a query.

"Sergeant Major, I cannot tell you who I am waiting on. That is privileged information." I stood my ground. He was going to either hit me next, like First Sergeant Alfonso, or threaten to bust me down.

"Count them, Lance Corporal. Name the ranks. Go ahead. Recite the ranks for me. Do it."

"Recruit, no rank. Private E1, no stripe. Private First Class E2, single stripe. Lance Corporal E3, stripe and a rocker. Corporal E4, two stripes. Sergeant E5, three stripes. Staff Sergeant E6, three stripes and a rocker. Gunnery Sergeant E7, three stripes and two rockers. Master Sergeant E8, noncombat command rank, three stripes and three rockers. First Sergeant E8, three stripes and three rockers with a diamond in the middle. Sergeant Major E9, three stripes and three rockers with crossed swords in the middle. Command Sergeant Major E9, three stripes and three rockers with a 'C' in the 'V' of the crossed swords in the middle."

"Well, where do you and I align on that scheme of rank?"

"I am barely on it, Sergeant Major. You are nearly pegged out." It was withering.

"Who are you waiting for, Private?" There it was. He just busted me down. He had the authority, without so much as a captain's mast.

"Sergeant Major, why? Is it the refusal of answering your question or are you truly interested in who I am waiting for? Has my quick rise in rank riled you to this unwarranted fury against me? I was invited to come to the Senior NCO Chow Hall unequivocally, but I can't wait to leave, and I promise I will never return. Is that what you want? I offended you by my presence?"

"I want you to tell me what I am asking you, Private. Who are you waiting for? Shall I make it the Discipline and Retraining Platoon next? I can have the SFP here to remand you in a matter of minutes and your CO won't know where you are for a month, thinking you went AWOL or deserted."

That was all he could do. Separation from service had to be completed by an officer, battalion level. Funny all this was coming to me from PNCOC. Usually a referral to the DRP came from company level, a loss of rank, loss of pay. Battalion was involved in General Court-Martial, a sentence to jail or prison or, if warranted, separation. A sergeant major was way out of the chain of influence, not that he couldn't do it. I had heard the Discipline and Retraining Platoon was Six Weeks Week One every day. *Just tell him. It's no big deal. Staff Sergeant Ginny, Echo 2/2/7. It's just a stupid club that you aren't even a member of. Heck, in a couple minutes, he was going to be able to see who it is anyway.* That's right. He can wait another five minutes and get his answer. The S2 major was in there, First Sergeants French and Clark, who said that Colonel Thompson was in my corner. A colonel beat a sergeant major, I was sure. I didn't know poker very well, but it was like a flush to a full house, or something. Stall.

"I can't tell you that, Sergeant Major."

He was cool, not becoming unhinged or showing signs of being stressed out. He turned to the other sergeant major. "Call SFP. We are going to admit one broke-down private to the roll of the Divisional DRP for a period of thirty days for insubordination."

The other sergeant major got up and walked behind the steam line into the kitchen to find a phone, I guess.

"That's it. I'm done with you. You feel like hitting me, Private?"

Oh man, I didn't have a witness now. He could say I struck him and I was finished. I backed away a step.

"Where you going? Stand fast, Private."

I looked around, but there was no one else in the room. I took several steps away from the sergeant major. I was scared. I knew this was a bad situation. I was toast.

"Please, Sergeant Major."

"The punishment for striking a senior NCO is five years in Salt Lake, Private. You escaped that one time, but your history of lack of respect to senior NCOs can't be denied. You're done."

I stood there. I didn't owe this group anything. A sergeant major asked me a simple plain question. That's it. He outranked everyone in there that I knew, except for the major. Thompson would get me out of this. French. Clark. I sat down in a chair; my head was reeling.

"Get up! Stand at attention in front of me," demanded the sergeant major. I felt like beating the crap out of him.

I simply said, "Up yours."

Duty, honor, brotherhood was ingrained in me. I was an OL Lifetime member. I earned that. They couldn't take it away.

CHAPTER 18

Captain Shupin was done playing games. He had lost a valuable lieutenant and a new private, a good corporal had suffered a LoL, and now a veteran PFC was wounded and out of the fight. This amateur sniper action was his limit. He was about to show the rebels why he was a Fleet Marine company commander.

He had ordered all guard shifts to six hours with only two marines. A corporal was on continuous shift, sleeping up in the guardhouse. Everyone else was ordered to sleep. He then pulled all NCOs except for the corporals on continuous watch to the CP for a meeting. Additionally, he pulled Lieutenant Howard from first platoon and reassigned him permanent XO at the CP. The patrols had shifted their pattern throughout the day, gradually, in an untrackable, random, meandering walk through our zones. What it was, in truth, was a laid-out reconnaissance of the previous night's FP by the rebels. Shupin was hunting.

At dusk, all marines not on guard duty were going to exit the bunkers and move to the rebel FPs and set up for ambush. His patrols were going to exit one at a time, spaced out, and remain several hundred meters from the FPs. His plan was contingent on the rebels repeating their previous stunt and thinking the marines were locked into routine. He was on the offensive to crush them.

We had been taught, educated on the dynamics of the colony. All of the settlements were laid out pretty much the same and occupied by the original colonists of the Mars Colonist Program, MCP, and their successors, the New Colonist Mars Program, NCMP. The first ring of the settlements was only a half mile in radius or one-mile diameter, encompassing roughly 503 acres. They were not domed and contained eight rather large buildings. These buildings still exist and are the original shelters and laboratory work areas for the original colonies.

As the colony grew and prospered, a second expansion was initiated, a domed one-mile radius, or two-mile diameter with over 2,010 acres under an artificial atmosphere. This was the real start of the terra forming project, and the colony grew to over one thousand residents including families. The objective was for these colonists to continue and expand the mining for minerals, growth of research and development R&D, sustainable farming, forest regeneration, and aquaponics. Once a colony reached a certain level of sustainability and profit for the "Company," the next dome expansion would extend to a four-mile diameter, over 8,042 acres.

This last ring was cut up in twelve pie slices, or a clock, with the dome stations at the o'clock on the perimeter. The outer ring was land grant property to the colonists for personal use. It was largely unused, vacant, and unpopulated. This was the area that the rebels controlled. This was our objective.

I patrolled out with four other marines under the leadership of Corporal Eddy. I didn't know him very well, other than the incident in the Corporal's Bay. He had a good reputation and was an experienced squad leader. I was just another marine. I was the team medic. We were to head toward Bunker Three and lie in wait.

Eddy set the watch. We were in a tight circle, facing outward, three sleep, three watch, rotating throughout the night if need be. The night before, the assaults started after midnight, so we were set up by dark, 1900. Captain Shupin had six marines in the CP to react as a decoy. Basically, he had thirteen marines secreted out in front of each bunker, six from the CP patrols and the remainder from the platoon of the station. Two marines and a corporal remained in each of the guardhouses. This was not SOP and our deployment had been quick and early in the looming darkness. The trap was set. We were rested, for the most part, but we were accustomed to long hours and any rest we got was a bonus. This was a cakewalk compared to last week.

It was my sleep time. I had just passed the watch off to a PFC I hardly knew in first platoon. I was the outsider, the medic from second platoon. We were all family, just cousins.

I was dozing when Eddy quietly reported, "We got a creeper, Six. He's moving toward number three at an angle out of old quadrant three. Advise."

The outer, latest, perimeter was divided into twelve sections, and the next inner perimeter was divided into eight quadrants.

"Maintain visual. Do not make contact. We will wait for the fireworks to start and snuff all candles at once. Copy."

"Aye, Six."

"All patrols and bunkers, we have movement toward number three. Maintain visual on any contact and report. Do not initiate return fire until approved, copy?" All units responded. Yeah, Shupin wanted them all. He wanted to hit them hard.

For the next two hours, we monitored several rebel snipers slipping into their FPs from the night before. We had four confirmed rebel shooters, waiting until their assigned kickoff. Shupin advised all bunkers that if fired upon, to return fire so as not to tip off the rebels of any deviation.

We had them, four in our area. I didn't realize it, but we actually had three former SS in the company, Ginny, I knew, but LaBoye and Oliver also. All had pulled sniper tours. Shupin deployed his hunters, and they were hungry. Each had their targets in sight, waiting.

The rebels waited until 0200, a little later than last night, and Stations Nine, then Eleven, Six, and finally ours were hit. Shupin gave the command. Three rebels were instantly hit with disabling wounds, but not killed. The fourth was furiously brought down with a hail of GLAR fire. He never had a chance. The three wounded were seized, stripped, and brought to the CP for interrogation.

The rebels quickly learned of the capture and defeat of four of their faction. The attacks on the other sections ceased within the hour. A negotiation for the release of the captured snipers was initiated before sunrise by the IL. The body of the dead fourth shooter was laid out in the second quadrant, under the promise from the Fleet Marines that it could be recovered and returned to his family without impediment. His picture, prints, and DNA were recovered and stored. All intel was removed, but no excessive malice was rendered. It was not our way.

The three wounded were given aid and water and nutrient supplements. Each of the staff sergeants had hit their marks precisely for effective damage, all received a single hit to the femoral saddle, close to the main largest artery in the body. The wounds caused massive pain, huge blood loss, and near-deliberating loss of movement. They were collected without incident.

I was involved in their treatment. The other medics and I did what we could. Captain Shupin along with Lieutenant Howard and Gunny Scott interrogated them. The more severe case was prepared to be returned to the rebels. We did everything we could to stem his bleeding, but he bled out, falling into a low-blood-pressure coma and slipped away. I hated it. I had no ill feelings toward this man, he wasn't able to do us great harm. There was nothing to do for him. I tried to clamp off the artery, but it was too deep and slipped away, and I couldn't get it again. We even did blood transfusions, three marines lined up, donating their blood to save him. Two other medics and myself worked on him for two hours.

Gunny Scott pulled me away finally, sat me down, and asked me, "Have you heard the three rules, Smith?"

I looked at him, dumbfounded. I had heard lots of rules, regulations, orders, but just three?

"No, Gunny. Just three?"

"Rule one for the medic, 'Good men will die.' Rule two, 'Doc can't save them.' Rule three, 'Doc will go to the gates of hell and back to change rules one and two.' Smith, you did everything you could. All of you did. There was nothing you could have done. You got me?"

I was covered in blood, and though the sun was up for over an hour, I never noticed. I shook my head. What was going on? Why did they hate us so much? We weren't fighting them. Heck, we could destroy them. Couldn't they see that?

"I want to take him out there, for his family."

"Sure, let's clean him up first, you too. You're covered in blood, Smith." I looked down. My utilities pants and T-shirt were soaked. I had removed my HECS so I could work on him.

"Gunny?"

"Yeah, Smith."

"Is this it?"

He looked at me. "What do you mean?"

"Tell me we are right."

"Yeah, Smith, we're right. I wouldn't lie to you, son. This is an old argument. We're trying to help. You're trying to help. You'll find it. You're right." He put his hand on the back of my neck.

I trusted Gunnery Sergeant Scott. I got up and walked to my bunk, stripped my utilities off, and headed for the shower. The body of the rebel was cleaned up. I didn't know his name.

Chapter 18

PRESENT

The sergeant major stood in front of me, his hands on his waist, waiting for the SFP to arrive and haul me away. I heard someone walking up, but I was staring icily at the sergeant major, still sitting in the chair, ready to defend myself if attacked.

"Sergeant Major, what is your assessment?"

I recognized the voice, so I turned toward the speaker. I was surprised to see not only Dixon but also several others from the meeting walking into the main chow hall.

"Sir, I find that Smith exhibits deep unconditional loyalty, placing trust and honor above his own well-being and status." The sergeant major was still facing me.

"How far did you go?"

"I busted him down and sent him away on a trumped charge for five years. His reputation of having uncontrollable violence issues is not correct, sir. He showed quite a bit of restraint, well, up until he told me, 'Up yours.'"

Laughter broke out in the group behind me. I was not sure what was going on, but I was beyond angry now. Had all this been some sort of a trick? A test? I was seething; the laughter at me was only getting me hotter.

"Smith, please return to the room with us. I think you want an explanation, maybe even a minute to calm down," the man known to me as Dixon said.

I angrily stood up and glared at the group. "This was a joke, some sort of a sick way for you all to push a marine to see if he would explode?"

Staff Sergeant Ginny walked in with First Sergeant French. "I trusted you two. This is despicable."

I started to walk toward the door, nearly pushing my way past men that I had no idea what rank they were.

"Do you know what the Spartan soldier had to accomplish to earn his shield, his place in the Syssitia? At the age of seven, he was taken from his family and placed in an Agoge, a state school. He was starved, beaten, taught to fight, and steal his food. As teenagers, the ones that showed leadership were admitted to a group that acted as secret police and were responsible for murdering the 'helot,' the slave class, to keep them in check. By the age of twenty, he became a full-time soldier and moved into the barracks and had to join a Mess Club, or Syssitia.

"Loyalty to the state came before anything else, including family. He was required to marry at twenty, but before thirty, and still had to live in the barracks and sneak away at night to visit his wife. To be caught was certain punishment, yet he was encouraged to have many children. Tests of courage, bravery, honor, loyalty, strength, and fighting were all expected to be endured. No man was greater than another in the phalanx. Each Spartan protected the man to his left with his shield, his life. You have shown, proved, that not only are you brave, loyal, skilled in combat, and your brother's protector, but also you can be trusted. We want you to join us, Smith. We want you to enter the Syssitia of Leonidas—a secret group, a strong group that can serve you as much as you serve it. Come, come back to the room with us," Dixon invited.

I was still very upset, angry, and confused. I didn't want any part of this group. Their tactics were abusive. Yet I saw men I knew, had trusted, among them. How could they belong to such a club that humiliated a fellow marine? No, I wasn't interested.

I continued to the doorway, but Ginny moved to block me. "I'm sorry you had to go through that, Smith. We all did, but I want you to think about it. Take your time. Cool off. Come talk to me when you have settled down."

I could barely look at him. Staff Sergeant Ginny, I respected this marine. "Remember what I asked you inside a while ago? Keep your word."

He moved out of my way and I walked out the door. The walk back to Second Training Battalion barracks was blind, achieved by automatic memory. I was in a rage. I found myself at the bottom of the steps and didn't know how I'd gotten there. I had walked right through a PT formation of First Week PNCOC students, the instructors evidently yelling at me, but I didn't notice. I climbed the steps and entered the barracks, walking right past Corporal Griffin and up to the second bay. Without realizing, I went straight to the head and into the shower and stood there, under the water, fully clothed.

Grigsby was talking to me, but I couldn't understand what he was saying. Someone turned off the water and pulled me out into the dressing room and sat me down. I saw Alvera, Cummings, Maliki, Campbell, and Grigs. What was going on?

"You all right, man? Something happen?" asked Alvera.

"Why am I wet?" I asked, regaining some awareness.

"Get out of that wet uniform. Help him," said Campbell. "Grigs, go get a towel. We got formation in a couple of minutes. Let's get him dressed."

My uniform was pulled off me, Grigs handed me a towel, and I dried off, trying to figure out what was going on. Alvera and Maliki wrung my uniform out. My boots were soaked, nothing to help that out. I got dressed, Campbell and Grigs helping me. They didn't ask questions and I didn't say anything, except once.

"Did you call Kate?"

"Yeah, man, promise. We're going to meet next Saturday after graduation."

"Okay."

That's all I said the remainder of the day to anyone. The day was basically only a roll call formation and a review class on range safety. We were headed to the range Monday for Quals. After dinner, we had study group and I just sat, lost in thought. I went straight to bed afterward.

CHAPTER 19

Second platoon rotated to the CP twice during the next week. I felt more at home here, practically, than anywhere else I had ever bunked. I patrolled out at least twice a day, coming to know every marine in the company since I was assigned to the CP for the duration of our tour as one of the six medics. *Funny, when I thought about it, that time I had told Larson I didn't know the marines in the company like he did.* We were scheduled to leave tomorrow, cross my fingers that nothing bad happened until then. Two weeks we had been here, so that means with the week we had spent charting Butch and Sundance and the near week on Butch, we only had less than two weeks to pull for the CR. I couldn't imagine that we would go in early. Captain Shupin wanted his men to earn their CR, but it was all up to battalion anyway.

The morning before the day we were scheduled to depart, when I returned from my patrol, Senior Corpsman Weaver was waiting for me. He had dropped by to run a med check on Echo, you know, if everyone was showering, eating, or treating their feet.

"I don't want you to get in the mind-set that this is going to become a regular routine, PFC Smith, but I have a letter for you, and Captain Shupin has informed me that Echo is pulling out tomorrow. I'm scheduled back at White Mountain next week for another course. If you want to send a reply, pass it to me on your way out of the colony tomorrow."

He handed me an envelope that felt pretty thick and walked out of the CP, joining his security team to continue their rounds.

I couldn't believe it! Wow, a letter from Donna! I had no duty or responsibilities. All the guys were sleeping or playing cards and chess or eating or talking. I walked to the small area we called the galley. A pot of coffee was always on and a pot of stew or soup or something. I ladled some rice soup into my cook pot and returned to my bunk. I dropped my GLAR on the bunk, pulled my HECS off, kicked off my boots, and stripped down to my UA shorts—I had cut them off at the knees—and a T-shirt. I sat down, tasting the soup. *Uh, okay, needed salt.* I set the pot on the deck. The cockroach thing was way over now. I opened the letter and two small pictures, photos, dropped out. Oh man, my mind was racing. That's what she looked like. My mind had to remember—recall—every second I was with her, a mental image, a movie. The mind wanders, loses some quality, skewing the image over time. The first photo was obviously her Space Fleet basic training grad pic. She was in her Dress Blues, a white shirt with a high collar, with a silly-looking black string tie in a bow; her coat was a dark blue, almost black, with a double row of buttons down the front, almost looking sharp. Her hair was short, as I've always seen it, the cowlick hidden under a goofy-looking white and matching dark blue pillbox hat with a short visor. She was tanned, a great big smile, obviously very proud or happy. The left sleeve somewhat facing out revealing a golden diagonal half-stripe or slash midway between the shoulder and elbow. Was this the first stripe that they got when completing training? The E1, Third Class Fleetman. There was a little cannon emblem under the apex of the half-stripe, Gunner rating. She also wore a little medal on her left above her…on the left side of… She had a medal over there. I smiled, recalling our first meeting. I turned the picture over and she had written a short description. "*I can see you laughing. Yes, I earned it! Gunner Third Class.*" I laughed. I turned it back over and stared at it a few seconds more.

I looked at the second picture. This was more recent, she was older-looking, more like I know her now. I looked back at the first one. Yes, definitely younger, just a girl. Wow, she had really grown up. I studied the second picture. She was standing inside a Betty. It had to be hot, she was in SF utility pants and a tan T-shirt loosely tucked in, darkened with sweat. She was holding a large, what appeared to be, very heavy spring. Her face was dirty and grease-streaked, her hands filthy. Her smile was as big as ever, the cowlick spreading her short black hair up like the wind was blowing. This was the girl I knew. I closed my eyes and felt, tasted, her kiss. I turned it over and read her note. *"Recoil spring for the cannon, about forty-five pounds! Death Valley, Crew Training Range. Right before I rated up to Gunner First Class!"*

I unfolded her letter; it was four pages. What could she have so much to say? I noticed the paper and envelope were very similar to her calling card, gold border, her name printed at the top in a fancy cursive.

> *Dearest John*
> *I was so surprised and excited to receive your letter today, but really, you couldn't have picked the worse person to send it through! How do you know Senior Chief Weaver? He is the hardest, rudest, instructor at White Mountain!*

I had to laugh. I could see that. Was he promoted? I thought he was a chief petty officer.

> *We were in the middle of Underfire Triage. And I had, I know boring for you, but I was dragging a classmate and thought I couldn't go any further. And he, the senior chief, yells at me and says, "This marine expects a corpsman to be able to pull his buddy to safety." And he drops this piece of cardboard on the ground and says, "All the way to here, Ramsey." I had a weird feeling and I was able to drag my patient the rest of the way! I looked down at the paper and it was for me! I didn't know what it was, but I opened it and read your note and I was so happy to know you were safe. It was such a surprise. I was so happy to hear from you, John. I miss you and think about you all the time.*
> *I really hope all the guys are okay. Please say hello to each of them for me, Carpenter, Larson, Lieutenant Green, Moon, Jackson, Grigs, Carlson,*

> *and Luke. I know there are others in your platoon, but I don't know them as well, though still say hi.*
>
> *Larson was so funny that day I met him the first time, remember? When we were heading to the beach? He teased me about being the "other" girl! What a clown. I bet he sweeps the girls off their feet.*

The letter just kept going, replaying her day, week. For a few minutes, I was with her, listening to her talk, rambling on about whatever, enjoying her company, back at the beach, watching her read or cook. I read the last page.

> *I really hope you can come to my graduation. It's still three weeks away, on a Saturday. Please, please come! If you can, I know you may still be out. I understand. But I want to see you again. I can't wait. Oh! Guess what? The senior chief pulled me out of dinner line earlier today and said that he was returning to where you were at the end of the week and if I wanted to send a letter back, he would take it! What? Seriously, this is the hardest instructor we have. I couldn't believe it.*
>
> *Stay safe, John. I love you. I really do.*
>
> *XXOOXX*
Donna

I reread the letter twice and was staring at the pictures. I had to write her back. What could I tell her? I looked up and around the room. Everyone was the same; we were only patrolling. The rebels had hit us again a third time the next night, just Echo this time, with what I'm sure they thought was a hard and concentrated effort, but Captain Shupin had anticipated that. The ambushes were set out as before, the staff sergeants deployed only after contact was made. Shupin didn't hold back this time, treating them to a full Fleet Marine company onslaught. The rebel casualties were incredible. We left them where they fell to be collected in the morning by the colonists. There hadn't been an assault on our positions since. I couldn't tell her any of that. Maybe I could tell her about the giant roaches? No, that might gross her out.

Larson was talking with Carpenter, Gunny, the XO, and Shupin in the Ops Room. He had been acting strange since he rejoined us, after his injury, but today he was anxious or something. Gunny came out of the room and looked around. "Grigsby, Moon, Smith, Rich, saddle up. Patrol gear, ready in five, long hump."

What? I just got in. This was a strange team anyway, all heavy hitters. Larson came out and started getting ready. Okay, so he was taking us out, but where? I topped my reservoir and a bottle and grabbed a couple energy bars and a gel. I slipped my Med-Vest over my head. Should I mix the bottle? I folded the letter back into the envelope and held it in my hand, contemplating whether to shove it inside my HECS or leave it in my CP hanging on my bunk. I quickly shoved it in the inside of the HECS. We were ready, no briefing, intel, ETA, RPs, or contingency plan. This was weird. Where were we going? We headed toward the hatchway and Larson suddenly turned and quickly went back to his CP and dug around and then rejoined us.

"Let's go. Rich, take point. Grigs, sweep, diamond." Out we went.

Diamond is just a basic offensive patrol formation, Rich at the point, Moon and I on the other corners, Grigs at the tail, and Larson in the middle.

"Take us straight up to the second ring, Rich. We'll catch the perimeter trail and head to Station Four's trail."

"Copy," replied Rich.

It was just another patrol to him, and it didn't bother him that we were headed out of our section.

Every marine had something, some little quirk or habit or hobby or whatever. Some guys collected rocks, small ones, or leaves, or old pieces of money. Some guys wrote or sketched or even painted. I read and tried to figure things out. Our CPs were private, especially on a CR, and no one questioned what another guy might be carrying all over the universe. Larson, it was funny, carried a little, I mean a small eight-inch or so, fuzzy light brownish-orange stuffed bear. He kept it in a plastic bag so it wouldn't get wet or dirty. I don't know how long he had been carrying this bear around, but it had to be for a long time because it was not new anymore. She had a little straw hat and a little flower print dress and a little basket in her paw. It had to be a her, with the dress. Anyway, it was no big deal. I'd seen it in his wall locker before and asked him about it. "Oh, that's CP Bear," he said. That's what he had turned back for to get out of his CP. He stuffed CP Bear into his HECS as we walked into the midmorning toward the center of Mars Colony Three.

I turned my focus back to my assigned section and watched for the slightest movement or out-of-the-ordinary objects. Daylight hours had been relatively safe for patrols, the colonists busy with their work or small farm plots. We were just another patrol from the out-of-the-ordinary section that had hit back hard. No one wanted to bother us, especially during the day. I hoped.

As we walked, I started noticing Larson behaving oddly, stepping out of his pattern and stooping down, as if looking for tracks or something. He would wander close to me or back toward Moon, all the while keeping the formation on line. Then I noticed he was collecting things, a twig or branch of a cotton plant that he broke off as we passed a field of it and then wild flowers or plants. We had been instructed not to disturb the colonist's crops, as much as possible. He started talking, randomly, not patrol-related, telling us about the early colony history, structure, and makeup.

"The Colony First Phase was just the innermost ring, about 502 acres. It was only a mile wide. No dome, so no atmosphere. The colonists were housed in four long dormitories, and there were four additional buildings for the labs and dining hall. Mining operation was the main focus, but aquaponics, animal farming, and crops sciences were also initiated. The true first colonists were the construction and security teams. A timeline, deadline really, was given to have the second ring dome stations up in three years. Of course, that's about the time the Martians hit, supported and equipped by the Galleens."

We walked on, listening. Some of this we knew already, but a lot was new information and it was interesting, Larson spoke very offhand, casually. This wasn't a class.

"By the time the colony reached a population of eight hundred, which was hard to maintain with the attacks and other hardships, the first dome was operational and terra forming became a high priority. The colony had to become self-sufficient, raise their own food, and produce their clothing and other necessities. Rotational crops such as potatoes, lettuce, broccoli, squash, cotton, flax, berries, and others were planted and harvested. Sheep, angora rabbits, chickens, dairy goats, honeybees, and of course fish were raised. Forestry was next along with orchards and vineyards. Everything was genetically altered for rapid and full potential. The soil was disked, pulverized and plowed, and given fertilizers and other nutrients. Water was processed through chemical bonding creating little molecular gel droplets, and the ground received its first drink in thousands of years."

We had reached the second ring and were continuing along the trail toward Station Four, the time passing quickly. The information was intriguing, but our attention never wavered from our scanning. A couple times Rich stopped us when seeing a colonist working in a field. Larson continued after each potential threat was evaluated and dismissed.

"Each colonist was entitled to his or her own piece of titled property, to be utilized however they wished. They had to have been on planet for three years, be sixteen, or married. And when the third ring was up and secure, the present-day guardhouses, that ring would be divided into the now twelve sections. The original contract stated four acres were to be deeded, but the Investor Companies rewrote the contract agreements and changed it to only two acres and it was land granted, meaning ownership could be revoked. That was probably the real start to the revolts. The sections were subdivided into squares or rectangles as much as possible, due to the curve of the perimeter, in two-acre plots. Instead of spreading out and utilizing all the sections and giving space, the land grants were all clustered in four sections, two, five, eight, and eleven. The other sections were plowed and terra formed as before and then just left fallow."

Larson stopped and looked around. "This is the boundary of Guardhouse Three. We're headed into Section Four. Advise First Division we are inside their AO."

"Copy, Patrol Two. Proceed," replied Gunny, who was no doubt listening in the entire time as well.

"Anyway," Larson kept walking and talking. "Colonists would refer to 'going to the country' when they were off and head to their little piece of land to try to make a home."

He looked around and gave a small laugh. "Yeah, they planted fruit trees and kept bees and planted gardens. Tried to act like they were back on Earth, lords of their own estates."

We eventually came to a new section that was remarkably different than the last two we had traveled. I had patrolled Section Two and I could see that it had been cultivated, like this one.

"Take the guardhouse trail, Rich. About a kilometer, you'll come to a cross trail."

"Affirmative, Corporal." Rich was finally realizing this was not an ordinary patrol. Larson was very familiar with the history here.

"Families were started from the beginning, and the quest to get more land in the family was a major objective. But it was hard. It took time. You had to be sixteen or married, with three years on planet to own a plot. The colony was barely ten years old."

We turned, and Larson had stopped picking flowers. He had a good size handful, a pretty collection from what I could see, plus that branch of cotton. He was more aware now of where we were walking, stopping and looking around, as if getting his bearings, like someone who was familiar with, but hadn't visited in a long time and the surroundings had changed. We turned again, we were getting close to the perimeter of the dome. I could see a guardhouse a ways off diagonally to our right. He stopped and bent down, digging into the soil and rolling the dirt in his gloved fingers. He set the bundle of flowers down and pulled off his gloves, again scooping up the dirt and then smelling it. His hand waved across the wild grasses, he stood and picked up the flowers, leaving his gloves, absentmindedly. I stooped down and grabbed them, as we followed him as he walked.

"There were guilds, specialty groups, clubs, you might say societal levels. Animal and crop science, textile and manufacturing, medical, science, mining, construction…food and nutrition science." He had paused with that group. "The Agriculture Guild made incredible advances in the soil productivity. Huge amounts of earthworms and beneficial insects were raised but limited to the common use, colony property sections. The Foods and Nutrition Guild produced materials for organic composting that were unbelievable."

There was a small igloo-looking object raised up from the ground in front of us. It was made of polymers, resins, or something similar. Larson walked around it and we came to an open doorway that led down into it. He started in.

"Wait, Larson!" I called out, afraid he wasn't altogether thinking. What was he doing?

He disappeared inside, and we followed. "Moon, stay out here," I said.

"Copy that. What's going on?" he asked. I shrugged my shoulders.

It was a small room, a cabin without the logs and in a circle. There was a little hole where a chimney once was, now lying on the floor. A bedframe, a little sink and counter, and a chifforobe were the only items. We looked around. It was so small that no one was hiding in here. Larson slowly passed his hand in the closet, though nothing was there, but he acted like he was touching something. He turned and walked back outside, we were right with him.

"There is a fruit tree grove over there, a hybrid of an apple and a pear, named prapple. Go see if there is any fruit-bearing, Grigs."

Grigs looked at me, he and Rich walked over. We could see a cluster of dwarf trees. Larson walked closer to the perimeter, toward a bramble of brush and vines. He walked straight in, pushing through and then kneeling and pulling and tugging at the vines and bushes with his bare hands.

He laughed. "It worked! I'll be. It worked."

Moon and I moved closer. Larson was kneeling in a slightly depressed pond covered with vegetation debris on the surface of the now disturbed muddy water. Years of leaves and dead branches and decayed berries—the vines and bramble were blackberries and strawberries—had created a messy pool.

"Larson, get out of that. Come on, man. What is this place?"

He stood up and pushed his way to the edge of the pond that was facing the outside of the perimeter and cleared away an area of grass and twigs and dead sticks. He knelt down and removed his helmet, pulling his mask and goggles down.

"It's me, Rebecca. I'm sorry I've been gone for so long. It's beautiful, isn't it? You said it would work. I brought you these, your favorites." He laid the bundle of flowers on the ground along with the branch whose bolls had recently broken open with enormous pure white cotton.

We were speechless, staring. Who was he talking to? Larson lived here? Grigs and Rich walked up quietly watching what was happening.

Larson scooted over just a little bit. "Hello, Savannah Jane, my beautiful girl. I have missed you so much. I brought you the bear I promised you. I call her CP Bear, but you can name her whatever you want. She's yours. Here, let me take her out the bag. Don't worry, she's okay."

He laid the little bear near the flowers to the side, just far enough where a child would be from her mother. *Oh man!* No, this was not happening. This was Larson's…

I pulled back, touching Moon who was lost watching. We all stepped back, moving toward the little house. We gave him some time with his family. He talked and knelt on the ground for half an hour, occasionally touching the ground or the flowers, picking some berries, and placing them in a pile.

After a while, he stood up and looked around, saw us, and walked over.

"She was a cook and I was a farmer. We had different plots. She was over in Two, and I was over that way." He waved back the way we came. "We got married and I was able to make a trade so that we could join our plots. This was not seen as a good area, but we worked hard. She snuck out gallons of compost and I stole a pound of worm casing and eggs." He started walking back up the way we came in.

"Two acres, from there"—he pointed—"to there, along the perimeter was not good property and we were two acres deep, from up there." He pointed the direction we were headed. "Three acres that way is the dome station. No one wanted to be that close. The man that owned that piece on the other side was not interested in the land, so effectively we had four secluded acres. We could develop it without attention. So we did."

He stopped and looked around and back to the pond and his wife and daughter.

"She said that the energy field would create and condense water vapor, and I told her that it wouldn't, but we dry irrigated that area and lined the pond with resin. It fell away from the perimeter, so the idea was that the water would collect. We mixed the compost and worms and planted the berries. She baked little pies and took them to the marines stationed at Guardhouse Five over there. She became friends with them. They watched over our farm when we were gone. She was so happy when she got pregnant. We would have a family."

He stopped talking, just walked on.

"She died in labor. Our little girl was so beautiful, she never saw her. Well, not here. Savannah Jane died a day later. I couldn't stay here without them. A young captain who really took to Rebecca came by as I was digging. He had missed her and was concerned about the baby. He sent two of his corporals to get me later that night and they smuggled me back to Earth. That was over ten years ago. I've never pulled this colony. This was the first time I've been back."

He stopped now and dropped to the ground. "I didn't know that I would miss it so much. I should have stayed with them."

Moon and Grigs picked him up under the arms and he stood up. I wasn't sure what to say, to say anything. "We wouldn't have met you, Larson, and that would have been a huge loss to all of us. I'm sure Rebecca would have wanted you to be happy and live the life you have."

"Thank you for coming with me. Let's get back."

The patrol back was uneventful, he was an excellent tour guide, pointing out things to us, explaining the crops and the inability to conduct free trade with the other colonies. The Companies didn't want that, this was how they controlled the colonists. That was another part of the fight. I was learning a lot.

When we got back, no one said anything, routine as usual. I rotated into another patrol that evening and Echo departed without incident the next morning, our relief asking what happened in Station Two. Captain Shupin replied that there was a ghost and weapons would randomly go off by themselves, but there was no mention of the roaches. We all laughed to ourselves, and the legend of the haunted bunker was born.

That same night before we departed, as I was leaving on my last patrol, I pulled Donna's letter out and handed it to Larson.

"I want you to read it, as if it was to you, from—" I pointed my head. I didn't want to say Rebecca's name in here.

Larson looked at me with surprise. "I don't need to do that, buddy, but thank you." I pressed the envelope into his hands.

"Okay, just hold on to it for me then, until I get back."

I walked away. Later, when I returned from the patrol, he was awake. He passed it back.

"I wrote your letter, fair is fair. Give this to Weaver in the morning." He handed me a sealed envelope addressed to Donna. "That was nice of you, Smith. It helped."

Six hours later, Echo was on Bettys headed back toward the Centauri system. Bad memories had to be dealt with.

Chapter 19

PRESENT

The third week of PNCOC was uneventful other than I barely qualified on the range with my GLAR. I only scored a dozen hits on the one-hundred-meter target in all four firing positions, killed the twenty-five-meter, and scored enough points on the fifty to have an all-around passing average. The incident in the shower passed, no one pressing me, and I kept the secret. Tuesday was spent in Self-Defense review along with our final PT test. Everyone passed that with no problem; even Simon had recovered and knocked out a hundred-percent score. Wednesday after morning PT, we loaded up on Bettys and flew back to Cali for the day. *Man, that was great.* It was summer now, and the water was beautiful. Pool work first then the ocean, it was nice to be back for a brief visit.

Thursday, we had classes on paperwork completion, regulations, new boot introduction to the platoon, payroll Q&A, proper uniform regulations, proper awards placement and recognition, and rank identification in the Space Fleet (we should already be aware of Fleet Marine rank, but just in case somebody slipped through, we covered that too).

Senior Training Instructor Gunnery Sergeant Chavez basically taught Third Week, and this was our real first contact with him other than morning PT. First Sergeant French was more active with First Week, and the staff sergeants handled their platoons primarily Second Week, except for the Nav check out on Wednesdays.

Gunny Chavez was the real deal, hard to the bone and expected us to behave like seasoned corporals even though most of us were barely lance corporals. Staff Sergeants Patte and Tzenski had started to treat us better, as co-NCOs, toward the end of the second week, even joking some, but not Gunnery Sergeant Chavez. All the classes Thursday were geared as if we were orienting a new boot into our squad. Chavez would role-play, the only time he placed himself below us, and would ask the dumbest questions—I mean, moronic-level stupidity—but we had better know the answer. After lunch chow, he reentered the classroom for the Dress Alpha, Rank ID, and Awards session. He wore his, I guess his, Alphas but his ribbons, medals, and awards were all messed up and his uniform was untidy and unregulation beyond hope. He stood there in the front of the classroom and called us one at a time to point out and fix one item. It was the only time he laughed all week, mocking us at the end, betting us a hundred push-ups if we found everything. We lost, since he was wearing a Space Fleet trouser belt dress buckle, SF to FM initials barely noticeable.

Friday, we called drill, reviewed Ceremony and Formations, went for fresh haircuts, and generally had an easy day. I remembered Corporal Larson the first time I saw him after he had completed PNCOC, with his brand-new, one-day old haircut, high and tight!

There was no final exam, so Friday night study group for us was Alpha preparation. Just like that night three weeks ago when I met those two other marines, we were walking on the clouds. Most of us were going straight to Drill Course on the third deck, some just going back to their units or to their new units in the Twelfth.

We were still sitting in the chow hall, no hurry now. It was around 1730. Cummings, Campbell, Maliki, Grigs, Simon, Alvera, and I were at our table. First Sergeant French walked up to the table, waving his hand down signally for us to not get up. He was making his way around to all the Third Week class, briefly talking and congratulating us. I hadn't had any contact with him the entire week. I was calmed down now, just feeling a little betrayed.

"Good job this week, Marines. Going to be happy to see all you in the NCO corps. Lance Corporals Grigsby, Maliki, and Smith, your immediate orders have been changed. Grigsby, you will report to Combat Medic B Course Sunday morning. Maliki and Smith, you have a meeting at 1800 at Seventh Division HQ with an officer from Fleet Marine Command. Just ask the CQ where to go. You better get moving."

I sat there stunned. I mean I hadn't thought much about becoming a drill instructor until the phase thing came out, and after I had decided to do it, it grew on me. This was a disappointment. Was this some sort of retribution from the secret society, teaching me to respect my superiors? French was looking at me, Maliki had already stood up and was walking toward the tray window.

First Sergeant French said in a loud and commanding tone, "The proper response is, 'Aye-aye, First Sergeant!' and to carry on with the orders that the Fleet Marine Command and unit structure have deemed necessary and beneficial to the overall mission. So why are you still sitting on your butt, Lance Corporal?"

"Aye-aye, First Sergeant!"

I popped up, embarrassed, and hastily walked to deposit my tray and join up with Maliki.

French called after me, "Lance Corporal Smith, stand fast."

I was away from the table midway to the window, no one nearby. He joined me, speaking a little more privately.

"I shouldn't have to explain myself, but I don't want you to think the wrong thing and to go into that meeting with the wrong attitude. This has nothing to do with Sunday, nothing at all. You have to believe that. You're finally going to get your long answer, Lance Corporal." He was not angry or talking down to me.

"Which answer is that, First Sergeant?"

"You're meeting with Colonel Thompson. Your purpose to him will become clear to you tonight. Good luck." I could tell he meant it.

"Thank you, First Sergeant." I started to turn away.

"Smith," he spoke with the same gentle tone he had with me on the steps when he invited me to the meeting. "When you finally pin those two stripes on, call me Top. You've earned it."

I turned back to face him. "Could I start tonight?"

He smiled. "Sure, Lance Corporal."

"Thank you, Top."

He laughed and turned back to finish his walk-around. That cleared that air.

Now, what did Colonel Thompson want?

CHAPTER 20

Our return to the Centauri system was uneasy for each marine in Echo Company. The overpowering emotion of guilt and sympathy to those who disappeared in the ravine and our inability to do anything to save them were not to go away the rest of our lives. The company inserted on a distant ancient land plateau, thousands of miles away from the mine site on Butch, and began a systematic patrol pattern.

We all anticipated, with dread, the fierce windstorms that would create hours of seclusion and uneasiness. There were no storms. The day was long, bright, and hot. The ground was baked hard and void of the sand that we had associated with Butch or even the terra-formed rich dark-red soil of Mars Colony Three. Heat shimmers waved and danced like a low-lying morning fog of the forests of Fraser.

A detailed exploration of the planet was being conducted, broken up into massive grids, patrolled by foot, and supported by Bettys. It was planned to take over a year involving numerous individual units. Toward late afternoon, Echo loaded back onto the Bettys and departed our site survey area.

The ramp dropped after nearly two hours of planetary flight or so, and we looked out to a vastly different environment than we had just left. The sky was darkening, and the wind was picking up in intensity, the sand dancing in swirling dust devils. My heart and soul dropped. We were back.

Orders were given to quickly off-load and form up in a company formation. This was it. This was the ravine. But it was different. There were several buildings, the ones we had observed being assembled before we left weeks ago now replaced with more permanent and secure structures. I looked around; this was completely transformed, it was an operational frontier post now.

Gunny Scott called Echo to attention and ordered, "Platoons, report!"

This was like a regular, normal formation.

Captain Shupin then addressed the company, "Fleet Marines of Echo, our assignment is to continue mapping and surveying the surface of this planet until we are relieved at the conclusion of our CR. I know each of you has questions that may not ever be answered."

The wind was really picking up. This was the beginning of the evening storm. The Bettys had departed to wherever they went when they left us.

The CO continued, "I want to welcome you to Camp Green, named in honor of our own First Lieutenant Green, Second Platoon, Echo Company 2/2/7."

I guess they had promoted him posthumously. He was not eligible for promotion to first lieutenant for another year.

"The ravine behind you has been excavated and stabilized. The remains of most of the marines who perished have been recovered. In honor of the men of Alpha Company 1/2/7, it has been named 'Alpha's Ravine' and a monument has been erected."

He continued for a few more minutes, the storm intensifying until we had to be dismissed and find our bunk assignments.

I stood, like most of the guys around me, gazing at the interior of the large hex dome bay that was our billets for the next two weeks or so. *Wow, what a stark contrast to both what we just walked out of and the Mars guardhouse bunkers.* This was well-lit, bright, and almost cheerful. Double bunks were lined up on facing sides of the structure, reminiscent of our barracks back home. There was another company of marines already bunked but leaving plenty of room for us and our gear, maybe even another whole company. The deck was smooth, bright white as the sand outside, was it? Sand melted into glass? The NCOs had been separated and had their own quarters, so nothing but lance corporals and below were bunked in here. We found our assigned bunks, grouped together by platoons, a note card on the foot of the bunks denoting company and platoon. This was nothing I had ever seen before.

Lance Corporal Rich said, "Yep, frontier post, always nice. Remember that one, Almond, we pulled on Luna? That was sweet."

Almond and Rich of course went through the Y together, while the remainder of the old platoon other than Larson and Murray had been lost before my group and I joined in. And now we had Clark and his group. The other platoons were talking among themselves, the older, more experienced vets commenting on their experiences with frontier posts as well. We settled in; there were no foot or wall lockers, our CPs and GLARs hanging off the end of the bunk frames.

One of the marines from the other company walked up and started talking to no one in particular. "Welcome to Camp Green, the pit of the universe, named after some bone LT that got himself swallowed up in that giant hole out front."

The entire company rushed him at the same time, and it was all that the more level-headed and experienced marines could do to pull the two companies apart! The NCOs had been alerted almost immediately, and a general riot ensued for several minutes, marines from two different companies fighting to defend their honor or the memory of a respected officer.

"Stand down! Stand down! Echo Company, stand down!" yelled Captain Shupin. Gunny Scott was in the middle of the fray, along with his senior NCOs, pulling men apart.

"Stand down, Hotel! Stand down!" yelled the other CO.

It was mayhem. Over four weeks of near continuous strain on Echo, mental anguish, erupted to a flashpoint. Finally, the NCOs and officers had managed to break up the brawl. Marines were bloodied, faces showing welts and bruises, uniforms and T-shirts and UA ripped. No one was seriously injured, and no self-defense or debilitating force was used, complete self-restraint to that end. It was just fighting. The two groups were separated, vaguely, the two company commanders and other NCOs in the middle, arms outstretched, attempting to quell and determine the cause of the mass physical contact.

I noticed that the COs both were down to T-shirts, having evidently started to relax prior to the fight. That was when I noticed Captain Shupin sporting a bloodied lip! Good for him! He had gotten into the fray too! I hope that whoever struck him was unknown. My jaw hurt, and I had been dropped to the deck with a blow that knocked the breath out of me. But I had scored a couple hits for the memory of Lieutenant Green too, my knuckles hurt and were cut a little, bloodied.

"Stand down, Gunnery Sergeant Scott! What in the name of sweet mother of little green apples happened here?"

"Staff Sergeant Dempsey! You better have an explanation of this mess, pronto!" yelled the CO of Hotel Company, of as yet known division.

Marines from both sides of the narrow demilitarized zone began yelling and pointing hands across the very narrow distance. The NCOs and company officers squeezed nearly to the point of being in contact with both factions. Abruptly another skirmish broke out, the two walls collapsing in total bedlam as before. Now the officers were in full contact as well as their NCOs. It was a full-on "caged match out."

Once again, the officers and senior NCOs managed to separate and regain order. This time the two companies were ordered to the opposite ends of the barracks, the NCOs and junior officers standing in a "no-man's-land" between the two.

Now I could see that all officers and NCOs were showing signs of physical contact, ripped blouses, T-shirts, or UA, swollen lips and eyes, bloodied faces, or knuckles. Honor. Pride. Esprit de corps!

"The next marine that moves forward will be brought before a full court-martial and God Himself have pity on your soul! Don't you move, not one inch! Gunnery Sergeant, give me a report! I want it yesterday!"

"Aye-aye, sir!" Gunny Scott nearly ran toward us followed by his entire corps of NCOs, and several lance corporals were pulled out of the gaggle and quickly interrogated. The same was happening across the DMZ of the chaotic single-deck barracks with the other company.

"Report Gunnery Sergeant Scott, I want to have an answer to this total reprehensible action that my company has involved itself in. Now, Gunny." He was hot.

Gunny Scott didn't even wait to arrive at a position of Post or in front of the CO; he made his report, or evaluation, of the initial findings of his investigation.

"Captain Shupin, it seems that the fight was started by a wayward derogative comment by a member of Hotel Company toward the demise of Lieutenant Green, sir."

The CO of Hotel was also receiving his report from his acting company sergeant, Staff Sergeant Dempsey. "Sir, the members of Echo Company attacked a member of Hotel, enforce, after a comment was made. The members of Hotel were defending their own. No prior knowledge of said Lieutenant Green was known to belong to Echo, sir. The marines of Hotel 2/3/5 wish to pay their sincere condolences to the memory and honor of Lieutenant Green, sir."

There, it was settled, a truce, a parley set out between two experienced and veteran NCOs. I'm sure Staff Sergeant Dempsey, hearing the report of Gunny Scott with the details from Echo, combined with his own quick inquiry, made the correlation and on the cuff offered face-saving to his own men while at the same time making an apology for the offhand comment. It was good enough, we were all Fleet Marines, and the fight was just about honor and pride and the remembrance of a hero.

There was some murmuring among our group. "Captain Shupin, sir," Scott broke the momentary silence and, I'm sure, the deliberations of the two commanding officers in how to proceed. "Sir, Echo wishes to offer a hand in friendship and forgiveness, a show of brotherhood toward Hotel."

Shupin spoke quietly to his coequal, a treaty of terms, I would surmise, a deal of forgiveness for strikes against officers and senior NCOs.

"I swear as loud and long as the universe, if a single man, either company, engages in physical contact, you will regret you were born. Am I clear?"

The entirety of the barracks snapped to attention and bellowed out, "Aye-aye, sir!"

"Carry on."

The two officers did a perfunctory salute to each other and the opposing companies cautiously approached the center, meeting and clasping shoulders, slapping one another on the back, laughing, becoming friends. Hotel 2/3/5 became our best friends for the next week, Mad Dog, Fifth Division.

Every evening when each of us returned, we would greet one another with our division motto, "Come and Take Them!" and "Loyalty to the End!" We mixed and ate chow together, played cards and chess, and even hit the new company that arrived prior to Fifth's departure, ganging up on them and making them recite the inscription on the obelisk before being allowed to settle in. That became the tradition for Camp Green and the initiation for every new company that arrived for their tour; they had to recite the poem.

The first morning after breakfast chow, right after the night storm faded away, before we loaded the Bettys to continue our daylong mapping and survey of the planet, Captain Shupin marched us to the mammoth black opal obelisk that had been erected in front of the vast ravine that every marine in Echo had in some way experienced. The sides of the ravine had been reinforced, the edges and steep cascading sand stabilized. The recovery and search for each and every Fleet Marine that had been lost in the ravine had been extensive. Of the fifty-three confirmed Fleet Marines of Alpha 1/2/7 that entered the ravine, all but three marines were recovered. Lieutenant Green and PFC Somersby were also not recovered, making a total of five Fleet Marines unaccounted for. Their status was and remains MIA/POW to this day. The names are recorded on the obelisk, in order by rank, and therefore Lieutenant Green is listed second, under Captain Stransky, also listed as MIA/POW. PFC Somersby was near the bottom, the lone Echo 2/2/7 listed besides Lieutenant Green. The ravine has become known formally as Alpha's Ravine and the obelisk a badge of honor to pull duty and visit.

A poem, an old poem from an earlier unreasoned charge, was inscribed on the opposite side of the list of names, the alternate sides were inscribed in an unknown text. It intrigued me to know what it said or what language it was. I stood gazing up at the beautiful, magnificent huge stone. It stood over ten feet high, solid black opal, a gem that was more precious than diamonds, yet this was solid and huge. The inscriptions were shining in a bright light, as if lit from inside, but weren't. The top glowed, as if it were acting as a lighthouse. The whole thing was incredible. I walked around it, amazed and awed. I read the names, each one, trying to record them in my memory, realizing that I couldn't. I walked around to the opposite side of the names and read the poem inscription,

The Charge of the Light Brigade
by Lord Alfred Tennyson

Half a league, half a league,
Half a league onward,
All in the valley of Death
Rode the six hundred.
"Forward, the Light Brigade!
Charge for the guns" he said:
Into the valley of Death
Rode the six hundred.

"Forward, the Light Brigade!"
Was there a man dismay'd?
Not tho' the soldier knew
Some one had blunder'd:
Theirs not to make reply,
Theirs not to reason why,
Theirs but to do and die:
Into the valley of Death
Rode the six hundred.

Cannon to right of them,
Cannon to left of them,
Cannon in front of them
Volley'd and thunder'd;
Storm'd at with shot and shell,
Boldly they rode and well,

G. VAN WALLACE

Into the jaws of Death,
Into the mouth of Hell
Rode the six hundred.

Flash'd all their sabres bare,
Flash'd as they turn'd in air
Sabring the gunners there,
Charging an army, while
All the world wonder'd:
Plunged in the battery-smoke
Right thro' the line they broke;
Cossack and Russian
Reel'd from the sabre-stroke,
Shatter'd and sunder'd.
Then they rode back, but not
Not the six hundred.

Cannon to right of them,
Cannon to left of them,
Cannon behind them
Volley'd and thunder'd;
Storm'd at with shot and shell,
While horse and hero fell,
They that had fought so well
Came thro' the jaws of Death,
Back from the mouth of Hell,
All that was left of them,
Left of six hundred.

When can their glory fade?
O the wild charge they made!
All the world wonder'd.
Honor the charge they made!
Honor the Light Brigade,
Noble six hundred!

I had to know where this was from and why it was penned. Surely this Lord Tennyson had witnessed as bold and heroic charge as the fateful marines of Alpha 1/2/7. What did the other sides of the obelisk read? I had to know. There were several men standing with me that I thought might know. Grigsby had gone to college before he was drafted. Larson was very well educated and wise. Carpenter was smart and well-read. Gunny Scott was wise and well learned. I didn't know Lieutenant Howard, but he was college educated. Staff Sergeant Ginny, who I knew somewhat, was of course very smart. Staff Sergeants Oliver and LaBoye, I didn't know.

I walked up beside Captain Shupin. "Sir, excuse me. What does that say?"

I motioned toward the panel to the immediate right of the names of the marines of Alpha. Gunny Scott was, of course, right beside him, GLAR always at the ready. He was amused by my boldness.

"It's the same as the preceding panel, Smith, the list of names, the same as the opposite panel, the poem." He was looking at the unreadable panel, as if reading the names.

"What does it say, sir? What language is that?" I asked, not sure I heard him correctly.

He turned to look at me and then looked around, as if checking to make sure no one else, except the gunny, who was right beside him, could hear. "It's the universal language, Smith."

I stared at him. We were the only three within conversational hearing. "Sir?" I asked.

"The language of God, Smith. Hebrew," he said, continuing to look at me. "The poem is from the Crimean War of 1853. Research it on your own. Get back to me on your results. You're dismissed."

Which was another way of saying, "Go away. I'm done with you now."

Chapter 20

PRESENT

I caught up to Maliki, who was waiting for me just outside the chow hall. He shook his head and gave a short chuckle. "Smith, man, you are a magnet for anything that can happen. Did French nail you again for your slow reaction to the change of orders? Any idea what this about?"

"Yeah, he told—"

"Hey, Maliki, Smith! Wait up!"

We both turned around and saw two more guys from our class exiting the chow hall and running toward us and then a third and a fourth stepping out the door. I looked at Maliki, the four others were all scattered from other divisions, but not in our regular group. We all knew each other; you couldn't help but get to know one another, just not closely.

"What's this about?" asked the marine who hailed us to wait. His name was Stevenson, from Fifth Division.

"Yeah. I was starting to look forward to another three weeks of chaos and screaming instructors," added a marine who wasn't much older than seventeen, the youngest in the class next to me. He was from Second Division, Akito.

They all were looking at me.

"Come on, Smith, everyone knows you have a rapport with the first sergeant. What did he tell you?" asked Stevenson.

I liked him, but I didn't talk to him much. He ran with his own group of guys, mostly all Fifth. There were six of us now and we stood looking at the door to see if anyone else was coming.

"That looks like it. What's going on?" Maliki was laughing, looking at me.

"Well, I guess you'll find out in a minute," I said, trying to figure out whether to mention Colonel Thompson's name or not. "What did French tell you guys?"

I started walking toward Seventh Division HQ, and everyone fell in an automatic file to my left. Habit. I laughed. "Come on, cluster up. I'm not marching you guys!" We all laughed, and they grouped up around me, Maliki right beside me.

"French said we were meeting an officer from Fleet Marine Command," I said.

"Yeah, we know that. He told us that when he broke the news about our order change," said Akito. "What did he say to you in the middle of the chow hall?"

"We're meeting with a colonel." I wasn't sure if I was supposed to say this, so I hesitated.

"All right, what about? If they were going to transfer us to the Twelfth, they don't need a colonel to tell us," laughed another marine.

"We're meeting a Colonel Thompson…"

Every marine stopped cold and starred at me. I had walked on another step or two and realized I was alone. I turned and looked at them. "What? You all know him?"

"You're kidding me? All of you know him?" asked Maliki, looking around.

"This was supposed to be hush-hush. This is," Akito was talking. "I'm going to go out on a limb here guys. Don't leave me hanging out to dry, but what do you guys know about Sparta?"

"Oh man, really? This is what this is about? The uh," Stevenson was unsure of whether to say it, "the Spartan…"

"Okay, clam up. Not here, bury it, right now," I said.

I was looking around to see if anyone was nearby, watching us or listening. "I think we all are on the same sheet. Let's get going. If this is it, we'll know soon enough."

We walked on, in silence, the six of us lost in our own thoughts, our own flashbacks of a meeting with a very secretive colonel. Without looking at the others, I started analyzing each one as much as I knew. Maliki and I were from Seventh, and he was one Y class ahead of me. Stevenson was the most senior of us, having completed four CRs, and was getting his stripes tomorrow. He was from the Fifth. Akito was Second Division and had missed his third CR by a week. Tough break. The other two, I think, were from First but I didn't know them that well. All of us were young, no one much older than eighteen, all volunteers, and each of us had prepared mentally to proceed onward to Drill Course after PNCOC.

I don't think anyone else had been to Seventh Division HQ before. I mean, okay, obviously the others hadn't, but Maliki was starting to act excited.

"Smith, I've never been here before. You?" he asked, stopping at the sidewalk in front of the beautiful building.

I didn't want to sound like I was bored, I wasn't, this place sent goose bumps over my skin. It was magnificent.

"Twice, it's amazing inside. I haven't been past the foyer though." They stared at me, each one.

"Lead the way, man."

"No, I can't. There's a CQ inside. It'll be a staff sergeant in Alphas, cut to the bone, ready to tear us to pieces if we don't have our A-game on. We're about to graduate from PNCOC and are reporting to meet with a Fleet Marine general officer, by the book. Stevenson, you're senior, aren't you?" Of course I knew he was, we all knew where we fell in line.

"Yeah, okay. What is it, Smith? Like reporting a detail?" he asked. I know he knew his stuff, but it never hurts to check the reference material.

"That's right. March us in. Report the detail. State your name and your business. The CQ will have a daily list. He shouldn't mess with us too much, send us to where we need to go. Good luck." I grinned, glad I wasn't in charge.

"Great. Detail, fall in." Stevenson, like all of us, was top-notch.

That was the other thing I put together—these were all good marines in their individual groups, squared away, motivated, and smart. Each of them had taken some part in the brawl with the cadre and had to endure a week back in their units of ridicule and blame prior to restarting the course. None of them had uttered a single negative comment to me for my part in the entire episode.

We marched in and came to attention in front of the CQ desk. I had given Stevenson a quick layout of the foyer, and he put us at parade rest while he reported to the Duty CQ. Just like my two previous visits, the staff sergeant who was on duty was about as tight and cut and squared away as any drill instructor on the quad for graduation. Stevenson was flawless, and the staff sergeant looked him over a good count of ten. He checked his list and in a bold voice that resembled Gunnery Sergeant Bryant on my first morning meeting him demanded the names of the marines in the detail.

Stevenson recited the names, rank, and division of each man under his charge. Wow, I had forgotten to think of that. I would have sunk us for sure. Stevenson was given the directions to the meeting room, the Brigade Ready Room inside the doorway—left down the corridor, up the steps to the third deck, to the right, second doorway on the left of the corridor. We were ordered not to deviate or explore, and if we needed to use the head, there was one immediately facing the stairs on the upper deck. Then we should enter the room and wait for further instructions and to remember to check out when departing or there would be a price to pay when we were found.

We marched inside the doorway and into the corridor. *Unbelievable.* It was almost 1800 and the hallway was bustling with senior NCOs and midgrade officers; a hurried, almost frantic, pace was evident. The corridor was lined with small offices and opened doors, everyone in Alphas. I felt totally out of place. No one gave us a second glance, as if a detail of Fleet Marine lance corporals was an everyday occurrence. I guess it was, but it was the presence of so many officers to me that was the oddity. We found our way with no problem, walking into the room within two minutes of our quest, finding several other marines already sitting or standing, quietly talking with one another. The room all jumped up and came to attention when we entered, and then they all relaxed, several exclaiming,

"Man, I can't take this much longer."

Or, "Holy moly, come on! Give us a little warning next time."

And, "Phew! How many of you guys?"

There were about eight or nine marines already here, but I didn't know any of them, never seen them. We only wore division patches on our Alphas, and everyone was in utilities, so I had no idea what units they were from. They could be other brigades or battalions of the Seventh or other divisions, like our group. The questions and talk and rumors and speculation all started again, and now there were close to fifteen marines in the room. I quickly took in everything I could, which was not much. Maliki and I stood together, but the rest of our group drifted and grouped up in twos and threes and two groups of four. Stevenson was talking to two other guys, almost like he knew them, and I soon put it together—they were Fifth Division, three of them. The door opened again and we all jumped up, but it was just two more marines. One of them was a corporal.

"What's going on? Anybody know what this is about?" he asked. I have never seen him before.

"Is this all Twelfth?" he asked. This guy was trying to make a place for himself, looking for a sergeant to impress.

"No, you Twelfth? We're First," responded another that was one of two groups that had four, including the two from our PNCOC class. They were all lance corporals, now that I could make out the other two.

"We're Twelfth," said a guy sitting, talking to another marine beside him. The newly arrived corporal walked over to them. The other marine that came with him stood in the doorway.

"Anyone Seventh?" he asked.

"Yeah, over here," said Maliki. Our new friend was from Charlie 1/3/7. Now there were seventeen of us.

"What is this, Smith? What did French tell you? You were about to tell me before Stevenson came out."

Maliki was checking out the room, just like I was. We had done a lot together the past three weeks, and I felt like he was a good friend. I didn't know this new guy from third brigade. He was just trying to grasp the situation.

"I think, like Stevenson was saying." I looked at the marine we didn't know, who introduced himself as Lance Corporal Lewinsky, and I continued, "This is related to the Spartan Agoge thing."

Lewinsky jumped.

"You guys know this Thompson guy?" he asked.

"Yeah, I think we all do, and it's Colonel Thompson."

The door opened and we all jumped up, but it was just three more marines in utilities.

"Oh, come on!" said one of the guys that was present when I had arrived. I guess his nerves were pegged.

One of the three newest arrivals was also a corporal, but he didn't make a big fuss, just gravitated to his division, since he knew one of them. It was the Fifth, and Stevenson was his buddy. We welcomed our fourth member to the Seventh. I looked around, we all had four in our groups now, each division had four members represented. This was it, twenty of us, for whatever was going on, this was all of us. The next time the door opened, it was going to be the start of the answer.

I tapped Maliki and said, "This is all of us. Any minute now."

His face was drawn, tense, worried. What experience had he had with Colonel Thompson? What was the situation with each of these men? I thought back to my period with this man, Jim as I knew him for almost three days. My time was mostly good, a quiet morning coffee, sharing breakfast with him and his family, a fun afternoon on the beach, playing cards, a cookout, and the two runs together. His knowledge of me was a little over the top, but I guess from what First Sergeants French and Clark had told me, he was about to make general, so I guess he had to check me out pretty good. What was going on?

The room we were in was not a classroom, not even close. The armchairs were padded green leather and comfortable, arranged around a large, heavy, deep mahogany-polished square table, with several chairs along the back wall. At the front of the room was a white board and projector and a pull-down screen, like in school. There was a small table in the front, off-center from the larger table, and it had two chairs tucked underneath. There were two stacks of manila folders on the smaller table and a third stack of papers. Whatever this was, it was long planned, and I would bet anything, those folders represented each marine in this room.

CHAPTER 21

It just always seemed to top itself, the boredom, the fear, the extreme fatigue taken to the physical limits, the hunger, the loneliness. Whatever situation we had already experienced was always pushed further the next time. Two weeks. Two solid weeks, fourteen days, Echo patrolled the scorched and barren landscape of Butch, physically mapping any oddity that was noticed in the aerial scans. Well, thirty-hour days, so really if you took that into account, it was, what, six additional hours times fourteen. Good night! Another three and a half days extra, I hadn't thought of that. But I guess you could consider it like dog years, it didn't matter. The physiological effect might affect the body in some degree, but to keep everyone on the same page, so to speak, calendar days were all calculated by Earth time.

Captain Shupin was dead set on his company maintaining physical conditioning the entire time as well. Daily PT and Self-Defense practice schedules were set up in the Rec Room, and we had platoon runs every morning. Even the patrols were coordinated with training objectives and a master schedule. We continued to develop our navigational skills, tactical formation, EPs, move and cover with live fire, and keep other skills sharp. There was no such thing as a simple day of patrolling, as each insert and extraction was treated as though we were in combat. I guess that was good. Each marine honed his skills and experience.

The morning after we had visited the monument at Alpha's Ravine, Captain Shupin addressed the company again. It was our last formal company formation until the day we departed. Phase Three was announced; this was almost our fourth week out on the CR. It seemed so long ago that we had all stood together in the battalion lounge and shared breakfast. It's amazing, really unbelievable what had happened in that time.

Phase Three contained basically two parts, and either one separately blew me away. The first part was the announcement of the general plan that would, at a later time, identify one battalion from each brigade of each standing division for reassignment, mostly to create the new division. Shupin told us not to fret over that, what happens would happen, and if our battalion was selected, we would move in whole and continue in the same manner and high level of professionalism and service. My gut was turning. I know every marine standing with me was as stunned as I was.

The second part was equally mind-blowing, an open call for "mentor" applications and drill instructor course slots to any lance corporal that met the guidelines other than time in service. All interested marines should inquire. A waiver on promotion, "fast track," was now available. The Fleet Marine divisions needed additional drill instructors to meet the anticipated huge influx of new recruits in the coming months. My inner desire to achieve a higher level of service and training tugged on my conscience. I'd never thought that I wanted to become a DI.

What the heck was I thinking? I laughed at myself. I'm not DI material. I'm too young to begin with, and then let's add the total lack of time and experience. I laughed again. What a stupid thought that was. I didn't even have two CRs yet, let alone barely six months' service. I looked around. I hope nobody saw me thinking about it. *Keep your mouth shut. PFC Smith, you won't make lance corporal for another six months, at least. You are not even in a class with Carpenter or Custer or Breemer or Carrington or Valmer.* All those corporals had five and six CRs. The company was dismissed, and we started our day of patrols.

That evening when we returned to the post and were eating chow with Hotel 2/3/5, the conversation was exceptionally loud and boisterous. The topic of course was on the announcement that morning. I was sitting with Grigs and Luke. Sergeant Carpenter walked up and handed me a sheet of paper.

"Fill this out," he said. He slid several other sheets on the table. "Grigsby, Luke, Moon, you guys might be interested too. Let me know." He walked on.

"What is it?" asked Grigs, picking up one of the sheets from the table. I was reading what Carpenter handed me. I laughed.

"Yeah, right," I said, laying the paper on the table.

The other guys were picking up the sheets to see what it was, laughing and putting them back down.

"Application for A Course Drill. Are you kidding me?" said Luke looking surprised. He went back to his dinner, talking to Moon and a guy from Fifth that was sitting with us.

Grigsby was reading the sheet. I was watching him. He laid the application back down.

"What you thinking?" I asked.

"I don't know, sounds interesting," he said, taking a bite of lasagna.

"Man, we don't have time in service or rank. Besides, you have to have gone through NCO school before you're eligible for Drill."

"Nope, look at it again. They're calling it Fast Tracking, waiving most of the time of service and promoting up. This is a good opportunity to move up with this new division."

I stared at him.

"Are you serious? You're going to do this?" I was hardly able to control myself.

"Nope, we're going to do it together," he said. We laughed.

"If I remember, you hated Six Weeks. Are you kidding?"

"That side of it, but we'd be doing the ordering and bunk flipping! It's got to be better from that side of the line." He was serious.

Two days later when second platoon was loading the Betty to start the day, Carpenter casually asked me, "Where's your application? Grigsby turned his in already."

"What? I didn't fill that out, Sergeant."

He looked at me stunned. "What? The CO needs that ASAP. I told you to fill it out. What part of that didn't you understand, PFC?"

"Seriously, Sergeant Carpenter? I don't qualify for that."

"Did you see me hand it to anyone else and tell them to complete it? What do you think that means? When we get back in, I expect that turned into me before chow. Understood?"

"Aye-aye, Sergeant."

Coercion, simple, plain, strong-arm tactics. Several other guys from other platoons submitted their applications, and we all received our orders to report to PNCOC on the Sunday following our return from the current CR. Oh, and promotion to lance corporal was effective immediately. Ha-ha!

A couple days before the end of the CR, Gunny Scott walked around, saying goodbye. He was pulling out early to prepare for his move to the Twelfth. Hugs and arm shots were exchanged with some of the NCOs and regular handshakes to others below ranks. He stopped in front of my bunk.

"Lance Corporal Smith, keep in touch. Oh, here," he said, reaching into his upper slash pocket of his blouse. "This came for you this morning on the supply run. Don't let this one get away, son. She's a keeper."

He tossed the envelope on the bunk beside me, and I looked at it. It was from Donna. I stood up and grabbed his hand.

"Thank you, Gunny. You've taught me a lot."

"Ahhh, get out of here. You're going to have to suck up to Staff Sergeant Ginny to get out of details now. Good luck with that. Read your letter."

He took my hand strongly and gave me a quick hard hit in the arm, laughing, and then turned to continue his walk-around. I watched him a second and then sat down and opened the letter. I was excited to hear what she had to say, how her Corpsman Course was going.

Dearest Larson and John,

I laughed. I forgot that he had written her. What did he say?

I thoroughly enjoyed your letter, how sweet of both of you to share your thoughts and time with me. Well, since I am writing to the both of you, I'll tell you both to stop sending your mail through Senior Chief Weaver! He is enjoying my torment way too much. Your latest letter cost me an extra mile on the run yesterday morning because he said I was "sandbagging." I've never heard of that before. What does that mean?

The planet you are on sounds wonderful, beautiful. I can't wait to see you so that you can finally tell me which one it is. I hope I can visit there someday and see the garden and pool of water.

~~There is a lot of~~ Never mind. I guess I can't say that.

My course is almost over! It's hard to believe it's been almost four weeks, not counting the two weeks of Preconditioning. Oh, that reminds me, John. Something has come up, a scheduling problem. I'm sorry, I don't think you can attend my graduation. You weren't going to be able to make it anyway, so I guess it doesn't matter. I hope I can make a stopover in Fraser before my first tour. Please tell me you won't be "grounded" again or have back-to-back B courses!

My heart sunk, but I guess she was right. How was I going to get away to her graduation? Her letter continued for another four pages, a whole page more than her first letter. I don't know how she could write so much. She talked about her different classes, how hard PT was in the gym, and the three weekly runs, not including the nightly runs on the jogging track they could do on their own. I shook my head. She ended by telling us both to watch after each other and that she really did enjoy writing to the both of us, so for me not to feel like I was the odd man out. I laughed. She drew a little smiley face and "Lol" beside it. I thought that was a weird thing to write, unless Larson had mentioned his hand.

She signed it, "*Love always, Donna (and yours too, Larson, whoever she may be)."*

I was touched. That was so thoughtful and gracious of her. I don't know what he had revealed, but Donna had been able to determine he was writing to her as someone else. There was a single picture included; she was sitting on a bench in a park or somewhere, and the flowers were in full bloom. She was dressed in jeans and a light jacket, her smile as big as always. I flipped it over, she had written, "*To Larson, you are a special friend, not just because you are watching over my Fleet Marine. Love, Donna.*" That was a nice picture. If I kept it, she would find out and I would be in trouble with both of them.

I got up and walked out of the EM barracks and down the small tube that acted as a connector to the other quarters and hex tents. Everything was open, a small dome had been activated a couple days ago, so no one wore their HECS inside the tents. My GLAR was secure on my bunk frame.

I entered the NCO quarters and walked over to Larson's bunk; he and Murray were double bunked. It was a few minutes before chow and we had returned from patrol not an hour ago. Larson was reading a book, while Murray was playing cards with Eddy. There were no formalities to jump through here, unlike back home at Second Battalion. If we needed to talk with an NCO, we just came in.

"Hey, Corporal, you got a letter," I said, not too loudly. I didn't want this to turn into a library. I was standing next to his bunk, holding the envelope out.

He grinned. "Seriously? You don't have to do that, really. It's all good."

"No, really. Your name is on it and everything. She even sent you your own picture." I couldn't help but laugh.

Larson sat up and took the letter hesitantly, giving me a smile. "Hey, look, I don't know what you wrote. But you can keep writing for me if you want. I don't know what to say."

Now he laughed. "No, Smith. You're going to have to do your own work, but I'll help you. What she say?" He looked around to make sure no one was listening, while he pulled the letter out. "Oh man, this is longer than the other one."

"Read it yourself, but we have to find another carrier. Weaver is having too much fun."

We both laughed. "I'll get this back to you at chow." He sat back and started to read.

"Yeah, whenever." I turned and walked out.

The next days passed slowly.

I was ready to leave Butch. I said goodbye to Lieutenant Green and PFC Somersby, and Echo loaded up on the Bettys for our trip home, back to Earth, to Second Battalion. This was a different homecoming than my first time, our last two weeks were hard and physically exhausting, but without the fatigue of battle weariness of that first CR. I guess to Clark, Hackney, and Woolsey, it was daunting. But with each future CR, growth and experience would continue. We were tired, but ready for the party, ready to hit Fraser, ready to unwind.

Of course, there would be B and A courses for a lot of guys, Division Duty rotation, daily training and battalion duty, formations and inspections, and eventually the Refit and Readiness training to prepare for the next deployment—never-ending cycles. At least Grigs and I had a couple days off before heading to PNCOC, along with Moon, Carlson, and Luke who had B courses. Jackson and Hackney had a specialist appointment, because they had developed a skin rash, which was thought to be linked to the contact with the roaches. Yuck.

Sergeant Carpenter, before we landed, was the one to break the bad news to second, I'm sure each platoon yelling and screaming with their own revelation. "Don't get out of control tonight. Company PT 0500 tomorrow. Company formation after morning chow. Let's hit that Camel fast and get cleaned up. I want weapons inspected before they're checked in, Corporals Larson and Murry. Welcome home second platoon. It's Tuesday afternoon. We had a good CR for the most part. We lost a good leader and a friend in both men. We got to move on."

The crew chief started his landing procedure, and then the ramp came down and we quickly grabbed our CPs and ran for the Camels. We weren't lucky this time. First platoon was already loaded and flying down the strip laughing and making gestures at us.

"That's okay," said Corporal Larson. "Lance Corporal Almond and Rich, secure the washroom. Listen, Second, as soon as you jump down, go straight for the Training Room and strip down. Dig down right now and pull out your shorts. Dump your CPs…"

The plan was put in motion. We might not get the showers first, but by the love of little green apples, we were going to get our wash done!

Chapter 21

PRESENT

The door opened, and as every other time, we all jumped up, some of the groups not so sure if there wasn't more of us arriving. My little group, the Seventh and Stevenson's Fifth Division, knew this was it.

A sergeant major dressed in Alphas stormed in and bellowed, "Attention on deck! Remain locked up! Why was there not a sentry posted at this hatch? I will deal with that later. Colonel Thompson, NNP Fleet Marine Command will shortly address this company. You will remain on your feet, at the position of attention, until he instructs you to take seats, upon which you will sit at attention. For the love of God's favorite planet, you"—he angrily pointed at a marine standing toward the back wall—"and you and you, pull these chairs in a semblance of a formation. Where did you all fall off from? Get this room in an orderly fashion! This is not a school picnic. I want two rows of orderly ranks, yesterday! I thought I had two corporals in here? Three feet off that table. Well hello, Buffy, glad you decided to wake up." He addressed one of the corporals, "Three feet off the table, Corporal. Three feet between the ranks. Why am I doing your job?"

"You and you, first and third, 'dress' your chairs off the table. Fifth and seventh…" The poor corporal who knew Stevenson jumped into action, known as Buffy from then on, while the other was momentarily caught like a deer in the headlights. Maybe he was the poor corporal.

"What are you waiting on, Corporal Snuffy?" He was caught in the full attention of the sergeant major now. "Move!"

"Twelfth, break up on the ends. Push these other chairs against the back wall."

He was in motion now, his brain catching up to the ordered and ritualistic obedience of structure and command. In less than a minute, the two rows were in a neat and evenly spaced formation, all extra chairs lined up in a perfect line along the back wall.

"Lance Corporal Stevenson," called out the sergeant major.

"Aye, Sergeant Major." He was as shocked as any of us that his name was known at all by the sergeant major.

"You will make rank tomorrow. Therefore, you are the next highest in rank of this company. Stand at the hatch and immediately announce officer on the deck when that transpires. Carry on."

"Aye-aye, Sergeant Major." Stevenson quickly moved to his post.

This was all formal knowledge and tradition, well-known to us. I knew this sergeant major, but I just couldn't place him. Salt and pepper close-cropped hair, of course. He was typically fit, barrel-chested, arms that could squeeze the breath out of three of us at the same time, about five foot ten. He wore three rows of ribbons and awards, and very conspicuously, he was an OL. Was he the other sergeant major in the senior chow hall at the table? I wasn't sure.

"Let's get this straight, girls, from the get-go, I am not your friend or your gunny or good 'ol Top. You will not attempt to be familiar with me, and I will break you in half if you disrespect the colonel in any way that I see as such. Am I clear?"

"Aye-aye, Sergeant Major," we yelled.

"His time is valuable, and although he may allude that he is interested in your comments or questions, do not waste his time. Major Hawkins is your acting company commander and he will be the one to further explain what the colonel will outline." He looked at us.

We were standing at attention, in front of our chairs, trying, to the man, to figure out what was going on. Yes, he was the second SM last Sunday, I could see it now. But I knew him from somewhere else.

"Sergeant Major," called out Stevenson. "He's coming."

The sergeant major stared at him with noticeable contempt.

"Well?"

"Officer on the deck!" called out Stevenson, pulling the door widely open and standing his post at attention, ready to close the door and then reopen it at the appropriate time.

Finally, Colonel Jim Thompson and I, as well as every other Fleet Marine in the room, were reunited. The man demanded attention and respect just by his stature and presence. I hadn't put it together before, the man in Bermuda shorts, a wrinkled T-shirt and flip-flops, drinking coffee from a Daffy Duck cup at my campsite table. He owned the room, his attitude and demeanor that of authority and command. Wow, he shook my hand in friendship once, treated me as a fellow marine, and called me his friend. What a story that was. This officer was heads and shoulders above my existence. I still couldn't help but admire the man. He was in utilities, surprisingly, just another officer, trying to blend in. He walked to the front of the room, followed by Major Hawkins and another marine, I wasn't sure what rank, I couldn't see.

"Take your seats. Hello, welcome. It's good to see each of you again." He gazed out at us, taking the time to actually look at each us. "Corporal Crisp and Saunders. Lance Corporal King, Stevenson, Smith, Maliki…" He called each of our names, without looking at a list or pausing in thought, making eye contact with each us as he did.

"I know Sergeant Major McCarthy has put the fear of death in you. That's his job, but I want you to feel comfortable for a few minutes while I explain why you are here. Sunday morning, the final phase will be announced, the initiation of the Spartan Project. Oh, by the way, this is all confidential. Do not discuss this information with anyone other than those in this room. As I was saying, you are about to begin an important assignment. You are the front line of the new and innovative growth of the Fleet Marines. You are Spartan Corporals and your mission is a combination of supervision and command in providing organization to the system of Agoge Academies that will be instituted in the coming months. Early Sunday morning, all state-sponsored orphanages will be raided and those responsible for abuse, theft, and other crimes will be taken into custody and held for trial. The NNP Fleet Marine and Space Fleet Command will be given authority to oversee and continue the daily operation of these institutions."

He paused, letting his words sink in. I was stunned. This was high level. I had only recently, with the little information that Jim, uh, Colonel Thompson, had shared with me on the beach, been able to comprehend the extent of illegal activity I had been subjected to while at Sansozo Orphanage. I had been talking to Maliki, of all people, who was also an orphan and he had told me several things that I had little knowledge of, including the forced labor and cheating of our wages.

"You all have endured the ridicule, jokes and sneers, the theft of hard-earned wages, and the abuse of neglect of the very necessities that were supposed to be available to you but were withheld or stolen."

I couldn't look around, we were sitting at attention and I really did fear Sergeant Major McCarthy, but it was dawning on me that each of us in this group were orphans.

"It is now time for you to act, to become responsible and return the benefit and privileges that the Fleet Marines has given you. In the next few weeks, the smaller orphanages will be closed and consolidated into larger homes. The existing larger institutions, some of which several of you came from, will become active Agoge Academies. The plan calls for twenty initial Agoges, each designated and representing the five standing divisions. There will be four each, hence four of you from each division. You, you." He pointed at a marine, then another, and then me and then to several of us. "You will become their Corporal, their mentor, their friend, their counselor."

He continued but I was only able to take in a small amount of information. I was stunned. I was… I didn't sign up for this. I'm not a counselor, a mentor, a… I couldn't do this.

"Some of you are even asking yourselves now, 'Can I do this? I can't be a floor advisor.' Yes, you can. You wouldn't be here if I didn't know you could handle it. You are each handpicked by me. You all volunteered for Drill Course, and you wanted to become DIs. So this is, well, not the same exactly, but just as important, just as hard. Each of you are the top of your units, showing leadership, self-motivation, valor, loyalty, above-average intelligence, and are independent thinkers, which, since I'm there, many of you never completed high school but you will now. During this duty assignment, you will complete course work to earn your diploma, no debate. Continuing."

Wait, what? I have to go back to school? What is going on?

"In a moment, I will wrap this up and turn the particulars over to Major Hawkins, your new company commander. You are all now TDY, reassigned to the Third Training Battalion, Spartan or S Company. Those of you who are currently enrolled in courses that are completing tomorrow can remain bunked there until Sunday morning. The rest of you that either just arrived to Fraser or are actively assigned have your bunks already. All of you will report to the S Company barracks Sunday morning at 0700. I will leave those details for Major Hawkins. During the next two weeks, you will undergo training and receive the information and materials to continue your assigned mission. I will meet with each of you during that time to reacquaint and answer your questions. I look forward to talking with you again. I do. It was fun to meet you the first time and—" I swear he looked straight at me and said, "Maybe we can go for another run."

I couldn't help but smile, remembering our first run together, just the two of us.

"Sergeant Major." We all knew what that meant, and before he could bellow it out, with respect to a general officer, we jumped to our feet.

"On your feet!" yelled Sergeant Major McCarthy, but we were already in motion.

Twenty former ragged, wretched, useless, street urchin, despicable, no count, rabble, thieves, and beggars but now formidable, proud, respected, veteran Fleet Marines stood at attention and gave due respect to a man who gave us notice. He was our 'dad'—only an orphan could understand that.

The sergeant major followed him out the door, and before we had time to think, Major Hawkins was standing before us.

"Take your seats."

I knew the major, he was our S2, or Division Intelligence officer. I didn't have an opinion about him either way. There was really no interaction with him other than the AARs and that was all cut and dry. His appearance and demeanor were indifferent following the colonel, and he spoke with no overt authoritative overcommanding voice. He was a major, and that alone warranted attention and respect of rank.

"I am Major Hawkins, your acting company commander, for the present time. This is Gunnery Sergeant Robinson. He will be your main contact for most, if not all, future dialog and needs. Your weekly reports, which you will learn more about later in your training, will come directly to me and I will respond, if needed, directly back to you. You will be divided up into two training platoons. I want to mix you up. You are no longer First, Second, Fifth, Seventh, and Twelfth Divisions. You are Spartan Company, Third Training Battalion for the duration of your TDY. I can see several of you have questions, but please hold them until the end."

Yeah, I had some questions, but I guess they would have to wait.

"At the completion of this training period, you will be assigned to an Agoge Academy, to which you will act as a trainer, counselor, mentor, coach, drill instructor, or headmaster. We will get into all the specifics during the course, but rest assured you will be fully prepared to carry out your assignment to the best of your ability. There is no 'getting out of it.' You have been ordered by Fleet Marine Command and this is your assignment, so reply with an 'aye-aye, sir' and carry on. Am I clear?"

"Aye-aye, sir," we responded.

"Good. You will be assigned an Agoge. Agoges in ancient times were Spartan state-run schools for boys from the age of seven, which served as their education and early military training. Unlike that, as some of you know, there are girls at the orphanages as well, and they are included in your responsibilities. This is not, per se, military training, until the higher grades but we'll cover that later also."

He continued on for a few minutes and then looked at the gunnery sergeant who called us to our feet, and the major departed. Now, I guess we were finally going to get some answers.

"I am Gunnery Sergeant Robinson. That is Gunnery Sergeant Robinson," he said, making it clear that we would not refer to him as gunny anytime soon. "For all practical purposes, I'm it. There will be several guest instructors and a few 'outings.' You may remember them as field trips," he said this with a little sarcasm and mockery. I was not sure if the gunnery sergeant was pleased with his task.

"You are all veteran Fleet Marines, well adapted and keen on the ways of the workings of what is expected and how to accomplish it. I should not have to hold your hand. Three of you, are, or are soon-to-be, corporals. The remainder of you tried and true lance corporals, figure it out. Due to your particular situations, you also have many virtues and skills. Get it done. Sunday morning, you will report to your new barracks at 0700 sharp, not before and certainly not after. You are Third Training Battalion. Your barracks is the Rosemont dormitory of the old YMCA. There is a field adjacent to it that will serve as your drill and recreation field. You should have that squared away. Company PT formation will be Monday at 0530. The barracks should be ready for inspection at that time, of course, and after chow, you will fall out for instruction in the classroom in the lobby of the Rosemont, which will serve as the company lounge as well. Are these instructions clear?"

He looked at us, a little bit of a smile slipping onto his face.

"Good. I will see you Monday at 0530, shorts and red shirt. On your feet. Dismissed."

"Gunnery Sergeant Robinson," spoke Corporal "Snuffy" Saunders.

"What, Corporal?" he replied with a gruff tone. "I thought I asked if the instructions were clear, that was your time to ask or speak."

"Yes, Gunnery Sergeant. I, where is—" He never finished.

"Figure it out, Corporal." He walked toward the door. "Pick through the folders. Everyone take a stapled pack there on the table. Corporal Crisp, return this room the way you found it."

He walked out. We stood there looking at one another. *Holy moly.*

CHAPTER 22

The morning PT and run weren't bad at all; either we had remained in pretty good shape or the CO didn't want to hurt us the first day back. It felt good to run in shorts, in the cool of the late April morning, without HECS or CPs or a GLAR in our hands. It was a comfortable run, just three miles. We stood for company inspection after chow, and Staff Sergeant Ginny made his appearance officially as the company sergeant, gigging uniforms, shaves, haircuts, and the like, each platoon sergeant following down his platoon, taking notes.

The divisions were going to be revamping. New marines, both boots, and veterans from dislodged battalions were going to be filling the ranks. Continuous training and reorganization would be the new norm from now until we deployed again. Any marine that didn't have B or A courses coming up should be prepared to pull company, battalion, or Division Duty. Off time would be given as it was available. Duty day, other than training, would try to remain in the 0500 to 1630 realm.

Captain Shupin had turned the company over to Ginny right after the inspection formation, allowing Staff Sergeant Ginny to pass along this InI, Information and Intelligence. Toward the conclusion of the formation, Ginny informed Sergeant Carpenter that Battalion First Sergeant Clark required a work detail led by a corporal, and then dismissed the company.

If it were possible to stand in the wide open and not have a single friend, not a place to hide, that was the feeling of the entire platoon as no one dared move, causing any attraction to himself. Each of us acted as if we were invisible, not breathing. Jackson decided to start scratching his back, a ploy to remind Carpenter he had a clinic appointment tomorrow and to take it easy on him. Corporal Murray was acting like he was a ghost. You could talk to him, but he wasn't there. Moon was too big to not notice, so he stared at the deck. All I could think of was that Grigs and I were going to be gone for several weeks and therefore were sure to get hit now before we were gone.

"Corporal Larson, pick your detail and report to Top ASAP. Let me know who you got and where you're going. I'll be in the TOE." He walked off, along with Corporal Murray, who was now free.

"Aye-aye, Sergeant. I'll tell you now who I have, Moon, Carlson, Smith, Grigsby. The rest of you head to the barber or back to the bay and start working on your gear."

Larson was unbothered, just another detail. He had four good workers and all he had to do was supervise the mopping, grass cutting, painting, steam cleaning, trash pickup, or whatever it turned out to be. Luke was approved for a three-day pass to go home to see his mother, who was sick. Almond, Rich, Jackson, Clark, Hackney, and Woolsey dodged the bullet, this time.

Larson left us in the hallway and reported to First Sergeant Clark. "Corporal Larson with a four-man work detail reporting as ordered, First Sergeant."

We could plainly hear the details of our soon misfortune.

"Corporal Larson, prepare for a sand detail. You'll be TDY, and I don't want my marines to fall out looking like a bunch of ragtags! You have until 1000 to board that Betty and then report to Gunnery Sergeant Britz at the pool for recert before you jump in. I want that missing key found if you have to stay out there all night. Dismissed."

"Aye-aye, First Sergeant."

What the heck was sand detail? A missing key, you mean an armorer's key? Good night! Someone lost their key? In the sand? We were standing at ease and Larson quickly walked out of the Ops Room.

"Listen up. TDY, that means all your gear. Grigsby, Smith, you have to get your new stripes sewn on yesterday. Everyone to the barber. Top does not want his marines looking like civilians out there. We have a little over an hour. I'll see if I can line up a scuvy. Meet at the CQ desk. Move it!"

There was no time to whine or complain. There was no time to accomplish what we had to do—pack our duffle, which we just unpacked when we arrived yesterday setting everything up for inspection; drop our Alpha jackets and at least one dress shirt at the seamstress and beg for an immediate job; jumping in line at the barber at the PX; purchasing the cloth stripes as well as the pins at the PX; and checking out our GLARs. And if Larson couldn't get us a scuvy ride, we were doomed.

Grigs raced for the PX to buy the stripes, while I ran with our jackets and shirts to the seamstress and begged her, promising her I would buy her lunch each week I was on Post. Grigs came running in with the stripes and we jumped line for haircuts. No one really cared. The longer it took for them, the more possible work detail they got out of. The four of us met back up after Grigs paid for the sewing job and we ran back to the barracks together, frantically packing our gear and cautiously making our way down the steps with everything we owned but the GLARs, which we signed out when I opened the Arms Room.

We were standing in the foyer at ten minutes to 1000. Top walked out of the Ops Room, fully aware of the great accomplishment we had achieved just to be here. He walked up to each of us, running the backside of his three middle fingers on our freshly shaved but sweaty heads along the top of the ear, whistling.

"Whish, nice. Looks good, Marines. Corporal Larson saved your butts from dying on that three-mile ten-minute run you were going to have to do. Don't show back up here until you find that key, you hear me? Scuvys are around back. Corporal's waiting on you. Get outta here."

We ran for the main door, circling around to the back parking lot. All I could think about was a key in the sand was much like a tack in a haystack. We were doomed for failure.

Chapter 22

PRESENT

Linda's was standing room only, the only table open was the little two chair table but no one even attempted to use it. The table was so piled with drinks and tacos that Linda finally told the marines who tried to order anything for it that she just couldn't take their money, since there was no room for anything more. After the early dinner rush, it cleared out some, and we finally grabbed a table. Grigs and Kate were standing against the wall going to the little hallway to the head. She was laughing and resting her hand on his shoulder, occasionally patting or slapping it as he evidently was telling some story or joke. Moon surprised me, showing up with Steph right after we scored the table. Alvera was talking to Simon, and they were both excited, Drill Course started in the morning for them. Maliki and I talked last night as we walked back after the meeting and shared our experience and knowledge of the colonel, along with the other four from this class. It was too much to figure out, so we decided to just make the best of it and have fun tonight.

    I had called Donna and left a message. She was flying, possibly on her first real op. She had told me the other night that she had met up with a team of SS and went over some SOP stuff. Basically, if she deployed with a heavy platoon with an SS, she was about to get into some hot and heavy business. I was worried about her, but I also knew that every marine in that platoon would be watching out for their Doc, as much as she would be watching out for them. I couldn't let it control me. I couldn't dwell on the possible "what could happen stuff." She was a trained and experienced operator, and she fully knew and accepted the risks. *I had to see her again, hold her, tightly, and tell her…*

"Hey, Smith, come on! Sit down. I got you a chair." Grigs and Kate had moved up and pulled three chairs with them to the table.

"All I can say is that when Captain Ramsey sees this place now, she's going to have a major meltdown!" laughed Kate, and Steph joined in.

"Oh yeah, this is like her favorite place to take Donna." Steph was holding her hand to her mouth, fanning it in mock laughter.

"What? Who is Captain Ramsey?" asked one of the guys.

"Donna's sister," said Grigs, also laughing.

"What? You mean that mean captain who scared the life out of us at the hospital is Donna?" replied Alvera, not quite hearing the whole conversation.

"No, no!" I said, laughing, along with Kate who was nearly turning red.

"No, her sister," said Kate and Steph at the same time.

"You're dating that captain's sister? Oh man." Alvera was rubbing his head.

Carpenter was standing at the edge of the table, trying to fit in, but he was not in his crowd. He fit in with Grigs and me and Larson, but not with these younger guys. I knew he was going to shove off soon.

"Is she coming?" he asked me.

"No, Donna's on an op," I said looking up and speaking a little more quietly.

"Yeah, I know that."

He was nervous. What the heck was wrong with him? I knew that in a couple weeks, he was headed back to Six Weeks as a drill. Larson was getting his stripes any day. I had mentioned to Carpenter about the order change, just that Maliki and I were temporarily reassigned for a couple weeks, but I couldn't say what for. He took it in stride and told me to do the best I was capable of and to keep in touch.

"What's wrong with you?" I asked. "You're acting weird. You need to go? I understand. Where's Custer?"

"No, I can stay a little longer. Custer's got another week on his Division Duty. He's put in to go back to Drill too. He asked about you, said he's going to kick the snot out of you for ruining PNCOC. He really did enjoy that course." Carpenter laughed. "He's a sadistic marine."

I looked up at him and decided to ask, "How did you two meet? He said something about riding the same bus together."

"Yeah, we came from the same place." He was thinking.

"Oh, no, I want to disappear," said Kate. I looked over at her. What was she doing now?

She was staring at the door and I followed her gaze. *Oh man*. It was Captain Ramsey and she was standing inside the door, looking around as if in horror. She recognized Kate and started to walk over. Now I wanted to disappear. I bowed my head, turning away, putting my arm up on the table. *Please don't see me. Please don't see me*, I repeated to myself. Grigs made an attempt to stand up and walk to the head, but his leg got caught in the clutter of chairs, and all he managed to do was trip, causing more attention to himself. Alvera, too late, saw her and all he could do was turn away and pretend to read a menu.

"Hello, Kate. When did this all happen? I haven't been here in a couple of weeks. Why are there so many people here? Did Linda change her specials for Saturday night?"

"Hey." Kate was at a loss. I knew what the captain's first name was, and Kate obviously did too, though she was unsure to say it in the mixed company of the table. Moon was quietly laughing; the whole incident was hilarious to him. Steph was trying to not be noticed.

The captain suddenly became aware of the identities of the others at the table. "I'll let you get back to your friends. Kate, Steph," she said trying to disengage.

"Ma'am," Steph automatically responded, knowing she was outed.

Captain Ramsey backed away, still unsure of what to do, whether to leave or act indifferent and find a table, now that a couple were open, marines having stopped in for a quick bite but heading to a bar for drinks and the hope of finding a girl to talk and dance with.

Carpenter stepped away from the table and walked toward her, starting a casual conversation. What the heck? The world was spinning backward.

CHAPTER 23

It was well past midafternoon when Corporal Larson had reported to Gunnery Sergeant Britz, the senior pool instructor for Water Training. He was not happy to see us so late in the afternoon on an already busy training day, with no advanced notice of our showing up for a recert. He questioned Larson concerning our orders and kept us waiting against the wall while he made a call. The humidity of the pool along with the overbearing presence of chlorine was nearly causing us to pass out. We were fully clothed in utilities, having run a mile to get here in the near desert heat of the Cali coast. Yes, we were back at the Water Training Week area, only a couple miles from the beach and somewhere Donna was attending White Mountain Corpsmen Course. *So close.* We had our CPs, duffle bags, and GLARs, which were sweating almost as much as we were in this environment.

Gunnery Sergeant Britz returned after several minutes and informed Larson that we were to secure our duffle bags in the pool Training Supply Room and then proceed to the Beach Training Area and report to Gunnery Sergeant McQuay of Charlie Company, First Training Battalion, for our search area. We were not to perform any in-water search with HECS until after we completed recert in the morning back here at 0800 sharp.

The run to the beach was horrific, with the heavy CPs, it was full-blown summer here, but the knowledge that we were going to hit the water shortly pushed us onward. It had been a long time since any of us had been here, even Larson, who had gone through many recerts, back to the First Training Battalion Beach Training Area. We recognized the shower house and tarped pavilion from a distance. Scuvys and recruits were on the beach, training and learning the skills that were so common to each of us now. We slowed and came to a march and a drill instructor saw us approaching his company and met us at the parking lot.

"Who are you? What are you doing here, Corporal? This is Charlie Company, First Training Battalion. Who are you looking for?"

"Corporal Larson, Echo 2/2/7. I was ordered to report to Gunnery Sergeant McQuay, for a search for an armorer's key that was lost," replied Larson, starting to feel the effect of frustration.

"I'm Gunnery Sergeant McQuay. I don't know anything about this. Stand fast. Put your detail at ease, before they drop out, Corporal."

"Aye-aye, Gunnery Sergeant." The gunny walked away. "Stand easy. Drop those CPs and get some water. Everyone all right? Pull out a gel or a bar if you got it," he said, dropping his own CP, pulling out a water bottle. We were soaked in sweat, our utilities darkened; the temp had to be in the nineties or better.

"Seriously, Corporal Larson, we're looking for a key in the sand?" asked Carlson. "Are we going to live here?"

We all laughed, as the task seemed impossible. I didn't know if we were going to be using a metal detector or not, it hadn't been mentioned.

"Here he comes. Fall back in."

"Here's the sitrep, Corporal. Last week, Fox Company had to shift down that way." He pointed down the beach. "And a corporal thinks that's where and when he lost his key. You will lay out a grid from the tideline up to the hardline, fifty meters wide, and conduct a thorough search. I would suggest using a shake box and going down four to six inches. I don't have time to babysit you, Corporal. It's your detail. You can use the shovels and rakes in the shower house closet. You will conduct your own daily PT and set up your Bivys on that AO. I will include you in my meal numbers until you are relieved or my company departs Friday afternoon. Until you recert, no HECS in the water. You are free to authorize your duty uniform. It's the beach and hot, so enjoy it. I have sent one of my staff sergeants to mark the general area. You will not interfere with my company training in any way. Is that clear?"

"Aye-aye, Gunnery Sergeant."

"Carry on, Corporal. Good luck."

He walked back to his company. We never had contact with him again. We could see a drill instructor walking out toward the area pointed out by the gunny, and he had a PHA in his hand. He stopped and looked back to the training area and kept walking, stopping again about a hundred meters away from the TA. He dug a small hole and then started back. We met him midway.

"I marked the near boundary, Corporal. Set your search grid off that away from our AO. Happy hunting." He shook his head, not even stopping as he relayed the information, I'm sure like us, thinking this was an impossible task.

We reached the hole he marked, and Larson told us to drop our CPs and pull out our PHAs. He pointed to the four corners, instructing Grigs and me to a corner and sent us out. He directed our position, from the suggestion of the gunny and we set our corners. This was going to be a monumental task. This was the search area. He sent Moon and Carlson back to the shower house closet to collect shovels and rakes and the shake box. They returned with three shovels and two rakes and a box contraption that set up like a table. It had a screen bottom and was about three feet square. We were going to sift the sand, methodically, in a spiral pattern from the middle outward to the tideline and hardline, about sixty meters by fifty meters, three feet at a time. My head was spinning.

Moon, when he gazed at the enormity of the search area, simply said, "You're yanking my chain."

"Change into shorts. Let's cool off and then we'll start. Maybe we'll luck out and hit it on the first shovel."

Yeah, right. Our CPs were on the outside of the search area, and that was also where we would set up our camp, at least for the first night. I thought Grigs and I would be out of here on Saturday afternoon, but these guys, or someone, were going to be out here for days.

The water was great, and we walked out after a few minutes and began the search, starting in the middle of the search area. An area three feet square was raked smooth and then the shake box was set up. Shovel after shovel of sand was thrown into the box while two men sifted through it. For the next three hours, we worked until Larson spotted Charlie preparing for chow. We had covered about twelve square feet. He ordered us to wash off and redress in pants and T-shirt and to grab our cook pots and we headed for chow.

We returned and continued our work until it was almost dark and then set up the Bivys. Larson set the watch rotation, a simple one-hour single-man post. We would PT when Charlie got up so that we could eat chow, work a couple hours, and then report to the pool. This was our schedule for the next two days. The sun and PT and mild labor with sparse training company rations and some ocean swims mixed in turned our bodies back into hard, tanned, and fit specimens of the perfect Fleet Marine. Larson, who was no PT nut, decided, probably out of boredom, to push it and we PT'd twice a day Thursday and Friday.

By Saturday morning, we were alone, Charlie long gone on the training assault on the Beach House, Gunny McQuay leaving us a case of Full Meals. We were drawing our daily water from the shower house. We had completed PT hours ago and were a third of the way in our search pattern. The day was already hot by midmorning. A scuvy drove up to the parking lot and then headed toward us along the beach hardline, the area of beach that bordered the road. A sergeant hopped out and yelled at Larson, "Hey, Corporal Larson, Echo 2/2/7?"

"Yeah, what's up?"

Larson was barely able to keep his shorts up; he was bare chested like the rest of us, dark bronzed by the sun, barefoot. His cap that he wore during the heat of the day had cut a noticeable tan line on his recent three-day shaved head.

"The key's been found. I have your duffle bags. Your detail is to clean up and prepare to represent the Seventh Fleet Marines at a function at noon in Alphas. I'll drop your bags up at the shower house. Someone will come back and pick you up in about an hour to drive you there. You better hurry."

He climbed back in the scuvy and drove back up to the shower house and tossed our bags on the sidewalk and drove off. We all looked at each other. What the heck? Moon pushed the sift box over, dumping the sand. I looked at the beach that we had covered. It was so nicely raked and manicured that you could clearly see the pattern.

"In the water, let's break camp, showers. I have never been so glad to be told to get dressed in Alphas, if it will get us out of here. Let's move," said Larson, heading for the water.

Chapter 23

PRESENT

Early Sunday morning, the small group of us from PNCOC got up and went to breakfast together before we started what was to be a long walk to the site of the old YMCA staff quarters. I had inquired to Staff Sergeant Patte as to the location, but he'd never heard of it and told me to ask First Sergeant French. Top asked me if I was sure that's where we had been told to report to, because as far as he knew, that area hadn't been used in years. It wasn't anywhere near the new Third Training Battalion site, which was just up the street.

It took us forty-five minutes to march there with all our gear, HECS, GLAR, CPs, and duffle bags. We met up with several other small groups, including Corporal Crisp, Stevenson's buddy. Crisp decided that it would be a good idea for us to fall in and march in route step, so we did. Our group was complete, all twenty of us, as we approached the barracks. It wasn't a barracks. Gunnery Sergeant Robinson had referred to it as a dormitory, but it wasn't that either. We all stared at it—this couldn't be the right place. There were two buildings, two stories; the other one had been in a fire and was, for all purposes, destroyed. "The drill field" he mentioned, possibly, was the overgrown old gravel parking lot, as there was no other area nearby that was clear enough of trees and huge rocks. We had arrived from down a gravel road over a mile from the main Post road. There was a sign back at the road when we turned that read Rosemont Lodge and there was another old sign in front of the building we were now standing in front of.

"Man, I have been in some torn-down places before, but this, I believe, tops the list," said Crisp. "Okay, drop those bags. Corporal

Stevenson, remain here in case the gunny shows up. Corporal Saunders, let's go take a look." He was in charge, he had just taken it.

They both dropped their duffles and CPs, keeping their GLARs and walked in. We could hear them, vaguely, as they walked around then climbed the stairs to the second deck, talking, cursing, and then laughing as they reappeared.

"Okay, this is it. We're pretty sure. I don't think Gunny Robinson is showing up today. He was pretty clear about our objectives and assignment. The second deck is the bay, main deck is classroom and lounge. There are two small heads, one each deck, one shower stall each. We'll designate an area on the main deck as a small galley. We have no bunks, no mattresses, no cleaning supplies, and no classroom equipment. We have water and electricity. I guess they forgot to turn those off before we got here." We all laughed.

He continued, "Our drill field needs a little work too. The closest chow hall is almost two miles away, so it looks like the plan is a lot of Full Meal boxes, oatmeal, or SOS and soups on the menu." He looked at us. "Let's just cut to the chase. They picked us because they know we can overcome these small obstacles based on our past experiences. We are evidently about to take charge of these Agoges, orphanages, and we had better be able to scrounge, adapt, and drive on with unflinching resolve. Who can drive a Camel?"

We broke up into three groups, stacking our duffle bags and CPs out of the way, and stacked arms and set a sentry. One group began policing the drill field, enlarging the area by removing the cement and decayed wooden pole parking space bumpers and other debris, pulling up weeds and out-of-place wild bushes. We would need rakes and shovels and sand or gravel to even it out.

The heads were disgusting, the urinals and toilets stained and foul, the shower stalls not much better, mold, stains, unsanitary. The sink basins and mirrors were cracked or missing. There was no galley, just a mop sink and cabinet in what used to be a closet. There were electric outlets for coffee, a microwave, and maybe a crockpot. There were shelves and a couple bookcases that had been left behind. The deck was a mix of old nasty carpet and ripped and torn linoleum. There were absolutely no cleaning supplies. We couldn't even start cleaning other than collecting trash and ripping up the carpet; it was decided it had to go. After that was ripped up, we went ahead and pulled up the linoleum, opting for the bare plywood decking.

Surprisingly, I was one of only three guys that could drive a manual transmission, which the Camel truck used. The problem was—well, one of multiple problems, but one at a time—we didn't have a Camel assigned for our use; and even if we did, how and where were we going to requisition the supplies and material we needed? A list was made, Crisp and Stevenson and a couple others ticking off, listing what was needed immediately. Besides the bunks and possible footlockers or wall lockers, the chairs, tables, and cleaning supplies, we needed food items, galley equipment, and field maintenance equipment. We had no way to acquire any of it. The list was daunting.

"Hey, wait a minute," I said. "In that packet, there was a sample Requisition Form on how to complete it at the Agoge for material we needed. I think it had the major's signature."

"You're right. But it was partially filled out as an example."

"We need to clean it up and hit the quartermaster this morning while they're getting rocked with the Sunday recruit outfitting. Master Sergeant won't be there," added Maliki.

"We need a Camel. We can't carry all this. How can we get a Camel?" another guy asked.

"The Third Battalion is still outfitting the barracks. We need to hit an unoccupied one for whatever we can get."

"We're all going to jail," laughed a lanky marine, a noticeable scar on his cheek, one replaced eye. He had been hit hard at some time, a testament to his character to be here.

"Okay, we can't all go, but we need a good crew for some fast heavy lifting and, well, you know." Crisp didn't say it, but we all knew, unauthorized borrowing, now known as military asset redistribution.

To the man, we all volunteered, but Crisp and Saunders picked out ten marines, while the rest would stay and continue with the work as best they could with no equipment. I was one of the twelve going, so was Maliki. We strapped our water bladders on, grabbed several RFs from the packets, and set off at a double time. None of us knew when we would return, if we would, or if we would be successful in our quest, but it was what we had to do.

CHAPTER 24

Before we even reached the shower house, Larson was laying out the plan. "As soon as we hit the building, drop your CPs and pull your shower kit out. Find your duffle and pull your Alphas, short-sleeve shirt, dress shoes, hat, and white gloves. Carlson, you'll shine leather. Lay your Alphas on the duffle and I will give them a quick press and starch. Smith, you clean GLARs. We'll be under arms during the function, so they need to be good, but we don't have time to conduct a full field strip on them."

He was rattling off the jobs as we were double-timing through the sand toward the showers.

"Grigs, you'll help me, so you can continue when I hit the shower. Moon, you shower first and then relieve Smith."

Larson pulled a small iron-looking contraption out of his duffle along with a small empty spray bottle and a small metal canister. He quickly mixed some powder with water in the spray bottle and started pressing the Alphas, steam wafting from the little iron. I stripped down the weapons and frantically, but methodically, wiped and cleaned each piece, dry brushing the straps, then gently leaning each cleaned GLAR against the wall on the windless side. Moon joined me, sitting on the short curb dressed only in his skivvies, freshly shaved, waiting to get dressed with the rest of us at the last minute, keeping his Alphas clean and crisp. I hurried into the shower, shaving, brushing my teeth, clipping my nails, and even running the razor around my head retracing the fairly fresh three-day haircut. I rejoined Moon and we cleaned the last GLAR together. The starch and press job were taking the longest; the little iron was a personal-size gadget not intended to do the job on a whole detail.

"Pack your gear and stack there." He pointed to the edge of the parking lot. "Get dressed in pants and shoes and T-shirt and let's practice some drill for a few minutes. I don't want to show up with a detail that doesn't know how to 'Present Arms' or 'Right Shoulder Arms.' Let's go! Let's go! Move it, Marines."

It had been a while since we had any formal drill under arms, other than simple marching for movement. The Fleet Marines were not accustomed to do much pomp and ceremony.

For the next few minutes, Corporal Larson maneuvered us through several orders of drill movement and weapon handling. Our ride appeared, and Larson was temporarily challenged as he tried to figure out how to fit the gear of five combat-ready marines dressed in Alphas and six riders into a vehicle that was essentially designed for a maximum of six occupants or four occupants and gear. There was just not enough room. The duffles were stacked and crammed as best they could in the back of the scuvy, while the CPs were hung on the outside along the frame and canopy. The seating was designed for two up front and two in the back seat, and the option of two in the back cargo area. Larson now squeezed three of us in the seats. The GLARs and our jackets laid on the laps of the men in the rear seat. I scrunched up front straddling the shifter. Moon wedged in beside me, the driver barely able to drive safely.

"You know what this is about, Lance Corporal?" asked Larson to the driver.

The lance corporal was reaching cautiously between my legs, pulling the short shift lever down, dangerously close to thrusting the billiard-ball-size knob into my crotch. We were both attentive to his movements, and the distracting question was not deemed too overly important at the moment. The shift complete, the driver now responded to Corporal Larson's inquiry.

"Yes, Corporal. Your detail is to attend the Space Fleet Corpsman graduation this afternoon representing the Seventh Division. I am directed to stand by and then drop you off at the airfield to return to Fraser at the completion of the ceremony. That's all I know."

My head was swimming. How did this get set up? Was this whole detail a set up for this, or was it all coincidence? Moon was laughing, figuring it out. The two and a half days on the beach were boring in one aspect, though somewhat relaxing and not overly strenuous, and we had a good time.

"All of this was to get you, us, to Donna's graduation? Man, that's killer. Did you know?" he asked.

"No, I swear, Moon. You guys, I didn't set this up. Corporal, you knew what was going on."

"Oh no. I had nothing to do with this. I would have come up with a better TDY than raking sand. This smells like Top or Gunny Scott. If Custer had any power and authority, I would have bet his sneaky hand was in it."

Everyone laughed. Yeah, someone fixed us up.

The lance corporal was driving in an efficient manner, taking the coastal highway's slight curves with finesse and experience. Our bodies wedged in so tightly that only our heads swayed from side to side, the only thing freely movable. We came to an intersection and I remembered it from my drive in with Donna to the beach. Now I knew where we were. Just a little over a mile was the entrance to the campground where we spent the week. We passed it, traffic becoming thicker as families were coming and going. We fell in line behind a procession of cars headed toward the Space Fleet White Mountain Base and Training Area.

"What is all this?" asked Grigsby, I assumed, to our driver.

"That back there was the campground. All this traffic is headed either toward the base or to town. Typical Saturday traffic. Probably another ten minutes, we'll get there in time. Traffic will peel off before the main gate and hardly anyone will be going to the Polo Grounds where this is being held today. How did y'all get this gig?"

"I don't know, maybe a new intramilitary cooperative venture," replied Larson, laughing.

It was hot all cramped up in here, the warm sea breeze giving us just enough relief. Larson had made the decision to not wear our jackets and we would square away, hopefully, out of sight when we arrived. The work in the blazing sun the past three days acclimatized us somewhat to the heat, tanning or darkening and toning our bodies.

I laughed to myself. Yeah, Donna was going to be really surprised to see all of us! That should get her back for her two appearances at my little graduations. The whole platoon was not here, but five of us from her normally assigned Betty were now eagerly talking and excited about the nearing ceremony. Grigs, Moon, Carlson, Larson, and myself, we had all witnessed her undaunting and relentless supporting fire on the guns, and each of us could point to a moment or time when her covering fire saved our skin. She was just as important and highly thought of to each of these guys as she was to me. She was our Betty gunner and hopefully would be our corpsman in the future as well.

The traffic split off and we approached the main gate, the Space Fleet guard stopping us and calling for his Sergeant Of The Guard, or Chief of the Watch, or whatever these guys called it, upon seeing our cramped and out of uniform condition. He waved us to the Inspection Lane, touching his GLAR subconsciously upon noticing our weapons in a semiconcealed arrangement, lying on top of our Alpha jackets. A lieutenant and a CPO approached, with a third Fleetman circling to the curb side. The chief stood now just off the lieutenant's left, I knew from my own gate experience, ready to take out the driver and render the vehicle disabled in the event of an attack.

The Space Fleet lieutenant stepped boldly up to the driver's door and demanded, "Where are you going, Lance Corporal? Why are your passengers out of uniform and in possession of weapons? I need you to keep your hands on the wheel and step out of the Betty."

"Lieutenant, sir, I am Corporal Larson, Echo 2/2/7, and we—" He was cut off.

"Remain quiet, Corporal. All of you in the back, keep your hands where I can see them," replied the officer. Man, this was no way to treat a detail assigned to attend a ceremony.

The driver stepped out and was directed to the front of the scuvy, where the chief performed a quick pat down.

"You're next, Lance Corporal. Slide out on this side. Keep your hands on the dash," he directed me.

Well, either way would have entailed me having to navigate over the shifter, but the steering wheel was now a further obstacle. I scooted out of the door and followed the lieutenant's instructions and received the same pat down.

After several minutes, we were all out of the vehicle, passing traffic slowing to stare at us, probably wondering if we had been caught smuggling or if a failed saboteur attack had been heroically quelled by the vigilant gate guards.

"Corporal, what is your reason for having your detail out of uniform on my base? What is your purpose for being here?"

"Sir, the scuvy was too confined to wear the Alpha jackets. We have orders to attend the corpsman graduation, and I did not want our jackets to get soiled or wrinkled, sir."

"Let me see your orders."

Larson was unfazed, didn't miss a beat. "Sir, we have spent the past three days on a sand detail searching for an armorer's key. The verbal orders came over this morning for us to attend the graduation. The corpsman is, was our gunner, sir. Seventh Division is showing respect and gratitude for her service."

"That's a good story line, Corporal. It might get you out of a bar fight, but you have entered the reservation jurisdiction of a Space Fleet Training Facility with unauthorized weapons, without written orders. You aren't going anywhere."

He turned to his chief petty officer and instructed him to call into the SFP HQ. We waited. The attention we were drawing to ourselves was starting to become irritating, if not demeaning. Several minutes passed and finally the CPO was talking with someone, I guess describing more in detail the situation. Shortly a couple SFP scuvys arrived and a senior chief pulled the lieutenant to the side and exchanged information.

"Okay," said the lieutenant. "You will follow the SFP. They will escort you to the Polo Grounds. Corporal, put your men in proper uniform when you arrive. The senior chief petty officer will now take over."

The lieutenant turned and returned to his guardhouse. A good twenty minutes had been wasted standing, waiting for confirmation.

"Corporal, your GLARs are all deactivated, yes?" asked the senior chief.

"Yes, Senior Chief, since the moment we came off CR, but please recheck them."

"That won't be necessary. Two of you hop in the back of that scuvy," he said pointing to the nearest one, the one he had arrived in. "I'm going to take you straight up to the Polo gate. You can get your detail squared away on the blind side. Don't worry, we got a couple of minutes before the start. Welcome to White Mountain."

Finally, a friendly and welcome word to our presence.

Chapter 24

PRESENT

Monday morning came way too quickly. We had been up most of the night, scrubbing, painting, constructing, shoveling, and moving. The extent of our success was a testament to our knowledge and experience as a group. The acquisition of the Camels was easier than we had feared, Corporal Crisp lamenting to the Motor Pool corporal the complete frustration and repetitive corrections he was subject to with the newly arrived second lieutenants to the Third Training Battalion. None of the barracks were ready to receive the recruits that were pouring in, this detail here was responsible for moving in and setting up bunks that hadn't arrived yet, and that's why we needed the Camels so we could pick them up.

The shopping spree at the main supply and distribution center was hair-raising but in the end proved to be richly rewarding. We had pulled up to the loading docks in the two Camels, ten marines falling out in standard work detail fashion, bored, angry, and aloof. Corporal Crisp along with Corporal Saunders gave us instructions to stay put and not wander off as they quickly entered the shipping office. The conversation and pure scavenging skills of these two were not witnessed firsthand, but Saunders stepped out of the office a minute later and ordered the Camels to back up to the docks and for all of us to "stand to" and get ready to load the materials and equipment we required.

Crisp spun a story, like the one at the Motor Pool. We were permanent party with Fox Company, Third Training Battalion, and the recruit bunk count had been delivered, but the permanent party quarters' equipment and furniture were missing, along with the lounge training room furnishings. The list was read off, the Requisition Form, RF, searched for, Saunders yelling out for a lance corporal to look in the notebook in the cab for the RF for the bunks, mattresses, chairs, tables, and additional RF. Quickly, a marine from the Twelfth, who knew Saunders, made a list of what he had just called out, a cue that we had scored.

There were a handful of supply clerks working in this section this morning and the combined chaos of Sunday morning recruits being run through for Initial Issue as well as the complete dysfunction of the newly organized and rushed startup of Third Training Battalion was a formula for our success. As clerks pointed out and counted off the requisitioned items from our list, a couple of us managed to wander into the inner shelves of the seemingly "giant catalog store."

Whatever we saw that looked like it could be used or be beneficial was secreted out—a thirty-cup coffee maker, a microwave, and a small refrigerator. It was amazing the craft and artistry of distraction and misdirection some of these guys had. We had twenty bunks with mattresses, folding chairs, two tables, and other supplies, including the cleaning equipment and even a couple of shovels and rakes. Our Camels were packed, barely room for the scavengers to climb in among the haul, and we returned to S Company, where we quickly unloaded and dashed away again.

Splitting up on the next trip, one group went to the Third Training Battalion chow hall in hopes of either finding a recruit work detail absent of the mess sergeant or the similar confusion of the start-up that we had enjoyed our previous success with. Neither case greeted us as I backed up to the rear of the chow hall. I recognized one of the cooks right away, a sergeant from the Seventh and he knew me. I wasn't sure how to proceed. Corporal Saunders was in my group.

"What do you need, Corporal? We're not expecting a delivery today," he said walking toward us.

"No, Sergeant, we're here to pick up some cookout supplies for the Fox Company kickoff." Saunders was scrambling to keep from getting busted.

"Fox Company? They're not scheduled to activate until next week. Are you sure?"

"Yeah, Sergeant. I got permanent party right here, and Gunny Robinson sent us over here to grab stuff for the lounge, you know coffee and soup and stuff."

The sergeant looked at Saunders then he glanced at me. "Hey, Smith, I thought you were in PNCOC and then going to Drill. How'd you wind up with this detail?"

"Uh, you know, Sergeant, next week I start Drill. Be here in Fox after that, I guess."

"Yeah, I know. Who'd you say, Gunnery Sergeant Robinson? You better not let him hear you call him Gunny. You'll be scrubbing the head with your toothbrush. What you got on that list? We been issuing the same stuff to the other companies. I can't give you a whole bunch extra, but we'll see what we got. You know, you guys can start chowing here you know."

"Yeah, Sergeant, we just want to get the barracks up, work through."

"Yeah, Robinson is like that."

We walked in the back and collected a bounty! Twenty-pound bags of rice, soup mix, a case of steaks, a crate of vegetables, a rack tray of bread, coffee, oatmeal, two gallons of milk, and other food stuffs. So much was perishable that we feared that it would spoil before we could use it, and we only had a small refrigerator. With the Camel loaded, we headed back to our new home.

The other group had explored the barracks quad, since most of the training battalion was still under construction. They collected several sheets of plywood, lumber, some hand tools that had been found in an unlocked JOBOX, and an as yet attached to the wall whiteboard, still in its cardboard shipping box. They also found paint, mineral oil, and brushes.

When 0530 arrived, we were all outside in formation, waiting for Gunnery Sergeant Robinson to appear. He drove up in a scuvy, parking beside the one Camel we didn't have a chance to return before the Motor Pool closed last night. He acted as if it weren't there.

"Corporal Crisp, are the barracks squared away and ready for inspection?"

"Aye-aye, Gunnery Sergeant. Will you be joining us for chow this morning Gunnery Sergeant? So we can include you in our meal count."

He gave a short laugh. "What's on the line, Corporal?"

"We have eggs, SOS over potatoes."

"I don't like my SOS over potatoes. I like it over toast, Corporal Crisp."

"Sorry, Gunnery Sergeant, no toast."

"I've never heard of a chow hall not having toast for SOS. What kind of mess are you running here, Corporal?"

The exchange was nearly hilarious, a gunny sparring with a corporal over a menu item in a barely functioning galley.

"No disrespect, Gunnery Sergeant, but if you don't like the offering, you can feel free to chow somewhere else this morning."

Gunny Robinson stood in front of the small company, ready to lead us in PT, on this warming first of June morning.

"How's my PT field looking? Better than no toast, I hope."

"We raked it all night, Gunnery Sergeant. We need several loads of sand or dirt to make it playable."

"Huh. No, no sand or dirt. You'll have to rough it up or plow it. Is the company all present, Corporal?"

"Aye-aye, Gunnery Sergeant. Permission for two marines to fall out and prepare company chow."

"Granted, Corporal, but I want chow duty rotated. This isn't cook school."

"Aye, Gunnery Sergeant. Johnson, Stevenson, fall out for chow duty."

The two men knew they were up for the assignment. They hastily ran back into the Spartan Company barracks to continue with their already in progress preparation for company chow.

"That'll be twenty-one for breakfast this morning, but I'm filing a formal complaint," said Gunny.

"Noted," replied Crisp.

"Company! Atten-huh!" cried Gunnery Sergeant Robinson.

"Riot, 'Ace! 'Ah-ward, arch!"

He marched us to our rocky but cleared PT field and began our simple exercise routine and an easy three-mile run. I had almost forgotten what a normal PT session was like.

After PT, Gunny Robinson sat at one of the two tables that was on the main deck, the general use room as it were. He looked around, taking in the bare plywood-sanded deck, treated with mineral oil. He watched as Johnson and Corporal Stevenson prepared several batches of SOS on our GG field stoves. He sipped his coffee while he took in the rotation of marines eating and cleaning up in the one of two small heads. He ran his hands across the shelves and cabinets that were crafted by several skilled carpenters of our group. He noticed the food stock that was carefully stacked and accounted for in our open pantry. He stood up, his breakfast complete, filling. He washed his plate and eating ware in the small field three-bucket sanitation system that was set up, and he refilled his coffee cup, tapping the new coffee maker as he walked away.

He motioned for Corporals Crisp and Saunders to accompany him as he walked to the upper deck, coffee in hand. His walk-around in our bay was equally met with satisfaction and approval.

His only remarks were, "I see Colonel Thompson picked the right marines for this assignment. You need to return the Camel this morning. All of this is small stuff, but they'll miss the truck. Class begins at 0815, utilities. Good job, Corporals."

CHAPTER 25

Larson stayed with our ride and sent me and Grigs with the SFP. The ride over with the senior chief was enlightening, to say the least. He pointed out places of interest, asking if we had ever been on base before. No, we responded, but I told him I had been to the campground. "Yeah," he said, "that was a nice place." He asked if both my parents were military. There was a brief pause, and then I told him I had been a guest of a friend, whose parents camped there.

"Oh, okay," he said.

He asked how we had gotten tapped for this detail, since this was the first time he had ever seen the Fleet Marines send an honor guard to a Space Fleet event. We weren't an honor guard, as far as we knew. We just had spent several days on a sand detail, and since our gunner was graduating this course, someone must have thought to send us as a gesture.

"Oh, okay, still shows a sign of respect and rapport between the two branches," he added.

We arrived after an enjoyable couple minutes' drive. The SFP pulled straight up to the gate, shielding us so that we could adjust our dress uniform and prepare ourselves without embarrassment.

"You know, Corporal, your men told me that you are not acting as an honor guard. You can secure your weapons with us or leave them with your driver if you choose," the senior chief offered.

Larson was in thought, I'm sure pulling every experience of formal rules and regulations and protocol that he could muster. He was weighing the options, there just had been no advance notification or direction on his orders. The senior chief was patient, realizing that the Fleet Marine corporal was processing.

"Corporal, it's well within regs for you to attend a function in formal uniform without your weapons. And if it will help you decide, there is a high-ranking officer in attendance today and his security detail would probably be happier if you were not armed."

"Okay, Senior Chief. We'll leave our driver to secure our GLARs along with the rest of our equipment. Where do we go? What's the deal here?"

"Just go through the gate. You'll see the seating, just find a spot. The ceremony will take place on the field itself. There is a reception following. You can hit that if you want. Then we'll escort you back to the airfield. Enjoy."

"Thank you, Senior Chief," replied Larson. He then ordered us to fall in and marched us toward the entrance.

"Look sharp, now. Lelf, lelf, lelf riot, lelf. Stand tall, Fleet Marine. The world watches you. Column to the riot, huh!" He turned us in a flank turn.

He had paused to let us pass and then quickly called, "Column to the lelf, huh!"

Again we turned back to our original line of movement, Larson now in the rear; single-file, we marched through the gate. He quickstepped back to his position to the right of the small file and maneuvered us up to the seating area. Nearly the entire crowd of over thirty watching us navigate under Corporal Larson's commands. He brought us to a halt and then a smart right face and placed us in parade rest. We were now facing the guests and visitors. Larson executed a flawless about-face and searched for a place for us to sit. The crowd clapped and whistled, I guess thinking we were part of the show! We were a smart-looking bunch, each of us groomed, tanned and dark, lean, and starched, with a small but noticeable collection of ribbons and awards.

People were standing around, talking with one another, laughing here and there, a backslap or handshakes with a greeting to those they knew. Larson found a group of vacant seats just up the only aisle, halfway back. He was just about to turn back around to face us when all of us spotted a Space Fleet officer walking toward us, leaving the group he had been engaged with in conversation. Larson turned his head to the side, as was customary when giving an order facing away from a formation.

He quietly said, "Oh boy. If you have ever pulled all the stops, do it now. That's a flag officer. Detail, atten-huh!"

We all snapped, kicking our heels loudly, slapping our hands against the side of our legs before clenching our fists, the thumb along the seam of the trousers, elbows slightly bent, chests thrust out, shoulders back, heads held with the chin parallel to the deck, faces blank and hard, eyes focusing on a distant object straight in front of each of us. Our dress caps pulled tightly down, the black leather brim two finger widths off the bridge of the nose. Every piece of leather shined in the bright, hot, early afternoon sun. Medals flashed and flickered, sending glare streaks in various directions.

The officer approached us and came to attention himself, giving us due respect that he was not obligated to show and returned Larson's salute. I did not know much about Space Fleet officer rank. It was more confusing and irrational than their EM ranks, but I did know that a "flag officer" was like our general. So this officer was a general, or I think they called it an admiral. At any rate, he was dressed in a spotless, absolute white dress uniform with three rows of ribbons and medals. The epaulets on his shoulders were dark blue with golden string tassels hanging down, and the flat board had three gold stars in a triangle pattern. *Oh, wow, this would be like a lieutenant general.*

"Absolutely spectacular, Corporal. What occasion does the Space Fleet have to owe this honor? The Fleet Marines have graced us with the presence of a highly decorated and sharp detail."

"Thank you, Admiral. Seventh Division Fleet Marines wishes to thank you and the Space Fleet for the service of one of its members, sir. We were ordered to attend this afternoon's Corpsman Class Graduation, Admiral." Larson was impeccable.

"If you don't mind my saying, Corporal, you are mighty low in rank for your obvious years and high achievements, yet your lance corporal is awfully young with an OL and Brotherhood Ribbon. This is a strange collection of marines you have here."

"Yes, Admiral. Best platoon I've ever served with, sir."

"That it seems, Corporal Larson." The admiral had acknowledged Larson's name by his name plate. "I have never been presented with such a fine group of Fleet Marines. I must ask that you and your detail join me for the ceremony. Is that okay, Corporal?"

"Most definitely, Admiral. We do not wish to impose on your plans, though, sir."

Like Larson was going to refuse the Admiral's invitation!

"No imposition at all, Corporal Larson. Both you and the lance corporal will make me look all the better, with your Freedom Medal, both your Brotherhood Ribbons, and his OL. You will sit with my party, as my guests. Follow me. Let me introduce you to my wife. She wanted to speak with you also."

The admiral turned and walked back to his party. Larson ordered us to follow in a peel from the left, and we stepped forward one at a time, me first, followed by Grigs, Carlson, and then Moon. Larson led the way, I'm sure his mind racing for the correct drill order to stop us in a line for a presentation. His orders were quieter now, soft, coaxing, as we marched up the right side of the seats, away from our original planned location.

"Detail, halt. Right face. Parade rest," he called, only loud enough to be heard, not overbearing or obnoxious.

"Corporal Larson, may I present to you and your marines, my wife, Mrs. Elaine Ramsey."

I didn't think I heard correctly. *Did he say Ramsey?* The woman was very stunning, elegant, and graceful, with a broad, happy, genuine smile. She was familiar looking, but I had never seen this woman in my life. Her long once-golden-blonde hair was showing signs of strands of silver, but she was not vain in her attempts to keep it blonde with dyes, letting it turn in its course. Her face was strong, her eyes a beautiful green. She was wearing a nice but simple light blue and pink flower-print dress, which just made her face and presence that more highlighted.

She smiled. Well, it never left her face from the time we were presented, her hand outstretched to Larson, who took it in his white-dress-gloved hand. He gave it a light kiss and bowed gracefully, releasing her hand without hesitation.

"Ma'am, may I present to you, Lance Corporal Smith, Lance Corporal Grigsby, PFC Carlson, and PFC Moon."

As each of our names were called, we came to attention and then back to parade rest. Thankfully, she did not offer her hand to each of us.

"Thank you all for attending this event. I have never seen the Fleet Marines send a detail like this before."

"Yes, ma'am. We are delighted that we could attend." Larson was pulling out all his grace and charm.

"Let me introduce you to my eldest daughter, Captain Ramsey," said the admiral.

Now I was sure I was in a bad dream. The captain was pulled away from a conversation with another officer of the small group. As she turned, I was able to recognize the dear captain that had seemingly made it her mission to expel me from the Fleet Marines. She was the twin of her mother, so I don't know where the evil came from, but her facial expression changed to an irritated although responsive acknowledgment of our presence.

She did not dispense with the same pleasantries of her mother but rather simply said, "Corporal, nice of you to join us today. Please excuse me," and she returned to her conversation.

The admiral introduced a couple others and then it was time for us to find our seats. He directed Larson to have us follow him and his wife down the row of chairs. Mrs. Ramsey sat on her husband's right while Larson and the rest of us to his left. The remainder of the party found seats to his rear and front and to his wife's right. I felt totally out of place and absolutely terrified with the realization that Donna's father was an admiral. I heard Moon and Carlson talking and laughing quietly on the end, and Grigs was poking me in the side, grinning from ear to ear.

Man, I was never going to hear the end of this. Now I understood why Donna was so set in making her own way, why she seemed to hide her family secret, why she was so dagone driven. Everything was fitting together, Chief Swan's behavior at Linda's, the campground, her complete... What was it? Her style, her standing. No, her mannerism. No, just her whole attitude and stature. She had grown up under complete authoritative control and structure. Her training from childhood to present was of a military service. Why was she taking an enlisted route instead of an officer?

I looked over at the admiral and then back to the field before us. Either she was doing this in rebellion against her father's wishes or she wanted to break the expectation and excel on her own. I don't think he knew who I was, so she evidently hadn't mentioned me. But he's an admiral. Surely, he had someone watching over his daughter in the squadron, ensuring her safety. Oh man, she was a door gunner on a Betty operating with a bunch of Fleet Marines! That had to be driving him crazy. Now she was about to become a corpsman, a much more dangerous occupation.

The admiral turned to Larson and asked him something, I could barely hear the question. "You said that you wanted to thank the Space Fleet for the service of one of its members. Who would that be?"

"Yes, Admiral. The gunner that operated with us two CRs ago is graduating. She really came through for us on several ops and the platoon owes her a lot, sir."

The admiral sat back and didn't say anything for several minutes, then turned, and spoke with his wife a couple times. The corpsman class finally marched onto the field followed by what were probably the instructors for the course and took seats that were set up on the right flank of the visitors and guests. A podium was positioned center of the audience. An officer, I think a captain, began the ceremony.

I was just trying to keep it under control. I zoned out, my mind racing to make sense out of an upturned situation.

Chapter 25

PRESENT

The very first class we would have for the week was with an officer from Fleet Marine Command S1, Personnel. He was a major, an instructor from the Officer Preparatory Candidate (Course), OPC, and taught a psychology course as well as a couple other subjects. When he entered the room, we all jumped to our feet as expected and he began after instructing us to our seats. He was odd, very casual, friendly, and he immediately took to several guys and called on them all the time. Then he seemed to be visibly irritated with a couple others, nearly yelling at them for the slightest reason. He spoke of early adolescent characteristics and development. Finally, after over an hour, he gave us a break.

When we returned to the classroom, he was visibly angry with the entire company, saying we were late and promising to inform Gunnery Sergeant Robinson of our dereliction and demand punishment in the form of double PT. He continued with the stages of adolescent development and the fundamental needs of youth, especially in a fatherless environment. The session was much longer than the first, and when he finally mentioned a break, we all couldn't wait. But before he dismissed us, he pulled a bundle of papers from his briefcase and informed us we would be taking a quiz first. It was a hundred questions, to be answered on a scan card for easy and quick grading. The "quiz" took us to lunch. Some of the questions were repetitive, asking the same thing in a different way. I knew this approach; it identified if you were guessing. Lunch was Full Meal boxes and the class resumed shortly after. Corporal Stevenson was just able to make a fresh batch of coffee.

The major was totally different now, more like an average officer, neither friendly nor standoffish. He passed back our quizzes and spoke to us.

"Let's discuss my behavior earlier today. Honestly, how did it make you react or feel toward me?"

This was a trick. There was no way anyone was going to say he was a complete jerk the entire morning.

"Imagine you behaving in this manner with your Agoge groups, picking favorites, mistreating others, threatening punishment, moodiness, or altogether behavior changes. Your scores are horrible, either you guessed or just didn't pay attention to the material I presented. That's how children are going to react. Keep your instructional time short, forty-five minutes tops for the older ages, no more than thirty minutes for grades eighth and ninth. Okay, let's start over."

The afternoon was much better, and he repeated for the most part what he presented in the morning, plus additional subject matter, breaking down the age groups, male and female. Child psychology. He gave us another quiz, only twenty-five questions at the end of the afternoon. I recognized the same questions from earlier, but I knew the answers this time. I scored a hundred, as did most of the company.

"There, same questions, nonrepeat, and you all pretty much aced it because you were listening this time. I hope this helps you."

He left, and Gunny Robinson came in and told us to hit the field. He broke us up into three groups.

"Okay, none of you, thank goodness, have attended Drill Course and all of you have PNCOC. You will not treat these kids like recruits or dirt. They're kids. Just kids. Some of them may not want to participate in the program. You can't force it. This is the rough schedule you will have with all youth in your Agoge. Daily Fitness period with all grades seventh through twelfth. Remember that school is separate in most of these institutions, so you will have to make contact with the systems to schedule that either in school time or after. Tuesday and Thursday from 0700 to 0800, you will conduct Spartan Platoon Drill for active members from ninth up. You will meet once a month with the eighth grade and have a class and once a week with the ninth grade and teach Military Introduction. With the tenth grade, each Thursday, you will instruct a Learning Tract. The eleventh grade meets Wednesdays and the subject is Fleet Marine Preparedness. The twelfth meets Monday, Wednesday, and Friday. All course material and lesson plans are already developed, and you just need to review it prior to instruction time. You will have additional duties and responsibilities. They include coach, teacher, dorm supervisor, security, mentor, and parent. This is a six-month tour."

I could hear the moans and grunts of disapproval and disbelief. *Six months? No way.*

"You will not actively recruit any of your Agoge kids. The age requirement is still sixteen." Several guys looked my way. It was well-known now.

"However, you will set up once a week off campus and operate a fixed-location Recruitment Center. The purpose of our presence in the Agoge is to train and make aware of the real advantages of military service. Any youth that meets the age standard may freely enlist, and if they complete a full year of Spartan Platoon training, they will enter Six Weeks as an E1."

What? A private in a training company. Unbelievable.

"Two-year participants that graduate from high school will be eligible to enter the new OPC program as an ensign, a new officer rank or enter Six Weeks and upon graduation have E2."

Now this was getting ridiculous.

"That is why this Spartan Agoge program must be well taught and demand excellence. You are training the new Fleet Marine, getting them ready prior to joining. This is a lot to take in, so let's take a breath and drill and PT some."

The remainder of the afternoon, we took turns instructing and breaking down simple commands and routines. The week continued with classes, trips to the schools on base for familiarity with kids, course material familiarization, and the general realization that we were all scared to death. No one was going to be assigned back where they came from, which was a mixed feeling. We all were not going to start at the same time either, since the Agoges were not all ready, so we could be sent back to our old divisions or move onto A and B courses until activated.

The school visits turned out to not be as bad as I thought they would be. A special program was scheduled, and we all stood on the stage and answered questions. The thing was all of these kids were military children. They had grown up under the rigors and expectations of proper behavior and discipline. We visited the schools once more on Thursday afternoon and held a little field day, breaking up into several groups and leading a short activity that the kids rotated through, Drill, PT, meal prep, CP packing (the word combat was excluded), HECS suit up (the smallest suits were found and still were too big!), and Navigation. It was a hoot! The kids loved it and we had a ball.

At the end of the day when we were wrapping up, one of the kids asked if this was what we were going to do next week after school. Gunnery Sergeant Robinson answered, "Aye-aye, sir. This and other stuff as well. Who is attending next week? Show of hands."

What was he talking about? About half the kids, middle school and high school, sixty or so, raised their hands.

"Great! Those of you that want to come that haven't returned your permission slips need to get those in. We want to see all you at Spartan Pre-Camp and the overnight Friday."

Now I know I was hearing things. *Did he say precamp? Like this was summer camp or something?*

When we arrived back at the barracks, Robinson broke the news to us. Next week after school, we would conduct the same activities as today but more detail or length as well as others, here at our company area. The culminating activity would be an overnight Op of sorts, with a graduation Saturday morning with parents. Some of these parents would be officers and high-level NCOs, so we should do a good job. The usual and expected grunts and growls and moans filled the little classroom. There was a lot of work to be done from now to next Monday. It was nonstop since we began. No one would admit it, but we were all beginning to enjoy this assignment and the responsibility we had.

Colonel Thompson stopped by every evening and met with us, taking a few minutes with each of us individually. Friday afternoon when he arrived, he pulled me aside and said, "Let's go for a light run in the morning. I'll meet you at 0600 out front. You have a light day tomorrow. Sound good, John?"

"Yes, sir."

"Good. How's Donna doing?"

"She's great, sir. Graduated Corpsman a couple weeks ago."

"Tell her I said hi. I'll check."

"Yes, sir. I know you will."

I couldn't help but grin. How did he know all of us so well?

CHAPTER 26

It looked like there were twenty-five Corpsmen graduates and the formalities of introduction—a brief overview of the rigors of the course, the honor and high expectation that the new corpsman were under, and the acknowledgment of the training instructors—were all completed. The names were called one at a time, in alphabetical order. Most of the time, someone in attendance as a guest would clap or yell a congratulation or encouragement, and each candidate walked the short way to the podium and was pinned with the one-inch diamond-shaped-looking award badge by one of several instructors for the course. I noticed that Senior Corpsman Senior Chief Petty Officer Weaver was among them.

Many of the Fleetmen First Class E3s were also getting striped to Petty Officer E4. That was the two inverted stripes with a bar making a triangle. I couldn't help but chuckle. It was an absolutely beautiful day on the Cali coast, a slight ocean breeze, bright blue clear sky, the smell of the freshly mowed grass, and a hint of horse. Yes, it was an active playing field of some sort, whatever polo was.

Moon and Carlson were really getting excited as Donna was getting closer to being called. Well, we all were. I was so excited to be here I could hardly breathe. I hadn't seen Donna in weeks and she looked great in her Dress Blues, all straight and proper. They started asking Grigs something, but he was trying to wave them off. Then finally, as discreetly as possible, he reached over me and tapped Larson on the forearm. Larson turned his head ever so slightly I thought he was going to burn holes in Grigsby. I had seen that look before by parents in church to misbehaving children or other formal functions when the misbehavior was causing unwanted attention. Grigs quietly passed the inquiry from Moon. I rolled my eyes. Larson was going to kill us on the flight home. Larson waved it off and returned to his attentive posture and tried to act like his detail was not embarrassing him.

The admiral had been observant and leaned into Larson and asked what the problem was.

"Begging the admiral's forgiveness, sir. My marines are young and crass, with limited social awareness. They wanted to know if it would be appropriate to acknowledge our gunner's achievement, sir."

"By all means, Corporal. You came all this way to honor her. I would expect no less than a Fleet Marine cheer."

"It won't embarrass you, sir, to be next to us? If I may also be bold, sir, am I correct that the gunner is related to you in some way, Admiral?"

"That she is, Corporal. She is my daughter, but I'm as proud of her as if she were being pinned with her first officer rank. Let her have it, Corporal Larson."

"Aye-aye, Admiral."

I couldn't believe my ears. This was about to get crazy. I shook my head. She was going to die. There was one Fleetman in front of Donna, she would be called any moment now. Larson leaned slightly forward and turned his head down the row.

"Keep it clean. Stand by."

He sat back, and we all braced, sitting at attention. I tried to think of what I could yell out, but nothing came to mind. I was blank. I was sure Moon, Carlson, and Grigs were having no problem of thinking what they were going to say, Larson would be the mature one.

"Detail," he said quietly, in anticipation of Donna's name being called.

"Corpsman, Petty Officer D. Ramsey," called the captain at the podium, totally unaware of the eminent raucous bedlam that was about to unfold.

You know, a small detail of unabashed, young, and mischievous Fleet Marines bent on treating their gunner like one of the guys did not fit in a formal ceremony in the company of a Space Fleet Admiral. The small party accompanying the Admiral and his wife offered a polite and cordial round of applause and congratulatory remarks, but it was lost and unheard in the next second as Larson let loose his nipping and long contained hounds!

"On your feet! Atten-huh!" he yelled.

The five totally squared away and Recruit Poster Fleet Marines stood in a perfect line, near shoulder to shoulder, backs and shoulders broad and strong, medals, ribbons, stripes, Wound Badges, leather shining and glittering in the bright sunshine. In a voice of one, loud and full, the famous "Hoo-aah!" penetrated the seats and the field to the front. Donna, who had made it halfway to the cluster of instructors, stopped dead, stumbling, nearing tripping with shock, dismay, and probably complete embarrassment or at the least surprise. She looked at the crowd and for the first time saw, to her utter confused and shocked mind, was now aware of the little group of Alpha-clad Fleet Marines cheering and hooting in wild exhortations.

"That's our gunner!"

"She's our doc, now!"

"We came to get our kiss, Donna!"

"Corpsman Ramsey, Echo 2/2/7 needs you back!"

"You are flying back with us, Doc Ramsey!"

We were all laughing and cheering, the dress gloves muffling our clapping, the crowd joining in with the clapping, laughing at our spectacle. I noticed that Mrs. Ramsey was standing, clapping and laughing, enjoying the moment. Larson put us back to attention and ordered us to take seats. Donna had managed to make it to the podium, and Senior Chief Weaver both pinned her badge and striped her, giving her a good pump to the arm on the new rank, a show of respect and honor. I was so proud of her. She made it and I couldn't wait to tell her, to give her a hug and hold her.

The event ended after a recital of an oath, "To service, care, courage, and perseverance to never quit," was repeated. The captain invited all guests to remain and meet with the new corpsmen and enjoy a reception under the tent. Photo opportunities would be available. He thanked everyone for coming, and the ceremony was concluded.

The corpsmen all clapped one another and hugged, as was the usual occurrence with a course conclusion. Parents, spouses, family, and friends then converged on the field to personally congratulate their loved one. We all stood and exited the row so that the Admiral and Mrs. Ramsey could join the celebration.

He touched Larson on the elbow. "You will stay a few minutes for the reception, won't you, Corporal Larson?"

"Yes, Admiral, but we don't want to take away your time, sir."

"Oh, I'm sure she is more excited to see you than me, Corporal." The Admiral turned and walked to greet his daughter.

We filed down onto the field, all of us excited. Grigs and Moon patting me on the back with Moon asking if I wanted to get my kiss first or if I could hold out to be last. They all laughed. Donna was standing with a small group of her classmates and was introducing her father, the admiral, to her friends. She looked over and saw us walking toward her and her smile and excitement grew. I guess she still really didn't know who we were. We were such a surprise and the Alphas kind of hid our identity until close-up.

She finally recognized us, we did look different, and she ran to us, Larson holding his arms out wide and catching her in a full embrace. She gave him a hug and then a kiss on the cheek and he let go. Then she wrapped her arms around Moon, giving him a kiss on the cheek. He gave her a big squeeze and picked her up letting her down so she could grab Carlson and Grigs giving them their kisses and then another. I waited patiently, not so sure how we would act with people watching. I so badly wanted to hold her, kiss her, run my hand through her hair, and look in to her eyes. She let go of both of them and started for me but was hesitant.

It felt awkward for me as well. I walked to her and we gazed into each other's face, our eyes. I held out my hand and she took it with her left while placing her right hand on my chest, tracing my ribbons and awards then down my sleeve and the outline of the freshly sewn red lance corporal stripe outlined in "wound blue." I knew she wanted to kiss me as much as I wanted to taste her lips, but I only reached over and gave her a kiss on the cheek. She closed her eyes for a moment her lips slightly parted, wanting more than I dared give and then she gave me a small return kiss on the cheek and running her free hand down to mine. We separated while we still could and rejoined our surroundings, afraid anyone saw us for what we were. Larson stepped between us.

"Easy now. The Admiral is watching, and I think he's figured you two out. Good to know both of you."

We laughed, and she started talking and asking the question that was burning a hole in her brain.

"How did you guys get here? Is the whole platoon here? I can't believe it, John! I am so surprised to see all of you! I bet you're mad, aren't you?"

She looked at me, just realizing she had been found out again hiding things from me.

"This is it, all that came. And, uh, yeah, not mad. But you have to start leveling with me." She was nudging me, standing almost as close as she could to me.

"I'm sorry. Have you met Mother and Daddy? I mean, I guess maybe you have. You were sitting with them. How did you—? When did you get here? What are you doing here?"

She was dragging all of us the short few steps back to her parents, where she had left them when introducing her classmates to the Admiral.

"Mother, Daddy—"

Her mother gave her a stern look. "Donna, we've gone over this. You must address him formally."

"Forgive me, Admiral and Mrs. Ramsey. Let me introduce you to some of the marines that I have lived with…" She worded it that way, on purpose, I'm sure, to get back at her mother for correcting her. "…for weeks. They are a great bunch, to the man fierce and brave and loyal to each other. All of them dear friends of mine. This is Corporal Larson. He's one of my pen pals! And then there is Moon, the biggest and strongest and best Fleet Marine you could want next to you when you are outnumbered five to one. And Carlson is just a sweetie pie, always has your back. And Grigs, Grigsby. He is the best friend anyone could want…wait? When did you and John make lance corporal? Anyway, and this is Lance Corporal Smith. He is just a great guy. They are all great guys! How did you all get here?"

A Space Fleet photographer was walking around, taking shots and catching everyone, recording the event for future prints and an article in the *Military Times*. He was distinctly aware of the Admiral's presence and was careful not to take any of our little group, as it was. He discreetly asked one of the attending officers, the captain that was evidently an aide-de-camp, if it would be okay to take shots of the admiral. He was given permission, within moderation.

"Admiral, can I get one with you and your wife and daughter?"

"Yes, that would be good."

Donna was pulled away and the photographer posed them quickly, knowing full well the Admiral's time was limited. He took several shots.

"Bring in the Fleet Marines. They came here to watch her graduation. Get one with her and them."

We were motioned to join the next set, the Admiral staying in with us. I was placed just by chance beside Donna, her father on the other side next to Mrs. Ramsey, and Larson beside her.

"Let's move to the reception tent. I will need to meet and speak with others there a few minutes. Donna, I am proud of you. Thank you, Corporal Larson. I will send my appreciation to Major General Williams for your attendance today."

We all moved to the reception. Donna rejoined her mother who was asking her about the course, but glancing back to us a few times, smiling as she answered. I was so close, so close and just as far away from her as I had been on Mars.

Chapter 26

PRESENT

Even though it was the first week of June now, and the days had been steadily warming up and becoming hot in the afternoon, the mornings in the Rockies were still chilly, comparatively. I was up and waiting on the main deck, the first one up this morning. It was a casual, relaxed duty day for us, and first call wouldn't be until 0700, no PT, and class at 0815. I went ahead and started the big coffee pot to brew so that it would be ready when the guys got up. Everyone was still sleeping topside, the CQ trying to remain awake, sitting on the stairs.

I walked outside and waited for the colonel to arrive and did some stretching and a few warm-up exercises. I heard the scuvy and then saw the headlights in the misty gray dawn. He parked and stepped out, bending over and stretching, swinging his arms, pulling his legs up to his chest, jumping up and down, higher and higher, dancing on his toes. I joined him, swinging my arms and pulling them across my chest, rotating my head, stretching my neck.

"Good morning, sir. Is this it?"

"Good morning, John." He gave a short laugh. "Yeah, just us. Sorry about the entourage the last time. They all wanted to meet you. You made quite an impression, I'll admit. You ready?"

"Yes, sir. You lead the way. I'm sure you know this area better than I do." We started off on a light jog.

"I don't know about that. Your attack and subsequent EnE on the training range during the Nav at PNCOC says you know this area pretty well."

"Just dumb luck, sir."

He laughed. "No, no dumb or luck to that, and call me Jim out here. I think of you as a friend, an equal. I respected you that week. You truly impressed me, and you have a maturity well above your age, John."

"Thanks, sir, sorry, Jim." It felt weird. "I don't know. I don't think I can do it. I mean, I know how you feel, sir. I do too, but I don't want to mess up later and call you Jim. I still think of you as a friend too, sir. Maybe I can do it over time."

"That's good, I understand. Tell me, are all the guys up on this assignment?"

We ran along down the road back toward the main road. I didn't think that this was about that, about him pumping me for information.

"Yes, everyone's good. It took a couple days, but yeah…yes, s—, Jim. They're all good. Now it's exciting wondering who's got an Agoge first. Do you have any ready to get started?"

I figured if he was going to pump me, I could squeeze him too.

"No, none of them will be ready to go for another two weeks or more. All of S Company will return to training or their divisions first. Several of you, you and your buddy Maliki, for example, will need to pull another CR also. I want all the Spartan Corporals to have at least a CR stripe, most of you are decently decorated, which, by the way, congratulations on the DLC. I read the AAR on the ravine John, you—" He stopped running, so did I, looking at him. "you are incredible. I'm sorry about your sight, about your loss." We started running again.

"You know, John, your vision is getting worse. You're not going to be able to pull many more CRs without causing more damage. But there is another alternative, you know."

We were running. I heard what he was saying. I knew from my latest checkup with Captain Ramsey—the witch was finally going to get her wish—that I was barely passing operation standards. If I was going to stay active, I was going to have to be reassigned a rear position. The problem was, without going through SS course and serving a tour as a sniper, I was locked in as high as staff sergeant.

Sure, there were other higher-level NCOs that obviously hadn't gone SS, but they were noncombat pogues to begin with. I listened to Jim.

"I want you to pull one more CR, and that's it. You're done as a combat Fleet Marine NCO. You'll have your corporal rank, three CRs, so no one can question your bravery or dedication." He was looking at me.

My head hung low. I could feel the pain of the truth, the hurt, the loss of fraternal bonding that only those that fought beside a brother knows in his deep inner soul—the separation of the feeling of true dread and fear on one hand and the complete self-sacrifice to be willing to give your life defending the man beside you on the other hand. It was a strange relationship, emotion, almost an addictive drug. You hated the possibility that you or any of your friends might die today, but good night! Men have sat impatiently, yearning to return to the battle, almost wasting away after they pulled their last CR, wishing to be young again, reliving the excitement, fear, a bond with the one next to you so strong that it would never be replicated.

"I know you think that there is nothing that can compare to that, that total feeling of service or accomplishment, but there is. You are about to do it. This and drill instructor, maybe even…"

He paused, letting me catch up to what he was saying, what he was putting forth. I looked up. The morning was breaking nicely. It hardly ever rained on the eastern slope, the high mountains stealing most of that precipitation for the western slope. Somehow, the snow was different. We had reached the main road and were headed toward the First Training Battalion area. The day would be another warm one. That was good.

"What, Jim? Stuck as a corporal until I'm deactivated? Is that supposed to be the alternative?" I was having a feeling of self-defeat.

He laughed. "You think that's the glass ceiling, John? You think the Fleet Marines are going to waste your talent and ambitions and skills and kick you to the curb as a corporal?" He laughed again.

"John, you are probably the highest decorated lance corporal ever, and you're barely sixteen. Your talents and personal drive are known throughout the divisions' officer corps, and if you were a free agent, you would have multiple offers. John, after you earn your high school diploma, I'm recommending you for OPC. You can command a platoon on a CR and get your first company in a couple of years. You are just starting your career and well ahead of any officer coming out of OPC. You thought you were done?"

"This doesn't sound right, sir. You're yanking my chain. I'm not officer material."

"No, not yet, and I don't want you sharing this, either. You complete your school work. Your knowledge and aptitude will get you a class spot. Not me, you."

We ran on a few more minutes.

"If you don't mind, how did you find me, all of us?"

"This definitely stays here. The Fleet Marines are too low in our recruitment numbers, you know that. But we had to create another division to…uh… Well, the Soviet States Union is just about to overtake us by a division, which means they will have a stronger voting block on JCS. Presently, the Western European Countries vote along with the NAC, us. The Pacific Nations split their vote depending on the moment. We could lose the Chief of Staff and with it some secrets and power. The SSU is not our friend. Of course we are fighting the same enemy, but they would love to see us out of control of the JCS. The Twelfth Division was created by crippling the others, but we had to make it strong and put it out there right away to show that it was a complete division. We have a recruiting and draft problem. You and the others of S Company are products of an untapped resource and potential proving ground. There are millions of orphans from the wars and civil unrest. You were just a happenstance until your background was run and it was found that you were underage. I followed you after your third week, and well, here we are."

"First Sergeants French and Clark said you are soon up for a general position, is that true?"

He gave a slight chuckle. "It's not a position, like I'm working at a store or something. It's a rank. Yeah, John, I'm up for it. I should be getting my star anytime now."

"Where will that put you? I mean, where are you now, Jim?" I said that as casually as I had spoken at the beach, even as I cringed inwardly.

"You mean what's my unit posting? I'm assigned presently as a special assistant to the Fleet Marine Command Chief of Staff, but I should be given command of the new training brigade of the First, Second, and Third Training Battalions. That's pretty much my specialty anyway. Are you ready to take this Agoge and run with it?" he asked, changing the subject.

"I don't know. I hope so, but what are we supposed to do? Teach these weekly lessons and do drill and PT. For six months? Really?"

"Yes, and the time will fly by, believe me. You're not going to be a teacher, and you won't know what you are doing at the beginning. But listen, John, pass this on to the rest of them. You guys are battle-hard, think on your feet, get it done any way you can, combat veteran marines. This assignment is nothing compared to the ravine, or the moon of Xavier, or Mars, or any of the countless battles and skirmishes and duties that you and your Spartan brothers have experienced. You'll be fine. Teach these kids what you know, be a role model, show them the benefits and rewards of a life in the Fleet Marines as opposed to a slave in a factory until they die. Lay out the truth. If anything, give them the freedom to make an educated decision. You'll do a great job. It's time to turn around."

We headed back, the conversation turning to Donna and the beach, the uproar and total pandemonium and comic relief of the COMM chatter over the assault on the training company, and the eventual defeat of the SS, even my creation of a living memorial at Linda's. Before I knew it, we were back at the Spartan barracks.

"Are you coming in for a cup of coffee, sir? The guys would love to see you this morning."

"I wish I could, but I promised Angie we would go shopping and catch a movie on my day off, and here I am with you, first thing." We laughed.

"Thank you, sir. It was nice to see you again and catch up. I know you're busy, so I better let you go." I stood, ready to salute him.

"I enjoyed it, Lance Corporal. It's been too long, and I hope to see you and maybe Donna the next time, soon."

I came to attention and saluted him, for multiple reasons, respect for the man and his rank for starters and, secondly, in case anyone was watching. The morning was well on its way. He returned my salute and walked to his scuvy and drove off. *Nice run.* I walked in the barracks, the smell of bacon and coffee filling the air.

CHAPTER 27

We were all standing around the outer area of the tent, other guests coming up and inquiring or just curious about us, asking questions, and engaging in light conversation. We stood together, after Donna had to break away from us to introduce several of her instructors to the Admiral, one of them being Senior Chief Weaver.

"You think she'll out him for his mail delivery service?" I said to Larson jokingly.

"Only if she wants to point you out," he said slapping me on the back.

"Listen, grab a small bite, I mean a small bite, Moon. Stay away from the punch or anything with sauce. It'll ruin your Alphas. One of those little roll-up sandwich bites is perfect," Larson instructed us.

Near starving was about the correct state of our condition, having been on the beach since Wednesday with small rations.

We approached the buffet table and our stomachs rumbled. I could fill two or three plates and still eat. I took a little paper plate and carefully picked up a triangle wedge of what looked like a club sandwich and a rolled-up slice of something and a small bunch of white grapes. I walked away from the buffet and back to where Larson was standing. The rest of the guys were still picking and hunting for the right item.

"You're not getting anything, Corporal?"

"I guess—what is he doing?" he looked over toward Moon, who was sampling an item and then putting one on his plate if he liked it. I couldn't help but laugh. "I'll be right back," said Larson heading to tow in his big marine.

The captain that I believed was the admiral's aide was saying something to him, the admiral nodding a time or two in response or approval or just in randomness. The aide stepped away and kept a respectable distance to his superior, just far enough for personal privacy but always within quick response to deal with any urgency. I now noticed that there was another officer that was acting the same with Mrs. Ramsey, her aide or security, or both, always close but not hanging on.

The Admiral walked straight toward me. I felt a sudden embarrassment, holding the plate, the food gone, just the small stems of the grapes remaining. I quickly looked for a bilge, then rolled the plate up with the stems, and crushed it in my left hand, freeing my right to salute. *Did I salute?* I had not noticed anyone else doing that. Man, I was so ill prepared for this encounter. I came to attention as he stopped in front of me.

"As you were, Lance Corporal. I wanted to come over and congratulate you on your OL and other achievements. I do not have much time to stay active on the Fleet Marine's achievements, with my own personnel being in my realm of priority, but I must say I do remember the AAR of a certain operation where my flight crews witnessed a sole marine keeping his position defending a fallen officer. The reports said he wouldn't budge from his defense, even after receiving multiple direct hits. It was this action that allowed my gunners to nearly decimate the Galleen position and ultimately led to the liberation of POWs. Is that where you lost your eyes, Lance Corporal?"

"Yes, Admiral." I didn't feel I needed to explain any more. He obviously knew it.

"This same marine was responsible for the capture of a Galleen Candias, later in the same CR. That was you also, Lance Corporal?"

"Yes, Admiral." I was feeling really nervous, but I knew that Larson was staying away. I was on my own.

"I noticed earlier, Donna seems to be reacting differently with you, a little guarded, maybe. You were the one that she disappeared with for a week prior to her course here, is that true, Lance Corporal?"

"Sir, nothing happened, I swear." I was sweating like I had run a training run with full CP, and my heart rate was so high I felt my head was going to pop off my shoulders. I couldn't breathe.

He stared at me, a stern face, a face of complete authority used to strict discipline and respect shown to him.

"Oh, I'm sure of that, Lance Corporal. I just wanted to clear the air and let you know that I will be watching you. Donna is too old for me to tell her what to do or try to force her into decisions. As a father, I have the duty to try to protect her from injury and steer her in the right decisions. As an admiral, I am way out of her chain of command to interfere with her personal life. You will not hurt her, Lance Corporal, I believe that. I believe your character is of a loyal and protective nature. Just remember she expects honesty and loyalty as well as safety and security even if she portrays this outward adventurous, gung ho flight operation path. Thank you for coming. I believe she was completely surprised and is excited about spending the remainder of her weekend with you."

"Thank you, Admiral, but we have to depart soon. Lance Corporal Grigsby and I begin PNCOC tomorrow, sir."

"Oh, sorry to hear that, Lance Corporal. She will be disappointed, but that is the way of the military. Best of luck to you in your upcoming course." His manner changed slightly, a sign maybe that our time was complete, I was unsure, but I came to attention.

"Sir."

"Carry on, Lance Corporal."

He turned and rejoined his wife and they continued their meet and greet making the rounds to guests, graduates, instructors, and other senior-level visitors.

The rest of the guys came back and joined me.

"We're going to have to shove off here soon, Smith. You better try to take a few minutes to say goodbye," Larson said while looking around to find her.

"Yeah."

"What the admiral say? He knows you have a thing with Donna, doesn't he?" asked Grigs.

"Yeah. Hey, you guys can't say anything about this, okay? Promise me you won't swing me."

"We got you, bro. No one needs to know that you are dating the Air Group Admiral's daughter," said Carlson, laughing.

"He's a what?" asked Moon.

"Fellow over there told me that the admiral is a three star, like a lieutenant general. You know, the flight of four Bettys support one of our companies. Then they have a squadron, battalion to us. Four squadrons make an Air Wing, brigade. You know, that's a brigadier general. Well, he, Admiral Ramsey, is what they call a Group Admiral. He commands three Air Wings, basically a division commander. So, yeah, I don't want anyone to know we were out here either." Carlson was smiling.

"Give me a few minutes, Corporal." I said walking to Donna.

She had been trying to pull away from the cluster of people around her parents. She saw me and made a feigned expression of inability to escape.

I came up beside her and leaned close enough for her to hear me say, "Can you get away for a couple minutes? We gotta shove off soon."

She looked at me with a stunned, hurt look. "No! You just got here. I thought you were going to stay the weekend. What do you mean you have to leave?"

She turned away from the group, including her sister and faced me.

"We been on the beach since Wednesday but Grigs and I start PNCOC tomorrow and—."

"What? When did this happen? PNCOC, wait, what?"

She was seriously confused and turned back to her friends and said, "Excuse me for a little bit. I'll catch up to you. Don't leave without me." She spoke to no one in particular, but touched her sister, the captain, on her arm for acknowledgment.

Captain Ramsey recognized me, I really believe for the first time the whole afternoon, and replied to Donna, "Do not take long. We have reservations at the Club. We do not have room for extra diners, Donna."

Donna grabbed my arm and led me away toward the backside of the tent, the service side, where there was a full side wall, blocking the view from the event participants. There were several catering vans, scuvys, and a Camel parked on the backside. We walked to the blind side of one of the vans and she suddenly hugged me and gave me a kiss. Well, I gave her a kiss also, so I guess we both were kissing. I held her tightly and she held me by my neck, rubbing the small of my back, a break, and she pulled back and looked at me with sadness and confusion.

"Why do you have to leave so soon? It was such a surprise to see you," she gave a short laugh, "all of you, but, what do you mean you start PNCOC tomorrow? You don't have enough time in service. Neither does Grigs. Wait. What's happening? When did you two get promoted?"

She was holding me, looking into my eyes, my face, rubbing her hands on my shoulders and then my arms, down to my stripes.

"It's part of the Phase Six program. They made a call for drill instructors with fast track—"

"What! Seriously? You're going to Drill Course? When did you decide you wanted to be a drill instructor? How can you do that? You have to be a corporal, don't you?"

"Yes, we are being what they are calling fast tracking, PNCOC then DI course, then corporal, and then to a training company. Aren't they doing the same kind of thing with the Space Fleet?"

I was rubbing her back then her temples on both sides, smoothing her hair, touching her lips.

"I guess, but ugh, I don't know. This is so fast. You start tomorrow? Why were you on the beach? Here, at the campground? Why didn't you visit me?"

"No, not at the campground over at the Water Training Area. We had a sand detail and were looking—"

"A what? What's a sand detail?"

"We were looking for a key, but I don't think it was ever really there."

"A key? You were looking for a key in the sand since Wednesday? Are you kidding?" She was starting to laugh, pulling me close and giving me a kiss.

After a few seconds, we stopped, and I continued, "Yeah, an armorer's key, but it was just a way to get us out here I guess. It was kind of relaxing."

"For three days, you have been digging in the sand for a key? That is too funny. The Fleet Marines really know how to use your time wisely, don't they? Who was with you? Larson, Grigs, Moon, and Carlson? Anyone else?"

"No, that was it. We flew in Wednesday afternoon and were out there until just right before the start of this. You look good. Gosh, I've missed you. I think about you every day, how you are."

"Me too, and your letters! I told you I was so surprised to get your first one. That was so, so amazing. We had heard about the ravine trap, but I didn't know if your company was there or not. It's so hard to get any information. Senior Chief Weaver, when he arrived back right after it had happened, he gave us some news. That was before I got your letter. Then he came back again, from Mars, with your letter and he told me later that day that you were all right and had done a great job treating a knee wound. I'm so glad everyone in your company was okay."

I looked down, subconsciously, not meaning to, but she read my reaction immediately.

"Oh no! Who? Not Sergeant Carpenter? Where's Luke? He's always with you guys! Who, John?" She was genuinely distressed.

"It was the lieutenant, Lieutenant Green, and one of our boots, Somersby. They were right behind us on the first assault, when it caved. I don't know. We searched. They never found…"

"I'm sorry. I'm so sorry, John. He…you…" She laid her head on my chest and I stroked her hair, rubbing her neck. We held each other. I thought I would lighten the moment.

"I'll let Larson tell you about his garden, if he didn't already in his letters." I heard her mumble something, but didn't understand. I pulled away a little so I could hear her better. "What?"

"What's his girl's name? Who's he sweet on?"

"Oh, don't push too hard on that, babe. It's, uh, it was a long time ago."

"Did she break his heart? Was he engaged or something?" I wasn't sure if I should say anything. Of course I was the dummy that brought it up.

"No, Donna. He was married, but she died, so did his baby. I shouldn't have mentioned the garden. Don't say anything to him."

"You are not doing so well on the news and information visit, John. Next time I see you, please don't have so much bad news to tell me, okay?"

She looked at me, her eyes wet with tears. *I shouldn't have brought it up, stupid.* The whole conversation has been nothing but bad news. I rubbed her eyes with my thumbs, holding her face in my hands. I gave her a kiss on the forehead.

"Okay, no bad news next time." She reached up to my hands on her face and held them in hers.

"I guess, well, you know Daddy now. Are you okay? I'm sorry. I knew I had to tell you, but I just… I couldn't find the right time. Does it scare you? Are you—? Do…? What are you thinking?"

"Am I scared? Yeah, I'm scared. Good night! He's an admiral, I guess you know that. Funny, huh? What? Do you think I'm going to run away? No, Donna. He isn't running me off. He doesn't want me to stop seeing you. He—"

"He said something to you? When? Did he threaten you?" she was getting agitated, angry.

"No, yeah. No, he talked to me. He knows, but he's, well… I'm not sure he's okay with it, but he's not interfering. He believes I'm an honest guy. He said he wasn't going to try to make your decisions for you. It's okay. You're just stuck with me, because there is no way I can get away from you now." I tried for a little humor.

"I'm so mad. I'm going to tell him this afternoon to stay out of my…"

"No no no no! Don't you say anything. No, no, it's okay, Donna. Please. He said you were too old for him to try to make you do anything as a father and as an admiral you were out of his command, so basically he's leaving it up to you already. Don't push it, okay? Okay? Don't push."

"Okay, I won't say anything, and he's never pushed his rank around on me before, so all right." She moved in for another kiss and…

"Donna, where are you? Donna!"

It was Captain Ramsey. *Oh man.* I broke away from her but not before the captain walked around the van and came right up to us.

"Donna, oh for heaven's sake, please! Get away from her before I have you arrested, Marine. What are you doing?"

I stepped back. This woman just scared the life out of me every time I had contact with her.

"Ma'am, we were… She's… It's not…"

"It's okay, Denise. He's my… he's my boyfriend. This is Lance Corporal Smith."

Donna was stumbling back, embarrassed, caught. I think afraid or maybe respectful of her older sibling.

"No, Donna, it's not okay. This is not the proper place or circumstances for you to be in this…this situation. You will embarrass the admiral, and this private is nothing but trouble for you. Stay away from her. Do you understand me?" she said the last part with true hatred and anger to me.

"Ma'am, we weren't doing anything—"

"Be quiet! Don't speak to me. You don't belong here. You will not have any further contact…"

"Smith, we need to shove off." Corporal Larson came around the van just then, the rest of the guys with him. "Excuse me, ma'am. I need to collect my lance corporal."

Captain Ramsey halted her tirade. I don't know, was her fit of rage against me personal? Was she out of line? Or was it with the appearance of a knowledgeable NCO, she realized she had no grounds for her behavior. Whatever it was, she became normal in her bearing, pointing her finger at Donna and then in a direction around the van to the end of the tent.

"I'm sorry. Call me. I love you, John. Thank you for coming. It was good to see all of you again," Donna said as she followed her sister's directions. They disappeared, and Larson grinned at me.

"We saw the captain looking around and then come around the back here where you and Donna came. Figured you needed a hand. Let's go. You and Grigsby have some work to do tonight. I hope we can get your shirts pressed." He gave me a punch on the shoulder. "Did you get to say goodbye a couple of times?"

All the guys laughed and hooped loudly. *Oh, jeez.*

Chapter 27

PRESENT

Maliki and I were sitting at a table by ourselves, off to the edge of the dining room of the Second Training Battalion chow hall. We liked it here, and by now, we had learned that as long as you didn't call attention to yourself, you could chow at any mess facility, practically, on base. I knew Master Sergeant Wright here, fairly well, and it was never crowded. It was Saturday afternoon and we had just finished up the Spartan Company training. We didn't have orders, so we were just in limbo, planning on staying in the Agoge barracks, as we called it, until someone figured out what to do with us.

The Spartan Pre-Camp had gone exceptionally well. Each afternoon this past week, three buses of kids had arrived at the S Company training area and we rotated them through a series of activities and classes, from barracks and equipment inspection, Nav, marksmanship, CP march, PT, military history and traditions, and, the finale on Friday night, the 5K road march and bivouac. The kids loved it. Along with a lightly loaded CP, the meal last night was from a Full Meal box and a "hot" this morning of scrambled eggs, SOS over potatoes, and coffee or hot chocolate. The little graduation was held several hours ago, with certificates and handing out of T-shirts to each participant. We even got one, "Spartan Company Third Training Battalion Pre-Six Weeks Training Camp." We all loved our shirts. Each of the twenty corporals and lance corporals of S Company had our pictures taken with every camper, shaking hands while presenting their certificate. The parents, a couple I knew, surprisingly, from the Seventh Division, were so glad to see their children have such a positive experience.

Wow, I was still on a feeling of euphoria, my mood and general attitude very happy and positive. If this was how the experience of the Agoge was going to be like, this was going to be wonderful. I wondered if drill was the same. I bet it was, maybe not all the time, but certainly on graduation, when all your bonehead, unbelievable stupid, and inept recruits turned into Fleet Marines.

Some of the other guys decided to stick around the barracks as well, some taking chow at our assigned chow hall, Third Training Battalion, and others just eating in the barracks. The past two weeks had been exciting as well as demanding. Sleep was premium, we always had lessons to prepare, classes to practice, barracks area development continuation, and meal prep.

Most of us were "dirty," meaning we had been marked by the quartermaster and senior chow hall sergeants as the culprits in an unauthorized requisition of supplies and equipment. Major Hawkins had been called before the commander of the new Third Training Battalion to explain his signature on multiple RFs that had been passed by an unknown group of marines with no apparent active unit designation. The major had offered no explanation, only pointing out that the RFs all had been altered and showed signs of obvious tampering. His unannounced and surprise visit with us during the first week to advise us that a small group of miscreants were being sought for the misappropriations of supplies from Third Training Battalion and that if any information was known as to the identities of the criminals, to report it directly to Gunnery Sergeant Robinson so that it could be passed up the proper channels. He added that he hoped that the misappropriations would soon cease, because his name and reputation were beginning to become soiled.

The intended message was clear—we should stay clear of the Third Training Battalion chow hall if we had been involved and to make future requests through the proper channels. We had achieved our first assignment of getting the barracks and area up, and all other needs would be handled properly.

The major, since he was on-site, performed an impromptu inspection, finding everything satisfactory, but was puzzled over several items, most notably on the main deck. The galley was outfitted with multiple items—the enormous coffee pot, two small refrigerators (it was soon apparent that the one was just not big enough), an industrial microwave, a small two-burner stove, and a well-used set of large cook pots. The near full-wall-size whiteboard in the main room also peaked his curiosity.

He queried the gunnery sergeant, "These items were not on the list of unauthorized requisitions, Gunnery Sergeant. Where did they come from?"

Gunny Robinson replied, "Sir, they must have been loaded by the clerks by accident." We could barely contain our laughter.

"Carry on, Gunnery Sergeant." The major departed, and we didn't see him again until last night for the march and bivouac.

A few marines drifted in over the next half hour, and we were just getting ready to head back to the barracks when a cluster of NCOs came in, not uncommon. They picked up their trays and took their turns at the serving line. Staff Sergeant Williams was among them and was casually looking around and saw me and immediately left his tray on the guide rail of the line and walked briskly to us.

"Uh-oh," I said.

"What is it?" asked Maliki, but Williams was already at our table.

"Where have you lance corporals been? I've been looking for you everywhere since Thursday. I thought you were in Drill Course. No one knows where you've been assigned. All division could say was that you were TDY with Third, but no one there knew where you were either." He stopped talking and was looking at both of us. "I never pegged you two as sandbaggers. Where the heck you been?"

"We've been TDY in S Company, Staff Sergeant, twenty of us. The last two weeks, since PNCOC," I said.

"There's no S Company, Smith. Stop playing me for a boot lieutenant." He was a little hot.

"No kidding, Staff Sergeant. It's new, part of the Spartan Project." Still, Williams wasn't buying it.

"Look, I'll play your game later. Right now I need to know if you're interested, both of you, on getting set up on a Riot Platoon

CR. Lieutenant Diaz, remember him?" I nodded. *Yeah, I remembered Diaz from Six Weeks.*

"He's pulling together a tight group, all handpicked, and he asked about you specifically, you and your little crew from that SS episode couple of weeks back. I got Grigsby and Alvera already. The lieutenant has some corporals from his old company and a few others. He split the numbers with me. Most everyone I knew unfortunately went to the Twelfth or are on CR right now. Who was on that team? It was you, wasn't it, Maliki?"

"Yes, Staff Sergeant, and Cummings. He's in Drill with Alvera and a couple of other good guys from PNCOC, all squared away," said Maliki.

"Yeah, but Cummings is First Division. That won't work, will it, Staff Sergeant Williams? I think he would go, just to stick with us."

"He was the third guy? Well, there is a way. Technically he's still TDY in Drill. The lieutenant just has to grab him for his TDY before orders are cut to send him back to his division or to a training company. I think we can get him. All right, now that I have found you two, I need you to report to the airfield at the big hanger tomorrow at 0800. Who's your platoon sergeant? Where have you been? Don't feed me this bull again."

"Gunnery Sergeant Robinson is our company sergeant. I don't know where he is," I said.

"Gunny Robinson, really? Where are you barracked? No one in Third knows anything about you."

"Try Major Hawkins. He's been our acting CO."

"Try again, Smith. Major Hawkins is Division S2, and he's no company CO. What the heck are you trying to spin here?"

"He's telling you straight, Staff Sergeant Williams. Maybe you should check with First Sergeant French. I think he knows what's going on," added Maliki, coming to my defense. Williams just looked at both of us.

"What are you two into? This is real?"

"Yes, it's part of the Phase Six Division Project. Twenty of us will be assigned shortly to oversee orphanages to prepare future enlistees."

"So that's where this is going."

A light went off in Williams' head. He knew the recruitment numbers were weak. His experience as a DI gave him insight in the shortage for the new division. It was clearing up for him.

"All right, I'll check in with Top French, figure out how to get up with Gunny Robinson and get you guys over to Riot Platoon for the next month. Any other guys you think are tight, ready for this assignment?"

We both looked at each other. "Yeah, there's Lance Corporal Budner," I said.

Maliki added, "Don't forget about Hughes. They just finished PNCOC with us. You said you got Grigsby and Alvera already?"

"Yeah, this is good. I got a couple of guys I know. We'll train and prep next week and begin the CR right after that. See you two tomorrow."

He got up and walked out of the chow hall totally forgetting about his tray or eating. He had to chase down a ghost.

CHAPTER 28

Before we boarded the Betty, we changed back into utilities, since there's too much chance of getting grease or hydraulic fluid on our Alphas. The march back to First Battalion Training Quad, where our barracks were, the near three miles, was not so much hard or uncomfortable, just time-consuming. Grigs and I had a lot of work to do to prepare for the start of PNCOC in the morning. There just had been no time to think about it. The last week of the CR when our orders came through, we were still patrolling Butch, mapping out the planet. Luckily for us, the PT regime that Captain Shupin had maintained and the last three days on the beach had kept us in good physical condition.

Talk was minimal on the hike back, everyone trying to keep the pace that Moon was setting, Larson had put him in front so that we would get back in time for dinner chow. All of us were hungry. The flight back was when we all talked, laughing about the beach, the graduation, and seeing Donna again. Everyone loved her, from the time she had crashed the company CR party to that night at Linda's and of course my stories at the beach. She was like their little sister now; forget about me, they would defend her to the death. Larson asked me what was going on with the captain and I told him that she was the doctor that I was having so much problems with.

"Wait. That's the eye doctor? She's Donna's sister? Let me get this straight. One, you are dating an admiral's daughter. Two, she has a sister that's a Space Fleet captain. Three, the captain hates you long before your connection with Donna. Four, she busts you making out with the younger sister. Man, you just keep it coming, don't you, Smith?"

The guys were laughing and joking and bumping me. The talk and jeers and general fun carried us to Fraser.

We made it to the barracks and dumped our gear, greeted the guys, took in the news, caught up on the duty roster, and headed to chow with the rest of the company. It was strange to see guys that we had only been away from for a few days. It seemed like a month. Jackson and Hackney had some kind of fungus infection and were under treatment with medications and were off the roster, no one wanted to get too close to them. Luke was back. His mother was doing better. He missed us as much as we missed him. Sergeant Carpenter was busy learning the ropes on being a platoon sergeant and was doing great. Staff Sergeant Ginny had been running the company as the company sergeant. His promotion was coming any day now.

Echo was slated to get two new lieutenants before the next CR, but which platoons was up in the air. The only lieutenant we had now was Howard with first platoon. Second had now lost two lieutenants in combat in the past three CRs. It was becoming a bad luck platoon, but no one came right out and said it. It was felt, though. Our battalion, Second Battalion, Second Brigade, had dodged the bullet of reassignment to the Twelfth, but everyone knew someone that had been transferred, like Gunny Scott. The emptiness was like a cloud in the air, but the division had to move on.

Chow talk was excited, the guys on sand detail spinning a massive story about the enormous search, the extreme heat of the desert, wind and rainstorms, the unseasonably large waves, the attack of seagulls on the camp, little water and no food for the first two days, the SFP being pulled in on the search, and girls from the nearby campground—yes, there is a campground right next to the training area!—walking down to sunbathe right beside us, even undoing their top backstraps! The rest of the company was eating out of Moon and Carlson's hands, some of the NCOs laughing and trying to pull the story apart, but Moon kept weaving a tale, his audience in full hypnosis. First Sergeant Clark had come in partway through it, leaning against the wall in the back, a cup of coffee in his hand, laughing at his until then unknown storyteller. Just when the story seemed to be falling apart, Top came to the rescue.

"PFC Moon, the First Training Battalion CO says that the key was turned in a couple of hours ago. Seems one of the sunbathers found the key when she was putting her top back on. He wanted to thank all of you in your efforts on the search."

He turned and walked out. The chow hall went nuts. The story had just been authenticated! Moon sat there, beaming with newfound focus. He was now the company yarn spinner. Every new boot would listen to Moon tell about the company brawl at Camp Green or the attack of the giant roaches, or the boot that managed to fall out of a Betty when the crew chief was activating the HITS, or a half-dozen others. What was so funny was they all had factual basis, but Moon could twist anything to make it big.

Grigs and I finally stood up and Larson followed us back. He assisted us with our work, even letting us borrow his little iron to press our shirts. It was too late to get our stripes sewn on professionally, so a couple of the corporals showed us how to do it, correcting and helping us. Everything had to be perfect. We did laundry, folded and refolded, packed and repacked, cleaned everything, and then cleaned it again. Sergeant Carpenter came by later and checked our gear, I guess waiting for Corporal Larson to correct the big stuff. Carpenter was a drill instructor by calling, knowing all the small hard-to-find gigs, or imperfections.

By 2000, Grigs and I were wiped out; the week was killer. Larson knew we needed to get some sleep, but everything had to be right, had to be ready. The Cadre expected perfection and attention to the smallest detail. Other lance corporals that had been to PNCOC came by and told horror stories, trying to scare us, others laughing at our impending plight.

"Come on, guys, cut 'em some slack. Stop blowing smoke."

Larson knew better than to outright chase them off, since that would only make it worse. Men had to grow up and handle what was expected of them. The initiation was about to start, the long-forged walk to PNCOC and the total mayhem of unparalleled misery not even experienced in Six Weeks. I was starting to feel that all this was just a big yarn, like Moon, just hype—a tradition of young E3s going away to a truly difficult and hard course, to train to become NCOs, but everyone came out all right. Look at all the corporals and sergeants and staff sergeants and up. They had completed the course and were none the worse for it. This was just like the stories told on the factory floor back at the orphanage, tall tales told by people about the military that had no idea, no knowledge, just to scare others.

There were a couple other guys from the other platoons getting ready also, the same stuff happening to them. Finally, after hours of work and preparation, Larson went to get Carpenter one last time. Carpenter's inspection went well, and he told us to get some sleep, the three weeks would pass quickly, and that we were ready. We would do fine. The company settled down, guys letting us try to get some rest. I looked over at Grigs, who gave me a wink and pulled his covers over his shoulder.

I lay on my bunk, thinking of everything that had happened up to this day—my enlistment, my first CR, Lieutenant Green, meeting Donna, all my friends, Sergeants Carpenter and Custer, my training at the Y, my second CR with the Galleen snipers, the ravine, and spending time with Donna for just a brief time today. It was massive, the events that had brought me to here, the night before PNCOC. *Ahhh, it couldn't be that bad, just stories. Tomorrow would be a great day, the start to a wild and wonderful new chapter.* I faded off to sleep.

Chapter 28

PRESENT

"...Grigsby! Pull Smith out of there..."

My mind was reeling. Everything was slow. I could see the blue and green of laser bursts weaving through the air, a full firefight still in progress. For some reason, I was drawn back to a training session of a surrounded fortified position. We had to dig in and let the Bettys blow a hole in the attacker's perimeter. It was becoming clearer to me now. We had to maintain our position. No, that wasn't right. We had to defend our position. We had possible wounded, and that was our mission, defend the position and evacuate the wounded.

Real time.

Puc! Puc! Puc! Zik! Zik! Zik!

I knelt on a knee and returned fire, Grigs beside me. Lieutenant Diaz was directing the Bettys to blast an enclave of rebels. First squad had managed to collect the three KIA marines that had made it out of the downed Betty and pulled them back to the ramp. Second squad was laying down pinpoint deadly return fire on the poorly trained and ill-equipped rebel fighters. This was like the Mars assault on our station bunkers—they were no match for us.

Staff Sergeant Williams was gearing up to break through the hole and decimate the routing remnants.

"Second squad, prepare to move. Shoot 'em down, no quarter. First, cover."

No prisoners, we would gain our intel on the downed Betty from elsewhere. This was my objective. These were my immediate orders. This was what I had trained to do.

"Go!" yelled Staff Sergeant Williams, and second squad rose and ran forward.

"Never hesitate in a fight, Smith."

I heard the words spoken to me by several of my mentors, Custer, Carpenter, Williams, Ginny, and Tzenski.

This was a turning point, I knew now. The struggle for the colonies was to get bloody and cruel, more than I had yet seen. The war had just been initiated. The Colony Wars had begun.

PRESENT: FIVE WEEKS LATER

I was watching the scenery out the window, not too unlike the desert out west or even some of the planets I had been to. I smiled. Old fences and dilapidated farmhouses and rusting cars and military equipment, dead towns—it all seemed such a waste, so sad. I was heading east, and the sunrise was breathtaking, the colors so vibrant, clean. I was sitting midway back on the bus, and a little boy was peeking over the next seat, watching me. He and his mother had boarded last night, she had carried him in her arms. He had been sleeping and I helped her get settled, even telling her I would watch him as she went to use the little head on the bus. She was worn out, tired, trying to make it back to her childhood home back east. He was five or six.

I had a banana left from my bag lunch yesterday and a little wrapped snack cake. I held them out to him, and he took both. His mother was finally sleeping. The boy ate the cake first and then the banana. I smiled. He had his mother, hopefully, that would not change. I looked back out the window again. I missed my friends. I missed Donna…

The traffic sign for Prairie slipped past, exit two miles. This was it. I was nervous, scared. Would I be all right? Could I adapt to a new life, a different setting? My tablet rang. *Dagone Grigs!* He had messed around and set all kinds of alarms and ringtones and laughed every time I yelled at him to fix it.

I smiled when I saw the caller ID. "Hey! I was hoping you'd call," I answered.

"…Yeah, just pulling in. Of course, I'm nervous," I replied.

"…I don't know. I told you it was a combined Agoge from two houses, about eighty kids total." My anxiety easing as I was talking to—

"…Okay, I'll call you tonight, really. Yeah, I'm scared! Okay, okay. But hey, we're here. I gotta go. I'll call, promise."

I hung up as the bus came to a stop. I looked out and saw a small familiar town, with little shops and stores, some open, some closed for a long time. The sidewalk was littered with trash, a homeless person sleeping against the front of a closed-down business. I stood up and collected my CP and GLAR, putting my jacket on, fastening the buttons, and slipping the dress belt around my waist, straightening my uniform, tracing my hand over my new CR stripe.

I stopped before I stepped down and talked to the driver, motioning to the woman with the small boy. I pulled out my chit card, and he slid it across his reader and handed it back to me, printing off a ticket. She would travel all the way to Charleston and I had paid for meal stops too. I waved at the boy, his mother just waking up, ready to get off the bus since she had no more credits. I stepped onto the street and got my bearings. I had never been here before, but it was so familiar. It was hot, the southwest wastelands, it was well into July but not even 0800 yet.

All my equipment and supplies had been sent directly to the Agoge except for what I had with me, what I needed for the immediate process. This was all new to everyone, and it was going to be either really easy or very difficult. I hoped for really easy but was prepared for being very difficult. I drew several stares from passersby and early commuters.

"Thank you so much." The woman stepped off the bus and gave me a hug and then a kiss on the cheek. "You didn't have to do that. Thank you." She was in tears, so relieved and happy.

"You're welcome, ma'am. You'll get home all right. Take care of that boy. You'll be okay." I held her hand and she squeezed it, then she turned and boarded the bus, waving from the window, wiping her eyes. I waved and then turned to walk down the dirty street, looking for an address.

I came to a diner and opened the door and stepped in. How many little towns all over the NAC had similar places like this? I was drawn back to a time, a place—.

The man behind the counter paused in talking with a customer eating his breakfast and watched me. The dirty cook through the service window glanced at me continuing his order prep for three men sitting at a table next to the window. I walked in and closed the door. I took in an area larger than it appeared from the outside. There were several tables, six, and a row of three booths along a side wall. The place was dirty; it hadn't been cleaned in quite a while.

"Where's the head?" I asked, setting my CP down against a chair at the counter.

"The wha—?" stumbled the clerk, waiter, owner, or manager, whatever he was. He then added, "You can't bring that weapon in here. It's against the law."

I found the sign for the head and walked to it. "I'll have a cup of coffee," I said over my shoulder, my GLAR slung over my shoulder.

I walked back out after taking care of business and washing up from the long bus ride and brushing my teeth. I had previously put my toothbrush in my pocket.

I walked back to my chair, leaned my GLAR against the counter on the deck, and dug into my CP pulling out a manila file folder. I drew out several heavy stock, almost poster paper, sheets and slid one across the counter to the man. I still didn't have a cup of coffee served to me.

"Here, you will need to post this announcement onto your front door by the end of the day. Where's my coffee?" I asked, staring the man in the face, not flinching, wavering, or in the least submissive.

"Your head is filthy. The deck and counter and tables are filthy. I would imagine your galley and service areas are also filthy and do not comply to Government Inspection Health Codes. You have twenty-four hours to bring this facility up to minimum health standards or you will be fined and shut down."

"Who do you think you are? Who are you? You have to leave before I call the Security Force."

"Are you the owner or manager of this business? Let me make this clear to you and you can pass it on to whomever you wish. The NNP Military Services are done fooling around with local intolerance and disregard of laws and policies. This establishment has been selected to serve as a Recruiting Center and will be fairly compensated for its use. I will perform business here once a week and run a tab while I am here and will pay it in full each visit. I require an itemized receipt of charges and let me warn you now that any false charges will be treated as attempted theft and you will be prosecuted by the law. I will not tolerate any badgering of my guests by you or your staff. This is for you." I slid a sheet of paper to him. "It spells out all of what I have informed you, along with the associated NNP regulations and law codes."

"I have already asked for a cup coffee, twice. Let me remind you that you have twenty-four hours to get this establishment up to health safety standards. The first offense is a two-hundred-fifty credit fine and one week in the nearest Military Discipline Barracks. I believe that would be Salt Lake here. There is no second offense. This place will be closed, and the Fleet Marines will move to another business location. Am I clear?"

The man had been browsing the sheet I gave him, and he looked up and replied, nervously, "I understand, but I can't get this place cleaned up that soon. You have to give me more time. I don't have any help."

"Twenty-four hours, you may have to pull an all-nighter. Now, hand me a clean rag and a bucket of water with some bleach added. I will start you off by cleaning that booth over there myself."

I took several minutes and thoroughly cleaned the table, seats, and wall adjoining the booth. I had removed my jacket and hung it on the back of a chair at a table. I was just finishing up, having swept a nasty pile of collected trash, crumbs, and other unknown objects from under and around my AO, putting my jacket back on. The breakfast diners had been watching me and talking quietly to themselves, very interested in my actions, one even commenting, "It was about time someone had actually cleaned up in here."

I sat down in my just cleaned booth, savoring my freshly brewed cup of coffee. The door opened, and I tensed momentarily, expecting the worst. A young boy and then a girl peered inside and then stepped in.

The boy turned to the girl and said, "See, Kelli, I told you that I saw him. I told you he was here."

Kelli was maybe fifteen, he was younger, only twelve at the most. I would bet brother and sister. She had curly short dark hair, dirty and unbrushed. Her clothes were too small, also dirty, and her pants were short and had holes in the knees, the T-shirt and work shirt not good for her. He was the opposite, his clothes too big, his pants legs dragging, making it hard to walk. The man at the counter was staring at them, I waved for them to approach me.

"Hi, you are looking for something?" I asked, knowing it was me they were interested in. "What are your names?"

"Are you the soldier that is coming to take us away?" asked the boy, no fear or hesitation.

"Shhh, Benji, quiet," said Kelli, grabbing him by the shoulder and pulling him back. He had nearly come right up to the table. Yes, she was the protector, his sister.

"Well, yes and no, and yes and no. I'm not taking anyone away, Benji, and I'm not a soldier. I'm a Fleet Marine. I'm here to supervise the Agoge."

"The what?" replied Kelli, relaxing a little, becoming more at ease with me.

They both had short hair, and I knew from experience that meant that they had not too long ago had a lice infestation in their residence. I could see where he had scratched until he bled. Her fingers had the telltale signs of nail polish, chipped and peeled, long since overdue for stripping down and repainting. The habit of young girls that did not groom properly. They both needed to bathe.

"The Agoge, or orphanage, but hey, you want something to drink? Will you join me? I'd like to talk and ask you some things."

"Yeah!" said Benji, scooting into the seat booth across from me, escaping from his sister's hold.

"Benji, no. We have to go." She was curious, smart, protective.

"It's okay, maybe another time."

She didn't make a move and Benji was looking at her, pleading. "Okay, but just for a minute," she said, giving in, hoping to get her brother a drink treat.

"What are you doing here, mister? What's a Fleet Marine if it's not a soldier?" he asked. I grinned.

"It's the army, Benji, for older boys, but you are not going in there." Kelli sat beside her brother.

"What do you want to drink? Have you had breakfast?" I wondered. I thought to myself, *I guess we all repeated what we knew, what we learned, and how we learned it. It spoke to the greatness of our teachers.*

"Call me, Corporal. The Fleet Marines is not the army and we are not soldiers. We're marines, but, Kelli, there is a branch that enlists females as well. It's the Space Fleet, and I personally know several great women that are serving. Here, let me show you—"

My uneasiness faded. I made two new friends that I would grow to love and instruct and mentor for the next six months and beyond. I was Corporal Smith, Agoge Academy Fourteen, Spartan Company, Third Training Battalion, First Training Brigade, and I was home.

EPILOGUE

The woman sat impatiently in the outer reception area. She was not accustomed to being treated like this. The table was turned in this instance, she was the one that usually kept people waiting past their appointment times. Her features were not what one would call attractive, her thinning, straight dirty-blonde hair fell just above her shoulder and she was not one to overly primp and maintain any sort of style, just straight and basic. Her face was neither attractive nor ugly, just plain, apart from her high cheekbones and a dimpled mouth, which gave her a swollen chipmunk look. It was inherited. She wore no makeup, used no perfume or deodorant, and wore simple clothes. That was probably the most unusual characteristic about her. She was well able to afford to dress and look nicer, but it served her no interest. She came from a rich and politically powerful family line; her grandparents had gained their fortune with the blood of patriots and those patriots' courage. Her grandparents and parents, of course, advanced by corruption, greed, and incompetence, which seemed to be a required attribute to be successful in politics. She glanced at her wristwatch. *Damn this man and his ego and wealth.*

A full hour past her appointment, she was led into the grand office of her host, the CEO of Energy United Corporation, Bert Goor. The marbled floor was Italian. Famous paintings of Van Gogh and Rembrandt hung between heirloom tapestries of Scottish origin. Sculptures and busts of Apollo and Aphrodite stood in the side wings of the doorway. She was instructed to have a seat at the desk and that Mr. Goor would be with her shortly.

What! she thought, *Another delay! Now I am subjected to waiting in his office like some street charity beggar?* This was intolerable treatment of a high positioned senator of her stature. He was now being overly rude and pestilent. She had meetings herself to head. Even later this evening a committee was convening to address some of the military overreaches and meddling into the orphanage kickback schemes and this unauthorized new Division Project. These generals were getting to be a real pain and disrupting the plan.

An inner state room door opened off to the right side of the giant desk and Mr. Goor finally made his entry. He walked straight to his chair and sat down.

"Senator, let's be brief. I am very busy today." She was immediately put off that he didn't even offer an apology for keeping her.

"Mr. Goor, the Military Services Committee has recently become aware—"

He cut her off with a quick and flippant wave of his hand.

"Senator, I am fully aware, more so than yourself, of what the military is doing. You and your assembly are spineless and weak. This is exactly why the Conglomeration took power in the first place. You are bought, selling your services like cheap street vendors, and you dare sit in my presence telling me that you are *aware*. Let me show you this, Senator, and let me ask if you are aware of this incident."

He touched a brain-pad on his desk and the room lights dimmed and a hologram video began projecting, suspended off to the side of the desk.

The video was raw, unedited, and had a feel of professional photo journalism, that being professionally shot. The angle was upward, originating in a concealed and lightly forested backdrop. Voices could be clearly heard, excited and calling out instructions. The flight of three BTTI craft came into view, low over the treetops, and then a surprising and loud explosion or bang or thunderous noise was heard, like a sonic boom. The senator watched as a streak of white yellowish fire stretched toward the aircraft and struck the middle one causing an instantaneous explosion and fireball, the BTTI falling nearly straight down. She was shocked, not at all by the possibility of loss of life to any service members, but that a BTTI had been taken down. It was impossible. She had not seen or heard of this incident.

Another angle of another footage showed the assault on the now destroyed BTTI on the ground and rebel forces mercilessly gunning down one, two, and then three crew members as they staggered out of the interior of the craft. There was laser fire coming from the door gunner and from the air as the remaining BTTIs attempted to aid the survivors. Yet another footage showed an intense firefight with a platoon of Fleet Marines in a defense perimeter and then finally the routing and slaughter of rebels as they attempted to escape. The hologram ended, and the lights came back up.

"Have you been made aware of this little bit of information, Senator? I don't think so. I wonder if your general of the Fleet Marines has volunteered to your committee that an entire platoon and a BTTI were destroyed. Has he? Keeping secrets from the General Assembly, are we?"

The senator was fit to be tied. He was mocking her, but she wanted answers, from this creature and from that conniving over-dressed pompous war hawk.

"How is this possible? I thought those flying boxcars were state-of-the-art, undestroyable technological advances? What took it down?"

"It seems that the death to this highly technological military equipment is exactly what made it. The Achilles heel, as it were, is its ultrasensitive defense system. The weapon that you saw is a late-twentieth-century antiarmor tank round, the M289 Sabot, the 'Silver Bullet.' It has in itself no electronic or laser guidance systems. The firing system can be an ordinary 120 mm artillery piece with no trackable system, making it an ideal anti-BTTI gun. The round melts through the armor of the aircraft at high speed and velocity and spews molten metal and tumbles around inside, igniting any flammables and generally making a mess of things. I'm surprised there were any survivors. These rounds will be used in conjunction with another little surprise for your boastful and cocky warriors. The new HECS armor to begin issuance with the new divisions is flawed. The cover story is that the GBL has been improved over our own technological advances. So you see, Senator, how the high and mighty are fallen? The Conglomeration is poised to wrest control from the NNP at any moment, when we choose, so I would advise you to take that to your little committee meeting."

The senator was seething. The deal was for the NNP to remain in control as a puppet, allowing the populace to believe that the billionaires were contained and a decent way of life was once again achievable. Many of the senators and World Council were on board with the arrangement and payments, but these infernal generals and admirals were tearing it all apart again, gaining too much power themselves. This had to be stopped. This humiliating defeat and crushing strategy just might be the way to keep the status quo. Yes, this could work.

"My time is up, Senator. I will be in contact. Goodbye."

The assistant that had showed her in was now at the door waiting for her to exit. The senator stood up and walked out, barely containing her composure and humility.

Back on the street in the front of the downtown high-rise office complex, she waited for her aide to summon her limo. She was devising a plan herself, a former disgraced marine had recently come to her attention, offering services of a special kind. The traffic was light that time of day, not that she cared or noticed, and she waited for her car at the edge of the curb, absolutely fuming and wanting to know why this dreadful limo driver wasn't already here, waiting.

She did not, therefore, see the work van run the red light fifty feet away, nor did her aide who was sending or receiving a text. The van sped up as it cleared the intersection and jumped the curb, unobstructed by any waiting taxis or limos, and struck the senator, barely missing the aide by inches, sending her, part of her, flying into the air and over a hundred feet down the block. Onlookers converged on the scene, sirens wailing and Security Forces arriving and taking reports of witnesses and trying to piece the horrible accident together. The driver of the work van had suffered a heart attack and died before knowing what was happening. It was how it was, a tragic accident taking the life of a prominent and respected senator of the people. The meeting that was scheduled for that evening was postponed and never rescheduled. Such a tragic loss.

NNP MILITARY RANK AND UNIT ORGANIZATION

Fleet Marine EM & NCO

Recruit, no rank
E1 Private, no stripe
E2 Private First Class, PFC, one V stripe. May command a Fire Team
E3 Lance Corporal, one V stripe and one rocker. Commands a Fire Team and occasionally a squad
E4 Corporal, two V stripes. Commands a squad and occasionally a platoon
E5 Sergeant, three V stripes. Commands a platoon
E6 Staff Sergeant, three Vs and one rocker. Platoon Sergeant may act as Company Sergeant
E7 Gunnery Sergeant, three Vs and two rockers, "Gunny". Senior NCO in a company, Company Sergeant
E8 First Sergeant, three Vs and three rockers with a diamond in the middle, "Top". Senior NCO in a battalion. Master Sergeant, same stripes as First Sergeant without the diamond, non-combat troop command
E9 Sergeant Major, three Vs three rockers with crossed swords in the middle. Senior NCO brigade. Command Sergeant Major same as SM with a "C" in the crossed swords. Senior NCO division.

Fleet Marine Commissioned Officer

O1 Second Lieutenant, commands a platoon
O2 First Lieutenant, commands a platoon, serves as XO for company

O3 Captain, Company Commander
O4 Major, Battalion XO, begins S1–S4 responsibilities
O5 Lieutenant Colonel, Battalion Commander
O6 Colonel, General Officer, Brigade XO, may have other responsibilities
O7 Brigadier General, commands a brigade, XO to Division
O8 Major General, commands a division
O9 Lieutenant General, member of Joint Chiefs of Staff, JCS
O10 General, Chief of Staff of the Fleet Marines

Fleet Marine Unit Organization

Four Platoons make one Company
Three Companies ABC, CSC, HQ make First Battalion
Three Companies DEF, CSC, HQ make Second Battalion
Three Companies GHI, CSC, HQ make Third Battalion
Three Battalions and HQ make a Brigade
First Brigade
Second Brigade
Third Brigade
Three Brigades and HQ make a Division
    For example, 2nd Platoon, Echo Company, 2nd Battalion, 2nd Brigade, 7th Division, or E 227

Space Fleet EM and NCO

E1 Fleetman Third Class, single diagonal slash
E2 Fleetman Second Class, two diagonal slashes
E3 Fleetman First Class, three diagonal slashes
E4 Petty Officer, two inverted stripes and a bar forming a triangle with the lower stripe
E5 Chief Petty Officer, Chief, three inverted stripes
E6 Senior Chief Petty Officer, Senior Chief, three stripes one bar
E7 Master Chief PO, Master Chief, three stripes two bars
E8 Senior Master Chief PO, three stripes, three bars
E9 Fleet Chief, three stripes three bars a star in the middle. Senior Fleet Chief, three stars in the middle

Space Fleet Commissioned Officer: Flight Operations

O1 Second Lieutenant, Betty Flight Ops/Navigator, Co-pilot
O2 First Lieutenant, Betty Co-pilot/Pilot, XO of a Flight
O3 Captain, Pilot/Flight CO
O4 Major, Squadron XO, other duties
O5 Lieutenant Commander, Squadron CO
O6 Commander, Flag Officer, XO, or Deputy Commander of Air Wing, Flight, and Ground Ops
O7 Wing Admiral, commands Air Wing, combined operations
O8 Group Admiral, commands Air Group, three AWs
O9 Rear Admiral, commands two AGs, Joint Chiefs of Staff (JCS)
O10 Fleet Admiral, Supreme Fleet Commander, JCS or CS

Space Fleet Unit Organization: Flight Operations

Four Bettys and a support craft make a Flight.
Four Flights and four "Jumpers" make a Squadron.
Four Squadrons and all support personnel and other equipment make one Air Wing.
Three Air Wings make an Air Group.

FLEET MARINE ORGANIZATIONAL CHART

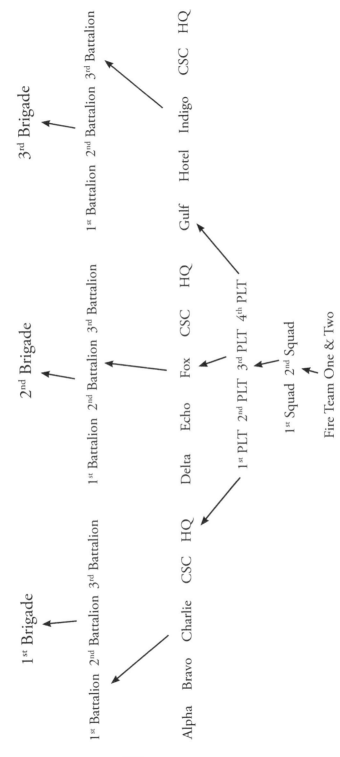

CHARACTER LIST FROM SIX WEEKS

PFC John Smith: Main character, orphan, joins Fleet Marines underage
Sergeant Tim Carpenter: Echo 227 Platoon Sergeant, recruiter, Bravo Training Co drill instructor
Sergeant Custer: Bravo Training Co drill instructor, transferred to Charlie 117 Platoon Sergeant
Corporal Larson: Echo 227 platoon medic, older than average Fleet Marine
Private Grigsby "Grigs": Smith's best friend, Y camp
Private Sam Moon: Smith's group of inner friends, Y camp
Private "Luke" Jones: Smith's group of inner friends, Y camp
Private Carlson: Smith's group of inner friends, Y camp
Private Jackson: Smith's group of inner friends, Y camp
Captain Shupin: Echo 227 CO, former Bravo Training Co XO
Gunny Scott: Echo 227 Company Sergeant
Lieutenant Green: Echo 227 Platoon Leader
Lieutenant Diaz: Bravo Training Co Platoon Leader
Sergeant Williams: Bravo Training Co drill instructor
Staff Sergeant Ginny: Echo 227 First Platoon Sergeant
Staff Sergeant LaBoye: Echo 227 Fourth Platoon Sergeant
Corporals Dettmer, Lietz, Muniz, and Eddy: Echo 227 squad leaders
First Sergeant Clark: 227 Battalion First Sergeant
First Sergeant French: Bravo Training Co First Sergeant
SF First-Class Donna Ramsey: Smith's girlfriend, Betty Door Gunner
Captain Ramsey: Donna's sister, Space Fleet medical doctor
Private Campbell: Charlie 117, Y camp friend
Jim Thompson: Met at campground
Lance Corporal Griffin: 227 Battalion CQ, Smith borrows his tablet

NNP Fleet Marine Colony Wars continues John Smith's saga as he matures and develops into a first-class Fleet Marine fighting an alien civilization in the not too distant future. His leadership skills and intelligence continue to push him to the forefront where he must prove himself. As the story progresses, Smith and others like him, begin to learn of a secret project—a plan in which they are integral part. The *Fleet Marine* series will grab you and keep your attention.

Mark Schuppin, Virginia State Park District Manager, retired

Reading this book, I am emotionally tied to John Smith's experiences even without first-hand military experience. Everyone that has had deep friendships and felt loss can relate to *Colony Wars*. The amazing way the author draws you into the action has you experiencing the highs of adrenaline fighting in the midst of a battle and the lows of loss. You are exhausted, hungry, thirsty, hot, cold, happy, sad, triumphant, courageous, and scared. It's hard to put this story down because you are living the action with John Smith. *Colony Wars* is very realistic—it's human nature, it's life, it's conflict, and it satisfies a need for heroes. John Smith is a hero and we need more like him.

Celeste DeVaney, RN, mother, grandmother, wife, and avid reader

Colony Wars is a masterful sequel to *Six Weeks* that will surprise you with each chapter. Wallace gives a firsthand portrayal of the trials of military service and captures the bonds of brotherhood that come from shared service and sacrifice. You will connect with the characters on an emotional level as they share their lives with you. You reach the end wanting Book 3 in a desperate way.

W.S. Smith, Virginia Conservation Police Officer, retired

ABOUT THE AUTHOR

G. Van Wallace is an Army veteran. After the Army, he earned his degree in Education from Liberty University. He had dabbled in a variety of careers, but he has found his passion in writing. G. Van Wallace makes his home in Buckingham, Virginia with his wife and two daughters. *Colony Wars* is his second published book in the *NNP Fleet Marine* series.

CPSIA information can be obtained
at www.ICGtesting.com
Printed in the USA
FSHW010605210320
68301FS